WEDDING ON
THE BABY WARD

AND

SPECIAL CARE
BABY MIRACLE

BY
LUCY CLARK

MILLS &
BOON

Lose yourself in a heartrending duet
from Lucy Clark...

SAVING TWIN BABIES

WEDDING ON THE BABY WARD
Delivering these premature conjoined twins
is neonatal specialist Miles Trevellion's
only priority—the compellingly
beautiful Dr Janessa Austen can be
nothing more than his colleague. For now...

SPECIAL CARE BABY MIRACLE
New mum Sheena's tiny girls
are fighting for their lives, and
paediatric surgeon Will Beckman is the man
to save them! Sheena's hoping for two little
miracles—but perhaps an unexpected
third dream might also come true...

Saving Twin Babies

*Only the world's most renowned doctors—
and a miracle or two—
can save these tiny twins.*

WEDDING ON THE BABY WARD

BY
LUCY CLARK

First published in Great Britain 2011
by Mills & Boon, an imprint of Harlequin (UK) Limited,
Eton House, 18-24 Paradise Road, Richmond, Surrey TW9 1SR

© Anne and Peter Clark 2011

ISBN: 978 0 263 88601 6

Printed and bound in Spain
by Blackprint CPI, Barcelona

Dear Reader,

Babies are always so cute but beautiful twin girls who are born conjoined can really capture your heart. Ellie and Sarah are two little girls who came into the world and unbeknownst to them, ended up uniting four very special people.

Janessa and Miles were so much fun to write, especially the part about making Janessa a pilot. After being given a joy-ride flight in a tiger moth biplane as a birthday present, we knew the experience was one that needed to be relayed in a book. The airfield where Janessa flies her plane is one of our favourite places to visit and part of the book was even typed there, sipping a nice cup of coffee on a pleasant Spring day while the lovely old planes take to the skies.

Sheena and Will brought their own set of unique challenges to the story. For Sheena, going through not only the pregnancy but the long awaited separation of her gorgeous twin girls was gut wrenching to write, especially after reading and researching how parents feel when faced with such situations. With Will by her side, loving and caring for not only her but the girls as well, Sheena was able to get the happily ever after she so richly deserved.

We hope you enjoy reading about these special babies who have brought together two couples who were made for each other.

Warmest regards,

Lucy

For Lili and Mat—
who share the same warped and silly sense of humour
as us. Thanks for making us feel normal!
—Hosea 14:9

CHAPTER ONE

'JANESSA. Phone,' an agency nurse called. 'It's the maternity ward. They say it's urgent.'

'I'm a little busy,' Janessa Austen replied, not taking her attention from her latest patient. The Adelaide Mercy NICU had quite a few of the regular nurses off sick today and while the nursing agency had provided staff to keep things running, these nurses weren't trained in NICU procedure. 'Find out what the situation is and I'll get someone to go to Maternity as soon as possible.'

Both Janessa and Kaycee, one of her top NICU nurses, stood next to the open cot of the tiny twenty-six-week-old baby girl who was in need of urgent medical attention. Baby Taneesha had been born only twenty minutes ago and had been intubated and rushed from the delivery suite down corridor to the NICU where the brave little soul continued to fight for her life. The staff were giving her breaths via the Neopuff to keep her alive while they organised the ventilator.

'Kaycee, we need some surfactant,' Janessa ordered. 'It works so well on these tiny stiff lungs,' she mused as she continued to work. Whilst it had been 'one of those days', Janessa wasn't about to lose a patient, not to fatigue nor interrupting phone calls.

'Come on, Taneesha,' Janessa said with loving determination. 'Hang in there, sweetie. You can do it.' While she crooned to the baby, Janessa's hands were working rapidly. 'What are the oxygen saturations?' she asked, her gaze focused on what she was doing.

'Eighty per cent,' Kaycee replied as she began to increase the oxygen levels.

'How's that surfactant coming along? We need to get that moisture into the lungs, stat.'

Kaycee was working quickly and handed the syringe to Janessa who administered the liquid into the endo-trachael tube. A few minutes later the oxygen saturations went up as Taneesha's breathing started to improve. Kaycee did the observations once more as the agency nurse came over to Janessa.

'Maternity don't need you to send anyone up,' the nurse reported. It was around lunchtime, her first day on the job, and she'd been thrown in at the deep end. Still, Janessa couldn't help that. They'd already had three babies born within the last hour, all of whom had come directly to the NICU, the ward clerk was out on her lunch break and the rest of the staff were either assisting in the delivery suites or monitoring other little babies. Today, the NICU's forty-four-cot ward was most definitely full to capacity.

'What's the problem, then?' Janessa asked, still focused on Taneesha.

'There was an emergency.' The nurse consulted a piece of paper in her hand. 'A baby by the name of Joey. Apparently, his lips started to turn blue.'

'Not again.' Janessa sighed and shook her head. 'Has he been attended to?'

'Um… They said the doctor is bringing him down.'

'The doctor? Doctor who?' Janessa asked.

'Excuse me! Assistance required. Over here,' a deep

male voice said from the entrance to the NICU, and Janessa glanced over briefly to see a man in a rumpled suit walking into the unit, pushing a baby's crib. She didn't know who he was but she knew who the baby was.

'That'll be Joey.' Janessa looked at the agency nurse. 'Go and bring him in. Put him…' she quickly scanned the NICU '…bay two for now.' She returned her attention to Taneesha, while checking the blood gas results. The agency nurse hovered uncertainly for a moment before heading over to where the man was already pushing Joey's crib into the NICU, not waiting for anyone.

'Come this way. B-Bay two,' the agency nurse stammered.

'Right. Bay two. Well…lead on,' the man said with a hint of impatience as he removed his jacket and tossed it carelessly onto a desk. Thankfully, his tone wasn't loud but it was definitely insistent and Janessa hoped the sensitive babies in the NICU didn't pick up on the disruption. The last thing any of them wanted right now was a chain reaction of one baby after the other crying in the need for attention and comfort.

'Had to happen on a day when we're short-staffed,' Janessa mumbled.

'Oxygen, stat,' the male doctor ordered. 'Baby is cyanotic. No, no, no. Thirty per cent oxygen,' he growled at the nurse. 'Don't you even know that much?' He shook his head and took over.

'Obs?' Janessa asked, concentrating on blocking out the larger-than-life man who was creating havoc in her NICU. She wasn't the type of woman to allow her temper to get the better of her—in fact, she prided herself on having good control over all her faculties—but today, with the lack of sleep and her very early morning start, the edges were starting to fray.

Kaycee started the obs as Janessa rechecked the fluids that would help Taneesha. She wanted to look up, to check out what was happening in *her* unit, but she remained steadfastly by Taneesha's side. 'That's it, Taneesha. Good girl. You keep fighting.' Janessa looked at Kaycee.

'Her oxygen saturations are now stable,' Kaycee reported after quickly doing the observations, and Janessa let out a sigh of thanks. 'I'll go see what the commotion is all about.'

'No. It's OK.' Janessa quickly pulled off her gloves and rubbed her bare hand over Taneesha's tiny body, pleased to note that the skin was not only a much better colour but much, much warmer than before. 'There you go, love,' she whispered to the babe, before glancing at Kaycee. 'Stay and monitor Taneesha for me.' Janessa reached for another pair of gloves. 'I'll go see what's happening with Joey.' She jerked her head towards the commotion. 'And can we perhaps see if Ray's finished assisting in the delivery suite? It would be great to have him back here in the unit.'

'I'll see to it,' Kaycee responded, and as Janessa headed towards the newest arrival in the NICU, she took one calming breath, knowing she could leave the running of things in Kaycee's more than capable hands while she pulled strength from thin air to concentrate on the latest event in her already overly hectic day. She'd been on the go since about four o'clock that morning and as it was now just after one o'clock in the afternoon, her exhaustion level was steadily on the rise.

'No. That's the wrong-size cannula. This is ridiculous,' the man was saying to the agency nurse, who looked completely flustered and about ready to burst into tears. 'Go away. I'll do it myself.'

'What's the status?' Janessa asked smoothly, after giving a dismissive nod to the agency nurse. The unit was stressful enough at the moment and the sooner she could defuse the situation, the better.

'The status is to find someone in this place to assist me, preferably before this baby dies.'

Janessa unhooked her stethoscope from around her neck and put the eartips into her ears, before listening closely to Joey's chest. She heard the rasping instantly and sighed at her little charge. Without another word she went to a nearby cupboard, pulling out the correct equipment they would need.

'He needs a chest X-ray. We need to see if this baby has aspirated.'

'What happened?'

'I was in Maternity, reviewing a patient, when I noticed this chap coughing. I went to check and noticed he was cyanotic. Naturally, I thought he needed treatment so had him brought down here, but apparently...' he glanced pointedly at Janessa '...this NICU is understaffed and no doubt requires a full review.'

Janessa tried her hardest not to bristle at the way he was speaking to her, the way he was looking at her and the way he was treating her. It was clear by the way he was handling the medical equipment that he was a doctor. In another brief glance, she took in his seriously creased navy trousers and crinkled white shirt covering his firm torso, a college tie, which was knotted loosely, and beneath that his top shirt button was undone. His whole attire screamed 'surgeon' and a dishevelled one at that. What on earth had he been doing before arriving here in her unit?

Dr Whoever-he-was had just finished rolling up the sleeves of his shirt, right past his elbows and was washing his hands. As he reached for a pair of gloves, Janessa gave him a quick once-over and although he appeared incredibly handsome, with short dark brown hair and a square jaw complete with a cleft in his chin, his attitude was too arrogant for her taste.

'All hospitals are understaffed,' Janessa remarked quietly and matter-of-factly as she looped the stethoscope around her neck. She wouldn't allow herself to be embroiled in a slanging match with this man. She was a professional and she had a job to do. 'Right, Joey, let's get you sorted.'

'Joey? My name is Dr Trevellion, not Joey,' he growled, his words clipped yet measured, indicating he knew not to raise his tone in case he upset the babies.

Momentarily stunned, Janessa met his gaze, her eyebrows raised as her insides did a little nervous flip at this news. Dr Trevellion! She'd known he was coming to Adelaide Mercy hospital for six months as she'd been the one to initially request his presence, and while she'd read his articles and followed his career, she never would have connected the photograph of the clean, crisp professional portrayed in medical journals to the crumpled, crabby man in her NICU.

Here he was. Australian specialist. The great and marvellous—and obviously arrogant and impatient—Dr Miles Trevellion. In *her* NICU! Great. It was just what she didn't need added to her impossibly draining day. Then again, she supposed as he was one of the world's leading NICU specialists, she should have expected the arrogance and self-importance he seemed to exude, but it didn't, however, change the fact that little Joey required their expertise.

'Joey is the baby's name, Dr Trevellion,' she pointed out, both of them busy as they prepared to treat Joey. 'He was here in the unit two weeks ago, doing this same old party trick, but apparently he's back for a repeat performance.'

'He's done it before?' Dr Trevellion clenched his square jaw in disapproval. 'Then why wasn't he here in the unit, receiving the proper treatment, instead of in the ward, in the hands of an inexperienced mother?' The exasperation in his tone was evident.

Janessa's muscles instantly tensed at his words and she ground her teeth. 'You may regard Joey's mother as inexperienced but I'll have you know that Adelaide Mercy prides itself on providing the best instruction and support for every mother who comes through our doors.'

'So you pushed him up to the maternity ward because there wasn't room for him here?'

'On the contrary. Joey's mother needs to learn how to deal with this situation. The fact that Joey's been having breathing difficulties is the main reason why they haven't been discharged yet. We couldn't rule out something like this happening again and I'll have you know that Joey was clinically stable before being released to the maternity ward.'

'Well, he's not now. Let's get an IV line in and monitor him properly.'

Janessa glanced at Dr Trevellion, noting that his tone had mellowed slightly and now, instead of looking annoyed and impatient, he simply looked tired and exhausted, and she wondered exactly when he'd arrived, not only at Adelaide Mercy hospital but, more importantly, when he'd arrived in Australia. She certainly hoped he hadn't come here directly from an international flight but now that she took in his attire, she guessed her assumptions were fairly accurate. He would have wanted to make his own assessment on the yet-to-be delivered conjoined twins he'd been appointed to care for. If their positions had been reversed, Janessa would have gone directly to the hospital from the airport as well.

The only words spoken between the two of them were instructions and Janessa found Dr Miles Trevellion to be clear and direct. That was good given that she'd be working with him for the next six months. A thrill of excitement swept through her at the realisation that she was standing opposite the great neonate surgeon yet she was grounded enough not to let it go to her head.

'There you go, little guy,' Dr Trevellion said softly about five minutes later when Joey started to stabilise, the rasping in his chest now beginning to settle into a more normal rhythm. Dr Trevellion took off his gloves and gently touched the baby's skin, showing such intense caring that Janessa was momentarily stunned.

He cared. He had a heart and it could be touched. Watching him, the way he interacted with little Joey, was enough to restore her faith in him. She'd never doubted his abilities but seeing him speaking so softly to the babe, watching the tender way he touched the little boy's body, showed her that he was a man who really did care about his patients.

'Hey, Nessa. Kaycee said you needed my help,' a man in his late forties, with slightly greying hair and the occasional hint of a lilting Scottish accent, said as he sauntered towards them. Janessa looked away from Miles Trevellion, only belatedly realising she'd been staring at him.

'Oh, hi, Ray. No. We're fine here. Situation stabilised. But allow me to introduce you to Dr Trevellion.'

Ray's bushy eyebrows shot up at the news. 'Trevellion? Really? *The* same Dr Trevellion who's come here to look after our Sheena's conjoined twins?' Without waiting for an answer, he continued, 'In that case, welcome to Adelaide Mercy and to the NICU.' Ray heartily shook the other man's hand. 'We're so glad to have you on our team, aren't we, Nessa?'

'Very.' Janessa pulled off her gloves and stepped back from the crib. 'Ray, would you mind calling up to the ward to let them know we'll be keeping Joey for at least the next twenty-four hours,' she requested.

'Right you are, lassie. Say, why don't the two of you go and have a cuppa, eh? I'm sure Dr Trevellion would relish the chance to talk about our Sheena, given that's the reason why he's come here in the first place.'

'You took the words right out of my mouth,' she agreed. 'We'd best do it while the unit is a relatively quiet and settled. Goodness knows, that can change at any given moment.' Janessa looked to the handsome newcomer and spread her hand wide, indicating the way to her office. 'Shall we?'

'What? You?' He looked from Ray to Janessa. 'You're joking, right? You're just a nurse.'

'*Just* a nurse?' She frowned at him. 'That's a phrase you'd better not bandy around too much, Dr Trevellion. I'll have you know that our full-time senior nurses are the best in Australia. There's Ray here, who is always so calm, cool and collected.' She pointed. 'Over there we have Kaycee, who is forever brilliant and a walking encyclopaedia, and the woman who's just walked into the ward, heading for the sink, is Helena.'

'She's going to retire at the end of the year,' Ray added. 'Not sure what we're going to do without her. She's such a mother-hen, always looking after her chicks, and I'm not just talking about the young mums who are constantly in the unit with their ill wee ones—she's a mother to the staff as well.'

'My senior three.' Janessa nodded.

Dr Trevellion was still looking at her but this time there was amused disbelief in his eyes. '*You're* really the head of the NICU? But you look about nineteen years old!'

Ray chuckled. 'That she does, but don't let the outward demeanour fool you. Our Janessa is well trained, highly in-telligent and always in control.'

'Thank you, Ray,' Janessa remarked, feeling extremely self-conscious.

'*You're* Janessa Austen?' Miles couldn't disguise his utter astonishment. His expression should have amused her, and probably on another day it might have, but now that the emergencies seemed to have settled down, fatigue and hunger were starting to gnaw at her again.

'I've heard all about you,' he continued as he followed her. 'Although for some unfathomable reason, I expected you to be...' He stopped, trying his best to be diplomatic but realising he'd already failed. His mind was still fuzzy from the travelling he'd done during the past thirty hours. 'Older,' he finished.

'I may look young, Dr Trevellion, but I can safely assure you,' she said as they walked into her office, 'that I am fully qualified to *be* the head of the NICU.' She closed the door behind her and motioned to the seat opposite her desk. Dr Trevellion stared at her and it seemed to take a few seconds for her words to sink in and for him to realise that she was indeed quite serious.

She *was* Janessa Austen and this *was* her NICU. 'Then it must be said, Dr Austen, that you carry your age exceedingly well.' His tone was rich, deep and smooth as he delivered the compliment. A complete contrast from the way he'd spoken when he'd first entered the unit, and for a second the change almost put Janessa off balance.

'Thank you.' She'd be unwise to put any credence in the compliment, even though she wanted to because, quite simply, no man had complimented her in such a very long time. However, this man was her new colleague, at least for the next six months that he would remain at Adelaide Mercy hospital.

He'd come specifically to guide the neonate team through

the delivery and subsequent surgeries of the conjoined twins who were due to be born within the next few weeks. He would also be doing some research, some lecturing and helping out in the NICU when his schedule permitted. Allowing herself to become distracted by his compliments, by his good looks and by his status was out of the question. Brisk, clear and professional. That was the only type of relationship she wanted with him.

'Please, won't you sit down?' She again proffered the chair. 'You must be tired.'

'Do I look tired?' he asked as he relented and sat in the chair opposite her, a hint of his earlier impatience returning. His back was straight, his shoulders broad and they really filled out the clothes he wore. Janessa swallowed and looked away from his body to his annoyed blue eyes.

'Yes, as a matter of fact, you do,' she replied honestly. 'My guess is that you've probably come from the airport straight to the hospital in order to check on the conjoined twins.'

'That is what I've been hired to do.'

'Of course.' She clasped her hands tightly together and placed them carefully onto her desk as she controlled her breathing. It wasn't what he was saying that was starting to grate on her nerves but *how* he was saying it. His tone was clipped and mildly annoyed and she didn't appreciate it at all but she could also hear the fatigue hidden beneath and that was reason enough for her to cut him some slack…that and the fact that she would be working closely with him. It would be ridiculous to get off on the wrong foot. 'Would you prefer a cup of coffee instead of tea?' she offered.

'I don't want a drink. I didn't come here for polite pleasantries.'

'Obviously,' she remarked under her breath.

'Pardon?'

She pasted on a polite smile. 'Nothing. So, I take it you've already seen Sheena?'

'Yes,' he grumbled with increasing impatience. 'That's why I was in Maternity and was able to bring that sick little baby to the NICU before things got worse.' Irritated, unable to sit, Dr Trevellion stood, his presence almost filling her small office as he paced back and forth.

She recalled the way she'd pored over the plethora of articles he'd written over the years, how he'd reported on his vast experience working with many different teams in the caring practices and surgical breakthroughs with conjoined twins. He was a highly reputed specialist, a man of incredible knowledge, and she had to admit to being a little disappointed in finding him so blusterous. She sincerely hoped it was merely the jet lag talking and that their entire working relationship wasn't going to be this antagonistic.

Thinking of her amazing friend Sheena, who was the mother-to-be of the conjoined twins, Janessa forced herself to take a calming breath before remarking, 'I do thank you for bringing Joey to the NICU. Your prompt action and attention were invaluable to his health and now we can continue to monitor his progress more closely.'

Dr Trevellion stopped pacing and turned to glare at her, his blue eyes even more piercing than before. 'Don't you dare hand me that polite diplomatic clap-trap. I don't appreciate it one bit. The fact of the matter is that if this NICU is to be the primary provider for conjoined twins, your unit needs to be run with a tighter grip on the expectations placed upon it not only by the hospital at large but by the needs of the patients.'

Janessa's eyes opened wider at his words. How dared he? And she'd been trying to be nice. 'And *I* don't appreciate,' she interjected when he paused to drag in a breath to continue his blustering, 'visiting consultants who barge into *my* unit, demanding instant attention and upsetting my staff. My unit runs effectively and efficiently and I'll thank you kindly not to come in here with your unfounded accusations and over-inflated ego.' While she spoke, she kept her voice clear but firm. Yelling and bawling people out was definitely not Janessa's style but neither was she a doormat. She hadn't achieved her position as head of unit simply by her good looks. She could be direct and as stubborn as the next man when it was called for.

Slowly she rose to her full height of five feet eight inches and placed her hands on her desk as she met his gaze with determination and veiled anger. 'You may have more experience than any of us when it comes to conjoined twins, Dr Trevellion, but that is no reason for you to believe that you're also employed to harness more productivity from the Adelaide Mercy NICU. You are not. You are here for the next six months as a visiting consultant, not head of unit, not even as a permanent member of staff and I'll thank you kindly to keep your comments to those of a professional nature without adding an insulting slur to everything you say.'

He raised one eyebrow at her and for an instant she thought she saw his lips twitch into a bit of a smile. The action confused her. Was he cross with her or was there something else happening here? She had the strangest feeling that he was testing the waters, trying to gauge her personality. If that was the case, she still didn't like it. 'In other words, if I can't say anything nice, don't say anything at all?'

She lifted her chin a little higher, defiance flashing in her eyes. It was then and only then that Miles actually started to realise that whilst his new colleague might indeed look very young, she most certainly wasn't. There was wisdom in her eyes that said he'd almost pushed her to the brink of keeping her temper in check. She was doing very well at controlling it, and he had to admit he admired her style.

'If you like.' Her tone was still controlled, still firm and still on fire—a fire that was directed solely at him.

'Well, then.' He inclined his head towards her. 'I'll bid you *adieu*.' He turned and had taken but three steps towards her door, his back ramrod straight, his broad shoulders square, the material of his white shirt pulled tightly around his firm torso, when Janessa spoke again, her voice brisk, efficient and polite.

'Thank you for your assistance, Dr Trevellion. I'll see you at the prep meeting tomorrow morning.'

Dr Trevellion didn't speak a word but merely continued on his way.

As she watched him go, Janessa didn't move. Instead she counted slowly to ten inside her head, hoping to calm her nerves. It didn't work. She counted to twenty and started to feel a little better. Exhaling and sinking back into her chair, she picked up a piece of scrap paper from the recycle bin and ripped it into tiny shreds, the action doing a lot to calm her frazzled nerves.

Miles Trevellion was one of the finest leading NICU specialists in the field. He was a qualified vascular surgeon who would be caring for Sheena Woodcombe's conjoined twins, which were scheduled for delivery by Caesarean section in two weeks' time. Janessa was the second NICU specialist in charge—a placement she was determined to keep given that Sheena was like a sister to her.

She sat there for a whole two minutes, her door open, making her feel highly exposed even though no one walked by. She simply couldn't believe how insufferable Miles Trevellion had turned out to be. She had been initially excited to learn of his appointment and then nervous at the prospect of working alongside the great man. Now, she wasn't even looking forward to their first preparation meeting tomorrow morning.

'It doesn't matter what you want,' she told herself sternly as she rose from the desk. Sheena was the one who mattered and she wasn't going to let her friend down. The two women had met on their first day of medical school and although Janessa had pursued neonatology and Sheena paediatrics, their friendship had remained solid.

They knew each other's history. Together they'd celebrated the good times and cried through the bad. Sheena had been the person who had helped rebuild Janessa's confidence all those years ago, who had supported her when her father had died and who had been the first person on the scene when Janessa's house had burnt to the ground eight months ago.

In return, Janessa had been there for Sheena, through thick and thin. Bridesmaid at her wedding, confidante throughout Sheena's rocky marriage and supporter through the present divorce proceedings. Sheena's life was now upside down, and Janessa was determined to be by her side.

Being an integral part of the neonatal team responsible for the care of the conjoined twins once they were born was not only going to be one of the highlights of her career but also an esteemed privilege for in the future she would be a strong presence of the twins' lives.

She hadn't been able to save her own child, the baby born far too early. At only nineteen years old, she'd given birth to a tiny premature baby who hadn't been strong enough to survive. She'd been a young, inexperienced teenage mother whose darling little boy, Connor, hadn't been strong enough to fight for his life. Her young marriage hadn't survived the death of the baby but her determination to specialise in the field of neonatology had started to evolve.

The staff who had looked after her when Connor had been born, the specialists who had cared for him, fighting for his life, doing everything they could, had been her inspiration to do well in her classes. She had wanted to be like them, to be able to make a difference in someone else's life, to help and support young mothers and to fight for the lives of the little tiny babies who were born weeks before their due dates.

With supportive parents, she'd started medical school, only to have her mother pass away within that first year. Ultimately, it was her friendship with Sheena that had helped her through those difficult years.

Now she would do everything she could for her friend and those beautiful babies. She would be a part of their lives, their Aunty Nessa, who would love them and spoil them, and that was an honour she didn't take at all lightly.

She was now a specialist, able to help young mothers such as she had been. She had the knowledge, she had the experience and she would provide the best care for those babies, alongside her new colleague. Miles Trevellion would no doubt be the thorn in her side throughout this experience, given the man appeared to have an ego the size of Australia. He was good looking—of that there was no doubt. He was highly skilled and intelligent—that was not in question. But in instilling confidence and gaining respect of his colleagues? On that front, it appeared he was seriously lacking.

Miles Trevellion was the specialist, the surgeon, the man who was going to ensure those two little girls were able to live normal lives, and to that end Janessa would have to bite her tongue if he offended or upset her. The babies and Sheena were the important ones in this scenario and there was no way she was going to let any of them down.

CHAPTER TWO

Much later that day, once life in the unit had settled to a more normal level, Janessa made her way to the maternity ward to check on Sheena.

'Did you meet him?' Sheena asked eagerly as soon as Janessa came into the private room. As Sheena was a practising paediatrician at Adelaide Mercy, now on maternity leave, it was only right that she have top-of-the-line care.

'Who?' She was fairly certain Sheena was referring to Miles Trevellion, the man whom she'd been hard pressed to stop thinking about ever since he'd made such a dramatic entrance into her life.

'Who? Are you blind, deaf and dumb?'

Janessa sat in the chair beside the bed and closed her eyes. 'I feel it. Who are we talking about?'

'Miles Trevellion, of course. Isn't he charming?'

Janessa frowned but kept her eyes closed, an image of the man they were talking about swimming easily to mind. 'Not exactly the word I'd use to describe him.'

'It is for me. And he's sexy and good-looking—and those eyes...' Sheena sighed with longing, and when Janessa opened her eyes to look at her friend she saw that the woman's hands were clasped romantically together and held close towards her heart...or as close as she could get due to her enlarged abdomen.

'He can check on me any time he feels like it,' she drawled, the words punctuated with little sighs.

Janessa shook her head then chuckled at her friend. 'You should already know what he looked like. Didn't you work with him years ago when you did your overseas placement in Philadelphia?'

'I did and that's where I also met Will.'

'Ahh…the real love of your life. No wonder you didn't talk about Miles that much when you arrived back in Australia. You were too busy pining over Will.'

'Yep. Will. The man who didn't want me,' Sheena continued, before flicking her fingers as though to rid herself of the memory. 'But Miles…now, he was always quite the catch, even back then. So gorgeous and suave, and let me tell you, Nessa, he's improved with age.' Sheena waggled her eyebrows up and down.

'Well, I'm glad you like him. It's important that you like him. After all, as far as conjoined twins go, he's the expert.' And, therefore, she told herself, probably entitled to be arrogant and insufferable. For the job he needed to do, he no doubt needed a big ego as well. Still, she couldn't help reflecting on the small smile she'd seen touch his lips and wondered what it might be like to see him really smile. She shook her head, as though to clear it.

'You don't like him?' Sheena was stunned.

'It doesn't matter whether I like him or not, Sheenie. I respect him for his intelligence and I'm happy to learn he clearly has a decent bedside manner, given the way you're gushing about him.'

'Oh, he's charming all right. It's been ten years since I last saw him. We worked together for just under a month and even back then he had the habit of setting every woman's heart fluttering with his striking good looks and deep voice and sexy walk and—'

Janessa held up her hands. 'All right, all right. I get the point.' Because she really did. She could quite see, in the looks department, that Miles Trevellion had a lot going for him, but for her money she was attracted to men who had manners, charm and intellect. Well, she had to admit that Miles also had intellect, of that there was no doubt, but manners and charm? She'd yet to see what Sheena was talking about.

'So why don't you like him?' Sheena asked.

Janessa paused for a moment, choosing her words carefully. 'It's not that I don't like him per se, I hardly know the man.'

'But you were looking forward to him coming? To meeting him. You were the one who suggested we ask him to come to Adelaide Mercy in the first place, remember? And then you brought in a swag of his articles for me to read.' Sheena pointed to the pile of medical journals in the opened top drawer by the bed. Janessa instantly leaned over and closed the drawer, not wanting to dwell on the way she'd gushed about the man and his genius.

She could see she needed to define her present feelings towards Miles Trevellion in order to get Sheena off her back. 'OK. I have no problem admitting I admire him as a professional. If I find him a little overbearing and slightly dictatorial, that's my personal problem. Our job—the job Dr Trevellion and I need to focus on—is looking after your girls, and that's something we'll be doing to the highest standards.'

'You're still being cagey and I know that means I'm not going to get much else out of you, so instead tell me all about the medical emergency that happened here around lunchtime. Is everything all right?'

'Yes. All under control. Baby is fine. Dr Trevellion saved the day.'

'Great.' Sheena didn't sound at all happy. 'And I missed it, of course, because I'm stuck here, not allowed to get out of bed and needing to have my catheter bag changed almost hourly because my bladder is the size of a peanut, which means I only heard the news second hand,' Sheena grumbled. 'The nurses, who usually gossip about everything, have told me hardly anything. It's entirely not fair that as a practising paediatrician and one who is a valued member of staff at this very hospital, I'm not all that impressed about whoever has given the "gag" order surrounding me.'

'That would be me and you're a paediatrician who is on *maternity leave*.' Janessa stood and instantly picked up her friend's wrist, checking her pulse. 'You're not allowed to be worried or stressed or concerned or anything else about the goings-on in the hospital, Sheenie, and you know that. We've discussed it.'

'My blood pressure is fine,' Sheena grumped.

'Actually, it's a little raised.'

'That's because you won't tell me what's going on. I'm just a human incubator. Nothing more. Nothing less.'

Janessa smiled. 'Don't say that. You know you don't mean it. You mean everything to these babies and they mean everything to you. Your girls need you, Sheena, you're their world. You're the only one who can really protect them and you do that by lying here and doing nothing. We can only do so much to help the girls and therefore need to keep you as calm and controlled as possible. The gag order is in place because I can't have you getting stressed about things you would ordinarily have some control over. You're an amazing paediatrician, Sheenie, but you're on maternity leave and I need you to *leave* hospital matters alone.'

'But sometimes telling me what's happening actually decreases the risk of my blood pressure going up because I'm not frustrated from being kept in the dark,' Sheena quickly pointed out.

Janessa paused for a moment before shaking her head. 'It's all under control. Nothing to report. Now, before I forget, the special baby clothes that we picked out from the catalogue should be here within the next few days. I received an email telling me they were being shipped so we can look forward to their arrival soon.'

'I can hardly remember what we ordered.' Sheena frowned, still not happy that Janessa had cut off her sources of information.

'Well, let me remind you. There was a pretty pink dress with frills and...' As the two of them sat there, talking about baby clothes, Janessa started to feel the stress of her day begin to ease. It had been a long, long day, made even longer with the arrival of Miles Trevellion, who she hadn't expected to see until tomorrow at their prep meeting.

'Now,' she said, standing to hug her friend, 'you'll be due for growth hormone injections soon because we need these little girls as fit and as healthy as possible, so settle down and get some sleep.'

'Ha. My girls may be literally joined at the hip but that doesn't stop them from doing their gymnastic double act any time I try to get some shut-eye. It's impossible to sleep through that.'

Janessa laughed. 'Well...if you can't sleep, at least rest.'

'I do little else, my friend, whereas you look as though you're about ready to drop. Have you been burning the candle at both ends again?' At Janessa's shrug, Sheena eyed her friend closely. 'When was the last time you went out to the airfield?'

Janessa sighed. 'At least a fortnight ago. I didn't manage to get out last week.'

'Make sure you make some time, soon.' There was a caring note in Sheena's words. 'I need my Nessa in top form to look after my girls when they're born.'

Janessa placed her hand on Sheena's abdomen and received a lovely fluttering kick in response. A smile came instantly to her lips. 'I'll be as bright as bright can be. Oh, I can't wait to meet them, Sheenie. I'm so excited.'

'Me, too. I know I whinge and moan but…' Tears glistened in her eyes and Janessa passed her a tissue. 'There I go again. My emotions are so unstable.'

'They're supposed to be,' Janessa dismissed with a smile, taking a tissue for herself and dabbing at her own eyes. She noticed that Sheena looked past her and realised it was probably one of the sisters coming in to take Sheena's obs. Glancing over her shoulder, she was stunned to see Miles Trevellion leaning against the doorjamb as though he'd been there for quite some time.

'Hey, Miles. Come on in. Janessa and I are just having a weeping fest. Care to join?'

'I'll give it a miss, but thanks for the offer.' He smiled at Sheena as he sauntered into the room and Janessa immediately put out a hand, grabbing hold of the end of Sheena's bed, in order to steady herself against the effect of his powerful smile.

He'd showered and changed out of his suit and in some ways she wished he hadn't. In a suit, he'd been just like all of the other consultants and surgeons she dealt with on a regular basis but now dressed in dark denim jeans that seemed to have long forgotten any shape but his own and a pale blue polo shirt, his dark brown wavy hair still a little damp from his shower, he was completely irresistible.

Up until now, the only dealings she'd had with Miles Trevellion had been when he'd been scowling or criticising her. Now…the smile that creased his face, the way his lips lifted to show off his white teeth, the intensity of his blue eyes as they sparked with life only enhanced his already naturally handsome features and, much to her chagrin, Janessa realised she wasn't as immune to him as she'd previously thought.

'H-How long have you been standing there?' she wanted to know, silently berating herself for stammering. She forced herself to look away from him, to concentrate on staring at the floor, but she found her gaze drifting back to his as he spoke.

'Long enough. I didn't want to interrupt your bonding moments. You two talk to each other in exactly the same way that my sisters talk to each other.'

'We feel like sisters,' Sheena answered.

'Is that so?' Miles raised his eyebrows as he walked slowly round to the opposite side of the bed from where Janessa stood. He was looking more at Janessa than at Sheena and quirked an eyebrow in her direction.

'We've known each other for years,' Janessa felt compelled to say, even though she wasn't sure why. It was just the way he was looking at her, as though he was accusing her of having too close a friendship with a person who was now a patient. Technically, though, Sheena wasn't her patient—the babies were.

'And neither of us actually *have* a sister,' Sheena pointed out, 'so we've ended up being the closest each other has.'

'Interesting.' Miles fixed Janessa with a curious stare. 'Does that mean it will be too much for you to look after the twins once they're born? You're emotionally involved with Sheena. What if something were to go wrong? Would you be able to cope with such an event?'

Janessa visibly bristled. 'Nothing is going to go wrong. That's why you're here, Dr Trevellion, and don't you dare think, even for one second, about removing me from this case. Whilst Sheena and I look upon and support each other like sisters, we are not biologically related, which doesn't make it at all inappropriate for me to care for her babies. Besides, our entire unit is like a close-knit family, so if you remove me from the case, you'll have to remove everyone, and that will benefit no one. There is nothing any of us, not only in the NICU but within Maternity and the other associated departments, wouldn't do for Sheena. She is beloved by us all and, in fact, I would go as far to say that *because* we all love her, the care we'll be providing for Ellie and Sarah once they're born and throughout their subsequent surgeries will be second to none.'

'Aw...' Sheena smiled at her friend, a fresh bout of tears gathering in her eyes. 'That was lovely. Thank you.' She reached for Janessa's hand and gave it a little squeeze, then turned to look at Miles, her voice firm but still personable. 'And you—don't you even dare think of moving me to a different hospital. I don't want to go to Philadelphia, even if they do have the highest success rate and experience with conjoined twins. These are my babies and I'll be having them right here, at Adelaide Mercy, with my extended family standing beside me, supporting me throughout the entire process. *I'm* the incubator and I have spoken.'

Miles looked from one woman to the other, his gaze settling on Janessa. She was standing proudly by her friend's bedside, her shoulders back, her chin raised, her eyes glinting with that defiance he'd witnessed earlier that day.

She looked…incredible.

After he'd left the NICU, he'd returned to Maternity and checked on Sheena before being directed to the hospital's residential wing, which was to be his home for the length of his stay. There was no point in trying to procure a furnished apartment close to the hospital as he'd be spending the majority of his time within hospital walls. Therefore, the one-bedroom apartment he'd been provided with was more than adequate for his needs.

He'd showered and changed his clothes, which had definitely helped him to wash away the long hours of travelling he'd had to endure. Once he'd unpacked, he'd headed out for a walk around the campus in order to get his bearings. The sooner he knew his way around the place, the better.

Throughout the entire afternoon, thoughts of Dr Janessa Austen had been niggling at the back of his mind, like an annoying noise he couldn't shut off. Twice, as he'd walked around, he'd seen a woman of her height and colouring and, thinking it might be her, had been astonished to find his heart rate increasing at the thought of enjoying another sparring match with her.

Then he'd wandered back to the NICU, in the hope of seeing her again, to get another look, to try and figure out exactly what it was about her that appeared to be intriguing him so much. When she hadn't been there, he'd politely asked one of the staff where she might be and had been told to check Maternity.

It was odd for his thoughts to be occupied in such a fashion, to be more than professionally curious about a colleague and now, as he stood opposite her, Sheena lying on the bed between them, Janessa Austen's rich brown eyes filled with determination, Miles finally realised the answer.

It was because she wasn't afraid to stand up for what she believed in.

It was clear that she believed in her staff, in her unit and in her bond with Sheena. She was a woman of substance and the more he spoke to her, the closer he was to figuring her out. Once he figured her out, he would be able to put her right out of his mind. He liked puzzles and the challenges they presented. That was no doubt the only reason *why* she'd even caught his attention in the first place. He was sure of it.

Miles slowly looked away from Janessa, his thoughts returning to the present. He smiled at Sheena, pleased she was still calm and controlled even though Janessa had become a little riled. 'Of course. You will stay at Adelaide Mercy. Dr Austen will be by your side, caring for your children every step of the way. Whatever you say goes, Sheena. You're the mother. You call the shots.'

'Good. Don't you forget it.' Sheena looked closely at Miles for a moment then grinned widely. 'You always were such a tease, Miles Trevellion. Always stirring. I see you haven't changed.'

'Why change perfection?' he asked, and gave a little bow. Janessa watched him and frowned again, confusion replacing her earlier annoyance.

'Stirring?' Janessa let go of Sheena's hand and placed both her hands on her hips. 'Do you mean that you were simply saying those things in order to get a rise out of me, Dr Trevellion?'

'You're in trouble now,' Sheena remarked to Miles in a sing-song voice.

'Not a rise, Dr Austen.'

'Then a test of some sort?'

'If you like.'

'You don't think that's a little juvenile? To test your new

colleagues? Colleagues who, I might add, are all highly trained professionals?'

'Colleagues who have shown me that they're not afraid to stand up for what they believe in,' he countered. 'Colleagues who I now know are doing this job for more than the money they earn. There are two types of medical professionals in the world—those who do it for money and those who are called to serve their patients. I've worked with both over the years and in throwing a few bones at you, I've been able to see *how* you bite, *when* you bite and *why* you bite.'

'I hope you're not implying that Janessa is a dog in this scenario, Miles,' Sheena interjected laughingly. 'If so, don't go hiding behind me.'

Janessa couldn't believe what she was hearing, what her new and esteemed colleague was saying. He'd been testing her? Trying to rile her to see what sort of doctor she was? Anger, frustration and disbelief warred within her but there was also a part, deep down inside, that understood what he'd done.

He was a man who travelled the world, offering and applying his assistance to highly specialised cases, such as conjoined twins. He was a fount of knowledge and expertise, but as his placements would no doubt be of three to six months' duration it would mean he'd have to develop a foolproof way of sounding out his colleagues in order to know what type of personalities he was dealing with sooner rather than later.

She took another calming breath, crossing her arms over her chest, and met his look. 'Have you collated enough data on me, Dr Trevellion, or can I expect another round of your potshots?' Although her words were calm, her tone was cool.

The answer she received from him was a bright smile and where the last one had been aimed at Sheena, this one was definitely aimed directly at her...and she felt its full effect.

Her mouth went dry, her heart rate instantly increased and she found her knees beginning to buckle. Without breaking eye contact, she gracefully sat back down in the chair she'd occupied earlier.

The man had straight, white teeth, a slightly crooked nose, a cleft in his perfectly square jaw, which was covered in a five o'clock shadow that only added to his air of powerful masculinity. All of that combined with his intense blue eyes, which now appeared to be filled with warmth and deep satisfaction, made a lethal combination.

'I'm very pleased to say that you've passed with flying colours, Dr Austen. Not only have you proved that you're willing to stand up for your staff and your unit, you've proved to be the perfect person to assist me in the care of Sheena's twin girls.'

'How magnanimous of you, Dr Trevellion.' She worked hard to keep her tone droll, as though she didn't care one iota about his opinion when in reality she did. Here was a man she'd looked up to in a professional capacity, reading his articles, interested in his research, delighted by his turn of phrase, and when she'd met him, she'd been disappointed to find him like so many other surgeons—overbearing and dictatorial. And then he'd walked into Sheena's room, smiling brightly, his eyes twinkling, his clothes fitting him to perfection.

Physically, he was gorgeous—and he no doubt knew it—but he was also showing her that he wasn't as unreasonable as she'd first concluded. Perhaps there *was* more depth, more substance to Miles Trevellion. Perhaps the man who had written those powerful articles, not only detailing the intricacies of neonate surgery but also somehow allowing his compassion for his little patients to bleed into the structure of his clinical articles, was making an appearance.

Sheena laughed at them both, her head turning from one to the other as though she were at a tennis match. 'Are you both seriously going to call each other Dr Austen and Dr Trevellion for the next six months? Seems a little old-fashioned and ludicrous to me,' she finished.

'Sheena's right.' Miles came around the bed and held out his hand to Janessa. 'I don't believe we've been properly introduced. I'm Miles.'

She stood, relieved when her legs appeared able to support her once more. Polite and professional. That was all she had to be towards him—polite and professional. 'Janessa,' she replied, and yet the instant his warm hand enveloped hers, she felt her logical thought processes fly out the window, and at the same time her knees started to buckle once more.

She stumbled a little and Miles instantly moved closer, placing his other hand at her waist to steady her. His nearness only seemed to make things worse, as she breathed in his subtle spicy scent and became all too aware of just how close they were.

Gasping, she looked up into his eyes and was surprised to find him staring back at her, his blue eyes wide and slightly shocked. His eyes were perfect, so blue and so…perfect. Just like a sky on a cloudless day where she could take to the air and escape her life for a brief spell.

Her heart started to beat a little faster in her chest and her tongue came out to wet her lips. His gaze dipped for a second to witness the action, his Adam's apple sliding up and down his perfect throat. The world around them seemed to pause, just long enough that they could take a quick breath, drawing each other in before slowly exhaling.

'Janessa.' Her name sounded incredible spoken in his rich, deep tones and a wave of tingles spread throughout her body. This was wrong. It was ridiculous that she should feel an instant attraction towards this man when she wasn't even sure she liked him.

Naturally, she appreciated him as a colleague, easily accepting his genius in their chosen speciality and, of course, she'd fallen victim to a bit of hero-worship of such intelligence, devouring the articles he'd written the instant her editions of the *Journal of Neonatology* had arrived. That, however, didn't mean she needed to act like a silly schoolgirl simply because he was touching her.

Becoming cross with herself, she quickly disengaged any contact and spun away from him, taking two wobbly steps towards the door, her increased heart rate causing her breathing to remain uneven. 'Uh…anyway. I'd best go and…uh… check on a few of the babies before calling it a night.' She spoke quickly…too quickly.

'Are you all right?' Sheena asked. 'You're all flushed.'

'Am I?' Janessa raised a hand to her cheek and tried her best not to look at Miles but when she did, she saw him standing at the foot of the bed, his hands shoved into the pockets of his jeans. He was looking at her as though something strange had just happened but he wasn't exactly sure what. Had he felt it too? If so, what did that mean? Or perhaps this was another one of his tests. She quickly returned her attention to Sheena.

'Oh, that's probably because I've been up since four this morning. That's when our first new baby for the day decided to arrive and as I live the closest…well, I don't mind being called in.'

'Where do you live?' Miles asked, walking back to the other side of Sheena's bed, putting more distance between himself and his new colleague who, when he'd been close to her, had sent shock waves throughout his entire being such as he hadn't felt in an exceedingly long time.

He had no idea how or why this had happened, which was unusual for him. He was the man in charge, the one they all came to when they needed answers, and he liked it. The spark of awareness he'd just experienced when he'd been close to Janessa Austen meant absolutely nothing. He was a professional…and he was jet-lagged. Yes, that was most likely why this awareness of her had flared up. He was jet-lagged.

'Janessa's been living in the residential wing of the hospital for the past six months,' Sheena provided. 'She says it's the easiest way to keep an eye on me and the girls.'

He was surprised at this news. 'Really? Why not find an apartment close by?' Miles wanted to know, looking at Janessa who was almost ready to sprint out the door.

'Her house burned down and it's being rebuilt,' Sheena offered, answering for her once more. Janessa was glad of that as she was still struggling to get herself under control and to *not* look at Miles. 'We were supposed to go apartment-hunting but that's when I found out the twins were conjoined. I crumbled into a blathering mess and Janessa picked me up.' Sheena smiled lovingly at her friend.

'You'd have done the same for me,' Janessa replied, then opened the door, this time keeping her gaze trained on Sheena. 'Riley will be around soon to do his evening checks on you, but call me if you need anything, all right?'

'Yes, I'm fine. I have too many people fussing over me, especially Riley. What a fusspot of an obstetrician he is. Go. Sleep. See you in the morning.' Sheena waved to her friend.

Janessa nodded and with a polite smile aimed at Miles she all but ran from her friend's room.

The instant she was gone, Sheena turned to look at Miles, watching him closely. 'I don't believe it,' she said softly.

'Believe what?' he asked.

'You. Janessa.'

'What?' Miles was a little taken aback.

'Oh, don't play stupid with me. I've seen that look in your eyes before.'

'What look?' Miles settled down into the chair beside her bed and took her wrist in his fingers in order to check her pulse, hoping to distract her from whatever it was she was about to say. Fifteen seconds later, he released her. 'Good. How's your blood pressure?'

'Wendy.'

'Pardon?' Miles looked at Sheena.

'When we worked together ten years ago, we also worked with a doctor whose name was Wendy. Do you remember Wendy?'

'Of course I remember Wendy,' he replied a little briskly, and stood to walk to the end of her bed, unable to stay calm and seated if Sheena was determined to take him on a trip down memory lane. Wendy. How could he ever forget Wendy? He couldn't.

'You were very interested in Wendy when we met ten years ago.'

'What? How do you know?'

'You had this twinkle in your eyes. Every time she would come into the room, you would let your gaze rest on her a little longer than usual.'

'Are you sure you weren't projecting the way you used to stare at Will? Honestly, the two of you were madly in love. I still don't know why it didn't work out. He would never tell me.'

Sheena shook her head. 'We're not talking about me and Will, we're talking about you and Janessa.'

'Janessa?'

'Yes. You have the same twinkle in your eyes now as you

did back then. You're interested in Janessa,' Sheena pointed out, then paused and tilted her head to the side, her tone a little softer. 'Whatever happened to Wendy? The two of you were such good friends back then but once my year was up I returned to Australia and sort of lost track of everyone.'

Miles looked down at his shoes for a second and then met Sheena's gaze. 'You were right in guessing I was interested in Wendy. I was, so much so that I married her.'

'What? You're married?'

'Widowed.' The word was spoken softly.

'Oh, Miles. Oh, I'm so sorry. I…I had no idea.'

He shook his head and touched her hand. 'It's fine. She died seven years ago in a train crash.' It was the night where his life had gone from wonderfully full to horrifically empty. 'I've had a lot of years to work through the different stages of grief.'

'That may be, but you're still alone, right?'

Miles nodded. 'It's not so bad. I have my work. I have strong bonds with colleagues.' He thought of his good friend Will Beckman and although he still wondered what had happened between Sheena and Will all those years ago, now was not the time to discuss it. There was no way he could risk a rise in Sheena's blood pressure simply to satisfy his curiosity. 'And now I get to hang out with you again so that's a bonus.' He smiled and watched as Sheena relaxed back against the pillows.

'And you get to work with Janessa, too. She's really quite amazing—don't let her youthful looks fool you.'

'Oh, I've already learned that lesson.' He shifted a little farther away from the bed and turned his attention to a large bunch of flowers on the shelf, pretending to be interested, hoping his words came out with the right amount of non-chalance. 'Janessa, while looking as though she's barely old enough to drive, has proved she's more than capable not only of running a hectic NICU but also of putting visiting consultants firmly in their place.'

Sheena laughed. 'That's our Nessa. And you like her.'

Miles breathed in deeply, the scent of the flowers reminding him of the sweet scent that surrounded Janessa, before slowly exhaling. 'I'm…interested,' he admitted.

Sheena clapped her hands and Miles couldn't help but smile as he looked at his friend. 'I knew it. The twinkle is unmistakable. So?'

'So…what?'

'So what are you going to do about it?'

'Nothing.'

'Nothing? Miles, how many women have you been interested in since Wendy died?'

He thought for a moment and then shrugged. 'A few, but nothing serious.'

'And I'll bet that none of them have captured your attention so completely and as quickly as Janessa, am I right?'

'Uh…' He shoved his hands into his pockets, feeling awkward. 'We don't need to discuss this, Sheena.'

'Hey. I'm the human incubator, who lies here day in, day out providing the best care a mother can for her babies, feeling as though I'm trapped in this room while the world keeps spinning without me. Throw me some crumbs, eh?'

Miles smiled at her words. 'All right, all right. I haven't pursued anyone since Wendy's death.'

'And now you're *interested* in Janessa?'

He exhaled harshly, his words tinged with a slight impatience. 'Do I like what I've seen of her? Yes. Am I intrigued to know more? Yes, but that doesn't necessarily mean I'm going to do anything about it.'

'What? Why not?'

'Because the life I lead is not suited to people like Janessa.'

'How do you know that? You hardly know her.'

'She has her world here. That's clear. She cares for her staff, her friends and most definitely for you, and my world is anywhere and everywhere. The fact that she's caught my attention is neither here nor there. I don't have the head space for any sort of romantic relationships.'

'Well, you at least be nice to her.'

'I will.'

'And take her out to dinner. She needs food. She's too skinny. But then again, maybe because I'm so fat and stuck in here all day like a beached whale, my perceptions are a little skewed.'

Miles laughed at her words but crossed to her side instantly, placing a reassuring hand on her arm. 'You're not fat.' His words were heartfelt. 'You're pregnant.'

'An incubator,' Sheena grumbled, but smiled back at him. Sighing, she looked at Miles. 'Janessa's special.'

'I'm beginning to realise that.'

It took the walk down the single flight of stairs to the NICU for Janessa's heart rate to return to a normal level as she tried not to replay every little minute detail of when she'd been dangerously close to Miles Trevellion.

He was turning out to be quite the chameleon. First he'd been brisk and arrogant, then supportive towards Sheena and then... And then what? Hot and heavy with her? No. The man had taken her hand in his purely as a form of greeting, and when her idiotic knees hadn't been able to cope with being so near to him, he'd placed a supportive hand at her waist in order to stop her from falling. He'd been caring and polite.

And what about the long and intense gaze they'd shared?

She closed her eyes for a brief moment, her heart rate once more picking up as she remembered the way he'd looked at her. Surprise, shock and sensuality. Until that moment, she hadn't thought it possible to get all three together but Miles Trevellion had pulled it off…with a bang.

Janessa shook her head, pushing the thoughts away completely. Work. Babies. Sheena. Sleep. Those were the important things in her life at the moment, not thoughts of Miles Trevellion, and with a deep breath she set off to do her job. After confirming that both Joey and Taneesha were doing just fine, and that the rest of the patients and staff were under control, Helena, who was on the night shift, shooed her away.

'You look completely worn out,' Helena said as she pointed to the NICU door. 'Food, shower and sleep. I'll see you in the morning.'

There was nothing else for Janessa to do than to head out of the NICU. She walked through the long corridors, the hospital catering team out in force as they collected all of the dinner trays from the various wards. Smelling the food reminded her she hadn't had much opportunity to eat today and as she headed outside beneath the sheltered walkway that led to the residential wing, her stomach grumbled. All she wanted was to get to her room, have some raisin toast and go to bed.

'Wow. I heard that. You must be really hungry,' a deep voice said from just behind her. Janessa didn't need to turn around to know who it was. She may have only known Miles Trevellion for less than a day but his voice was instantly recognisable. 'That's one growly stomach you have there, Janessa.'

It was strange to hear her first name coming from his lips,

the deep rich tones somehow making her name sound sexy and sensual. He fell into step beside her. 'I guess it is.'

'Busy day?'

'How can you ask that? You saw first-hand what the NICU was like at lunchtime.'

'Yes, I did, and from what I can recall you handled everything beautifully. Especially impatient and demanding visiting consultants.'

She stopped walking and he stopped right beside her. Janessa looked up at him, wondering if this was another one of his tests or if he was being serious. She searched his eyes, looking for a clue to help gauge his mood, and then immediately wished she hadn't.

His eyes were so blue, so bright, so clear, like the sky on a cloudless day, and even though the light outside was starting to fade, looking into Miles's eyes made her feel the same way she felt when she was up in her plane, soaring above the ground, without a care in the world. It was odd. No man had ever made her feel that way before. She sighed slowly and then closed her eyes, not wanting to be affected by him and cross with herself because it was clear that she was. He was her colleague and she had to remember that, to treat him with the same level of polite indifference she treated the other surgeons who slipped in and out of her unit.

When she opened her eyes, she made sure she didn't look at him directly in case she lost her train of thought again. 'What do you want, Miles? I'm off duty, I'm tired—'

'And you're hungry. I was thinking…dinner? I'm new in town and have no clue which restaurants are the good ones.'

She shrugged. 'You can get a list from Reception at the residential wing.' She started walking again, wanting to get back to the privacy of her own room so she could relax and unwind and forget all about Miles Trevellion and the way he seemed to fill her entire body with tingles every time he looked at her.

'Actually, that was my attempt at asking you to join me. Sorry. Should have made that clear.'

Janessa stopped short and stared at him. 'You want to have dinner with me?'

'Yes. You're hungry. I'm hungry. I thought we could eat together. Clear the air a little.'

'If you're referring to the way you bawled out an agency nurse earlier to the effect that she's now requested never to return to the NICU again, consider the air cleared.'

'Good.' He shoved his hands in his pockets. 'Good. Well, now that the air is clear, I guess we can just have dinner and get to know each other better.'

'Why? You're a colleague and I—' She stopped arguing when her stomach growled again.

Miles decided enough was enough and gently put his hand beneath her elbow and directed them towards the taxi rank at the front of the hospital where he'd arrived that morning. 'It's just food, Janessa. I would like to sit across a table and eat food. I'd like to have some company while I do it and I also have some questions about the conjoined twins I'd like to ask you.'

'Oh. A business dinner.' She shrugged, easing away from his gentle touch, hoping the warmth currently spreading through her body would cease when she wasn't so close to him. She should turn him down, return to her room, eat her toast and sleep. That was what she needed to do and it would definitely put a bit of distance between them. However, she hadn't left the hospital grounds in over a week and the thought of having Giuseppe, the owner of her favourite Italian restaurant, cook her a huge plate of *fettuccini* made her mouth water. 'Do you like Italian food?' A taxi was driving by the road closest to the residential wing and she put her fingers in her mouth and gave a loud whistle. 'Taxi!' she yelled, and the car instantly drove up to the kerb.

Miles was stunned and pleasantly surprised at this turn of events. Who was this woman? She was well liked and respected by her peers, she was exceptional at her job, she was a caring friend to Sheena and now she was whistling loudly for a cab. Smiling, he opened the taxi door for her and as she slid inside he shook his head, even more delighted and intrigued by this amazing woman.

CHAPTER THREE

THE short taxi ride to her favourite Italian restaurant was completed with Janessa pointing out some of the immediate sights of Adelaide, which looked beautiful at dusk, just in case Miles asked her anything personal. She needed to keep reminding herself that this wasn't a date, it was just dinner with a colleague, and yet she was completely aware of him sitting so close beside her in the back seat of the taxi.

At the restaurant, they were warmly welcomed by Giuseppe and seated at a small table for two, their waiter lighting the candle in the centre of the table, giving the whole setting a more romantic atmosphere.

They read the menus, ordered and then sat looking at each other. Janessa tried not to fidget with the cutlery, telling herself again that this was not a date, just a dinner between colleagues to discuss Sheena's twins. At least if they were discussing work, there wouldn't be any of those long and awkward silences that often accompanied two people who didn't know each other on a personal level. Awkward silences…like…the one she was experiencing now.

'So…' Janessa cleared her throat, eager to get this meeting off on the right foot. 'Uh…regarding the girls, I know we'll be doing a lot of scans once they've been delivered.

However, what would happen if it's discovered they share a femoral artery?'

Miles leaned back in his chair and considered her for a moment. It was clear Janessa wanted to ensure this *was* a business meeting and while he was still highly intrigued by her, wanting to ask her more personal questions, he'd play along for now.

'Well, my professional opinion is that we should cross that bridge if we come to it.'

Janessa blinked, hiding a smile before trying again. 'But what if there is a vein that's hidden, that isn't picked up on the scans, and it gets severed during the separation?'

'Then I suture it closed.' Miles leaned forward onto the table, his gaze intent, his words earnest. 'Janessa, I know you're concerned about the upcoming surgeries for the girls, I understand how much they mean to you, but nothing is going to go wrong.' He shrugged. 'I'm here.'

She tried again. 'But what if—?'

'Janessa, there are too many variables to discuss right now, right here, at dinner, especially with your stomach grumbling and growling. We'll cover all eventualities and discuss every scenario in the coming weeks before the scheduled delivery of the twins. Right now, though, I'm hungry. You're hungry. Let's enjoy this meal.' He picked up his wineglass and took a sip. 'So…have you lived in Adelaide long?'

She blinked slowly at his obvious arrogance and the abrupt change of subject. 'But what if the girls—?'

'How long? One year? Ten years? Or have you always lived in Adelaide? It's not a difficult question, especially for someone as intelligent as you are.'

Janessa huffed and crossed her arms. 'Born and bred.'

'Travelled much?'

'We're here to discuss the twins, not talk about me.'

'I beg to differ. If you're going to be part of my team, I need to know a bit more about you.'

'And so discovering where I've lived helps you do that?'

'It gives me a sense of who you are and what's important to you. So...have you travelled much?'

'A bit.' She noticed that he seemed completely relaxed and at ease but, then again, a man as good looking and as intelligent as Miles would be quite used to meals like this. It was she who felt so odd, so naked and exposed.

'Would you like to do more travel?'

'Not at the moment. Especially with Sheena needing me.'

'Of course. It's clear that the two of you are very close.'

'Yes.'

He put his wineglass down and leaned forward, a bright smile on his face. 'Am I making you nervous?'

'A little.' The words were out of her mouth before she could stop them and she immediately closed her eyes in confusion as embarrassment washed over her. He was so smooth, so relaxed and charming. How was she supposed to keep herself under control when every time he looked at her he made her feel as though she was the only person in the world who mattered to him. She knew it was his *magnetism* that was drawing her closer with every word he spoke.

'You don't date much?'

The feeling of embarrassment instantly left her and her eyes snapped open. 'This isn't a date, Miles. It's a business dinner.'

'True. So, tell me about Sheena. How has she really been feeling? Sleeping much? What's her emotional status? As her friend, I'm sure you can give me a much clearer picture than what her chart and notes tell me.'

'True.' Relaxing a little, Janessa sipped her wine. 'She's... hanging in there. I guess that's the best way to describe it.

Naturally, her emotions are like a roller-coaster ride, but that's to be expected. She's also scared, nervous, worried— again, just like any other mother-to-be. But I think she's also concerned about the publicity the babies will garner once they're born. I mean, I know and you know that conjoined twins happen more frequently than people realise—'

'One in every two hundred identical twin pregnancies is conjoined.'

'Exactly, and each one of them has their fair share of publicity, although thankfully nowadays the publicity is more centred on the health of the babies and the subsequent operations to separate them rather than the "freakish" angle. Still, Sheena's worried about that.'

Miles nodded. 'It's a natural concern and one I've dealt with in different ways depending on the different services of the hospital where the babies are born. I think, in this instance, with the way your NICU is set up, we'll be able to secure the girls in a private bay, with screens and curtains so they can still receive the specialist treatment they deserve. Once they're stabilised, we can move them to a private paediatric ward, but that may not be for some months. It all depends on how healthy they are when they're born.'

'What about photographers and paparazzi? What about the other mothers in the NICU? What if one of them takes a photo of the babies and sells it to the newspapers? I'm not saying that any of them would, but I'm—'

'You're just trying to be prepared,' he finished for her, nodding. 'I completely understand. My suggestion is to take photographs of the girls within the first twenty-four hours, have your hospital PR people release them with an update on the girls' health and that should at least stop the temptation for people on the ward taking photographs and selling them.'

'Excellent idea. So clear, so straightforward, so simple. Brilliant.'

The waiter arrived with their entrées, the minestrone soup sending her gastronomic juices into overdrive. She grinned at Miles as she sipped the hot, tasty liquid, glad to finally be able to eat.

'When was the last time you ate today?'

'Um…' She swallowed her mouthful and broke off a piece of fresh, crusty bread which had also been brought to the table. 'Some time early this morning? I'm not sure. I know I've had several cups of tea and coffee.'

'Some days are busier than others.'

'Some days I eat more than others.'

He nodded, knowing exactly what she was talking about. 'It all pans out in the end.' Miles lifted his wineglass, holding it out. Janessa picked hers up and chinked it with his. 'To finding time to have a meal,' he toasted, and she smiled, relaxing a little more.

As they ate, the conversation turned to different topics ranging from politics to health-care funding, to recent breakthroughs in medical science and back to Sheena and the twins. By the time they said goodnight to Giuseppe, thanking him for a splendid meal, and had caught a taxi back to the residential wing, Janessa's stomach was full and her guard had dropped.

She'd discovered tonight that the brilliant man who had written all the journal articles she liked was also interesting, charming and very funny. Quite a few times he'd made her laugh as he'd recounted antics from some of the experiences he'd had.

'As with all new parents, it's customary to name your children at birth,' he'd recounted. 'But with the second set of conjoined twins I was fortunate enough to assist with, the parents, who were from Tarparnii, called their boys Ticanegia and Tocneshla. Then they shortened the names to Tic and Toc.' His smile had been bright, his eyes had twinkled with humour and Janessa had found herself just enjoying being with him as they'd laughed together.

He'd been a perfect gentleman, holding doors for her, insisting on paying for the meal and transportation, and now as they exited the taxi and headed for the residential wing, he walked close, his hand hovering in the small of her back as a means of protection and stability.

She swallowed as they walked into the reception area of the residential wing, feeling as though every eye in the place was on them.

'Evening, Janessa,' Arthur, the night-time receptionist-cum-security-guard, called, waving to her. 'And Dr Trevellion. Good to see you again.'

Miles guided Janessa over to the elderly but still fit man who had worked at this hospital far longer than either of them had been alive. Miles shook hands with the man, treating him with polite respect.

'Good to see you again, and please call me Miles.'

Arthur nodded, then asked, 'Did you manage to find somewhere good to eat?'

'Actually, I did. Janessa here was good enough to share her favourite restaurant with me.'

'Giuseppe's,' Janessa offered as she noticed Arthur's bushy eyebrows rise in surprise. She could see that he was intrigued by the two of them being out together.

'It's good to see you getting out and about, young lady.' He turned his attention to Miles. 'She works too hard, this one.' He looked back at Janessa. 'You should get away from the hospital more often. Go for a drive in your fancy car.'

Miles's eyebrows rose at this information. 'You have a fancy car?'

Janessa shook her head, not wanting to talk about her car or the fact that it had belonged to her father. That car was part of her personal life and therefore had nothing to do with Miles Trevellion. 'It's just a car.'

'I like cars. A lot,' he offered.

She looked at him for a moment, tilting her head to the side in a considering manner. 'I'll bet you like to drive them fast, too.'

Miles's smile increased and he winked at her. 'You'd better believe it. Helps to keep the heart pumping. Makes me feel alive.'

Janessa was sure she should have said something, come up with a retort that he, as a member of the medical profession, should know all about the dangers involved in such daredevil behaviour, but her thought processes had turned to mush the instant he'd winked at her.

'Surely,' Miles continued when she didn't make any reply, 'you have ways of dealing with your stress? Tell me you escape from this place every once in a while and remember how to live life like a normal person, rather than a medical professional tied to their work?' When she still made no reply, he exhaled slowly. 'Life's too short, Janessa.'

'I keep telling her that,' Arthur agreed, and Janessa snapped out of her stupor, having forgotten for a moment exactly where she was. She straightened her shoulders as Arthur continued. 'I keep telling her to ease up a little.' He tut-tutted, his words spoken in a caring and familiar way.

'And I *will* ease up, once Sheena's babies are all healthy and well on their way to living normal lives.'

At the mention of Sheena, Arthur demanded an update and she was more than pleased to give it, especially as it meant she could stop fixating on how one simple wink from Miles had turned her into a dim-minded twit. 'These aren't just Sheena's babies,' he said to Miles. 'They belong to the whole hospital. Sheena's one of our own and here at Adelaide Mercy we take care of our own.'

Miles smiled. 'So I'm beginning to realise. It's great to work at a hospital that has such a close-knit community.' He looked at Janessa, remembering how she'd been firm and direct with him earlier on that day, protective of her staff, her NICU and her friends. He noticed that her eyelids were growing heavier and when she tried to stifle a yawn, rather unsuccessfully, he shook hands again with Arthur and led a tired Janessa towards the old lift.

'Which floor are you on?' Miles asked as he pressed the button to call the lift down.

'Three. Ordinarily I'd take the stairs but...' She yawned, then shook her head. 'This always happens. Now that I'm out of the hospital, it's as though my brain switches off and my body gives in to exhaustion.'

Miles nodded. 'Happens to me, too.' The lift arrived and he held the door for her, waiting politely while she went inside. He pressed the button for the third floor and they both waited while the old lift creaked its way upwards. 'Perhaps the stairs would have been safer,' Miles remarked cautiously as he looked around the old lift.

'Probably.' Fatigue was really starting to hit. She needed to get out of this lift, escape Miles Trevellion's enigmatic presence and settle down to a hopefully uninterrupted night. Even standing here with him, just the two of them, there was a strange awareness, being alone together in such a confined space, that seemed to surround them.

When the lift finally stopped, Miles once more held the door for her and Janessa thankfully stepped out into the hallway. She was about to turn and say goodbye when she realised he, too, had stepped from the lift.

'Are you staying on this floor as well?' she asked.

'Yes.' He dug into his pocket and pulled out a key. 'Apparently, the residential wing used to be the old nurses' home many moons ago.'

'Correct,' Janessa said as she made her way down the corridor.

'The third floor was where they converted some of the rooms into small apartments with a kitchenette and their own bathrooms, although I was told that the plumbing hasn't been all that crash hot lately.'

'True. I can ask for you to be moved to the first floor where they actually have a lovely two-bedroom apartment, complete with a proper sitting room and dining room. Much bigger. Nicer for you and the plumbing on that level is fine.' She wasn't sure she could deal with working *and* living so close to him. The fact that she'd been looking forward to his arrival and the realisation that the impatient doctor she'd met earlier in the morning was that of a man exhausted from international travel was now clearly evident. Since they'd headed out to dinner, he'd been nothing but kind, cordial and caring towards her. Still…living and working in such close proximity to him would make her far more aware of him than she already was.

'Thanks.' He stopped outside a door—the door that happened to be right next to the door Janessa stopped outside. 'But here will be fine for the next six months. I don't need that much room. Contrary to popular belief, I'm not one of those surgeons who is dictatorial and demanding.' He smiled at her and she noted the same teasing glint in his eyes that she'd seen when they'd been at the restaurant when he'd been relating some of his more humorous stories.

'Good to know,' she countered as she pulled out her key and inserted it into the lock.

He lifted his eyebrows in pleasant surprise. 'Neighbours, eh?'

'Looks that way. Hope you don't snore too loudly.'

He laughed, both of them standing there, looking at each other, the world around them disappearing. Even though she'd told herself all evening that their dinner hadn't been a date, she couldn't help but feel like he was about to kiss her goodnight.

Slowly, the smile slipped from his lips as they stood there, staring, the awkwardness mixing with the awareness that seemed to all but sizzle between them. Janessa looked up into his soothing blue eyes and found herself sighing, knowing that if she let herself go, she could look into his eyes all day long and never get bored. It had been a very long time since she'd been attracted to a man in such a way and the sensations he was evoking were making her feel all warm and tingly.

'Uh…' She swallowed over her dry throat. 'Well…thank you for dinner.'

'My pleasure. Thank you for coming with me. It was nice to spend my first evening here at Adelaide Mercy in such fine company.'

A shy smile touched her lips at his words. 'Oh…er… thanks, I guess.'

His rich, deep, chuckling laughter rumbled through her. 'Listen to us. So polite, so full of thank-yous.'

She nodded. 'Our mothers would be proud.'

'Yes. Yes, they would.' He shoved his hands into his pockets, unsure whether he should shake her hand, give her a polite hug or just nod and turn away. It was odd. He wasn't used to being unsure of himself.

'Well…' she said, uncertain what to do next. Her mind, which was usually fairly sharp, seemed to have shut down through sheer mental exhaustion…and the fact that he was so close to her.

'Well…' he repeated, knowing he should move, go into his apartment and let her do the same. When she smothered another yawn, he nodded, decision made, and held out his hand in a polite form of saying goodnight. 'Get inside and get some sleep,' he said softly as she slipped her hand into his, pleased that he'd made the decision as to how they should end this evening. A handshake. Nice, polite, formal… maybe too formal. Perhaps a quick kiss on the cheek. Yes. A bit less formal, a bit more familiar but still professional.

She looked down at their hands, clasped firmly and perfectly together, the warmth from his touch spreading up her arm to burst forth and heat the rest of her insides.

At the slight tug on her hand, she looked up and realised, belatedly, that he was leaning towards her, heading in to kiss her cheek. However, the moment she moved her head, Miles's lips connected—not with her cheek but with *her lips*!

She gasped in shock and surprise but didn't immediately pull away, the world around them slipping and sliding and faltering a little as the pressure of Miles's mouth on hers remained intense, intoxicating and intriguing.

Her eyelids fluttered closed as his spicy scent wound its way around her, drawing her in, heightening every sensation now zinging throughout her. Pleasure, confusion, excitement, doubt.

He was kissing her!

She was kissing him!

Neither of them were moving away.

With her heart pounding so wildly against her chest, she thought it was going to break right through her ribs, Janessa stayed very still, scared that if she shifted, even slightly, he'd think she didn't like the sensation of having his mouth against hers.

Accidental? Yes. Powerful? Yes. Eager for more? Definitely yes.

He hadn't meant to kiss her, not like this, not on the lips, but she'd turned at the wrong moment and then…and now… and how was he ever supposed to think coherently ever again? He'd simply been intent on a firm and polite handshake, combined with a small peck on her cheek to let her know that he appreciated her going to dinner with him, and now it had turned into something unknown and electrifying.

He closed his eyes, either to memorise every moment they were sharing or to fight the urge to develop this impromptu kiss even further. The need to haul her close, to hold her firmly against him, to part her lips with his and—

Janessa jerked back, letting go of his hand and stepping back against her apartment door. Miles opened his eyes and looked at her, unable to believe the repressed desire and complete confusion he saw reflected in her rich, chocolate depths.

'Goodnight.' The word was choked and dry against her throat. Quickly she turned her back to him, her heart still hammering wildly against her chest, her breathing erratic, her cheeks flushed and her legs threatening to fail her. She fumbled with her key but another second had her door open and she was soon safely on the other side of it.

Breathing a sigh of relief, glad she'd been able to break free from the overwhelming sensations Miles had evoked deep within her, she stayed where she was, head back against the door, eyes closed, eager for her lungs to once again be filled with the appropriate amount of oxygen.

'Goodnight, Janessa. Sleep well,' she heard him say

through the paper-thin walls, and then she heard him open his own door and walk into his apartment. She closed her eyes again and allowed his rich, deep tones to wash over her, delighting at the way her name seemed to sound like a caress from his lips.

Slowly, she opened her eyes and pushed away from the door to walk on unsteady legs towards her bedroom. Miles had just kissed her! The man's lips had been pressed to hers and *she'd liked it*!

Flopping face down onto her bed, she whimpered in confusion. How on earth was she supposed to face him tomorrow at their nine-thirty meeting? How was she supposed to pull herself together and sit across the table from him and talk about work when all she would be able to think about was the way his mouth had felt so warm and perfect against her own?

She had no idea.

Miles put his key down on the empty bookshelf by the door and closed his eyes. Shaking his head, he couldn't believe what had just happened. He'd kissed another woman. Sheena had been right. He *was* interested in Janessa in the same way he'd been interested in Wendy. He'd loved and lost and the pain had nearly killed him. He couldn't...*wouldn't* go there again.

Whatever he felt for Janessa was irrelevant. He was there for the twins. All his relationships at Adelaide Mercy must remain professional. It was a matter of survival.

CHAPTER FOUR

JANESSA woke up upon hearing a noise and checked her alarm clock.

'Ten past three,' she muttered as she flopped back onto the pillow and sighed. With her eyes still closed, she fumbled around for her mobile phone and pager, which were on the nightstand next to her bed. Squinting, she looked with bleary eyes at the bright display on both of them but she hadn't received any messages or calls. Unsure what noise had woken her, she decided to ignore whatever it was and go back to sleep. Her alarm would be going off in just under three hours and after her hectic day yesterday she deserved all the sleep she could get.

Snuggling into the covers, she allowed her mind to settle back into dreamland where she'd been out at the airfield, flying in her plane, coming in to land, only to find someone was waiting for her. A man. A tall man. With dark brown hair and blue eyes, greeting her with a warm, welcoming smile. As she drew closer to the ground, she could see his features more clearly and was momentarily stunned to discover the man in question was none other than Miles Trevellion.

Her eyes snapped open at the realisation. She was dreaming about him? No. Ridiculous. He meant nothing to her. He was just a colleague…a colleague who had kissed her.

She moaned and buried her face in the pillow. Ever since the man had walked into her NICU, turning her world upside down, he'd been nothing but a harbinger of change and change was something she didn't like in her world. Change had brought her nothing but pain, trouble and, in the end, loneliness. First her baby, Connor, had died, then Bradley had left, her mother had died and later her father had become sick. She was fine if the change was initiated by her, that way she could control it, but Miles Trevellion was something she couldn't control and as such he posed a threat to her well-ordered life.

The only way to deal with this change was to treat him as nothing more than a professional colleague. The next time they met there would be no long stares, no touching and definitely no kissing.

She turned over, settling into a new position, forcing her mind to think of a different scenario to soothe her back to sleep.

She'd just started to settle, thinking about driving her father's beloved Jaguar E-Cabriolet through the lush, green Adelaide hills, the top down on the car, the wind in her hair as all of her stresses floated away, when she heard a noise again. She instinctively knew it was the same noise that had initially woken her and it was coming from next door.

It was the beeping of Miles Trevellion's mobile phone, no doubt alerting him to the fact that he'd just received a text message. She huffed impatiently as she heard him move around next door, wanting him to be as silent as possible so that she could get some sleep. Didn't the man have any idea how thin these walls were?

Janessa waited for a few minutes, listening to him, trying to picture the way he'd be moving around the apartment she knew was the mirror image of her own. As she lay there, she began to wonder what he would be wearing. It didn't sound as though he had shoes on and he was obviously in the kitchen, making himself something to eat.

After another few minutes the noises seemed to settle and she once again started to relax, hoping he'd finished his pre-dawn snack and head back to bed. Then, in the next instant, his mobile phone rang, followed by the crash of a chair falling and then the kettle whistling to signify it had boiled.

'Oh, for heaven's sake,' she growled, and flipped the bed-covers back. Stomping to the wall, she banged her fist on it. 'Can you keep it down, Miles? Some of us are trying to sleep.'

'Janessa?'

'Who else would you be waking at three o'clock in the morning?' she demanded.

'Sorry. Didn't realise you could hear me.' A pause then, 'No. No. Not you, Marta. Someone else—my neighbour.'

Marta? Janessa stepped back and looked at the wall in confusion. Through her sleep-deprived brain she belatedly realised he was talking on the phone to Marta von Hugen, who, she knew from the articles she'd read, was one of his colleagues in America.

Shaking her head, she stomped back to her bed and buried her face beneath the pillow, trying desperately to drown out the sounds from next door. She almost sky-rocketed through the ceiling, though, when someone knocked on her door. The pillow was tossed aside as she flicked back the covers and pulled a robe on over her short nightshirt. Usually, if there was an emergency in the NICU, she would be called or paged but sometimes they knocked on her door.

A second later she stood there, blonde hair loose and di-shevelled, robe knotted at her waist, legs and feet bare, door open as she stared into Miles's wide-awake blue eyes.

'Didn't mean to wake you,' he began, 'but now that you're up, I was wondering if you have any herbal teas? I only have coffee,' he continued, 'which doesn't sit too well with jet lag.'

Janessa stood there, glaring at him, one hand on the door, the other over the knotted robe, ensuring that it didn't accidentally come undone. 'It's three o'clock in the morning, Miles.'

'I know, but we're both used to being woken at ridiculous hours and I really could do with that tea. One good strong cup of herbal tea will have me sleeping like a baby in no time.'

He smiled at her.

The combination of his eyes sparkling, his lips curving, his straight white teeth shining brightly at her caused her knees to tremble momentarily. Her hand tightened on the door, more for support than anything else. Damn, but he was good looking. She had to be strong. Resist his natural charm. She had to focus and be professional.

'I apologise once again for waking you and now for disturbing you,' he went on when she made no reply. 'My body clock is still on American time and I probably should have remembered to turn my phone to silent. If it's at all possible that you have some herbal tea, I just need one tea bag and then I'll be on my way, back next door, leaving you alone to go back to sleep. I promise.'

Again, Janessa didn't move, didn't say anything, just stared at him as though he was some sort of apparition. Was she still asleep? Sleepwalking? Sleep-pounding on the wall? Sleep-annoyed?

'One tea bag,' she finally murmured, before turning and walking towards the kitchen. As she hadn't actually invited him in, Miles stayed where he was, but by not following her he was treated to a wonderful view of her smooth, silky legs and the swish of her hips as she sashayed up the hallway. He swallowed, taking in the slim build beneath her silky robe, wondering exactly what she had on underneath.

He shook his head, trying to clear his mind. She was his colleague and the fact that he was clearly attracted to her was something he would need to fight. Then again, what red-blooded male wouldn't be attracted to Janessa Austen, especially when she looked so young and tousled, fresh from her bed, her hair all messed as it wildly framed the smooth skin of her face, her chocolate-brown eyes half-open and still sleepy? Certainly not him.

She returned a moment or two later, a box of herbal tea in her hands. 'Take it. Keep it. The whole box. Drink as many as you need.'

'But I only need—'

'Take it,' she said clearly as she placed it in his hands. 'Consider it a welcoming gift.'

'Thank you, Janessa.' His smile was as bright as the early morning sun. 'That's very kind of you.' She could tell by the way he spoke and the look in his eyes that he was being sincere.

'It's not *that* kind, Miles. More like self-preservation.' Her words were still sleepy, tired and he could tell she was trying to hold on to that sensation where you were half awake and half asleep. It was common amongst doctors, especially when they had a callout. If there was any possibility at all of getting back to sleep, even for an extra twenty minutes, they clung to it. 'Now, if that's all, goodnight…or morning… or whatever.' She yawned and covered her mouth with her hand.

'Yes. Of course. Sorry to have bothered you and woken you and generally annoyed you.'

'Uh-huh.' She was starting to close the door to her

apartment, needing desperately to shut out the sight of him standing there, dressed in only a pair of jeans and a T-shirt that clearly outlined his firm, muscled torso. He was good looking, intelligent and far too appealing for this hour of the morning.

She was almost there, had almost managed to deal with the situation and close the door, desperately eager to get back to her bed, when her own phone started to ring.

'No. No. No,' she whimpered, closing her eyes and momentarily leaning her head against the open door.

'If it's an emergency, I don't mind going,' Miles offered. 'It's quite clear that you need your sleep, Janessa. Sheena told me that you've been working longer hours than usual of late.'

'I may as well give up on the whole sleeping thing,' she mumbled, leaving the door ajar as she headed back to her bedroom to answer the phone. 'Hello?' she said after connecting the call. She listened for a moment, closing her eyes. 'That's fine. I'll be right there.' She pressed the button on her mobile to end the call.

'Problem?' Miles asked and Janessa returned to the front door.

'It's Sheena. She's crying.'

'Crying? Why? What's wrong?' Miles was instantly alert.

'Nothing's wrong. She's just crying.' Janessa rubbed a hand over her eyes. 'Excuse me, Miles. I need to get dressed and go see her.'

'I'll go put shoes on,' he remarked, and before she could say another word, he'd disappeared next door. Giving up, Janessa headed back into her room, dismissed the comfortable bed, which was calling her back, and quickly got dressed. Two minutes later there was another knock at her door and Janessa knew it would be Miles.

'Here,' he said as she opened her door, pocketing her keys,

phone and pager. He held out a cup of what smelled like steaming black coffee. 'Black. Two sugars.'

'Coffee? How did you know how I drink it?'

He shrugged. 'I noticed at the restaurant. Anyway, I brewed some before I thought better of it and came to annoy you for some tea. I thought you could use a cup now, wake you up a bit more.' She was dressed in a pair of jeans and a baggy knit jumper, which looked warm and cosy. She'd brushed her hair, pulled it back into a ponytail and slipped her feet into a pair of flat shoes. She looked gorgeous, comfortable and very homely, and he realised that whether she was dressed as professional Janessa, sleep-tousled Janessa or comfortable, homely Janessa, she was an incredibly beautiful woman.

She wore no make-up and he detected no pretence about her. Miles couldn't believe how drawn he was to this woman. He'd worked with all different types of people over the years and ever since the death of his wife he'd been able to keep the lines between business and his personal life completely separate. Why couldn't he do it with her?

'Thank you. That was very thoughtful.' She gratefully accepted the cup and took a sip, trying not to be too affected by his kind gesture. She would have coped better with him being so close to her if he'd remained as lacking in charm and chivalry as she'd first thought, and of course before he'd kissed her. 'Mmm…just what the doctor ordered.'

Miles couldn't believe how pleased he was at her appreciation as they headed to the stairwell, both of them sipping the rich brown liquid as they went. 'You're more than welcome, especially after you gave me the whole box of tea.'

'What's a box of tea between friends?' she said as a throw-away line.

'Friends?' The word was spoken softly and with a hint of

surprise. Janessa simply glanced at him over her shoulder and raised an eyebrow.

'You *do* know what friends are, don't you?'

Miles smiled, liking the teasing lilt in her tone. 'It's been so long, I'm not sure I remember how to make friends. I know how to deal with colleagues, patients, emergencies, but friends…?' He shook his head as they exited the stairwell, letting the sentence trail off.

'Well…' she drawled as they walked through the quiet residential wing foyer, Janessa waving to Arthur as they went by, 'it looks as though there's something to teach the great Miles Trevellion after all.' The words were delivered with a bright smile and Miles almost choked on the liquid in his mouth. He swallowed quickly and coughed once as he continued to stare at her.

In the artificial light of the hospital grounds, dressed casually, demeanour more relaxed than he'd previously seen, Janessa's smile was wide, bright and completely encompassing, her tired brown eyes twinkling with merriment.

'Good to know you're human, like the rest of us,' she added before they entered the hospital building and made their way to Maternity, several staff members greeting them with a quick hello or a polite smile and nod. Miles could tell that Janessa was not only well liked but respected and he was pleased that he'd be working alongside a colleague of her calibre.

He'd read dossiers on Janessa and other members of the Adelaide Mercy senior team who would be assisting with the various aspects of the twins' delivery and future surgeries. It was a policy of his to know as much about his teams as he could, and to know that Janessa not only had the skills but the caring personality to match this sort of work was definitely a bonus. Far too often he'd worked with surgeons and physicians who were only interested in the prestige and fame associated with something as unusual as separating conjoined twins. Thankfully, the team at Adelaide Mercy were all invested in this project and perhaps the main reason behind that was Sheena. She was one of their own, a staff member, a colleague, a friend—and even, as Janessa had declared, a sister.

Upon entering Sheena's room, Miles was once more able to witness the bond between the two women. Janessa crossed instantly to Sheena's side and put her coffee cup down on the bedside table before immediately embracing the bed-ridden woman, handing her a tissue at the same time.

'What's wrong?' Janessa asked in a soft, caring tone.

'Nothing,' Sheena blubbered. 'Everything. Oh, I don't know any more,' she wailed. Miles came and stood on the other side of the bed, watching, deciding it was best to step back and let Janessa handle this, given that she certainly knew Sheena a lot better than he did.

As Sheena continued to cry, apparently for no reason whatsoever, Janessa held her and stroked her hair, murmuring soothing noises until the tears began to stop. Miles couldn't help but notice that Janessa was very maternal, as well as so caring and patient. He wondered if she planned to have any children of her own in the future. Her dossier had stated that she wasn't married and, again, he was curious as to why not. She was only thirty-six years old, although she looked years younger, she was intelligent, funny and so incredibly beautiful. So why wasn't she already spoken for?

'There, now. Feel better?' she asked Sheena.

'No? Yes?' Sheena smiled through the final tears that Janessa was wiping away. 'I still don't know.'

'Pregnancy blues,' Janessa remarked, brushing hair from Sheena's eyes. 'That's all it was.'

'I was lying here and I started thinking about everything, about things that could go wrong, about the surgeries, about how on earth I was going to cope…'

'Doubts and concerns are very natural,' Miles said, and Sheena quickly turned her head, surprised to find him there.

'Miles? I didn't see you come in.'

'He came with me,' Janessa said.

'With you?' Sheena wiggled up the bed and stared at them both.

'Not *with me* with me, it's just that Miles woke me up and then needed tea and then after the phone call, he made me coffee and as we were both awake we, uh…came together. Not *together* together but…' Janessa fumbled over her words and started to blush as she realised the more she explained, the more incriminating it sounded.

'I'm staying in the residential wing, next door to Janessa,' Miles interjected, his tone smooth and commanding. 'I'm still jet-lagged and was receiving phone calls from overseas. My phone woke Janessa. It's all very simple and quite innocent.'

'Exactly,' Janessa said, not wanting to talk about it further, given that Sheena had a knack of seeing straight through her emotions. 'Now…back to you. Do you want to talk about some of these concerns?'

'They're the same ones I've had all along.'

'Well, now that Miles is here, perhaps if we go through them again, he'll be able to give more information.'

'Good idea.' Miles came back round the bed to the same side as Janessa, pulling out a chair for her before getting one for himself. Settling down, he finished his coffee and looked expectantly at Sheena. 'I'm here to help.'

'Uh… OK. Let me see…where to begin.'

Janessa could see Sheena was trying to get her mind in

gear. 'Let's start at the beginning. With the birth. From what Riley—Sheena's obstetrician,' Janessa added in case Miles hadn't met Riley yet, 'has said, there's no question of a natural birth and that is why the C-section has been booked for two weeks' time.'

'That's right.' Miles nodded. 'With the growth hormones we're administering to the twins each day, this should help their bodies to develop a little faster than usual. There's a chance, as they're sharing the same placenta, that one is being more nourished than the other. However, after taking a good look at the data gathered on the twins so far, it appears that this is well under control. The stronger they are when they're born, the better chance they have when it's time to perform the first of the surgeries.'

'And the delivery? Riley said it's a straightforward procedure. Is that really true?' Sheena wanted to know. 'I've been there for plenty of deliveries before, I know what it's like, but I still keep thinking that so many things could go wrong.'

'They can, and you're right to be concerned. In some ways, because you're highly trained in the medical field, this can be seen as a disadvantage. You *know* what can go wrong and so you may tend to fixate on that. However, you have to trust this team.'

'Miles is right,' Janessa added. 'Riley is a brilliant obstetrician and you've worked with him long enough to know that he's able to think fast and clearly on his feet.'

'True.' Sheena sighed and nodded. 'So the actual birth of the girls is the easy part?'

'Precisely. Depending on their status at twenty-four hours, nothing will be done for the first few days, unless it's absolutely necessary. We'll be taking in-depth radiographs and CT scans of the girls but these will be done while they're mildly sedated.'

'And when will the first lot of surgeries commence?' Sheena yawned and Janessa could see that in discussing these issues with Miles, Sheena's mind was starting to let go of some of her concerns. This was good. What Miles was saying to her, keeping everything straight forward, honest and simple, was exactly what Sheena needed to hear. Keeping Sheena calm meant that her blood pressure would stay under control. If it shot up, they would need to perform the Caesarean sooner.

'There's no exact time frame for the surgeries as it all depends on the health of the girls. One set of twins I worked with weren't finally separated until they were almost two years old. Each set is unique and, as such, needs to be treated in the same manner.'

'OK.' Sheena closed her eyes and Janessa stood.

'That's enough for now. I know you have more questions for Miles, but he's not going anywhere so don't stress.'

'Good idea.' Sheena yawned and slowly opened her heavy eyelids. 'Thank you. Both of you.'

'You're more than welcome,' Miles stated, moving the chairs he and Janessa had been sitting on out of the way. 'We'll see you in a few hours' time.' He leaned over and squeezed Sheena's hand. Janessa couldn't help but be impressed by him. He really did care.

As they tiptoed out of Sheena's room, heading towards the nurses' station, Janessa turned to face him. 'Thank you.'

'For?'

'Putting her mind at rest. Not giving her platitudes. Being supportive.'

'The same could be said of you.'

'Yes, but I'm her friend.'

'So am I.'

'Ahh…so you *do* have friends,' Janessa teased, a small smile on her lips. 'Good to know.'

Miles returned her smile. 'Amusing.' His tone was droll but the look in his eyes let her know they were on the same wavelength. The realisation stunned her. The same wavelength? First she was attracted to the man and now she was connecting with him?

The smile slid slowly from her face and she swallowed over the realisation. Distance. She needed to find a way to distance herself from him, to stay professional but still be polite and friendly.

'So…are you ready to head back to bed?' The words out of his mouth were warm, deep and husky and Janessa felt a blush instantly come to her cheeks, especially when the night sister, who was sitting at her desk, gasped in surprise.

'Uh…he doesn't mean… We're not…' Janessa began, but stopped. She closed her eyes for a second, then took a calming breath. When she opened her eyes, she was determined not to be so flustered by the man who was now regarding her with keen interest, obviously waiting to see what she would say.

'Dr Trevellion and I are both staying in the residential wing,' she informed Sister. 'Not together…' She shook her head. 'He's in one apartment. I'm in another.'

'We're neighbours,' Miles added, as though trying to help her out. 'But the walls between our apartments are so thin we may as well be living together.'

Night Sister nodded politely, but the wide smile on her face said she was still highly interested in the dynamic that seemed to clearly exist between the two neonatologists.

Janessa groaned and shook her head. 'You're no help at all,' she muttered, before heading from the ward. She didn't wait for him and he didn't catch her up. For all she cared, he and his wide-awake, jet-lagged mind could stay in the hospital and do whatever he wanted. She still had a couple of hours before her alarm went off and she was going to get some sleep, even if it meant wearing earplugs in order to drown out the noises of Miles on the other side of the paper-thin walls!

You may be able to drown out the noises he makes, the little voice in the back of her mind told her, *but there's no way you'll be able to stop thinking about him.*

CHAPTER FIVE

JANESSA jolted instantly awake when the sound of an alarm clock buzzed all around her.

'What?' She sat bolt upright, the journal she'd been reading to help her get back to sleep flying across the room. She reached out a hand to turn off her alarm clock, but to her astonishment found that the sound wouldn't stop.

'What?' she said again, her brow puckering in tired confusion. She rubbed her bleary eyes and focused more clearly on the clock: 5:59 a.m. As she stared at the numbers, they changed to read six o'clock and with it came the sounds of the morning radio show she usually woke up to. The buzzing, however, still persisted and she stumbled out of bed, trying to figure out if it was a fire alarm or an evacuation alarm. Should she be grabbing her clothes and important case notes and rushing from the building?

Janessa walked bleary-eyed around the apartment, following the sound of the buzzing, now desperate to track its origin so she could stop it. She walked towards the kitchenette and it was only then that she realised the buzzing was coming from next door. From *Miles's* apartment. Did the man have it in for her? Was he intent on disturbing her any way he could?

She stared at the wall. 'You have got to be kidding me!' What was he doing? Why wasn't he turning it off?

Tired and still a little groggy, she pounded on the wall. 'Miles!' she called. No reply. Concern started to prick at the rear of her mind. 'Miles?' she called again, pounding a little louder on the wall. 'Are you in there?'

'Huh? What?' His sleepy voice, all rich and deep and completely yummy, came through the wall. 'Whaddya want?' he called again, and this time his tone was slightly muffled and impatient, as though he'd put a pillow over his head in order to block out the noise.

'Turn your alarm off,' Janessa yelled, starting to feel silly talking to a wall. She crossed her arms over her nightshirt, her feet now starting to get cold as she hadn't put on her slippers.

'What? Janessa?'

The way he said her name, all dazed and confused and sexily sleepy, made her close her eyes as a wave of comfortable warmth washed over her. When she'd returned to her apartment, she'd still had a bit of trouble getting to sleep, thoughts of Miles and his gorgeous smile, his hypnotic eyes, his firm, contoured body keeping her awake.

Now, to hear him mumble her name as though he couldn't quite figure out exactly where she was but wanted her to come closer, it only made her awareness of him escalate. In order to get back to sleep she'd picked up the latest copy of the neonate journal she subscribed to and begun reading…until she'd come across an article written by Miles Trevellion.

She'd felt a little strange, reading the words written by the man who only last night had kissed her! She closed her eyes, reliving the sensations, astonished at her own reaction. Why hadn't she pulled away sooner? Why hadn't he? It was the first time in such a very long time that she'd been kissed by a man in such a way and while she knew she shouldn't, given that he was a colleague, she wanted more.

More kissing, more touching, more talking, more being with him. It was silly and schoolgirlish but she couldn't help the way she felt. Thoughts of Miles Trevellion had been constantly on her mind since he'd walked into her NICU. Janessa thought back to the way he'd been at dinner, respecting that she'd wanted to keep things on a more professional level but excited when he'd shared some of his thoughts with her about the research he'd undertaken. He'd made her feel smart and worthy of his attention. It had been nice.

When she'd heard him return next door, she'd sighed, listening to him move around in his apartment. He'd started whistling softly to himself and Janessa had lowered the journal and closed her eyes, deciding to enjoy the sweet sound. Relaxing more, she'd eventually drifted off to sleep where visions of the man had infiltrated her dreams…nice dreams…dreams in which he was smiling down into her up-turned face, holding her close and pressing his lips to hers as though he thought her the most precious and gorgeous woman in the world.

And then the buzzing had started…the buzzing that was still going.

'Turn the alarm off, Miles,' she called through the wall.

'Janessa?' Again her name from his lips was one of deep confusion, as though he wasn't quite sure where she was.

'You woke me up. Again!' she accused, shaking her head and opening her eyes. It was better for her to be standoffish with him, to keep him at a professional arm's length because if she allowed thoughts of him to intrude into her already over-burdened mind, things could get sticky. Yes, he was brilliant; yes, she enjoyed being with him; yes, she couldn't help but fantasise about him pressing his lips to hers again and again—but the simple fact was that Miles was her colleague and one who would leave in six months' time.

She thumped once more on the wall. 'Turn it off,' she called, and stomped over to the sink where she filled the kettle and switched it on. She needed tea, preferably one of the calming, herbal varieties, in order to get her mind back to a more neutral place. It wasn't until she opened the cupboard that she remembered she'd given him the whole box of tea earlier that morning.

Closing the cupboard, she couldn't help but growl, her frustration increasing. The man really was impinging on her life. She had to keep things polite and impersonal. She was expected in the unit in an hour's time and she had hoped to get through quite a bit of paperwork before then. It looked as though this was yet another day in her life that wasn't going to plan.

Sighing heavily, she put two pieces of raisin bread into the toaster and settled on having a glass of juice, pottering around in her kitchen until finally the buzzing of Miles's alarm eventually stopped.

'Thank you!' Her words were called loudly, tinged with impatience. The man was disturbing her enough *without* his alarm clock joining in the fun.

'Sorry. Didn't want to oversleep. Forgot where I was,' he returned, and his words made Janessa feel a little contrite at having been so annoyed with him. She didn't envy him the jet lag at all.

'It's fine.' All she wanted now was for him to keep quiet so she could get her head back on track and get ready for the day ahead. A quick breakfast, a quick shower, then dress, collect her paperwork and head to the unit. As she pulled out a plate and knife from the cupboard, waiting impatiently for the toaster, she almost jumped when Miles spoke again.

'Were you able to get back to sleep all right, Janessa?'

This time, though, he wasn't yelling through the wall. He was speaking quite normally and she actually looked around behind her to check that he hadn't somehow wondered into her apartment.

'Yes,' she answered hesitantly.

'That's good. These walls really are quite thin, aren't they?'

'Yes.'

'This is so odd. It's as though if I were to punch my fist through this plasterboard I'd be able to see you.'

'Don't do that,' she called urgently, looking at the part of her kitchenette wall where his voice was strongest. If he did that, he'd see her dressed in her thin nightshirt and bare feet. Even the thought of him looking at her now made her cheeks tinge with colour. 'Uh…it would take for ever to get someone to come and fix it,' she added, trying to cover over the embarrassment she felt. 'Besides, you'd no doubt do an injury to your hand and we can't have those surgeon's hands damaged, now, can we?'

His answer was a rich, deep chuckle. 'No. We can't have that.'

The toast popped up but Janessa didn't move. She was glued to the spot, staring at her blank wall where she was sure he stood. He really was so close and yet so far. She walked to the wall and placed her hand against it, almost wondering if she'd feel the heat radiating from his body, but that was plain ridiculous.

'No. What's ridiculous is the way you can't seem to stop thinking about him, the way you hang on his every word and the way you're letting him affect you,' she murmured to herself.

'Did you say something?' he asked.

'Uh…' She moved away from the wall and backed out of the kitchenette. 'I'm going to have a shower,' she remarked, deciding to eat later at the hospital rather than staying in the apartment any longer than she had to. She couldn't believe how aware she was of a man she'd only just met and one she barely knew at all.

As she turned on the taps in the shower, the pipes groaned and creaked and moaned before the water spluttered out in nothing but a trickle. 'Ugh. Not now.'

She felt highly self-conscious of the fact that Miles could hear every little move she made. Why she should feel so… self-conscious about it all she wasn't quite sure. It was illogical to think he would smash a hole through the wall and if she'd learned anything about him both through his journal articles and the ridiculous tests he'd put her through yesterday, it was that Miles Trevellion was a logical man.

As she waited for the water pressure to increase, she still felt as though he could see through the walls, could see her standing naked in her shower, and the thoughts made her entire body flush with sensual embarrassment. What on earth was wrong with her? Usually, she could disregard any feelings of awareness she felt towards colleagues, preferring to admire them in a professional capacity. So why was she unable to do it with Miles? What was so different about him?

Until yesterday, when they'd met, her life had had a steady rhythm. Sleep, work. Sleep, work. The occasional day off where she would go to the airfield, fly in her plane and release her stress. Now Miles was in her life and he seemed to bring a different beat, a different rhythm to her world, one that made her heart go *pit-a-pat* with excited awareness and she wasn't quite sure what she should do about it.

Sighing, she turned off the taps and dried herself, knowing the sooner she headed to the NICU, the better off she'd be. Space. Distance. Separation. That was what she needed from her new neighbour and colleague, and the sooner the better.

Janessa quickly dressed in a pair of dark blue trousers and a pale pink knit top. Her hair was pulled back into her usual ponytail, out of the way and easy to put up into a surgical cap if necessary. Slipping her feet into flat, comfortable shoes, she quickly tidied her kitchenette and picked up the papers she'd brought over from her office the previous night.

She was about to walk out the door when she heard the squeak of the taps being turned on next door and the pipes shuddering as though they resented the fact that they had work to do. Janessa stopped, holding her breath as she unashamedly listened to the sounds from next door. Miles was in the shower. The water was running and she swallowed, closing her eyes, the picture of him standing with water dripping down around his brown hair, his angular face, his broad shoulders before sliding sensually over his firm torso and then down—

Her eyes snapped open and she swallowed over her thoughts. This was wrong. Him being so close to her was wrong. Miles and his enigmatic presence, his deep voice, his sexy body, his heart-stopping grin. She was a doctor, for crying out loud. The human body was just that to her—a body—and the fact that Miles Trevellion seemed to have a very nice specimen was of no concern. None whatsoever. Shaking her head, she grabbed her keys and opened her door. The sooner she was out of there the better.

And then he started to sing. Janessa paused, her hand

curling tightly around her keys as she listened. He had a lovely voice. His smooth baritone made easy work of the notes and as she forced herself to move forward, closing her apartment door behind her, she found she was humming the same song as she headed down the stairs. Darn Miles. How had he managed to get so stuck inside her head so quickly?

She liked her space and Miles seemed to have infiltrated it at almost every turn. With Sheena, with the NICU and with her accommodation. Well…at least she still had her flying to herself. Escaping from the world and flying in her plane on her days off was by far her most favourite thing to do. Not only did it remind her of great times she'd spent with her father but also whisked her away from the pressures of hospital life. She hadn't managed to get away enough lately but now, with the latest stressful addition to her little world, she was looking forward to heading out to the small airfield as soon as possible.

'Morning, Janessa,' Ray said brightly as she walked into the ward half an hour after Miles's alarm clock had woken her up. 'I was just about to make coffee. Can I get you one?'

She nodded, her stomach growling due to her aborted breakfast. She didn't want to think about it because that meant she'd have to think of the cause of her aborted breakfast and she'd already thought way too much about Miles Trevellion this morning. 'Thanks, Ray. How was last night?'

'Helena's handover recounted a non-eventful night. You've just missed her.' He headed to the unit's kitchenette and pulled out two cups before using the small espresso machine which had been a gift to them all from very grateful parents.

'Taneesha's stable? Joey didn't turn blue again?'

'Everything's fine. A good night—which was a godsend, given how full the unit is.'

'Still, there are quite a few babies who can be transferred to Maternity to be with their mothers today, so that should give us a bit of wriggle room.'

'Great.' As Ray made their drinks, he gave her a few more details about the handover from Helena, knowing that as soon as they'd had their coffee, they could do a quick round and make firmer decisions regarding the precious little ones in their care.

Ray handed her a cup that had a big red love-heart on the side and the words 'Fill my Heart' written beneath it, and for some reason she immediately thought of Miles. Janessa shook her head as though to clear it before sipping at the liquid with grateful thanks, deciding she really didn't want anyone to 'fill her heart' and that she was more than happy to keep her life exactly the way it was.

The awareness she felt towards Miles Trevellion was nothing but a reaction to being out of the dating game. Besides, she wasn't looking for any sort of romance in her life, especially not with a man who would be leaving Adelaide Mercy in six months' time.

As she walked to her office to read over the notes and reports from last night, sipping her coffee as she went, she told herself to be satisfied with everything she had. She was head of the NICU, a job she'd worked long and hard to achieve. The people she worked with on a daily basis were some of her closest and dearest friends. They'd supported her through her father's cancer treatments, had been there for her when he'd decided he was through with fighting the debilitating disease and had passed away.

They were a family. Kaycee and Ray and Helena and Sheena. Arthur was over in the residential wing, always looking out for her, just as her father would. There was also the staff on the maternity ward and Charisma, the hospital director who was an advocate for the right person in the right job. Janessa may not have any blood relatives, she may be all alone in the world as far as biological family went, but here, at Adelaide Mercy, she had her *real* family and she didn't need anything more…especially not romantic or sensual thoughts about Miles.

So the man had kissed her. It didn't mean anything. He'd simply meant to kiss her cheek in a polite gesture of thanks for a nice evening. The fact that their lips had met meant nothing…nothing at all.

With her mind firmly back on track, she was able to focus on her work. She had a meeting about Sheena's conjoined twins at nine-thirty, and headed to the maternity ward to say good morning to her friend just after nine. By this time the breakfasts would have been served, the ward rounds would have been done and Sheena would no doubt be ready for a soothing cup of herbal tea.

Janessa stopped off at the maternity kitchenette, made two cups and headed towards Sheena's room, calling various hellos to the staff as she went. She was humming happily as she nudged the door open to Sheena's room.

'Hi. Sorry I'm a little later than usual, this morning,' she said, her hands full with the two drinks. As she turned and looked towards her friend's bed, she was startled to see Miles Trevellion sitting in a chair by Sheena's bed.

'Oh. Hi. Sorry. I thought you'd be free.'

'Miles was humming that same song when he came in this morning,' Sheena pointed out.

Janessa looked at Miles, feeling like a deer caught in the headlights. The fact that she was humming the same song as him meant he knew she'd heard him singing it in the shower earlier that morning and for a split second it was as though the two of them were transported to another world, away from the hospital room, away from Maternity—back to when they'd been having a conversation that morning, only plasterboard and paint between them. Intimate. Indulgent and completely insupportable. She simply had to stop her mind from contemplating her new colleague in such a fashion.

'We both must have heard the same song on the radio,' Miles eventually murmured, his lips curving into a small smile that told Janessa that he knew exactly where she'd heard that song this morning and it hadn't been the radio.

Sheena held out her hands for the cup of tea. 'Ah, thanks for the tea,' she remarked, seemingly oblivious to the undercurrents passing between Janessa and Miles. 'I've been waiting for an eternity. I was starting to become quite desperate for my morning Janessa cuppa-tea-time.'

Janessa smiled at her friend, blatantly doing her best to ignore the tall, dark and sexy man in the room. 'I see the exaggeration hormones are working well this morning,' Janessa remarked.

Sheena laughed, but sipped the tea as Janessa put her cup down on the bedside locker, knowing that if she didn't she might drop it. She could feel Miles's gaze on her, watching everything she did, taking in the camaraderie between the two women. It was quite astonishing that he had such an ability to unsettle her, especially as she hadn't even known him for twenty-four hours.

Janessa pulled up a chair on the other side of the bed from him and looked at her friend. 'Did you keep sleeping after we left?'

'On and off, but no more waterworks, thank goodness,' Sheena admitted with aplomb.

'You told me you'd managed to sleep well,' Miles immediately interjected with instant indignation.

Sheena sighed. 'Yes, but I can lie to you. I can't lie to Janessa. She knows me far too well for me to get away with it.'

Janessa picked up her tea and hid her smile at Miles's reaction behind her cup. 'But Sheenie, you shouldn't lie to any of us,' she said after a moment. 'You don't like it when your patients lie to you,' she pointed out calmly.

'My patients *can't* lie to me. In fact, nine times out of ten they can't even talk, given that they're babies and young toddlers,' Sheena felt compelled to point out, but looked from Janessa to Miles. 'Oh, all right,' she grumbled. 'I won't lie to Miles any more, and it wasn't technically a lie, more like a nice exaggeration of the truth.'

'Thank you.' Miles nodded, seemingly satisfied, then turned to Janessa. 'Would you like to examine Sheena?'

Janessa shook her head. 'I'm sure between you and Riley, Sheena and the girls are well cared for. Besides, the nurses keep me up to date with anything out of the ordinary. We've got a good team here.' She sipped at her tea. 'I'm just here for a chat before our morning meeting.'

'Yes, and it's a meeting,' Sheena remarked indignantly, 'that I'm not allowed to attend, even though it's about me and my girls.'

'You're not the doctor, remember. You *are* the important incubator.' Janessa's words were not unkind but spoken with utter respect. She held out her tea cup and the two women chinked their mugs together. 'No one else can do your job.'

Sheena scoffed at that. 'Ha! Job? I lie here and do absolutely diddly-squat.'

'And that's the most difficult job of all,' Janessa agreed. 'See? We keep the tough jobs for those who can handle them.'

'Yes,' Miles agreed. 'It's important for your blood pressure to remain constant and as such...' he waggled a finger at her '...no cajoling the staff for information about patients.'

Sheena grimaced. 'It wouldn't work even if I wanted it to. Janessa's put a gag order in place.'

'A gag order?' Miles looked from Janessa to Sheena.

'I'm not allowed to know the ins and outs of what's happening in the wards because if I knew I'd get all bothered and impatient and want to go and help.'

'Really?' His eyebrows were raised in surprise.

'I know.' Sheena rolled her eyes. 'Can you believe it?'

Miles met Janessa's brown gaze and smiled, nodding slowly. 'An excellent idea, Janessa. Gag order. I've never heard it called that before. Well done.'

Janessa raised her eyebrows in surprise at the compliment. 'Er...thank you?'

'It's good to see that you're not only looking out for your friend in a personal capacity but in a way most doctors wouldn't have even thought necessary.' He stood from his chair and straightened his jacket, buttoning it up. 'I give credit where credit is due.'

'Nice to know,' she murmured, only glancing once or twice in his direction. If she looked at him, really looked across and met the deep blue of his eyes, she wasn't sure she'd have the strength to look away, especially given how gorgeous he looked in that suit.

There was a silence in the room for a second and an uncomfortable one at that, with the awareness she had of her new colleague. She sipped her tea, glad of something to do. As the room clock ticked on for another ten seconds, Miles eventually cleared his throat and addressed his comments to Sheena.

'I'll come by later and check on you again. Better go get ready for that meeting.'

'OK. Thanks for visiting,' Sheena replied as he headed around the bed and walked towards the door.

'Janessa, I'll see you at the meeting,' he remarked.

'Yes. See you there,' she sort of threw over her shoulder, looking vaguely in his direction. When he was gone, Janessa visibly relaxed in her chair, closing her eyes for a moment, only to encounter Sheena's interested stare when she finally looked at her friend.

'What was *that* all about?' Sheena asked with astonishment.

'What?'

'You and Miles. Honestly, you could cut the air with a scalpel the tension between the two of you is so palpable.'

'I have no idea what you're talking about.' Janessa feigned innocence and continued drinking her tea.

'Oh, seriously? There were sparks flying between the two of you from the instant you entered this room.'

'Sparks?'

'Janessa. He's not like Bradley. Miles has been through things and, unlike Bradley, he'll stick around. I know you were devastated that Bradley wasn't there for you, to be with you as you both grieved for Connor's loss, but not all men are like that.'

'All men? Meaning Miles?'

'He's a great guy, Nessa. Strong and dependable. You two are good together.'

'Together? No. We're not together.' At her words, Sheena gave her a disbelieving look. 'You think there's something going on between Miles and myself, don't you?'

'Is there?'

'Yes.'

At this word, Sheena sucked in a breath and clenched her hands at her chest, excitement in her eyes.

'It's you. *You* are why we're here, why our worlds have connected. We are both here, working together because of your girls. They deserve the best care in the world and that, if I may be so bold, is Miles and myself. So technically, Sheenie, it's all *you*. There are no sparks, no tension. Just real honest concern for you and your girls.'

'Now you've made me disappointed.' Sheena dropped her hands back to her rub her belly. 'Hear that, girls? Aunty Janessa is trying to fool herself into thinking that she's not attracted to Uncle Miles.'

'*Uncle* Miles? When did he get promoted to uncle status?' Janessa wanted to know, feeling mildly indignant that he should get the same level of honorary title as herself, and yet Sheena didn't know him nearly as well. She finished her drink and stood, hoping that leading Sheena down this track might also prompt a change in topic. The awareness she had for Miles was definitely there but that didn't mean she had to do something about it, neither did she want to discuss it.

'Hush. I can say what I like and assign titles to whomever I choose because I am the incubator and I have spoken.'

Janessa shrugged her shoulders as though she didn't have a leg to stand on with an answer like that. 'You are absolutely right. Anyway…' she collected Sheena's cup '…I have to go. I don't want to be late for the meeting.'

'You'll come by later and give me an update?'

'On most things, yes.'

'Good.' Sheena lay back and closed her eyes, getting ready to settle down for a nap. 'Nessa,' she said softly as Janessa headed to the door, 'don't push him away. He's not Bradley.' The words were spoken quietly and with complete seriousness.

'Understood,' Janessa replied, realising she hadn't fooled

Sheena one bit with her attempt at changing the subject. Her friend knew her far too well. 'Thanks, Sheenie.'

Sheena yawned. 'That's what friends are for.'

As Janessa returned to her office and gathered the papers she would need for the meeting—the first of many on the conjoined twins—she pondered Sheena's words. Was she resisting the attraction she felt for Miles simply because of the way Bradley had pulverised her heart? Was she too afraid to even take a tiny step outside her very comfortable comfort zone in case she once more ended up in tiny pieces? Was she that much of a coward that she would deny herself happiness simply because she'd been burnt so badly in her past?

Possibly.

CHAPTER SIX

THREE days later, after several meetings with key person-nel as well as the hospital administrator, Miles arranged another one-on-one meeting with Janessa in her office. He had initially suggested that they meet in his apartment to discuss the upcoming operations the twins would require over a soothing cup of herbal tea, but even the thought of being alone with him, in his apartment, made her entire body quiver with nervous apprehension. Her office was definitely safer.

Ever since the kiss, Janessa had been overcome by masses of tingles every time she'd seen him. She'd constantly thought about him on the other side of her apartment wall, her curiosity about him increasing, and although she wanted to keep him at arm's length, she also wanted to know as much about him as possible.

Every look he gave her seemed to linger just a fraction of a second longer than normal. If he accidentally touched her hand or brushed past her during the normal course of any day in the NICU, she wasn't able to hide her quick intake of breath as her body suffused with heat.

'As you know, in order to separate the girls, they'll need extra skin to cover the actual incision site. Therefore, one of the first procedures we'll be performing once they're stable and healthy is to insert tissue expanders beneath the skin in order to grow extra skin in that area.' Miles lounged in the chair, relaxed and completely comfortable in her presence. Janessa had to admit that whilst he had the ability to set her body on fire with just one look, she, too, liked spending time with him in this way.

Under the guise of work, even though it was necessary work, for her to know exactly what procedures and steps would be taken with regard to separating the twins, she liked that she was able to spend time with him...like this... alone. He never talked down to her, always explained things thoroughly and answered any and all questions she had. Sometimes she thought she asked too many questions but he never became impatient, insisting that he would rather answer her questions a hundred times over so she knew what to expect than risk making mistakes.

He was thoughtful, too, and always the gentleman. Tonight he'd arrived in her office with a bag full of take-away Chinese food. 'Thought we might get hungry,' he'd stated as a means of explanation when she'd raised her eyebrows at the gesture. And so there they sat, papers and documents spread out before them on her desk, the scent of Chinese food filling the air as they ate and discussed the various aspects of the different surgical procedures.

'I have to confess, I have very limited experience when it comes to tissue expanders. It's just something I haven't come across that often. I have, however, read every paper you've written on this subject and the techniques you've used during the surgical procedures,' Janessa remarked quite en-thusiastically, and was rewarded one of Miles's heart-melting smiles. Tingles flooded her body as she smiled shyly back at him. She still felt strange admitting she was such a big fan of his work.

Apart from that very first day in her NICU, when he'd been jet-lagged and completely exhausted, he'd been re-laxed and friendly, as well as being totally in control of the specialised neonate team they were pulling together to care for the girls post-delivery. No one in either the NICU or Maternity had a bad word to say against him and half the women would swoon every time he came near. Janessa, however, hoped she wasn't as obvious whenever she was near him.

'Have you ever seen the operation performed?' He used the chopsticks with ease as he lifted another mouthful of food to his lips.

Janessa sipped her green tea. 'Many years ago, in a two-year-old. Never in a baby. I think it's fascinating how the body can grow extra skin through this means.'

Miles nodded, impressed with the way she seemed eager to know everything about the twins' upcoming surgeries. 'It's much the same as how the skin expands in a pregnant woman.'

'Where do we order these special little bags?' She looked at the picture on the information she'd been studying then back at Miles. 'They're made of silicone, right?'

'That's right. They have a tube attached to them. In some of the older children we might leave the edge of the tube showing outside, making it easier to fill, but for the twins it's easier if the filling tube is just under the skin, thereby decreasing the risk of infection.'

'Which is the last thing we want.' She finished her noo-dles and used a napkin to wipe her face, before sipping the last of her green tea. Miles watched, delighted that she was the type of woman who didn't worry about her figure but instead seemed to have a very healthy appetite. Even when they'd been at the Italian restaurant, Janessa had eaten each course with appreciation instead of nibbling on a salad. It wasn't that she needed to watch her weight, far from it. She was perfectly proportioned...very perfectly.

He forced his thoughts back to the present, to the operation details they were discussing. 'Exactly. The bags will be gradually inflated over a number of weeks.'

'How long will the whole procedure take? I mean from the time the tissue expanders are inserted until there's enough new tissue for them to be removed?' She started to pack away her rubbish, tidying up, making things ordered and neat again.

'Approximately two months. We want to grow this new tissue slowly and carefully. Then, after another small operation, the expanders are removed and *voilà*—new tissue.' He, too, finished his food, and she held out her hand to take the empty container so she could dispose of it. 'Thanks.' He smiled as he wiped his face with a napkin.

Janessa smiled widely. 'That's what I love about medicine. The new breakthroughs in technology that make so much difference to the lives of our patients.'

Miles couldn't help but smile at her words, at the excitement she seemed to exude in discussing these surgeries. 'You really do love your job, don't you,' he stated.

Janessa met his gaze, feeling a little self-conscious. 'Of course. Don't you?'

'Most days.' He paused and sipped his green tea thoughtfully, watching her closely. 'Tell me, Janessa, have you ever thought of expanding your horizons?' At her blank look, he continued. 'You're excited by surgery. Have you ever thought of doing more training?'

Janessa was stunned by this idea. 'Uh...no. I'm more than happy where I am.'

'Don't get me wrong,' he added quickly. 'I think the work

you do here is brilliant. You're well respected, you're highly skilled and Adelaide Mercy is lucky to have someone like you in charge of their NICU, but there's still more you could learn.' He leaned in a little closer, closing the distance between them, wanting to get his point cross. 'I could teach you.' His tone had dropped a level and the look in his eyes was more intimate than professional.

She was sure he could teach her, and not just about surgery! The way this man made her feel was something she'd never felt before. With Bradley, the love she had thought would last a lifetime had run its course in a matter of years, and even though he'd initially made her feel all special and nice, it was nothing compared to the far more adult feelings she was constantly experiencing with Miles. Just one smouldering, sexy look from his deep blue eyes and she was almost hyperventilating with repressed excitement.

She eased back in her chair, needing to put a bit more space between them. Breathing out slowly, determined to get herself back under some sort of control, Janessa nodded slowly. 'Thank you for such a generous offer, Miles but… um…I'm fine here. Doing my job, working alongside my friends and, at present, caring for Sheena.'

Miles held her gaze for another split second and then eased away, watching her carefully. 'Family is very important to you.' It was a statement, not a question.

'Very.' She paused and then found herself saying, 'Especially when you're left all alone.'

'Do you mean Sheena? I don't mean to pry but where is the father of her twins?'

She hadn't been referring to Sheena but she was more than relieved he hadn't realised she'd been talking about herself. 'Jonas? He's long gone.' Janessa rolled her eyes in disgust.

'So he's alive?'

'Oh, yes. Alive and well and living with his new wife in Brazil or Mexico or some other sunny place where he can be selfish and demanding and ruin other people's lives.' Her eyes were dark, filled with intense dislike. Miles hadn't thought it possible for her beautiful features to be marred with such emotions but it was quite clear in both her expression and the way she talked of the unknown Jonas that she didn't like him one little bit.

'But he knows she's pregnant? He knows about the babies?'

'Yes—yes, he does.' Janessa sighed heavily, not really wanting to blurt out Sheena's past to Miles but also knowing that anything she said to her friend's doctor regarding the babies father would remain confidential.

'Jonas high-tailed it out of Adelaide the instant Sheena told him she was pregnant or, more to the point, when Sheena was determined to see the pregnancy through.'

Miles raised his eyebrows, both perplexed and puzzled by this information. 'He didn't want to have children?'

'Correct. It was part of the reason why they married in the first place. Sheena had been told years ago that she would never have children. Jonas didn't want children, either. When Sheena discovered she'd actually been able to conceive, she was so happy, so ecstatic. It was like a miracle.'

'She thought Jonas would feel the same way.' Miles nodded.

'He didn't. Instead he took it as grounds to file for divorce. He told her that if she didn't abort the pregnancy, then as far as he was concerned their marriage was over because he wasn't throwing away any of his money or time or any part of *his* life on a bratty little kid. He left when six weeks later we discovered she was having twins. Another eight weeks down the line we discovered the twins were conjoined.'

'You say "we". Don't you mean *she*?'

Janessa smiled. 'No. I mean *we*. As you've already come to realise, Sheena is well loved, respected and protected by the staff in this hospital. What she's going through is huge and none of us are going to let her go through it alone. That's what family is all about, hence the *we*.'

'You don't plan on having a family of your own one day?'

Janessa was momentarily stunned by his question and the image of Connor flashed before her eyes. Her Connor. Her baby boy. The child that never was. 'I…don't know.'

'Surely you've thought about it? Marriage? Children? Quiet weekends? School runs? Real family time?'

'Once, perhaps, but not any more.'

'Once? Bad experience?'

'You could say that.'

'You were…married?' he fished. He knew it was wrong to delve into her past but the more time he spent with her, the more curious he became. Why wasn't a woman as incredible as Janessa involved with someone?

'Briefly.' She sighed and stood, turning her back to him. 'It didn't work out.'

'Do you know why?'

She laughed with a hint of irony. 'We were young. Too young. But we were so sure that we were really in love, that we were mature enough to understand the commitment we were making to each other, and when our parents realised we weren't going to be talked out of it, we tied the knot.'

There was sadness in her eyes and a despondent tone in her voice.

'How young?'

'Eighteen.'

'Both of you?'

'Yes. I guess we thought it was the real thing but we were wrong.' She shook her head and sighed. 'When things became too intense, too scary, too grown-up, I think we both knew we'd been kidding ourselves. We separated when we were twenty and were divorced by the time we turned twenty-one.'

'Hard lessons to learn. You've never thought about marrying again?'

She held his gaze. 'No. After that it was far easier to remain married to my career.'

'Which has obviously worked out well for you?'

'Yes.'

'Focusing on work can take your mind off a lot of things. Work is always there to see you through, no matter what disasters life throws at you.'

'You sound as though you're talking from experience.' It was her turn to fish.

'I was married.' He spoke the words quietly, surprised to find that he wanted her to know about his past. The fact that he was becoming more and more interested in this woman with each passing hour he spent in her company, it seemed only right to tell her about Wendy.

'Didn't take?' Janessa was secretly thrilled he was sharing this with her. Miles had such a knack for not making her feel as though she was the only one walking out onto a unsteady ledge all alone.

'Quite the opposite.'

'Oh.' She was surprised by that statement. Was he hiding a wife somewhere? She'd always just assumed he wasn't married. Sheena hadn't said anything about him being married but, then, Sheena hadn't stayed in contact with Miles during the past ten years since they'd worked together. Was

Miles still married? It only confirmed how little she knew of him but before she could question him, he continued.

'My wife, Wendy, and I worked together for years, just colleagues, just friends, and then things slowly started to change into something more. We'd been married for almost two years when she died.' Miles stared off into the distance, remembering his past.

Janessa wasn't quite sure what to say for a moment but she knew what she wanted to do. She wanted to go to him, to put her arms around him, to say she was sorry for the loss he had suffered and the heartbreak he must have felt. She stayed where she was, keeping her physical distance from him whilst emotionally she felt more connected to him than before. 'You were lucky,' she stated.

'Yes.' He nodded and slowly exhaled any tension he may have felt in sharing his past with Janessa. 'Yes, I was.'

A more comfortable silence seemed to envelop them both, Janessa sighing as the tension and anxiety from her past slipped away. 'My parents were lucky.' She spoke the words softly, looking off into nothingness as she remembered. 'Their marriage was real and strong and I guess Bradley and I thought we'd be the same. I thought that my marriage would be as happy and as honest and as open as that of my own parents.'

'Where is Bradley now?'

Janessa shrugged. 'In Tasmania. We exchanged Christmas cards for about ten years but then it drifted off. We're both very different people now from who we were back then.'

'It was an amicable divorce?'

Janessa thought about the pain and heartbreak they'd both suffered when their son had died. Poor Connor. So little. Too premature to survive, and medical science hadn't been as great back then as it was today. It was because of her son and the amazing team of specialists that had treated him that she'd entered this speciality, as though to honour his memory and to help mothers who were praying for their babies' lives. Both she and Bradley had been stunned at Connor's death and things had never been the same between them after that. She'd put her hope and trust in their marriage, that together, as husband and wife, they would find a way through their pain, but he simply hadn't been able to cope.

'I guess you could say that,' she finally answered. 'I certainly don't hold any malice towards him. He wasn't to blame for what happened to us and neither was I.'

He sensed there was probably far more to it than she was admitting. No divorce, however amicable, was ever easy. Besides, he'd pried enough for one night and finding out more about her didn't help the way she made him feel. He still had to work alongside her, the sweet, summery scent she wore winding itself around him, drawing him in, enticing him to know more.

Living next door to her in the residential wing, knowing she was so close yet so far, sitting reading a book, overcoming the plumbing problems as she showered, sleeping peacefully in her bed…was also starting to become something of a problem and he'd started to wonder whether perhaps he should look around for a place to rent, outside the hospital grounds but close enough that he was readily available.

He would continue to tell himself that Janessa Austen was just another colleague, in another hospital, in another city that he would soon be leaving. The fact that she was the first woman who had piqued his interest since Wendy was a miracle within itself. She'd built a family for herself here and it appeared she had no intention of leaving. He needed to move, needed to be challenged with his work because that way he didn't have to consider what might happen should he choose to, once more, spend his life alongside someone permanent…and Janessa was just the sort of woman who would fit that job description.

He'd tried the happy family road before and it had ended in loneliness. Moving around, shifting every three to six months to a different location, a different country, going where the work took him, was the life he'd chosen and one he wasn't giving up simply because he was attracted to the intelligent and incredibly beautiful woman sitting opposite him.

'I'm sorry if you felt I was prying into your past. I most certainly didn't mean any offence by it,' Miles remarked after a moment, attempting to bring their thoughts back to the here and now.

'You were curious about me.'

He shrugged, feigning nonchalance. 'It's not uncommon for me to be curious about those I work with.'

'But I'm guessing you rarely follow through on that curiosity. You'd rather keep yourself to yourself, do your job and then leave. Which piques my own curiosity. Why? Why do you move around so much, Miles? What is it that you're running away from?'

'Who says I'm running away from anything?'

It was her turn to shrug. The man had just told her his wife had died and perhaps that had been enough to keep him on the move. 'I guess it appears that way when facts show that for the past six or seven years, you've never stayed in any one place longer than twelve months.'

'How do you know that?'

'Oh, come on, Miles. You're the man that everyone wants when it comes to conjoined twins. I can look you up on the internet and find a dozen or so different photographs of you and your team celebrating another successful spate of operations to separate conjoined twins, and most of them are at different hospitals around the world.'

'Maybe I just go where the work is.'

'Yes, but why? I'm guessing you're not bored with the work you're doing so if you're not running away, are you looking for greener pastures? A place where you fit? Where you feel comfortable? At home?'

'Why do you want to know?' he asked after a moment. She was getting close. She was asking him questions that he hadn't been asked by anyone in a very long time. He'd suggested that she expand her horizons, that she learn more, perhaps even travel with him so he could teach her more about the complicated and challenging world of conjoined twins. It shouldn't be such a stretch that as a homebody she would be curious as to why he didn't seem able to settle in one place. He couldn't blame her. He'd pried into her life and asked questions, so it was only fair.

'I'm…intrigued by you,' she remarked honestly, holding his gaze for a long moment. The atmosphere between them began to intensify and after a second she breathed out slowly and walked towards the door. She opened it and leaned against it, looking out into her unit. Some babies were crying, others were sleeping and some were being fed. They didn't understand time—they didn't care if it was the middle of the night or the busiest part of the day. They all had needs, special needs, and she and her staff were on hand to provide them.

'We're a pair, Miles. Both determined to stay in control of our lives. Both wanting to focus on our careers and not risk even the slightest bit of compromise…and yet, whenever we're in a room like this, together, intimate, quiet, the tension is so tight it would take more than the sharpest scalpel to slice through it.'

Janessa looked over at him, tipping her head back against the door, revealing her smooth long neck, her hands behind her back giving her a relaxed and open posture. Her guard was down and the look in her big, mesmerising eyes was one of complete honesty. 'Do you think there's any real hope for people like us, Miles?' Her tone was free and soft and tired. 'People who are always trying to control the world around them?'

Miles swallowed, his heart beating wildly as he drank his fill of the vision she made. He wanted to go to her, wanted to close the remaining distance between them, wanted to take her into his arms and to press his mouth firmly to hers. Didn't she have any idea just how alluring she was right now?

He shook his head, more to steady the burning need inside him to go to her than to answer her question.

She sighed again and looked away. 'I didn't think so.'

Another four days passed with, both of them confused by the emotions they felt for the other hiding behind their professional personae. The special clothes that had been ordered for the twins arrived and both Janessa and Sheena had a wonderful time looking at the gorgeous little outfits. There had been meetings every day, Miles going over the finer points of what to expect once the twins were delivered.

'The actual C-section is straightforward, but once the twins are out we'll need to be focused on stabilising them as soon as possible,' he'd said to Kaycee, Ray and Janessa who, along with Miles, would make up the initial postnatal care team. As far as planning for Ellie and Sarah's arrival, things seemed to be well on track.

Tonight, though, Janessa sat in her office and looked at the mound of paperwork before her. She had planned to spend most of today out at the airfield, up in her glorious Tiger Moth biplane, whisking away the cobwebs and setting her world to rights. Instead, she'd been in the unit for almost twenty-four hours straight, desperately concerned about a little baby, Philip, who had made his appearance in this world far too early at twenty-three weeks. Now, two weeks later and after a couple of doses of indomethocin to close the hole in his heart, it appeared surgical intervention may be necessary.

'Twenty-five weeks is not good,' she'd murmured to Kaycee as she monitored Philip's oxygen intake. 'Plus he's developed necrosis of the bowel.'

Still, the NICU staff would monitor him closely in the hope that the struggling baby would continue to fight for his life. For now, though, they'd managed to stabilise him as best they could but Janessa knew that if tiny, tiny Philip was going to survive, he would have a long and hard fight ahead of him. If he did require surgery, though, Miles, as the most experienced neonate surgeon they had, would perform it and Janessa was relieved to have him here at such a time.

While they were in the hospital things seemed to be under control, but in the evening, when she returned to her apartment in the residential wing, Janessa needed to call on all of her self-control *not* to think about him. Whether it be in her dreams or trying to guess what he was doing on the other side of the paper-thin walls that separated them.

She'd even taken to putting on headphones and listening to soothing music in order to help shut out images of Miles, next door...preparing food in the little kitchenette, sitting reading on the second-hand furniture, fighting with the taps to get the plumbing to work properly, lying in his bed at night...half-naked...hands behind his head, his muscles flexing, the blankets only partially covering his firm torso...

'Nessa?'

'Hmm? What?' She looked up from the work at her desk and met Ray's worried gaze. She shoved aside the ridiculous fantasies of Miles and focused her thoughts. 'Philip?'

Ray nodded. 'He's not improving. His oxygen requirement is thirty-five per cent and slowly increasing.'

Janessa sighed with sad resignation. 'I'll call Miles. It looks as though he'll have to operate on Philip after all.'

'Someone say my name?' Miles asked as he headed towards Janessa's open office door. His eyes met hers and for a fraction of a second they gazed at each other, veiled acknowledgement of the repressed awareness still coursing between them, before shifting their focus away and back to more important matters.

'It's Philip.' Janessa's face twisted as though little Philip's pain was her own, and in some ways it was. Philip's mother, Violet, was a seventeen-year-old girl who hadn't even known she was pregnant until two weeks ago. The fact that Janessa had been a young teenage mother herself meant she could empathise with poor Violet.

Miles nodded, already aware of the seriousness of Philip's case, and slowly exhaled, feeling the weight of the situation.

'Let's go and review him again,' Janessa replied. Philip was too young, too premature, too sick, and yet she wanted to do whatever they could in order to give him the best chance at fighting. They headed over to where Kaycee was closely monitoring Philip.

'We have to try,' she implored, looking directly into Miles's blue eyes, almost pleading with him to make things better. 'We have to try.' This time her voice broke on the words. Miles nodded and placed a hand on her shoulder. The touch wasn't romantic or sensual. While the warmth from his hand seeped into her body, she understood the show of support and solidarity his touch evoked.

'You're right, even if that means surgical intervention.' Thoughts of being unable to help his own little baby, the eight-month-old dying in his mother's arms during the horrific train crash, came back to haunt him. Miles knew he would do everything he could in order to give Philip the best chance possible. 'We owe Philip that much.'

With his words and his touch, Janessa felt a certain level of relief from her exhausted and frazzled nerves. Miles understood. Miles was also concerned about Philip and he knew they had to try.

Swallowing over the dryness of her throat, she breathed in a cleansing, calming breath and nodded. 'Thank you, Miles.' There was another beat where the two of them just stood, just stared, just absorbed, before he quickly dropped his hand and turned away.

'I'll go and speak to the mother.'

'Violet,' Janessa said.

'Pardon?'

'The mother. Her name is Violet and… Do you mind if I come, too?'

'No. Not at all.' Miles was pleased she wanted to join him as it only proved once again just how much Janessa cared about her patients, not only the babies but the mothers as well. Miles turned to Ray. 'You're trained in neonate theatre procedures, aren't you, Ray?'

'Most certainly, sir,' Ray replied, rolling his 'r's. 'I'll go and prepare the theatre and contact the anaesthetist.'

'Excellent.' Miles returned his attention to Janessa and swept his arm across his body. 'Shall we, Dr Austen?'

Janessa nodded and together they headed to Maternity where the young mother was lying in a bed, staring unseeingly out the window. Janessa drew the curtain around the bed, giving them some privacy from the other mothers in the ward.

'Hi, Violet.' Janessa smiled at her. 'How are you feeling? Any pain?'

'I'm fine.' She tossed the words out carelessly as though she didn't care about herself but sat up in the bed, gripping the sheets with both hands. 'Philip? What's happened? Is he all right? Has something gone wrong?' Her words tumbled out too quickly and Janessa instantly went over and put her hand reassuringly on the young mother's white knuckles.

She hated giving people bad news but she'd learned over the years that the best way was the direct way, combined with heart-felt compassion.

'Philip isn't doing too well at the moment. The hole in his heart is causing him more problems than his little body can deal with,' she began.

'We need your permission, should surgical intervention be necessary,' Miles continued, and went on to explain to Violet why Philip might need this surgical procedure. Throughout the entire discussion Miles was intrigued by Janessa, watching the way she seemed to relate on a personal level to Violet. There was vehemence in her words and repressed pain in her eyes. It wasn't only that she was being considerate to her patient, there was something deeper in her words, in the way she was making sure that Violet understood everything, in not talking down to the teenage mother. The compassion Janessa offered was complete to the point of perfect and it made him wonder whether something had happened to Janessa.

After they'd obtained Violet's permission, they headed back to the NICU, Miles still curious about his colleague. Janessa was quieter now, subdued but still direct in her actions and steadfast in her determination to do everything possible for Philip.

On entering the NICU, Miles headed off to the theatre and Janessa washed her hands thoroughly before heading over to Philip's humidicrib where Kaycee was still keeping vigil. She reached in and touched the little baby's stomach, stroking gently, crooning to him.

'We'll help you, sweetheart. As much as we can. We'll do everything possible. Be strong.'

'It doesn't look good,' Kaycee said a moment later.

'I know but even admitting that doesn't feel right.'

'He's too young. Even now, the risks are...' Kaycee trailed off, realising she didn't need to voice the thoughts both women were thinking. Janessa sighed, pain piercing her heart for the tiny life.

Soon it was time for Philip's surgery and after Ray had collected the baby from the NICU, Janessa went and scrubbed, pulling on her professionalism, ready to assist Miles. When he started performing the keyhole surgery on the tiny anaesthetised baby, Janessa found herself becoming more fascinated by his skill, and by the end of the surgical procedure, which had been undertaken with such precision and grace, she stood in compete awe of Miles and his abilities.

She'd read his articles and she'd always known he was the best. It was the reason why she'd requested he be the neonate surgeon in charge of Sheena's twins, but being here, watching him...it had only helped to solidify in her mind just how incredible Miles Trevellion really was. He was perfectly suited to this work, and although, through his publications, she'd been able to learn of his academic career and the way he'd become so specialised in this field, she had no idea what had prompted him to enter into neonatology in the first place. As a surgeon and colleague, he had her utmost respect but even as they degowned, she couldn't help but wonder what it was that made the man tick.

That, however, was an area she'd already marked as dangerous to enter. Hadn't she lain awake at night, wondering about him? Hadn't she tried to school her thoughts so she didn't dwell on the unanswered questions that didn't seem to want to leave her mind?

Deciding she needed a distraction and to get out of the NICU, and knowing she was leaving Philip with the best possible care, she headed up to the maternity ward to check on Sheena.

'He was amazing,' she said to her friend, her face alive with appreciation.

'I thought you weren't allowed to discuss patients with me,' Sheena remarked.

'I'm not discussing the patient, I'm discussing Miles and the way he performed the surgery.'

'Sounds as though you're really becoming…attached to the man.'

'Purely in a professional capacity,' Janessa quickly pointed out. 'It only proves that he is the most perfect doctor to be looking after your babies. It's right for him to be head of this team. Your girls…' Janessa reached out and put a hand on Sheena's abdomen, and one of the girls instantly kicked her, as though to say, *Hello, Aunty Nessa* '…are going to be just fine.'

'I know. With you and Miles looking after them, I *know* everything will be perfect.'

The two friends hugged and Janessa stayed for a few more minutes. 'I'd better get back to the unit.'

'Do you think Philip has a chance now?' Sheena asked as Janessa headed towards the door.

'A better chance than before but he's so…prem, Sheenie. So small. So weak.'

'And how are you holding up throughout it all? Teenage mother? Very sick baby? This can't be easy for you, Nessa.'

'I'll be fine. What happened to me happened a long time ago.'

'Mm-hm.' Sheena didn't sound as though she believed her. 'Just know that if you need me, I'm here for you. I may be just a human incubator to my girls but for you I'm forever your friend.'

Janessa smiled. 'I know. You're the best, Sheenie. Anyway, I'd best get back to the NICU.'

'You will let me know what happens? Either way?' Sheena's words had been calm but firm. 'Lift the gag order for this one. Please?'

Janessa looked at her friend, seeing the concern, knowing Sheena had seen these same or similar circumstances before. They both had. They both knew the odds. Even with Miles's brilliant surgical skills, it might not be enough to tip the scales in Philip's favour.

'OK. Rest, though. I'll talk to you later.'

Janessa headed back to the unit and after getting an update on Philip, who was still heavily sedated, she headed to her office. She had a lot to do but didn't want to do any of it. She sat there for a good half an hour, trying to concentrate, trying to get her brain to focus on the mounds of paperwork before her but to no avail. At a knock at her door she immediately looked up, glad of the interruption.

Miles opened the door. 'Sorry to bother you.'

'It's fine.' She beckoned him in and indicated the seat opposite her desk, the one he'd sat in all sharp and direct on his very first day here. This time, though, he was more relaxed, more calm. He'd obviously showered and changed after surgery and his casual trousers and polo shirt seemed to fit him to perfection. Janessa worked hard to ignore the way he moved, ignored the way the man was the whole package—handsome, intelligent and caring. Everything she'd ever wanted in a man, sitting before her. She clenched her hands tightly beneath the desk, more as a way of releasing her own frustration at being so drawn to him than anything else.

'How is he?' She didn't need to say anything else. All of them were equally concerned about Philip.

Miles frowned. 'Not doing as well as I'd hoped.'

Janessa nodded. They both knew the outlook wasn't good but they were still determined to do everything they could to help him.

'I've just come from seeing Sheena.'

'I was up there earlier. Just needed a break.'

'Me, too. She told me you've lifted the gag order on this one. Do you think that's wise? The chances that Philip could die are extremely high. You don't think news like that will elevate Sheena's blood pressure?' There was the slight hint of censure in his tone and Janessa felt the sting.

'No. I don't. Not this time. This time it's different and we both know it. She knows Philip's prognosis isn't good. The gag order mainly pertains to the running of the hospital, especially anything from the paediatric unit. This… Philip… he's different. Sheena and I have always shared these deep exchanges with each other. It's what we do. It's how we support each other. It's why we're such good friends.'

'You've obviously been through a lot with each other. Anyone can see how strong the bond is between the two of you. It's nice. Deep, abiding friendships. They're rare.'

Janessa couldn't help but wonder if he was referring to his

wife, the fact that he'd mentioned they'd been good friends before the relationship had progressed. 'Yes, they are.'

'Do you think we might be able to have that?'

'A deep, abiding friendship?' she wanted to clarify.

'Or something like it.' There was an earnest tone to his words.

'I've only known you for just over a week, Miles.' She spread her arms wide. 'I've known Sheena for almost twenty years.'

'We certainly have a good grounding for a friendship. We like each other. We respect each other. We seem to share a similar sense of humour.'

Janessa pondered his words for a moment, deciding that if they simply agreed to remain friends for the duration of Miles's stay, it might actually help them to deal with the electrifying pull they felt towards each other.

'It's one thing to be colleagues and neighbours but friends would be nice,' he added when she didn't immediately answer.

'Friends.' The word was spoken slowly, as though it was filled with deep reflection. Sighing, she stood and walked towards the door, gazing out into the unit for a long moment. Then something changed. The hairs on the back of her neck started to prick and she closed her eyes, listening closely, her back straightening, her entire body tensed. Everything else, trying to define her relationship with Miles, trying to control the way he made her feel whenever he was near… everything disappeared as she concentrated and listened to her intuition.

Miles noted the instant change in her demeanour, shifting briskly from open and sultry to one of instant apprehension. 'Something wrong?' he asked, standing up but not moving towards her. Distance. He needed to keep his distance.

'It's quiet.' Her tone was filled with concern.

'It's not that quiet. I can still hear a few babies making noises.'

'Not that sort of quiet.'

'Ah. You mean…something is about to happen?'

'Yes.' She looked at him and this time, all he saw was the look of a concerned neonatologist following through on an instinctive reaction.

'Philip,' they said in unison, and walked quickly over to where the little baby lay. He was sleeping, his breathing shallow and rapid.

If Philip was strong enough to survive, then young Violet would have her work cut out for her as babies born this early often ran the risk of neurological complications, such as autism or cerebral palsy. Her heart went out to both mother and child for whatever might happen within the next twenty-four hours.

'Something wrong?' Kaycee asked as she continued to monitor Philip.

'I don't know,' Janessa responded.

Kaycee picked up Philip's chart and handed it to Miles, who read it. 'I only did his obs two minutes ago. He's as stable as he can be, poor little lamb.'

Janessa accepted the chart from Miles and glanced at the information before looking at Philip once more. 'I don't know. There's just…something not right.'

'Instinct.' Miles nodded. 'The best weapon we doctors have and on the rare times that we don't trust it, heavy prices can be paid.'

Janessa could hear something, a tinge of sadness, a strong dose of regret coming through in what Miles was saying, and while she agreed with him one hundred per cent, she also noted that he was talking from personal experience. Had ignoring his instincts led to his wife's death? She pushed the thought aside, focusing on the wee baby struggling to fight for his life.

'Janessa has amazing instincts,' Kaycee confirmed.

'What do you think it is?' Miles asked.

'Seriously, I don't know. Something is…off. There's something not in line with normal parameters yet all his obs are fine.' She returned the chart to Kaycee and shook her head.

'So you're going to stand here and watch him?' Miles asked as Kaycee headed off to deal with another baby who'd just woken, his healthy little cries filling the nursery.

'Yes.'

'Fair enough.'

'What about you?' Janessa glanced across at him, both of them standing on opposite sides of their patient.

'You're right. Looking down at him now, there's some-thing…niggling…something not quite…'

Before Miles had finished speaking, the machines moni-toring Philip's heart rate started to beep noisily, Janessa noting that the tiny chest had stopped rising and falling. She quickly touched the baby, tickling his feet in order to stimu-late a response. Sometimes babies needed to be reminded to breathe but this simple stimulation didn't appear to be working.

'No response,' she reported as Kaycee rushed over. Miles had already pulled on a pair of gloves and was hooking his stethoscope into his ears. Kaycee grabbed the Laderal bag and handed it to Miles so he could resuscitate Philip. Miles gently squeezed the bag to give the baby some breaths as Janessa pulled on a pair of gloves.

'He's still desaturating down to fifty per cent.'

'He's just not picking up.'

'We can do this. We can help him.' Miles's words were firm and controlled. He looked over at Janessa. 'Let's do our jobs.'

CHAPTER SEVEN

'OXYGEN at forty per cent.'

'No more apnoeas,' Janessa told Philip. 'Caffeine, Kaycee. Wake him up.'

'I'm on it.' Kaycee was already injecting the caffeine into Philip's drip in order to stimulate a response.

'His hypothalamus is too immature. It's not receiving the signals, not computing,' Ray murmured as he brought the intubation trolley over.

'Oxygen desaturating.'

'Increase oxygen to sixty per cent.'

'Are the umbilical lines clear? Still working?'

'Yes.'

'Prepare dexamethazone.'

'No response to caffeine stimulus.'

'Oxygen still desaturating.'

'Boost to one hundred per cent. Prepare adrenaline.'

'Chest X-rays?'

'Get the machine ready.'

'He's still not responding.'

'Bag him.'

They all worked together, each of them doing their utmost in order to save Philip's life. It wasn't looking good and they all fought harder.

'Body's changing colour. Going grey.'

'No. No. Let's get him ready to intubate.' Miles was still pushing. Janessa was working equally hard.

'Administer adrenaline. Come on, Philip. Hang in there.'

Janessa took over the bagging to give Kaycee a break, putting her finger over the hole of the Neopuff mask and lifting it again, getting the oxygen into Philip's brain. Her fears that it was already too late, that even if they were able to save him right now, it might be too late to stop severe trauma to the oxygen-starved brain. In the distance, as though it was far, far away, she could hear the noise of a young girl crying. Violet. Violet was there. She'd picked a terrible time to come and see her son…then again, maybe it was the right time after all.

'Colour still grey,' Ray murmured, and Janessa could hear the dismay in her colleague's voice.

'Ready to intubate,' Janessa said, and received a quick glance from Miles. He shook his head, the movement almost imperceptible, but she caught it. 'We have to try,' she urged him.

'Lips are turning blue,' Kaycee reported, her tone as despondent as Ray's.

'It's over, Janessa.' Miles's tone held complete sadness.

'No. We can do this. We can save him. We have the skill.' She reached for the laryngoscope but Miles put his hand over hers.

'It's over.' He took the instrument from her and met her gaze.

'No.' The word was torn from her, filled with anguish and sorrow. 'No. We have to—'

'Nessa.' The use of her nickname, hearing it come from Miles's lips, his deep voice laced with resignation, managed to break through her denial. 'It's over. Let him rest in peace.'

Janessa looked over at Philip, his lifeless little body just lying there, and her mouth went instantly dry. Flashes of Connor lying in almost exactly the same position… She blinked and swallowed. 'Call it,' she rasped.

'Time of death, ten past two.' Miles's voice was hollow as though it was an effort to force the words out.

'He was too premmie. Poor little love didn't have the strength to fight,' Kaycee murmured as she and Janessa stood looking down at the tiny, lifeless body. It wasn't easy. It was never easy to lose a patient but when they were so new to the world, so young and helpless, relying on the doctors to do their very best to save them…

The tears wouldn't stay where she wanted them and despite her most valiant efforts, they started to blur her vision. She swallowed over the lump in her throat and tried not to sniff. 'I'll go and tell Violet.'

'No.' Miles's tone was firm. 'I'll do it.' He met Janessa's gaze and she almost gasped at what she saw. The pain, the raw, grinding emotion seemed to flood from him directly into her. There was no hope in his eyes, no promise of any kind, just a well of deep, personal heartache.

She swallowed again, her dry throat not making it at all easy. As their eyes held, somewhere in the back of her mind she realised that he was waiting for her agreement to his statement. He would go and deliver the bad news.

'No young mother should have to face this.' With that, he turned and walked over to where Violet was with Helena, near the front desk of the NICU. Janessa watched, waiting for the moment when utter heartbreak would come over Violet's features. As Janessa stood there, watching, waiting… Miles's words penetrated her mind. 'No young mother should have to face this.'

What did he mean? Was he going to stop Violet from

seeing Philip? From achieving closure? No. She wouldn't allow it. All those years ago, after they'd told her they hadn't been able to save Connor, she hadn't been able to face seeing his lifeless little body lying there. Bradley had gone, had said goodbye, but she had been too distraught.

It hadn't been until that night, that first night without him near her, after Bradley had gone home, that Janessa had changed her mind. She'd needed to see him, to see for herself that he was really gone, to achieve the closure the staff had encouraged her to find. When she'd spoken to the nurse, they'd arranged for her to be taken to the mortuary, to a small viewing room with comfortable chairs and soothing pictures on the wall.

There, the medical examiner had brought out her little boy. He'd been wrapped in a white blanket with little blue aeroplanes on it. She'd sat. She'd held him. She'd kissed him goodbye.

She wasn't going let Miles stop Violet from seeing Philip. Violet needed closure. She needed to be able to say goodbye to her baby, otherwise she might well live the rest of her life carrying around the scars of grief and mortification.

'Janessa?' Kaycee's soft tone brought her thoughts back to the present. 'Do you want to go fill in the paperwork? I can get him ready for his mother to see—'

'We'll do it together.' Janessa nodded, and as a strained, uncomfortable silence fell over the NICU she and Kaycee worked quietly and efficiently to remove the attached equipment before wheeling Philip's crib into the empty emergency bay. This way, the young mother would be afforded the privacy she would need.

Janessa looked over to where Miles was still standing next to Violet, the young mother crying on Helena's shoulder. She wasn't going to allow anyone to stop Violet from having access to Philip. Drawing in a deep breath, squaring her shoulders and clearing her throat, Janessa wanted to let Violet know that Philip was ready for a final cuddle.

No sooner had she taken two steps towards them than Miles helped Violet to stand and started to escort her in Janessa's direction. Janessa stopped. He was bringing her over? At that moment, Miles looked up and saw her.

'Ready?' he asked softly.

'Ready?' Janessa was momentarily confused. When she'd presumed Miles hadn't wanted Violet to see Philip, it was obvious now that she'd grabbed the wrong end of the stick.

'For Violet to say goodbye?'

'Yes. Yes, of course. Right this way.' When Miles had said, 'No young mother should have to face this,' Janessa now realised he'd been referring to the entire situation of losing a child. It showed her once again how wonderful Miles really was. He was so kind and caring and… She shouldn't be thinking about him in such a way but right now she couldn't help it. Seeing him so considerate, so compassionate stirred something deep within her. He was quite a man.

Poor Violet was as white as a sheet as they led her to where Philip lay, peaceful and quiet in the crib. Janessa felt her eyes starting to sting with tears again and she pushed them away, quietly trying to clear the lump in her throat, pursing her lips tightly together in order to keep herself under control. Professional. She had to somehow remain professional.

'We're very sorry for your loss.' It wasn't a platitude that came out of her mouth but heartfelt words as the young girl looked at her lifeless son, wrapped in a small baby blanket.

'Can I hold…?'

'Of course.'

Miles ushered Violet to a chair and Janessa tenderly picked Philip up and handed him over. The girl looked at him for a moment, before rocking gently to and fro. She bent and kissed his little head and then started to sing a soft lullaby.

With the sweet, innocent sound filling the air around them, Janessa found she wasn't able to hold it in any longer. Tears ran silently down her cheeks, her heart filled with pain and anguish for what this brave young girl was going through. Without looking at Miles, she said softly, 'Take as long as you need, Violet. Excuse me.'

She managed to make it to her office and was able to shut the door before a gut-wrenching sob erupted from her body. She didn't seem able to stop the free-flowing tears and she blindly made her way to her desk in search of tissues. She dabbed at her eyes and quietly blew her nose but the tears and pain didn't stop. They would, eventually, she knew they would, but for now, if she didn't let this emotion out, she would burst.

She heard her office door open but didn't turn round, knowing it would be Kaycee come to join her for a quick cry. This wouldn't be the first time they'd shared their grief when losing a patient.

'Janessa?'

She gasped at the sound of Miles's deep voice, her vision still blurred as she glanced over at him. She couldn't believe he was seeing her like this, all red-eyed and sniffly, being highly unprofessional and giving in to her emotions because one of her patients had died. It wasn't the first time. It wouldn't be the last. But each one had affected her in the same way.

'Oh, Janessa.' His words were almost wrenched from him, and before she knew what he was about he'd closed the distance between them. 'Come here, honey,' he murmured, and gathered her into his arms.

She went willingly.

Janessa knew there wasn't anything romantic or suspicious in Miles's offer to hold her. She told herself that all he was doing was offering comfort, sharing a moment that had touched both of them. She swallowed over her dry, scratchy throat and leaned against him, unable to believe just how being held by him, feeling his warm, firm arms around her, was giving her back her strength and self-control.

Neither of them spoke. Neither of them moved. Her tears started to quieten and she hiccupped a few times. Throughout it all, Miles simply held her. It felt glorious and wonderful and she couldn't believe how much she'd missed having someone to just hold her.

The warmth of his body, the beat of his heart beneath his chest, the whole aliveness of him radiated through her and for the first time in a very long time she felt as though she might actually be able to cope with her past. Comfort. Relief. Hope.

'I was prepared,' she said after a moment, 'for her to hold him, to kiss him, to say goodbye.' She breathed in, still hiccupping a little and allowing his glorious scent to wash over her. 'But I wasn't prepared for her to sing to him.'

'A child singing to her child,' he murmured, his deep voice rumbling beneath her ear.

'She grew up. In that one instant I watched her go from being a scared teenager to a young woman who had already lost too much.'

'She has family,' he stated. 'They'll help her through it. It's what families do.'

'Yes. It's what families do,' Janessa agreed, knowing she needed to move from his arms, to break free of his hold because it would be far too easy to stay there, to keep drawing comfort from him… But the comfort was already starting to change to total awareness of being held against his firm, muscled chest.

She glanced up at him, swallowing when she saw the way he was looking down at her. His gaze dipped momentarily to her lips and she felt the sweet whisper of his desire wash over her. He still wanted her, was interested in her. Nothing seemed to have changed since the last time he'd been this close to her…the night he'd kissed her.

Sighing, the warmth from his gentle visual caress causing the butterflies in her stomach to take flight, she licked her lips, unsure how they had become so dry suddenly. He closed his eyes for a brief moment, clenching his jaw before once more looking at her. Did she have any idea of the allure that surrounded her? The way she was drawing him in, making him want to throw caution to the wind, to forget that they were colleagues, that they were supposed to be professionals, and kiss her—properly this time, instead of the accidental meeting of their mouths, which seemed to have been burned on his brain?

Forward. She was urging him forward, somehow pulling him from the past, his deep, darkened past where he'd ended up all alone, and was drawing him into the future. Forward. Giving in to the urge to kiss Janessa, to draw her closer into his arms, to devour her mouth with his own, was a definite step towards moving on with his life. So many of his close friends, people he worked with on many different conjoined twin surgeries, had been telling him for at least the last twelve months that it was time.

He hadn't known it himself until he'd met Janessa.

Now here she stood. In his arms. Looking up at him while

he was looking down at her, the mood between them becoming more and more electrified with each passing moment.

'Nessa.'

The instant he breathed her name, the instant it came to his lips and filled the silence around them she started to tremble. She also eased away, spinning from his arms, breaking the contact, needing the space as she rubbed her hands up and down her arms. Miles shoved his hands into his pockets, cleared his throat, and took a step back as Janessa moved behind her desk and pulled another tissue from the box. Even as she performed the action, he could see that her hands still weren't quite steady. It gave him hope. To know that it wasn't just him who was feeling this way but that she was as much affected by him as he was by her.

'Thank you, Miles… For the…er…comfort. It was…appreciated but just so you understand, I'm not in the habit of losing my control on a regular basis.'

'I understand completely. Special circumstances.' He swallowed, his Adam's apple sliding up and down his long neck. Janessa glanced at him then and noted that not only was there the hint of repressed desire but something else… there was something else hidden in his tone…something she'd seen earlier… What was it? It only took another moment of looking at him for her to remember the way he'd looked when he'd insisted on breaking the horrible news of the baby's death to Violet. There had been something there… something deep and moving and highly personal.

Janessa angled her head to the side a little. 'Wait a second.' Her words were soft and in no way accusatory. 'You were affected, too, weren't you?'

At her words, Miles closed his eyes for a brief moment before looking at her once more. 'More than you know.'

'It's never easy to lose a patient.'

'No. No, it's not.' Gone was the desire and out came the hurt. She'd never seen his eyes reflect such a hidden yet incredibly powerful emotion. Most people in the world made every effort to repress things or events that had happened to them in order to function with some semblance of normalcy. It appeared Miles was no different.

She paused, noting the hint of gut-wrenching pain in the way he spoke. He wasn't just speaking from a personal angle, he was speaking from his heart, and it was a heart that had been shredded. She recognised the anguish, she felt the pain he was exhibiting, she could read the symptoms because she'd felt them herself…felt them when her own son had died. Following through on an instinct, treading very carefully, she asked softly, 'Miles? When you lost your wife…was there…? I mean, did you have any…children?'

'Yes.' The one word was covered in heartache.

'Oh, Miles.' Janessa sighed, her heart turning over for him.

'One child. One baby boy. He was eight months old. We had eight glorious months with him. Although he was a bit sickly to begin with, in the NICU for the first two months, after that he was a strong, healthy, strapping baby boy…who died in his mother's arms.'

'It must have been devastating for you both.'

'No. Not for Wendy.'

Janessa frowned, unsure what he was trying to say. Miles looked at her, his blue eyes, which were so usually filled with joviality and direction, now bleak and cold. 'We were travelling by train in Europe,' he said. 'There was an accident, a bad one. A horrific train crash. We were all involved. Wendy was holding Patrick and when the train derailed…' He stopped for a moment. 'I was thrown around, multiple fractures, lost consciousness. When I woke I was in hospital. Wendy and Patrick were listed among the dead.'

'Miles.' Janessa's heart wrenched with sorrow for him and she walked to his side, taking his hand in hers, linking their fingers together. 'I'm so, so sorry.'

'We were in the middle of nowhere. That stupid train crash robbed me of my family.' He shook his head. 'I was alone.'

Janessa squeezed his hand. 'I know how you feel. I do. I really do, and I'm not just saying that to make you feel better. I know what it's like to lose people you love...*babies* you love.'

Miles looked at her, recalling the way she'd been so vehement and determined to help Philip, the way she'd spoken to Violet as though she really did understand. 'You had a child, too?'

'I did. A boy. Connor.' As she spoke his name, she smiled. 'He was wonderful.'

'How old?'

She shrugged. 'Newborn. Twenty-five weeks' gestation. Just a touch older than Philip, but almost twenty years ago they didn't have half the equipment we have now. Today he might well have stood a fighting chance but, also like Philip, he was just too prem.'

'Is that why your marriage ended?'

'The loss of a child is never easy to cope with.' She shook her head. 'Bradley and I were just children ourselves, pretending to be grown-ups, but it was no good. I made impulsive and irrational decisions back then and it's taken me years not only to trust my own judgement but to trust others, not necessarily in the medical field but on a personal level. Any marriage break-up makes you really question yourself, makes you cautious of opening yourself up again. After

Connor's death, we were both floundering in a sea of confusion, too young and too inexperienced in life to cope with the emotions we both felt, and in the end we realised the wisest thing we could do was to call an end to our marriage, to admit that we'd failed and move on. It was one of the hardest things I've ever done, to admit to that failure.'

Janessa dropped Miles's hand and moved away.

'Oh, Janessa.'

'So, you see, I *do* know how you feel. I know how Violet feels right now. Sitting out there, holding her baby, saying goodbye.'

'It still hurts.' His words were a statement, not a question.

She nodded in agreement. 'After all these years, it still hurts.'

Both of them were silent for a moment before Miles said softly, 'It appears we have more in common than we originally might have realised.'

'Perhaps that's what drew us together in the first place?'

'Janessa—' He stopped and raked a hand through his hair before continuing. 'What do you say about becoming friends?'

'Get to know each other better?'

'Exactly.' He shifted and put his hands into his trouser pockets. 'We're going to be working closely together once the girls are born. Co-ordinating treatment, practical hands-on care, not to mention the preparation for the surgeries.'

'What are you suggesting?'

'That we spend time together because then that way we have some hope of finding common ground where this attraction isn't the first thing coming between us whenever we're together here at the hospital.'

Janessa thought for a moment. It would be good to be able to be in the same room as Miles and not be so aware of

126 WEDDING ON THE BABY WARD

him. Perhaps he was right. Spending time together in a social capacity might actually benefit them rather than hindering their working relationship. 'You make a fair point. Well…I guess we could go flying.'

Miles blinked once. 'Flying?' He paused, remembering that she'd mentioned something about flying before.

'Sure. It will get us out of the hospital. We'll be out in the open, fresh air, blue skies, destressing and letting all our troubles float away on the wind.'

'Flying? You're serious?'

'One hundred per cent. I'm not talking about the big commercial jets that take you interstate or overseas. Just a nice small aircraft. Gliding around in the blue sky, enjoying the sensation of a complete carefree existence…if only for a short while.' Janessa sighed. Even thinking about it was helping her to relax, to calm down, to push the past back where it belonged. Miles, however, was still looking at her as though she came from a completely different planet. 'Or we could do something else. We don't have to go flying. You can think about it if you—'

'Sounds great,' he interrupted, still astonished to discover that Janessa liked flying. It wasn't the type of hobby or activity he'd have thought she would choose to do on her days off but, then, he was coming to realise that Janessa Austen was unlike any other woman he'd ever known. 'Flying.' He nodded once, accepting the decision, especially as Janessa seemed quite keen on the idea. 'In a small aircraft.'

'You're not claustrophobic, are you?' There was nothing worse than taking someone up in her Tiger Moth who had a fear of confined spaces.

'No. I'm fine.' He nodded again. 'So…flying. Good. Different, but good. When?'

'Good question. Um…' Janessa mentally went through

her schedule. They were now in the very early hours of Wednesday morning and given everything that had happened with little Philip, there would be quite a bit of red tape to get through. 'Thursday morning?'

Miles pondered that for a moment before agreeing. 'Nine o'clock. After ward round. I'll meet you here.'

With that, he turned and headed out of her office, gone before she could say anything else. Janessa stood there, not moving, and stared at her open door. She'd just invited Miles to come and spend time with her in a small and confined space! Was she completely insane? Even being here in her office was bad enough. The close confines of the Tiger Moth, the two of them, up in the air, able to talk to each other via the headsets…sharing an exhilarating experience…

But that was a good thing, wasn't it? His suggestion that they should get to know each other better, that they should stop trying to guess, stop trying to figure out what made the other one tick, was a good thing. The more time she spent with him, the sooner she'd discover some facet of his personality that would irritate her and therefore break the dynamic fascination that seemed to bind them together.

She would be taking him to her special place, the airfield where she'd spent so much time, with her father as a child and later learning to fly. So many of her personal memories were bound up in that place.

With exhaustion weighing heavily on her shoulders, Janessa sank down into her office chair and closed her eyes, unable to believe her own stupidity. Had she really just opened herself up to share part of her life, a very important part of her life, with Miles Trevellion? Was she completely insane?

Apparently so.

CHAPTER EIGHT

AFTER writing up the paperwork for Philip and ensuring that Violet had finished saying goodbye to her baby, a weary Janessa escorted the young woman back to the maternity ward. Violet's obstetrician approved a sedative for her but Violet wanted Janessa to stay with her until she fell asleep.

Even sitting in the chair beside Violet's bed, Janessa's exhaustion level continued to increase. Once the young woman was asleep, Janessa headed to Sheena's room to check on her friend, surprised to find her awake.

She gave Sheena the sad news about Philip, and then checked Sheena's blood pressure, pleased that it was stable.

'It can't have been easy for you.' Sheena spoke softly, caressing her abdomen lovingly.

'It wasn't, but Miles…' Janessa yawned '…was a great help. He's so…' she sighed and closed her eyes for a moment '…comforting.'

'Really?'

Janessa didn't reply and Sheena chuckled. 'What?' Janessa asked a moment later.

'You are so exhausted, Nessa. Go to bed. Get some sleep.'

'I'm fine. I've been more tired than this before.'

'True but you weren't battling an attraction to your gorgeous colleague before.'

'You have a point.' Janessa's eyes were still closed as she sat in the chair.

'You're admitting that you like Miles?'

'Yep. Like him. A lot.' She yawned. 'Strange, isn't it? Never thought I'd be attracted like that to someone who won't hang around. Can't keep liking him, though. He's going to leave and I'll be all…' another yawn '…alone again.'

'You have me. You'll always have me, but I know what you mean.'

'I know.' Janessa opened her eyes and went to stand, wobbling a bit as she stood leaning on the chair until her balance returned. 'This always happens. When I finally stop, especially after a hectic day, my body just seems to go into complete shutdown.' She walked over and hugged her friend. 'You're the best non-legally-adopted sister I've ever had.'

Sheena laughed. 'Likewise. Now, go. Sleep.'

'I will, and just so you know, you're doing a fantastic job of being a human incubator. In fact, I'd say you're the best human incubator in the world. My mother was bedridden the entire time she was pregnant with me and I turned out fantastic.'

'Yes, you did.'

'Just think of how fantastic your girls are going to be.'

'I do. Now go and sleep before you fall down and hurt yourself.'

'Good advice. I feel so light-headed. 'Night, Sheenie.'

Janessa made her way out of Maternity and headed for the residential wing, very pleased that she was staying so close to the hospital. Sheena was such a wonderful friend and being raised an only child meant Janessa had often yearned for a sister. Now she had one. Although her parents had been able to have two babies before she'd arrived on the scene, both boys had been born with congenital heart defects. They'd both died within the first few months of their lives and back then the care for sick babies hadn't been as advanced as it was today. She'd often wondered whether Connor had a similar problem and perhaps that was why he'd died.

It was another reason why she'd chosen to specialise in the neonate field. To be there for women like Violet, to support close friends, like Sheena, to assist incredible surgeons, like Miles, and to read about the breakthroughs in research and technology.

Her mother had often told her how special she was, that she was their little miracle. A lump came instantly to Janessa's throat as she thought about her mother and in that split second, even though her mother had died almost eighteen years ago, her heart longed for just one more moment with her. To be held by her, to hear her mother's calm voice, to hear her sing a soft, soothing lullaby.

The image of Philip being held by Violet swam into her mind as she took the three flights of stairs up to her apartment. It was an image that came with its own sweet soundtrack and one that would no doubt remain with her for a very long time. Such loss, such heartbreak, such loneliness.

Janessa knew what it was like to be lonely. With no aunts, no uncles, no cousins, no siblings, no parents, it could have made for a very lonely life but all around her, here at the hospital, was a family she loved most dearly.

Then she had her friends out at the airfield, the friends who had known her father for most of their lives, who had watched her grow up, who had grieved with her when her father had lost his battle with cancer. Everyone around her combined together into one crazy big family and Janessa knew that she was truly blessed to be in such a place, but at the same time she would give anything to have one last hug with her mother or one last flight in her father's beloved Tiger Moth with him at the rear, flying them through the skies as though there really wasn't a care in the world.

Tomorrow, at nine o'clock, she would be meeting Miles to take him to the airfield to share her passion for flying. As soon as the thought entered her mind, she pushed it aside. It was almost four o'clock in the morning now and she was exhausted. It wasn't wise to think about the man when she was this tired because all of her defences were down. Add to that the memory of Philip's young mother singing to him and she felt emotionally drained. With her eyes blurring a little due to her sentimentality as well as the fact that she'd hardly slept in the past thirty hours, Janessa opened the stairwell door and exited onto the third floor, walking slap bang into someone.

'Oh, sorry,' she mumbled quickly, reaching out to rebalance herself and coming into contact with a wide, firm chest. At the same time, warm hands clamped around her waist and the weirdest sense of *déjà vu* settled over her. She breathed in, only to have Miles's spicy scent wind around her, drawing her in.

'This is starting to become a habit, Dr Austen.' His deep masculine voice murmured near her ear. 'You. In my arms.'

'Sorry.' She glanced up, looking into his eyes, and instantly wished she hadn't. He was looking at her as though she were the most important woman in the world. His pupils were wide, his irises more blue than she'd ever seen before, and the care and need and desire she could see there made her body suffuse with anticipatory tingles.

'Don't apologise,' he added quietly. 'I'm not complaining.' His words were deep, rumbling through her, adding to the tingles by causing goose bumps to spread over her skin as his breath fanned her neck. His hands were at her waist, hot and warm and feeling as though they could burn right through her clothes. The sensations radiated throughout her, adding a flush of fire to the tingles and goose bumps.

When he touched her like this, looked at her like this, wreaked havoc with her senses like this, it was all Janessa could do to hold on to some semblance of rational thought. Working alongside him, being near him, watching his brilliance as he'd performed surgery on little Philip, had only served to enhance the delight and admiration she had for him.

Swallowing over the dryness of her throat, she worked hard to ignore the way her hands were pressed up against his chest, the firmness of his body beneath his shirt making her fingers itch to explore the area, to touch and caress every contour, to commit them to memory.

Even though she'd already been in his arms once that morning, this time was completely different from the platonic, friendly way he'd held her as she'd cried out her grief for the loss of the little life.

Ordinarily, he'd discovered Janessa to be strong and self-assured but now, as he looked down into the upturned face of this stunning woman, he could see tears glistening on her dark eyelashes. There was a vulnerability about her he'd witnessed when he'd walked into her office and seen her crying. A powerful, protective urge had overcome him then and now, standing here in the deserted residential corridor, was no different.

He wanted to protect this woman. From pain, from suffering, from being alone. He, of all people, knew how bad loneliness could be, and whilst he'd been surrounded by his parents and his sisters after the death of his wife and his child, it was the small hours of the morning—like now, when loneliness could be at its most powerful.

During his first week at Adelaide Mercy, Miles had been fighting the inexplicable, burning need he felt for Janessa Austen. Perhaps it was the fact that she'd taken him into her office on his very first morning there and told him off, showing him that she wasn't afraid to stand up for what she believed in. Perhaps it was the fact that she cared for not only her patients but for her staff as well, showing them unfailing loyalty. Perhaps it was the fact that she was like a petite dynamo who still looked far too young to be head of such a high-powered unit.

Or perhaps it was that she seemed to fit so perfectly into his arms.

He wasn't at all sure why he appeared to be so drawn to her. She was starting to open him up, starting to make him believe there could possibly be more to his life than simply working and travelling. Even now, as he held her, her body so close to his, her scent winding around him, enticing dormant senses back to life, he couldn't help awareness coursing through him. He swallowed and watched as her gaze flicked to his throat before settling on his lips for a brief moment then returning to his eyes.

His mind went blank as he realised she was looking into his own eyes, revealing emotions such as confusion, intrigue and veiled desire. It was the way she'd looked at him in the lift last week but this time the emotions were deeper, richer, more intense. He'd been out of the game so long, out of the need to seek female companionship, and now here was Janessa, causing him to want, causing him to experience, causing him to feel.

It was as though everything during the past week had lead to this one moment. It was the moment when Miles slowly began to realise that, for the first time since the death of his family, there were other possibilities in life than living it on the run from his past, hiding from his guilt.

Janessa swallowed and licked her lips, causing Miles to want to lower his head, to brush his mouth across hers, just for a second, just to see how she tasted. It wasn't the first time he'd wondered that and it wouldn't be the last. He was attracted to her. Powerfully and strongly. Now, though, right at this moment in time, they were both vulnerable. He could see it in her eyes. She was heavily exhausted and her defences were low.

This time, though, the tug, the invisible bonds that seemed to be binding them together were most definitely harder to resist. He really wanted to kiss her and that want was starting to grow into a need…a desirable need.

Although it felt as though they'd been standing there for an eternity, in reality it had just been a couple of minutes, but even during that short period of time he could feel Janessa's body starting to relax more heavily against his.

'Miles?' she murmured, her desire-filled eyes looking up at him. 'What's happening between us?'

'I don't know, honey, but I do know that now is not the right time to discuss it. You're exhausted and it's time for you to get some sleep.' With a valiant effort he tried to step back, to release his hold on her, but as he did, she stumbled and leaned against him again. 'Whoa, there.' He slid his arm more firmly about her waist. 'I think your exhaustion has most definitely caught up with you.'

Janessa yawned and nodded, feeling lethargic and sleepy and nice, being held so close next to Miles. 'Excellent diagnosis, Dr Trevellion.'

'Right, then. Let's get you settled. Where's your key?'

'My what?' She raised her eyebrows to look at him.

'The key to your apartment.'

Janessa frowned for a moment, then patted the pockets of her trousers. 'Not there. Darn. I must have left them in my office.'

'Oh.' Miles's quick mind filtered through his different options. He could leave Janessa in the corridor, run downstairs and get a spare key from the residential desk. He could put Janessa in his apartment and then go down… No! That one was instantly dismissed. Even the thought of having her sitting in a chair, waiting for him, no doubt sound asleep… the mental picture was too alluring.

Walking her closer to her door, feeling her lean into him as sleep started to claim her, he decided to try a different option, ridiculous as it seemed. He inserted his own key into her door. The lock clicked. He turned the handle. The door opened.

'Interesting,' he murmured.

'What is?' she asked, her words slightly slurred and as he looked down at her, realised her eyelids were already half-closed.

'Nothing. Come on, honey. Let's get you into bed.'

'Bed?' She roused as he walked her into her apartment. It took him a split second to realise the set up was the mirror image of his own apartment and he headed for the bedroom. 'I can't go to bed with you. I can't, Miles. I want to but we can't. You'll be gone in six months and my life will be here with painful memories and…' She yawned as he carefully guided her to the bed and pushed aside the covers.

'We're not going to bed together. Just you in your bed. Me in mine. It's safer that way.'

'Safer,' she repeated as she pulled the band from her hair, blonde locks spilling out against the red satin pillowcase. He pulled the covers over her, his gut tightening at the glorious picture she made. Eyes closed, body resting, face

devoid of emotion. Unable to contain himself, he reached
out and brushed her hair back from her face, allowing the
pale strands to sift gloriously through his fingers. So silky,
so soft.

Swallowing, he bent over her, pressing his lips to her
forehead, knowing he shouldn't but powerless to resist. He
breathed her in, closing his eyes as he committed the sensations to memory. The feel of her skin against his lips, the
way her subtle scents surrounded him, the rhythm of her
steady, even breathing.

'Sleep sweet, Nessa,' he whispered, before standing and
striding firmly from her apartment, desperate now to push
aside the longing and the loneliness that swamped him.

'Ready?'

Janessa turned and watched as Miles walked into her
office, taking in the more casual attire of blue jeans, navy
blue polo shirt and top-of-the-line running shoes on his feet.
He looked so relaxed, so casual. Even the way he usually
wore his hair was different, more ruffled and slightly spiked
on top rather than brushed into a neat and ordered style.

On the first day she'd met him he'd been wrinkled and
tired and ruffled and exhausted and even then he'd looked
incredible. Today, though, his jaw seemed squarer, possibly
due to the light stubble enhancing his good looks. It made
him seem more relaxed, more rugged, more sexy.

She blinked once, twice and then forced herself to stop
ogling him and to snap back into functioning mode. 'Uh…
yeah…um, I mean yes. Sure.' She was standing at her desk,
having just finished writing up some notes on her little patients. Five babies had been well enough to go home and
seven had been moved to the maternity ward near their
mothers. The unit was now back to a more reasonable level

of occupancy and she knew her staff were more than capable of handling any emergencies that happened, although she seriously hoped for a quiet day.

'I'll get my things,' she murmured, and as she turned her back on him Miles couldn't help but take in her more casual attire. Up until now he'd only seen Janessa wearing tailored suits. Her skirts had all come to mid-calf and on the days when she'd worn trousers, she'd looked even more crisp and efficient.

He'd idly wondered if she wore the power suits in order to make herself look older and now, seeing her dressed casually in a pair of denim jeans and a knit top, her feet enclosed in brown leather boots, her hair still pulled back into a ponytail, he *knew* that was the reason for the stiff and starched suits because right at this moment she really did look about nineteen. All fresh faced and brimming with nervous energy.

Even when he'd tucked her into bed very early yesterday morning, he'd been mesmerised by her youthful appearance. Thirty-six? She looked anything but that old, and as she came towards him, a white scarf around her neck and a backpack slung casually over one shoulder, he was once again struck by how incredibly beautiful she was.

'OK. Let's go.' They exited her office, Janessa closing the door behind them, feeling the warmth of Miles's presence close to her.

'Can I take that for you?' he asked, holding his hand out towards the backpack.

She smiled politely. 'It's fine. It's not that heavy.' She felt so self-conscious, standing here in the unit, on her day off, feeling as though she was about to head out on a date with her new colleague. It wasn't a date. They both knew it wasn't. Didn't they? Her eyes widened imperceptibly as she wondered whether Miles thought that today was a date.

It wasn't but she had no idea how to make that clear to him without running the risk of making a fool out of herself.

'Right. I guess we'll take my car.' She felt strange walking out of the unit with him, conscious of all eyes upon them. Why did it feel as though the two of them were getting ready to embark on something that would take their relationship from professional to personal?

At the door, she stopped and looked at Ray. 'You'll call me if—?'

'Yes, yes,' he muttered, shooing her away. 'Go. Fly. Relax. That goes for you, too, Miles. The two of you need a break, and with Sheena's due date creeping up on us, this might be the last free day either of you have in quite some time.'

'Good point.'

'Now, scoot. Some of us have got work to do.'

'Quite the instiller of confidence,' Miles remarked as they headed out of the hospital. The day was big and bright and the sky had barely a cloud. Perfect April day and perfect flying weather. As they walked to the rear of the residential wing, passing several staff car parks along the way, Miles couldn't contain his confusion. 'You did say we were taking your car, not walking to this airfield, right?'

'It's just in here,' Janessa remarked, a slight smile tugging at her lips. 'Charisma gave me permission to use one of the old ambulance sheds to store my car. Here we are.' She took a set of keys from her pocket and opened the side door to what looked like an old work shed. As they headed inside, she flicked on a light, illuminating the work benches, which were covered with various bits of machinery and all kinds of tools. The scent of oil and grease hung in the air as well as dust.

'Who does all of this belong to?' Miles asked.

'Hospital Maintenance. This is sort of a storage shed-cum-workshop for them. Through there…' she pointed to the closed door on their left '…is where the bigger machines, such as the lathe and the bandsaw, are kept.' Janessa walked to another door, waiting for Miles to catch up as he looked around at the paraphernalia.

'Do you like this sort of thing?' she asked, her lips twitching at the way he was taking in the equipment. 'Are you a handyman as well as a surgeon?'

Miles smiled. 'I used to spend a lot of time in the shed with my dad when I was growing up. He was always inventing and making and building.' He nodded. 'They were good times.'

Janessa was surprised to hear him talk so openly of his father. 'That sounds nice. Memories like that are wonderful.'

'They are,' he agreed as he followed her through to another room.

'I used to help my dad out a lot, too. He was a mechanic,' she remarked as she flicked on the next light. With a flourish she'd practised a lot as a teenager, she whisked the protective cover off the car, then watched as Miles's eyes almost bugged out of his head at what he saw.

'That's a Jaguar E-Cabriolet.'

'I know.' Janessa set about opening the old wooden doors in order to get the car out. Miles, however, walked around the car, running his hand lovingly over the paintwork, peering inside at the wooden dashboard and making the same appreciative noises Janessa's father used to make. It made her smile.

'This is *your* car?' Miles slowly shook his head. 'You are a constant source of surprise, Janessa Austen.'

'Thank you…I think. You obviously appreciate cars.'

'I do. I race them.'

'What? And you call me a constant source of surprise.

You said you liked to drive fast but race? As a doctor, I would have thought you'd understand the inherent dangers involved in car racing and—'

He held up a hand to silence her as the daylight flooded into the room. 'Controlled track race days. That's all. Nice and controlled. Emergency crews on standby just in case. I know the risks involved, Janessa, and I'm not so stupid as to ignore taking the necessary precautions. But this baby…' he stroked the car again '…is magnificent.' He looked up at her. 'Who did it belong to?'

'Why would you think it wouldn't belong to me?'

'Because it's a guy's car.'

'That's such a stereotype, Miles Trevellion.'

'I know. Sorry, but—'

'It belonged to my father. As I said, I used to help him.'

Again Miles stared at her with a new and enlightening appreciation. 'You really are a constant source of surprise.' He also hadn't missed the past tense in her words when she'd referred to her father.

She opened the car door and climbed behind the wheel. 'Do you mind switching off the light and closing the shed doors behind me?'

'Sure.' After that was done and when he was settled in the car, seat belt on, sunglasses covering his eyes, wind in his hair, Miles grinned and nodded. 'It purrs like the most contented of cats. Good to see you keep it in top-notch working order.' As he spoke, he again ran his hand over the leather seats. 'So nice.'

'Would you like to drive it?'

'Yes.' The answer was immediate. 'Will you let me?'

'So long as you realise that we're not on a race track.'

He gave her a look that said he wasn't that stupid.

'All right,' she relented. 'You can drive home.'

'Excellent.' Miles grinned and eased back into the leather, and as they drove through the city traffic, making their way south, he felt for the first time, in a very long time, mildly content. Was it the car? Was it the chance to get out of a hospital into the fresh air, to do something completely different? Or was it the woman beside him who was proving that he should never judge a book by its cover?

CHAPTER NINE

BY THE time they arrived at the airfield, almost an hour later, Janessa felt the weight of the past few days lift from her shoulders. When she'd checked on Sheena that morning, she'd discovered her friend had had a great night's sleep. She had listened to the twins' heartbeats and checked Sheena's vital signs, pleased with the results.

'Go. Have a day away from this place,' Sheena had encouraged. 'I promise to be good and do exactly as I'm told so that nothing goes wrong and you don't have to come back early.'

'Thanks. I'd appreciate it.'

'You and Miles deserve some time away from this place to figure out what on earth is going on between the two of you.'

'Wh…? Huh?' Janessa was robbed of speech and stared at Sheena.

'I lie here, in this bed, all day, all night. People come. People go. People talk—not about hospital cases,' she added quickly just in case Janessa thought that someone had broken the gag order.

'I see you. I see Miles. I see you and Miles. Both of you are dancing and it's the same dance. Both of you are moving in time with each other to the same beat. That's a good thing, Nessa. Good for him and good for you.'

'But he's going to leave,' Janessa blurted out.

'Maybe. You don't know that for sure.'

'Of course I do. Look at his life. Ever since his wife and son died, he's been an emotional nomad.'

Sheena's eyebrows hit her hairline. 'He had a son? Uh… he told me he'd been married when he first arrived here but he didn't say anything about a son.'

Janessa instantly paled. 'Oh. I thought you knew. I mean… The two of you were friends. You knew each other.'

'I worked with Miles ten years ago and he was as personable back then as he is now, although I do have to say that now that I think about it he's definitely more subdued but, then, most people seem to settle a bit more with age,' she'd pondered. 'But the fact that you know that about him, the fact that he's obviously felt he can confide in you, is huge, Ness.' She paused. 'Have you told him about…?'

'Bradley and Connor?' Janessa nodded and Sheena sighed a deep sigh.

'Well, well, well. In that case, the two of you *really* need to get away from this hospital. Head out to the airfield, whisk away the cobwebs of the past and look forward to the future.'

'*What* future? I don't know what this thing is that exists between Miles and myself and neither does he.'

'Then it's time to find out. Go. Go, go.' Sheena shooed her away, but as she headed out the door of her friend's room Sheena called, 'Oh, and take some photos for me. Perhaps just looking at them will help keep my blood pressure under control.'

Now, at the airfield, the warm, fresh air filling her lungs, Janessa climbed from the driver's side of the car and retrieved her backpack from just behind the seat.

'This is an airfield?' He lifted his glasses from his eyes and gazed out at the flat, wide open space, which had a backdrop of yellowy-brown hills and clear blue sky. There were large sheet-metal-clad hangars and about twenty cars in the car park. An old fire engine stood ready to do its job and about ten small aircraft peppered the immediate landscape.

'Doesn't it look like one? I thought the planes would have been a dead give-away,' she teased, feeling more like herself than she'd felt in a long time. She loved this place, so very much.

'I…well, yes, you have a point.' Miles smiled at her, intrigued with this new Janessa he was seeing. From the instant they'd entered that old shed, revealing her incredible car, she'd been one surprise after the other. He was thoroughly enjoying it. 'It's just not what I expected.'

Janessa called a greeting to a young man of about eighteen years old who was walking by, a pair of large headphones in his hand. He waved back and Miles followed Janessa into what appeared to be a small café.

'Hello, Nessa,' a woman with silvery-blonde hair said from behind a large wooden counter, coming around to envelop her in a warm motherly hug. 'How are all your babies? And Sheena? Should be soon, shouldn't it?'

'Sheena is doing well,' Janessa replied, not even wanting to think about the past few work days and the way they'd all fought so valiantly to save little Philip. She stepped away from the embrace and indicated Miles, who was standing just behind her. 'Myrna, this is my new colleague, Miles Trevellion.'

'Hi. It's nice to—' Miles had been about to say more when he found himself enveloped in a warm maternal hug, which took him completely by surprise.

'Welcome. Welcome. Any friend of our Nessa's is very

welcome here.' Myrna looked at Janessa and winked, saying in a stage whisper, 'Ooh, he's a right looker, this one.'

Janessa looked at Miles then back at Myrna, and couldn't help the blush that tinged her cheeks. 'Um…yes.' She walked round to the other side of the counter and picked up some papers, reading them. She did it in an effort to hide the way Myrna had embarrassed her, needing just a few moments to pull herself back together.

Miles leaned onto the top of the wooden counter and she could feel him watching her closely. 'Do you work here?' he asked. 'Is this what you do on your days off? Come and work here?'

'Work here?' Myrna laughed. 'Good heavens, no. Janessa's one of the shareholders who keeps this place open and functioning.' Myrna returned to the other side of the counter. 'Davie's been over *Ruby* and she's all ready to go, love. I know how eager you are to get on up.'

'Thanks, Myrna.' Janessa went to the shelf and pulled out a hardcover book, opening it up and beginning to write. Miles watched her, intrigued by this new facet of her personality. He saw the writing on the front of the book, which said 'Flight-plan/Logbook—Janessa R Austen'.

When she was finished, she left the book with Myrna, Miles still watching closely. She met his gaze. 'I'll be back in a moment.' But before she moved she tipped her head on the side and looked at his broad shoulders, his firm torso and then nodded. 'Yes. I think it'll fit,' she rasped, her voice sounding a little husky, or was that just his imagination? The impromptu visual caress only increased his awareness of the undercurrents of emotions coursing between the two of them.

'What? What will fit?' he asked, but she'd disappeared into a back room. 'What's she talking about?' he asked

Myrna, feeling a little dazed and confused. Janessa had invited him here for a bit of a joyride but he was yet to be introduced to his pilot. Janessa was obviously going up with someone called Davie. Perhaps he would be going up with Ruby? It was all very cryptic at the moment.

Myrna smiled at him. 'Ever been flying before?'

'Of course. I flew from the US to Australia last week.'

'Not like that, ya daft one.'

Miles raised his eyebrows. Daft? The last time he'd been called daft he'd been a teenager. Janessa returned before he could question Myrna further. She held out a leather bomber jacket to him. It was old, a bit frayed around the edges here and there, but it held a lot of character. 'Here. Put this on.'

'On? Why?'

She looked at him as though he was indeed daft. 'So you don't get cold. I doubt Sheena or anyone at the hospital will thank me if you return to work with a cold because you weren't adequately prepared for your flight,' she remarked as she pulled on a similar jacket, which she took from her backpack. She repositioned the white scarf around her neck then inclined her head towards the door, repressed excitement in her eyes. 'Come and meet Ruby,' she said with a cheeky grin, before walking out of the sliding glass door, across the wooden veranda and out the small gate that led to the planes.

'Ruby?' Miles followed Janessa and was astonished to see her walking over to a yellow Tiger Moth biplane with the words 'Ruby' painted in cursive on the side. '*This* is Ruby?'

'Who else would it be?' Janessa stroked the plane lovingly, much in the same way he'd stroked her car.

'In love with the old plane? Again, you are so full of surprises.'

She smiled. 'In love with my dad's old plane.' The look on her face was wistful with a hint of sadness.

'You really miss him.' It was a statement, not a question.

'I do. It was just the two of us for so long and now that he's gone...' She let her sentence trail off. She stroked the name 'Ruby', which had been painted on with a loving hand many years previously. 'Ruby was my mother. This plane was my dad's saving grace after my mother died. He bought it, restored it, spent so much time talking to the plane, as though he was still having conversations with my mother.' Tears of happiness and regret came into her eyes as she smiled sadly. 'He loved this plane. We both did.'

Both parents gone. Bad marriage. Stillborn baby. All alone. Miles pieced together everything he'd learned about this amazing woman and his heart turned over with yet another wave of deeper caring. 'You really are all alone?'

Her answering smile was tight-lipped as she moved around the plane, stroking it, checking it, making sure everything was in working order. 'Not really. I have close friends both at the hospital and here.'

'But no blood relatives?'

'No.' The word was small but audible. 'But I have memories.' When she spoke, there was a slight wobble in her tone and Miles watched her closely for a bit longer.

'Like flying in his plane? Or driving his car?'

Her smile instantly brightened. 'Exactly. He loved classic things, my dad.' She headed to the front of Ruby and spun the propeller around a few times, checking. 'Well, Miles,' she said with a heavy sigh, 'I think we're about ready.' She walked to the side panel and opened it, handing him a leather flying helmet, large goggles and a pair of large aviator headphones, with microphone attached.

He held the items in his hands for a moment, watching

as she pulled out one for herself. First, though, she took out the band from her hair, the blonde tresses falling loosely around her shoulders, framing her face, the wind blowing them slightly, making her look like something out of a hair commercial.

His gut tightened with need and longing. He clenched his jaw in an effort to control himself against the absolutely stunning woman before him. She looked so young, so beautiful, so…untouchable.

'Problem, Trevellion?'

'Huh?' He blinked as though he'd just been dazzled by the sun. Instead, he knew he'd been dazzled by Janessa.

'Put them on,' she said, indicating the helmet, goggles and headphones he still held in his hands. 'Come on. I'm itching to get going.'

He stared at her for another long moment, her words slowly registering. '*You're* the pilot?'

'I thought that was obvious. I do remember saying I wanted to take you flying.' She shook her head. 'Here. Let me show you how to get in.' She started to give him instructions and Miles knew he had to click his brain back into gear otherwise they wouldn't be doing any sort of flying today.

He followed her directions, making sure he only stepped where she'd indicated, and all too soon he was sitting in the front seat of *Ruby*, Janessa standing on the wing beside him. She knew how to fly? First the Jaguar and now the Tiger Moth? When he'd walked into Adelaide Mercy last week, he'd never, in his wildest dreams, thought he'd be going flying with his neonate colleague.

So much had happened in such a short time and as Janessa leaned over him, reaching for the five different straps that would secure his body and buckle him into the seat, keeping him safe, all Miles seemed to be conscious of was the way her hair floated around her face, the way her scent enveloped him and the way her hand brushed his arm.

He was highly conscious of this woman and being this close to her yet again was not helping him to understand such a feeling. After Wendy's death, he'd vowed to concentrate on work, to help save the lives of others, as he'd been unable to save his wife and baby.

Now here he was, interested in another woman, a woman who had experienced pain and loss herself. Janessa was a woman who seemed to understand him, who seemed able to gauge his moods, to know what to say and what not to say. Ever since the other day, when they'd discovered just how much they had in common, their discussions about the conjoined twins had taken on a new level of power. It was as though now they understood each other's pasts, their drive to ensure everything went smoothly for the twins increasing.

'Miles?' Janessa's sweet voice penetrated his thoughts. There she was…beautiful Janessa with her flowing blonde locks and her sunshiny scent, the woman who was pulling him from the past into the present.

'Sorry,' he murmured, and shook his head. 'I missed that last bit.'

Janessa eased back, tilting her head to the side as she regarded him more closely. 'Is something wrong? You don't have to come up if you don't want to. I don't want to pressure you. I didn't tell you what we'd be doing in case you decided not to come at all.' And, she realised now, she'd *really* wanted him to come. Bringing him here, sharing this part of her life with him seemed the right thing to do…the next step in becoming friends.

'I'm fine with the flying. I just…zoned out for a moment. I'm fine, really. I'm already starting to relax.' He forced a smile and gave her his full attention.

He was enjoying all the wonderful new things he was learning about Janessa—the way she was not only extremely good looking but also incredibly intelligent; she also knew how to fly a Tiger Moth—that showed him how closed off his world had become. Since the death of his wife and child, Miles had brought in the boundaries his world, only letting in touches of light when it was needed most, just enough to keep him from tipping over into complete darkness.

Now, when he looked at Janessa, when he realised how smart and funny she was, it was as though she'd walked into his life and yanked open the curtains. Heavy, powerful sunlight seemed to flood into his life…opening the locked door to his heart.

'OK. What I need you to do is to put your hands either here on the side of the plane or up here above the instruments, but other than that, don't touch anything.'

'You'll be doing all of the flying behind me?'

'Yes. These planes are very finicky.' She secured the seat belt then pointed to the leather hat, goggles and headphones she'd handed him earlier. She plugged in the end of the headphone set so they could communicate. 'Put them on. The microphone will be close to your mouth. It's a little difficult to hear due to the wind but we'll get there.'

Being so close to him, giving him instructions and securing the harness had meant she'd come into close contact with him yet again and this time she hadn't tried to analyse the sensations such an action caused. She'd breathed in his scent, allowing it to wash over her, invigorating her entire body. Her mouth had been quite close to his own as she'd angled herself to make sure the straps weren't twisted. Her fingers had brushed the soft leather of the jacket he wore as she'd secured the belt at his waist.

She needed to right her thoughts, to brush away the effects of this man, or else she might not be able to fly the plane properly. Whilst she'd flown many of her friends in *Ruby* over the years, this was the first time she would be flying someone she was attracted to. Wanting to impress him suddenly seemed important. She knew it was crazy but that's the way it was.

Before she stepped off the wing, she turned her face into the wind, letting it blow her hair back and out of the way before she put the leather flying helmet on, quickly adjusting her goggles and aviator headphones. With her white scarf and leather jacket, she looked every inch the sexy pilot.

'How long have you been doing this?' he murmured, his voice deep, as though he was as affected by her as she was by him.

'Wearing sexy headgear?' she asked with a little smile.

He grinned. 'No. Flying.'

'Since before I could drive a car. Relax, Miles. You'll be fine. Just remember, don't touch anything. No levers, no gauges, no dials and leave those pedals on the floor alone.'

'Touch nothing. Got it, boss.'

'Hmm…boss, eh? I like the sound of that!'

With that, she jumped down off the wing, climbed into the seat behind him and waited for one of her friends to come and turn the propeller at the front of the plane to start it. Soon they were taxiing down the dirt runway, Janessa's clear voice requesting permission to take off.

'Ready, Miles?' When her voice came through his headphones, it was filled with wonderment, excitement and adrenaline. He didn't blame her. It was highly contagious.

'Ready,' he returned, and the biplane taxied down the runway before heading up, up and away.

* * *

Thirty minutes later, after flying over the sea, rolling hills and farmland surrounding the airfield, Janessa brought the aircraft in to land. When the wheels had safely touched down, Miles couldn't resist clapping and even gave a whoop of delight, which she heard through her headphones.

'Enjoy that?' she asked.

'Amazing! That was incredible. The wind on my face, the sun all around me, feeling as though I was one with this awesome machine… Yeah, Janessa, I enjoyed it.'

Janessa's own smile was bright and she was pleased she'd been able to share her love of flying with Miles.

She brought *Ruby* to a stop right next to the café. 'Door-to-door service,' he joked.

'We aim to please,' she said, before pulling out the connection on her headphones and pushing the microphone out of the way. She did a quick post-flight check before flicking open the buckle that had held her harness securely throughout the flight, the straps falling away. Climbing out, her goggles and headgear still in place, she bent over Miles to undo his large metal buckle but found he'd already done it. She turned to look at him and only then realised just how close they were.

'Thanks,' he murmured as he flicked the microphone in front of his mouth out of the way. Janessa swallowed, unable to move. She was standing on the reinforced part of the wing, hanging on to the rim of the plane, leaning over into the front passenger seat, her mouth literally millimetres from his.

'You're welcome.' Her heart was hammering wildly against her ribs and, given her present location, she was actually having a hard time breathing. Was it due to the way she was contorting her body or the fact that if she edged the tiniest bit closer, her mouth would touch his? She swallowed, knowing it was the latter.

He was looking at her lips, she could see quite clearly through her flying goggles that he was looking at her lips. The tension surrounding them crackled to life once more. They were colleagues; they would be working closely together for the next six months while he was here in Adelaide and then Miles would depart. Vamoose. Leave. She'd followed his career long enough to know he rarely stayed in one place. He was a man who shifted states and countries and continents, following the emergency calls of neonatology. She couldn't fault him for that.

She licked her lips, feeling self-conscious, and was about to move when she heard him groan.

'Don't.' The word was barely audible.

'Don't what?'

'Do that.'

'Do what?' she asked again, her gaze flicking from his eyes to his mouth and back again.

'You know exactly what you're doing.'

'I do?'

'You're drawing me in.'

Janessa swallowed again, her mouth and throat dry with anticipation, her heart pounding out such a quick tempo she thought she might become light-headed. 'Drawing you in?'

Her breath mixed with his, combining together along with the warmth of the day. Up in the air, with the breeze surrounding them, it had been exhilarating. Now, back down to earth, being so close to him, having him speak to her as though she were the most precious woman in the world, Janessa found him equally as exhilarating.

The spark was there, hot and powerful and refusing to be ignored. It was always the same when they were this close, when they were alone, when everything else in life seemed to disappear into oblivion.

Why did she have to be so close, so gorgeous, so…appealing? There was far more to Janessa than first met the eye and Miles couldn't help but acknowledge just how important she was becoming to him.

He should ease back, look away, make a move, something—*anything*—to break the bubble surrounding the two of them. How was it possible that within such a short time she'd been able to break through the walls, the barriers he'd spent years putting in place?

After Wendy's death he'd vowed to become one of those doctors who was more interested in his work than anything else. He wanted to help, to heal and to harness the potential of the people around him before high-tailing it. Allowing himself to settle down in one place wasn't on the cards. He wasn't meant for a life of domesticity. That point had been proven years ago when he and Wendy had tried to settle down.

And then he'd secured a job in Vienna. Head of Vascular Surgery. It had been too good to pass up but Wendy hadn't liked to fly so they'd taken the train.

His life had changed. The world he'd known had disappeared and from that moment on he'd made sure that he'd lived his life on the fringe. He'd completed more training, become a neonatologist, assisted with breakthrough surgery, written articles and papers, given lectures and presentations. He'd worked hard to get to where he was and now he liked his life and most definitely wasn't in any hurry to change it, or he hadn't been…until he'd met Janessa Austen.

From the beginning she'd been an enigma, appearing too young, too strait-laced, too appealing. He'd vowed to keep his distance from her, to have his walls and barriers firmly in place, just as he always did, and yet here he was, in her Tiger Moth, having enjoyed every moment he'd spent with her from the instant they'd left the hospital.

How had she battered down his walls? How had she managed to get under his skin so quickly, so effortlessly? What was it about her that made him completely unable to resist her allure? He shouldn't be looking at her. He shouldn't be reacting to the way her pink lips parted to allow her tongue to wet them. He shouldn't be almost desperate to taste her... but he was.

He'd wanted to kiss her so badly yesterday morning when she'd been so exhausted that she'd all but stumbled into his arms. He'd wanted to kiss her after holding her close in his arms, comforting her after Philip's death, unable to believe they'd both been parents of children who hadn't survived. He'd wanted to kiss her as she'd stared at him across the conference table, and if he was honest with himself, he'd admit that he'd wanted to kiss her the moment she'd bawled him out in her office not one hour after they'd met.

He'd been drawn to her from the start and although he knew he'd be leaving in six months, although he knew the feelings he had for her couldn't really lead anywhere except to pain, he also knew he simply couldn't fight her allure any longer.

'Don't look at me like that, honey.' And before she could ask what he meant, before she could utter a word, her mind filled with excitement and confusion and trepidation, Miles had closed the minute distance between them and captured her mouth with his own.

Their flying goggles clanked together and at the sound Janessa went to pull back, realising this was wrong, that it wasn't meant to be happening, that she and Miles were colleagues...perhaps even friends...but not this.

Kissing was wrong.

Miles, however, was having none of it and merely angled his head a bit more so their goggles didn't clank as he pressed his lips to hers more firmly. Her body came to life at the touch, at the pressure, at the need that seemed to burst forth from somewhere deep within her.

She had no idea where such intensity had come from. She had no idea what it might mean. All she knew was that Miles had given in, had stopped fighting the internal struggle she'd previously witnessed in his hungry blue eyes, and for that she was incredibly glad.

Glad. She was glad he'd kissed her and as his lips continued to hold hers captive, she was struck with the realisation that she hadn't been glad—truly glad—about anything for quite a long time.

'Janessa.' He edged back ever so slightly, her name a whispered caress from his lips.

'Mmm?' Her eyes were closed, her mind was spinning, her body felt as light as a feather. The way he made her feel was as though she'd breathed in helium and was floating up towards the sky, content just to be. The only other time she'd ever felt that sensation had been when she was up flying *Ruby*, forgetting the cares of the world… And now Miles made her feel that way with his addictive kisses.

Slowly, she opened her eyes and breathed in, his spicy, earthy scent tantalising her senses even more. He still had his goggles on, his headphones and his leather flying helmet—as did she. The sounds of the airfield, other small planes preparing to taxi down the runway, the smell of aviation fuel in the air as another plane refuelled, the wind blowing a gentle breeze around them…the world at large started to return into focus and she blinked as though to clear her mind.

'Uh…' She straightened up too quickly, almost knocking her head on the upper wing, and as she swerved to miss it, she overbalanced. 'Whoa!'

With a thud she fell to the ground, landing in a tangle.

'Janessa!' Miles quickly removed his headgear and goggles before carefully levering himself out of the seat and standing on the reinforced part of the lower wing. 'Are you all right?' But even as he asked the question, his gaze taking in the unruly sight of Janessa sprawled on the ground, trying to untangle herself from the headphone cord, which had wound itself about her leg, he felt his lips start to twitch into a smile.

She looked up at him and glared. 'Don't you dare laugh at me, Miles Trevellion.'

'Why not?' He stepped to the ground and without even offering her a hand up—which she would have most definitely refused—he bent and slipped his hands beneath her arms and lifted her to her feet in one easy move, the headphone cord untangling immediately.

'Let me go. I'm fine. I don't need any help.' She shifted away from him, completely embarrassed and annoyed for letting him kiss her, letting him touch her, letting him get under her skin. She pulled off her headphones and goggles before unbuckling the leather strap on the helmet and removing it, shaking out her blonde hair. Without another word, she stomped off through the gate and into the café without waiting for him.

He watched her go, sauntering along slowly behind her, knowing it was best to give her some room…give them *both* some room.

Why *had* he kissed her? Why had he given in to the urge and actually kissed her? Was it because their lives had run along similar paths? Was it because she knew exactly how he felt, surviving the death of a child? Was that a bond only people who had been in that situation could share?

It was definitely true, but he also could admit to himself that he'd been attracted to her, impressed by her, long before he'd discovered that piece of information. Knowing what drove them, understanding why they'd chosen to specialise in the field of neonatology, had opened the doors he'd kept locked for far too long.

Spending too much personal time with Janessa might actually become hazardous to his health, especially if she continued to be this constant source of surprise. She drove an incredible car, she flew not only a plane but a Tiger Moth and she tasted like strawberries. He liked strawberries.

As he headed inside, she was nowhere to be found, but Myrna was behind the desk. She held out her hands, accepting the headgear he still carried.

'What have you done to our Nessa, eh? She was all hot and flustered when she came in just now. That's not how she usually returns when she's been up for a relaxing flight in ol' *Ruby* so what have you done to her?'

Miles looked at the older woman, the woman who appeared to be in mother-hen mode, protecting her young. There was a determined look in Myrna's eyes that told him she wasn't in any mood for teasing. His own mother had worn the same look from time to time and he knew when to toe the line. It appeared honesty was the name of the game.

'Uh... I...' He cleared his throat, feeling like a recalcitrant teenager, especially as he shuffled his feet. 'Uh...I kissed her.' He didn't know why he'd confessed it, especially as when all was said and done it was no one's business but his and Janessa's. What he hadn't expected was Myrna's eyebrows to shoot up in surprise and a smile to spread across her face in utter glee.

'Really?' she asked with incredulity.

'Uh…yeah.' Before he could say another word, Myrna had come round the counter and embraced him in a large bear hug, even tighter than the one she'd given him when he'd arrived.

'Oh, I'm so happy. That's wonderful news,' Myrna babbled as she let him go, but slipped her arm through his, leading him gently to look at some of the photographs up on the wall. 'Come and take a look at some of these photographs. She was such a cute little poppet.' Myrna pointed at one of the photographs.

It was a black and white photograph of a man standing next to an old Tiger Moth, one arm resting on the plane, the other around a girl of about six or seven who was missing her two front teeth, grinning widely, her blonde hair flying in the breeze. Neither of them looked as though they had a care in the world.

'That's Janessa?'

'You guessed it. Her mother took that photograph. That was the day her father bought his first plane. Came out here a lot, they did. Then, of course, when his wife died, he sold that first plane and bought a different one.' Myrna showed him a different photograph. 'That's the glorious *Ruby*. Named the plane after his late wife. Never got over her death and it was over a decade later before he went to join her. Ahh… I tell you, Miles, that wee girl was born to be in the air.' She pointed to a different photograph in colour, one of Janessa taken only a few years ago, standing with the same man, although this time he looked sick and frail. Both of them were smiling but it was more for appearances than with the carefree spirit of years before.

'Over a decade later,' he murmured absent-mindedly as Myrna continued to talk. He shook his head. The poor woman. To lose her mother, her baby, her husband and then her father, too. For someone to come through such pain, such intense suffering gave him an indication of just how strong Janessa really was.

'A strong sense of family,' Myrna continued. 'That's what our Nessa has here, and we're all fiercely protective of her. And…' Myrna glared up at him '…none of us want to see her get hurt.'

Miles nodded. 'Understood.'

Myrna slowly shook her head. 'Did you *really* kiss her?'

Miles's smile was automatic. 'Yes, ma'am. I didn't mean to. Just sort of…happened.'

Myrna leaned in closer and patted his arm. 'That's the best way,' she whispered as Janessa walked back into the room.

'Ready to go, Miles?' she asked, brisk and efficient and more like the doctor he'd met on his first day at the hospital. There didn't appear to be any sign of the woman whose mouth had responded so ardently to his. He'd kissed Janessa! A colleague! He still wasn't sure why he hadn't been able to keep his distance, still wasn't sure what was going to happen next, still wasn't sure how Janessa felt about it.

Myrna turned to face Janessa. 'Leaving so soon, Nessa?'

Janessa smiled sadly at her friend. 'Sorry, Myrna, but duty calls.' She looked at Miles, her expression returning to one of complete seriousness. 'I've just received a call from the hospital.'

'Problem?' Miles was instantly alert, turning away from gazing at the photograph of Janessa as a little girl, so cute and adorable.

'Possibly.'

'Who called you? Ray? Kaycee? Is it one of the babies?'

Janessa shook her head. 'Sheena called me. She's worried.'

'Sheena's worried?' The look on Miles's face indicated how serious this might actually be.

'Yes, and you know Sheena. She's not the worry-wart type.'

'Get going, then, Nessa.' Myrna handed Janessa the car keys, which she had put on the counter when she'd arrived. 'Go and do what you need to do. Don't worry about *Ruby*. Davie will take care of her. You go and look after Sheena and those babies—and give her our love.'

Janessa nodded and hugged her friend close. 'I will. Thanks, Myrna.' She gathered up her backpack, jacket and scarf and headed for the door.

'It was lovely to meet you, Miles,' Myrna remarked, giving him a sly little wink that wasn't at all sly, as Janessa witnessed the exchange. 'Come back again some time. Soon!'

'I intend to.' Miles held the door for Janessa and as they headed to the Jaguar he was surprised when she handed him the keys. 'Are you sure you want me to drive?'

'Safest and fastest way back, please.' She slid into the passenger seat and put on her seat belt. Her fingers rubbed at her temples, trying to calm the headache that had appeared the moment she'd heard Sheena's worried voice down the phone line.

Miles slid behind the wheel, adjusting the seat before turning to face her. 'Are you all right, Janessa?'

'No. No, I'm not.'

'Worried about Sheena?'

'Yes.'

'Has she called Riley?'

'She wasn't going to so I did. He's on his way to review

her. He'll call me the instant he knows what's going on, given that it'll take us some time to get back to the hospital.' She shook her head. 'I shouldn't have come down here today. I should have stayed close. Sheena isn't given to overstatement and fuss. In fact, she abhors it so for her to call and tell me she's worried means there's definitely something wrong. Something bad.' Her voice cracked on the last two words, fear and panic, mixed with self-anger, lacing her tone.

Miles reached over and took her hand firmly in his. 'We'll get to her. Riley will call us. It'll be fine. Sheena and the girls will be fine.'

'But it isn't time. If the girls can stay put for at least one more week, things will be better,' Janessa protested irrationally, drawing an immense amount of comfort from Miles's touch. She should be withdrawing from him, she should be keeping her distance, especially after the way she'd responded to his kiss.

Miles had kissed her...*really* kissed her! The first time had been just a press of his mouth against hers and both of them had been surprised at the level of intensity that that brief moment had brought forth. Now, after his mouth had devoured her own, she couldn't believe how much she wanted a repeat. Being so close to him, having his mouth on hers, seeing that burning look in his eyes, caused her heart to pound out a powerful rhythm of want she'd been denying for...well, for ever.

She met his gaze. Even the thought of leaning over and kissing him once more had the ability to bring a blush to her cheeks. How was she supposed to reject his offered comfort, his support, when now was the time when she really needed it? For so long she'd had no one except Sheena to comfort her when things went wrong, and now, right when she needed him, Miles was there for her.

She closed her eyes for a moment, finding it was all too puzzling, too confusing, and she'd be better off focusing her energies on Sheena rather than on trying to decipher the incomprehensible way Miles made her feel. He gave her hand one last little squeeze before letting go and turning the key in the ignition, the Jaguar's engine purring to life.

'Everything's going to be fine.' His tone was sure and firm and steadfast. 'We'll get to Sheena. We'll be there to help her, to give her what she needs. Everything will be fine,' he repeated. 'Believe me.'

Janessa opened her eyes and looked into his dynamic blue depths. She recognised the complete truth in his words. He wasn't just saying them to calm her down. He really *did* believe that Sheena and the girls would be fine, and Janessa believed him. She believed him! She was stunned to discover that she not only believed him but that she'd somehow become reliant on him.

The thought made her tremble and she quickly slid her sunglasses in place as Miles drove out of the airfield car park. She believed in him. She relied on him. What was next? Would she wake up one morning and discover that she'd fallen in love with him? In love with the man who would one day leave her?

No. She couldn't do that. She had to remain strong, remain in control. She swallowed as he took her hand in his again and gave it another little reassuring squeeze, the sensation helping to calm her nerves but heightening the way she was drawn to him.

This wasn't good. If she continued to be affected by him in this way, she would be in real danger.

CHAPTER TEN

By the time they arrived back at the hospital, Janessa's mind had worked through almost every scenario there was. She'd had to stop herself from going to the worst-case scenario first because even *thinking* it had brought tears to her eyes.

Sheena was going to be fine. Sheena and the girls were going to be fine. Miles had said so but both of them knew that until they stood before their friend, until they could see face to face that she was indeed all right, everything was mere speculation.

Under Janessa's directions, Miles drove the car into the emergency bay at the front of the hospital, handing the keys to one of the orderlies who was more than happy to accept the job of parking Janessa's pride and joy back in the old shed.

As they rushed to the maternity ward, Miles could see the stress and strain on Janessa's beautiful face. His protective instincts kicked in and he found himself reaching out to hold her hand as they made their way through the long and busy hospital corridors. He was silently pleased when she didn't reject his touch and, gripping her hand tightly with his own, they continued to walk fast, closing the distance between themselves and their friend.

When they arrived in the ward, the sister gave them a look of relief.

'There you are. She's been asking when you'd both arrive. Riley wants to get her to Radiology to do an ultrasound to check on the twins because according to the foetal heart monitors, nothing seems to be wrong and—'

'We know,' Miles remarked, keeping calm, even though he could feel nervous and anxious tension radiating from Janessa. 'Riley's already called us to let us know Sheena's status.' It was only as he stopped to speak to the sister that Janessa disengaged her hand from his and entered her friend's room. Miles didn't miss the sister's look of interest at the fact that they'd been holding hands. No doubt there would be fall-out, gossip, rumours circulating, given that they'd walked halfway through the hospital holding hands, and while he didn't care what people said about him, the last thing Janessa needed right now was to be the hot topic of discussion at every coffee break. For now, though, it was paramount that he get his head around what was happening with Sheena.

'Where's Sheena's chart?' he asked, holding out his hand. There were already too many people in Sheena's private room and the sooner Miles read the observation charts and reports, the sooner he'd have a better idea of what might or might not be happening. Janessa had been very quiet on the drive back and he hadn't tried to get her to open up or talk. That was one thing he'd learnt over the years—women would talk when they wanted to but when they were quiet and contemplative it was best to leave them to their thoughts.

When Riley had telephoned information through, instead of relaying it to him Janessa had put her phone on loud-speaker and the two of them had been able to hear and talk to the obstetrician about what was happening. He'd appreciated that because it also showed him that where Sheena and the babies were concerned, Janessa really did trust him.

'Everything is within normal parameters.'

'That's what we can't figure out,' Sister replied.

'Riley's right. We need to ultrasound the babies. Sheena's blood pressure seems to be slightly raised but that could be simply anxiety. However, if we can't get Sheena's blood pressure under control, Adelaide Mercy's first set of conjoined twins will no doubt be born tonight. Pass me the phone. It's going to be far easier to have the ultrasound equipment brought to Sheena than the other way around. We need to keep her as stable and as settled as possible.'

Sister did as she was told and within ten minutes the sonographer entered the ward, accompanied by orderlies carefully wheeling the equipment into Sheena's room. Miles headed into the room after them to find Janessa standing by her friend, holding her hand, ready to offer whatever support was required.

'There you are, Miles.' Sheena smiled at him but even Miles could see how tired the mother was. 'Where have you been?'

'Doing my job,' he remarked as he came closer and kissed her cheek. 'Conferring with Riley and a lot of others.'

'Is that why he kept going in and out of the room?' Sheena sighed, leaning back against the pillows, showing her exhaustion. Miles knew right then and there, just looking at the mother, that it was time. Even as the sonographer squeezed lubricant onto Sheena's abdomen and started to give them pictures of the girls, Miles knew. He'd seen it too many times before.

He looked over at Janessa who, unlike everyone else in the room, wasn't looking at the screen but was looking at him. There was a question in her eyes, a question of concern, a question of vulnerability, a question of doubt. Miles's first instinct was to cross to her side, to take her into his arms and to tell her that everything was going to be all right, to reassure her, to give her the strength she'd need so that she could pass it on to Sheena.

He was only mildly surprised at such a need to protect her, to be there for her, given that it wasn't the first time he'd felt it. Too many times in the past week he'd wanted to do exactly the same thing, to protect and comfort her, and now that he knew how it really felt to have her lips pressed against his, how her mouth was the most perfect fit to his own, the sensations she evoked within him were definitely increasing.

She raised her eyebrows questioningly, as if to say, Is it time? Miles nodded, the action small but conveying so much. Janessa's beautiful brown eyes were filled with worry before she closed them, drawing in a deep breath and letting it out slowly. Then, when she opened her eyes, Miles recognised the professional neonatologist he'd worked with during the past week. She'd pushed her trepidation and anxiety aside, knowing she wouldn't be any good to either Sheena or the girls if she wasn't completely focused on what was about to happen. She'd told him on his first day here that she had the ability to do the job, and now he was seeing her words being put into action.

'Everything looks fine with the girls,' Riley commented, but looked at Miles for his reaction.

Miles, instead, looked at Sheena. 'You're exhausted. Your blood pressure hasn't improved in the past hour—in fact, it's increased.'

'The incubator has finished her job,' Sheena remarked, nodding as though she knew this was the way things would go.

'Almost,' Miles replied with a smile.

'You're the expert here, Miles,' Riley returned. 'What's your verdict?'

'Based on my experience, now that Sheena's blood pressure has started to rise, it means the girls are in danger and that things will start to break down. It's time. If we operate today, we'll get two healthy girls. If we leave it and monitor Sheena, we run the risk of the girls starting to fail. The thing with conjoined twins is that while you have to acknowledge that mentally they are two separate people, both with their own little personalities, the fact is that if one of them starts to fail, so will the other one. We want *two* healthy babies.'

Janessa nodded. 'Agreed.'

'Agreed,' Riley added. 'I'll head to Theatre and get organised. Oh, and someone had better let Charisma and the PR people—'

'Already taken care of,' Miles remarked.

'Excellent.' Riley nodded and continued out of the room. The sonographer had packed up her equipment and the orderlies were wheeling it out again. The nursing staff had headed out too and within a matter of minutes it was only Janessa, Miles and Sheena left in the room, everyone busy doing what they needed to do in order for these babies to be born safely.

'Charisma. *Pfftt.* PR. *Pfftt,*' Sheena grumbled. 'Why can't I just be left to have my babies in peace? Why am I this big three-ringed circus?' Tears bubbled over and Janessa instantly comforted her friend.

'It's not fair, is it?' She wiped away Sheena's tears and looked at her. 'Everything's going to be fine.'

'Is it?' Anxiety, worry, confusion, pain and heartbreak were in Sheena's tone. She looked at Janessa and then at Miles, her lower lip wobbling. 'I'm scared,' she whispered, and Miles moved closer to place a hand on her shoulder, wanting to reassure her in every way he could.

'Janessa and I are going to be there every step of the way,' Miles confirmed. 'And just think, soon, very soon, you're going to be able to touch your baby girls. They're both doing well, Sheena. They're both as healthy as they can be and you've done the most incredible job of carrying them for so long.'

'Miles is right,' Janessa agreed. 'You've been the most incredible and powerful incubator. The best in the world.'

Sheena gave her a watery smile and then a little laugh. 'Thank you.' She looked at Miles. 'Thank you both.' She sighed heavily and then rubbed her abdomen. 'It's time, girls. It's time for the three of us to meet. Oh, what fun we're going to have.'

Janessa leaned forward and spoke in a stage whisper. 'And Aunty Janessa promises to buy you both lots of noisy toys to drive your mother crazy.'

Miles laughed and looked at the woman he'd kissed only a few hours ago. She was funny and smart and caring. Strong and brave and sensual… And she was becoming far too important to him.

Sheena's C-section was performed without complications. Riley, the obstetrician, was not bothered by the cameras in the room, which would record the event for posterity. Miles had always told her that the delivery was the easy part but the reason they'd had meetings to discuss the postnatal care so intricately was so they were completely ready the moment the babies were out.

'My fifteen minutes of fame and you can't even see my best angle,' Sheena had joked as Janessa and Miles, Kaycee and Ray had stood by, waiting for the moment the twins were handed over to them. The instant the girls were carefully placed into their loving care, the neonate team focused on their special little patients. Ray and Kaycee worked closely alongside Miles and Janessa, inserting umbilical lines, steadying the girls' oxygen as they worked on them beneath large heat lamps over the specially designed crib.

'The first twenty-four hours are critical,' Miles had said at the different briefings they'd had during the past week. 'Even more so than with other babies. Only once Ellie and Sarah are born can we accurately determine exactly what we're dealing with. All of the ultrasounds and X-rays to date don't show us everything, hence we need to be as prepared as possible.'

Even now, as Janessa focused on working alongside him, Kaycee putting little knitted beanies on the babies' heads— one that had 'Ellie' stitched in and the other 'Sarah', so that staff could tell the girls apart—she recalled Miles's instructions.

'One-minute Apgar?' he asked.

'Five for Sarah. Four for Ellie,' Ray reported.

'Let's get them moved to the NICU.' Miles was firm, determined, completely in control of the situation. Janessa was as much in awe of him as before. He had knowledge, he had understanding, and as Ray and Kaycee worked with the orderlies to move the girls and the equipment they were attached to out of the delivery suite, Miles quickly crossed to Sheena's side.

'You did good. I'm so proud of you for carrying them for so long. You've given them an incredible start in life.' He brushed some hair out of Sheena's eyes and smiled at her. Janessa came up and kissed her friend on the forehead.

'Miles is right. The girls are doing very well. Rest now.'

'Good advice,' Sheena remarked, her eyes closing. 'Think I'll do just that.'

They were only a few steps behind the girls and once they were settled in the NICU in a room off to the side, enclosed by a curtain to afford privacy, the observations and checks began again.

'They're both in much better health than I had hoped,' Miles remarked after the ten-minute Apgar score on both babies was a nine. They stood there, the two of them, looking at the little girls, tubes and wires attached to them, lying on their backs, arms and legs spread, the specially made cloth nappies fastened in place.

'Yes.' She nodded, looking at the little girls who were her goddaughters. 'And they're beautiful.' The instant she said the words tears welled in her eyes, but where before she might have walked away from Miles in the hope that he wouldn't see her exhibiting such raw emotions, now she didn't bother.

He knew the truth about her past. He knew she'd lost a baby of her own and he knew, first-hand, the pain she'd suffered. Even though time had moved on, even though the world continued to revolve around them, the pain and the memories and the burning need to be a parent still continued to pulse through both of them.

'So incredibly beautiful.' She said each word slowly, carefully and with the utmost meaning. 'I love them both so much.' She smiled through the tears that were pricking at her eyes and when Miles placed his arm around her shoulders and drew her close, she didn't even think of pulling away.

He could feel the emotions coming from her, the love radiating from her for these beautiful babies…babies that weren't her own.

It seemed right and natural that he should comfort her. It

seemed right and natural to stand there with her, the two of them alone for the first time since they'd arrived back at the hospital earlier in the day. The two of them, looking at two little miracles lying joined at the hip. Ellie and Sarah. Both of them breathing rapidly in the oxygen-controlled environment, the machines around them beeping and displaying their vital signs.

'It's definitely good,' he murmured.

'I can even tell them apart,' she said with a small smile. 'Look, Ellie's face isn't as round as Sarah's.'

'Where?' Miles peered closer but still didn't remove his arm from around Janessa's shoulders. He was offering her comfort, true, but he was also a red-blooded male who was powerfully attracted to this woman. The last time he'd offered her comfort he'd been able to find the strength to pull away. This time, though, he wasn't finding it easy. Was that because he couldn't stop thinking about her? Was that because she was becoming incredibly important to him? Was it simply because he'd given in to the burning desire to kiss her? Now that he knew the flavours and sweetness of her lips against his, of how her plump pink lips seemed to have been designed to fit so perfectly against his own, he wanted to keep her as close as possible.

Although she might not want to talk about their kiss, about the sensations and emotions which had been evoked, awoken as though from a long and weary sleep, Miles couldn't ignore the way he felt for Janessa any more. Where he'd thought he'd never be able to move on from Wendy's death, here he was, desperate for some sort of signal from Janessa that she felt the same way, that she'd enjoyed the kiss, that she wanted more.

Instead, he used the excuse of leaning forward to peer more closely at the baby girls, to shift his body nearer to hers, to settle her within the circle of his arms, to have the curves of her body pressed to his, moulding as though they were meant for each other.

'Just there.' She pointed, not wanting to move away from the strength of his arm about her shoulders and angling her body towards his in order to fit more snugly against him. She knew she shouldn't. She knew she should find some sort of self-discipline to ease herself away from him, to draw back, to create distance between them because it would be far too easy to continue to snuggle in closer, especially now she knew how powerful and masterful he could be when his mouth was pressed to hers.

As though his thoughts mirrored her own, Miles angled her even closer and when she glanced up at him, it was the easiest thing in the world to lower his head a fraction, close the short distance between them and capture her lips once more in a kiss.

This time there was no initial surprise, his senses recalling with perfect clarity how she tasted. This time there were no flying goggles to distract them so they could focus on the powerful explosion of desire that existed between them. This time it was even more perfect than before.

She almost sighed into him as he once more brought her body to life. When she'd dated in the past, when she'd been interested in other men, she'd always managed to stay in complete control of her emotions. Not so with Miles. He seemed to have burst into her life, strapped her to a seat and taken her for a ride she hadn't known existed.

She'd been a pilot for many years. She'd competed in aerobatic competitions and done a multitude of extreme sports, such as parachuting, hang-gliding and para-sailing. She loved the sensation of being up in the air, of losing herself to the experience and exhilaration of such activities, but none had prepared her for the way she felt when being this close to Miles Trevellion.

Her breathing increased, her heart pummelled a wild rhythm against her chest, her mouth ardently seeking his, wanting to match him moment by moment, her knees beginning to weaken as he continued to create havoc with her equilibrium.

She was vulnerable. She was emotional. She was becoming too close to a man who would one day leave her world. She'd thought she'd been in love with Bradley all those years ago but she'd been a young and naïve teenager. She hadn't listened to the advice of those closest to her and then disaster had struck. Her son had died, her marriage had ended and then her mother had been taken from her.

Control had been her answer. To gain control over her life, she'd set off on a career of medicine, determined to specialise in the neonatal field to be able to help others. She'd worked hard, keeping any possible romantic connections strictly under control…until Miles had burst into her life.

Earlier today, this man's mouth had been wreaking havoc with her senses, just as it was now, and she was loving every moment of it. Kissing Miles, having his mouth on hers was like a dream come true, and it was a dream she'd had every night since he'd first arrived, since that first accidental kiss.

She was enjoying, far too much, the way he made her feel, the way his mouth seemed to know exactly how to tease and elicit a response. She could feel the way he appeared to be straining to keep himself under control, to keep things slow and steady, but it was there…the powerful, hot and heavy need to draw her even closer, to take the natural chemistry that existed between them out for a spin.

That was why she had to pull back. That was why she needed distance from him. He was starting to break down the heavy protective wall she'd built around herself, to keep her safe from ever giving her heart to another. The way he made her feel wasn't just physical attraction—it was an attraction of their souls. Miles understood her, appreciated her, respected her, and those special qualities would be able to completely expose her heart if she wasn't careful.

When she'd accepted the position as head of NICU years ago, Sheena had been adamant that it had been time for Janessa to start dating. Reluctantly Janessa had agreed but after about a year of the odd date here and there, her father's illness had required her attention and she'd split her time between caring for him and working round the clock at the hospital.

And now she had Ellie and Sarah. Two beautiful, precious, wonderful babies to help care for. It wasn't going to be an easy road. She knew she'd have to be there to support Sheena, to be strong for her friend, but when Miles held her like this, kissed her like this, when he touched her, held her hand, offered comfort, she wanted this to last for ever. She would be there to support Sheena and Miles could be there to support her. Couldn't he?

She knew that he would leave—eventually—and that if she did rely on him to renew her strength, she would run the risk of being even more hurt than she had been all those years ago when her marriage had failed.

Miles was kissing her. He'd opened a part of her she'd thought she'd locked securely away, and she knew, she knew full well that if she didn't start finding a way to distance herself from him, there was a fair chance she'd fall in love with him before she'd realised it.

Dangerous. The man was dangerous. Dangerous, powerful and overwhelmingly addictive.

Even though the kiss felt as though it had lasted an eternity, in reality it had been less than a minute. Janessa eased back, resting her head against his chest for a moment as she allowed her breathing to return to normal. She looked at the girls. The two darlings lying there, sleeping, their machines beeping in a steady and controlled rhythm. Thank goodness their eyes had been closed and they hadn't seen their Aunty Janessa kissing their Uncle Miles. It took another moment of gathering her strength before she pulled back, turning away from him.

'Everything all right?' Miles asked, his deep tone filled with desire.

'We need to monitor the girls.' Her tone was more brisk than she'd intended but even though the kiss hadn't lasted that long, she felt guilty at giving in to her weakness for Miles when she'd been supposed to be monitoring the girls.

'The girls are fine. In fact, they're better than fine.' His voice was calm but his words were insistent. 'They're about the healthiest set of conjoined twins I've seen delivered in quite a few years. Janessa, we need to talk.'

She glanced at him. 'We can't, Miles,' she said softly, surprised at the huskiness of her own voice.

'Can't?'

'You know what I'm talking about.'

'Do I?'

'Please? Don't do this.'

'Do what? Question you? Comfort you? Hold you? Kiss you?' He raked a hand through his hair, knowing full well that what she was saying was the right thing to do but not wanting to do it.

'All of the above.' She spread her arms wide, shifting around to the side of the humidicrib, putting a bit more distance between them. She pretended to check the machines, to be doing anything other than standing there, looking at him. Especially when the pull to return to his arms, to press her entire body against his, to run her fingers through his hair, to urge his head down until their mouths met in hot and hungry passion were becoming the only thoughts in her mind.

'We can't.' She kept her back to him, knowing that if she looked at him, she would give in. She wasn't as strong as people thought. 'We're colleagues and we have a busy few months ahead of us with the girls and getting ready for their many surgeries.'

'Do you know how many women I've kissed since my wife died?'

'Miles.' She looked at him, even though she'd just told herself not to. 'Don't.' She shook her head, definitely not wanting to know the answer. Even the thought of him with another woman made her insides twist with distaste and jealousy, and that was precisely the reason why she needed to keep her distance from him.

'One. You. That's it. Wendy passed away seven years ago and you're the first woman I've been really interested in since.' He gestured at the distance between them. 'This sort of thing, this instant attraction, doesn't happen every day, you know.'

'I know. Do you think I don't know that? But you're in my head, Miles. You're clouding my thought processes and right now I need to keep them focused on the girls. They need me. Sheena needs me. Being around you, when you touch me, hold me, comfort me…kiss me…' She'd said the last words softly, looking away from him, unable to continue to look into those hypnotic blue eyes of his. 'You mix things up.' She took another half-step away.

'I don't know what it is that exists between us and quite frankly I don't want to know because I don't have the time for it. And neither, for that matter, do you. We've run out of time and now we have a job to do. You came to Adelaide Mercy for a very specific reason.' She pointed to the small little girls. 'Two very specific reasons, and you have the knowledge and the know-how to lead this team forward so that these little darlings can enjoy happy and normal lives. Then you and I will go our separate ways. You'll head off to the next set of conjoined twins who need your expertise and I'll stay here to help Sheena in every way I can.'

'And we'll never know what this frighteningly natural chemistry that exists between us means?'

'Exactly.'

'And what if I'm not happy about that? What if I don't agree to your terms?'

'Then that's tough.'

Miles couldn't believe what she was saying and neither could he believe how much her words were hurting him. He'd grown close to her, he'd been intrigued by her, he'd come to admire her, and yet, as she stood on the opposite side of the small private room from him, it felt as though she was skewering his heart with the sharpest scalpel in the world.

CHAPTER ELEVEN

Two weeks later, as Janessa and Kaycee finished returning the twins to their special crib after Sheena had finished cuddling them, making sure all the tubes and wires weren't twisted and everything was in the right places, Janessa came and sat by her friend. It might be two o'clock in the morning, but being here in the NICU meant she didn't have to be in her apartment, listening to Miles, thinking about Miles, dreaming about Miles.

Since the day the girls had been born, both of them had ensured that they were never left alone in a room, that they sat as far away from each other as they could during the continued meetings pertaining to Ellie's and Sarah's separation operations.

'They're so incredibly beautiful,' Sheena said, looking at her daughters with complete awe. 'I look at them and can't understand why Jonas wouldn't ever want to have children and how he could possibly disown his own daughters.' She shook her head.

'He wasn't strong enough. Not like you,' Janessa answered.

'Probably. You know, lying there in that hospital bed, being an incubator, definitely gave me a lot of time to think.'

'And?'

'And a lot of the pain and heartbreak and disbelief I felt when Jonas left isn't worth dwelling on. He was weak, selfish and stubborn. Definitely not the sort of father a mother would want for her special girls.'

'And they are special.' Janessa sighed as she looked at them. 'You're right, Sheena. It's not worth dwelling on.'

'I know I have my work cut out for me. Single mother. Raising twins. On her own.'

'You won't be alone,' Janessa protested strongly. 'You are *not* alone.'

'Oh, I know I have everyone's support here at the hospital, but people come and go, they have their own lives, their own problems. The bottom line is these are my girls. My girls. Isn't that amazing? They're my babies. No one can take them away from me. Not ever.' Sheena sighed and looked at her babies with complete adoration. 'They're mine.'

A lump sprang instantly to Janessa's throat at Sheena's words. *No one can take them away from me.* Sheena had her babies and while Sheena would share and need help and support from Janessa, the fact still remained. They were *Sheena's* babies. Not *hers*.

'Anyway…' Janessa said, pushing the pain away, determined not to intrude on Sheena's wonderful moment. Her friend deserved so much happiness, so much love, so much joy and now she had it. 'Now that the girls are fed, changed and sleeping, I'd better go do a round of the nursery and get caught up on some of my paperwork.'

'Nessa? Are you all right?' Sheena asked, yawning a little.

'I'm fine. Make sure you don't stay too long. You need your rest, too, Mummy.'

Sheena smiled at the title. 'I will, but I'd like to stay a little longer and just watch them sleep. They're such angels.'

'OK.' With that Janessa headed out into the NICU, checked on a few other babies and then headed to her office, and throughout the entire time Sheena's words were in her mind, repeating themselves over and over, niggling at her.

Ellie and Sarah were *Sheena's* babies.

Janessa didn't deny her friend the happiness of saying those words but at the same time they pierced her soul, dredging up her painful past. She hadn't been so lucky.

Pressing her hands to her temples, she could feel the beginnings of a bad headache coming on…a migraine. She hadn't had one in well over a decade. Terrible, stressful, debilitating migraines. If she didn't take care and head straight to bed, she'd be useless in the string of meetings scheduled to start at nine o'clock next morning.

Knowing it was the right thing to do, she ignored her paperwork, said goodnight to Kaycee and the other nightshift nurses, pleased to hear that Sheena had just returned to Maternity, before heading out of the NICU.

They're my babies. No one can take them away from me.

The closer she was to the residential wing, the more Sheena's words seemed to turn in her mind. It was as though hearing them had unlocked the past, unlocked the memories of her son, memories she didn't want to remember.

When she exited the stairwell on the third floor, she tried to be as quiet as she could, not wanting to wake Miles. It was as though they were sharing a house where none of the rooms actually interconnected but they could hear everything that happened.

The pounding in her head was becoming quite fierce now and she walked carefully to the kitchenette, drawing her emergency medical kit from the cupboard. She had nothing stronger than paracetamol, but for now that would have to do.

They're my babies. No one can take them away from me.

The words repeated as though on a constant loop, and Janessa was unable to choke back a loud sob. She tried to fill a glass with water in order to take the tablets but found her hand was shaking too much, the water sloshing everywhere. She put the glass down before it slipped from her hand, pain piercing her heart so intensely that she wasn't sure she would ever breathe properly again.

Sliding to the floor, she hugged her knees and started to cry, the pounding in her head becoming worse with every stifled noise she made. The pressure, the pain, the pounding…on and on they went, before she could take the throbbing around her mind no more and, dashing to the bathroom, was violently ill.

Rinsing her mouth and brushing her teeth, she was startled when Miles called through the wall, 'Janessa? Are you all right?'

'I'm fine,' she called back, not wanting him to intrude on her pain. She was trying to keep her distance from him, trying to make sure she didn't get hurt by not becoming involved with him on a personal level. 'Didn't mean to wake you. Go back to bed.'

Her vulnerability was at an all-time high right now, and if Miles came over, if he held her, if he—

The sound of her front door opening caused her heart to jump into her throat.

'Janessa?'

'Miles? How did you get in? The door was locked. I checked it. I made sure,' she said, walking out of the bathroom, catching a glimpse of her red eyes and blotchy skin in the mirror, to find him standing in her front hallway.

'My key works in your lock. No doubt yours works in mine but none of that is relevant right now.' He walked towards her, taking in her features. 'You were sick. Are you all right? Did you eat something wrong? Have you been injured?' He reached out for her but she backed away.

'I'm fine. Go back to bed.' It was only as she said the

words that she realised he was dressed in a pair of denim jeans, a T-shirt still clasped loosely in one hand, as though he hadn't had time to dress in his rush to get to her. 'I didn't mean to disturb your sleep.'

'Janessa?' Miles was now clearly puzzled. It was obvious that she wanted him to leave but it was also obvious that she wasn't being completely truthful with him. 'It's clear that, contrary to what you're saying, you are not *fine*—in fact, you're quite pale.'

'Ugly, you mean.' She turned her back to him, not wanting to look at the incredible sight he made. She walked through to her room, now just wanting to lie down on her bed and cry herself to sleep.

'No. A little red around the eyes maybe, but most definitely not ugly.' There was a strength to his words and she wanted to believe him. Instead, she kicked off her shoes and climbed into her bed, laying her head on the pillow and closing her eyes.

'I just need sleep. You let yourself in. You can let yourself out.'

'So you're not sick?'

'If it's the meeting you're worried about, don't be. I'll be there at nine o'clock sharp.'

'I don't care about the meeting, Janessa.' There was impatience in his tone and she opened her eyes to look at him, very grateful that he'd at least put his T-shirt on and covered his tempting upper body. 'I care about *you*.'

'Well, don't.'

'Why? It's not something I can switch on and off any time I feel like it. You know there's this thing between us…this attraction that we're both working so desperately to fight.'

'I thought it was merely an attraction. I didn't know there was caring involved.' Her words were careless and tired but they triggered an immediate reaction when Miles closed the distance between them and lifted her into a sitting position, his hands firm on her arms but not to the point where he was hurting her.

'Of course I care about you. How could I not when I can't stop thinking about you? Don't you have any idea how you get to me, how you manage to get under my skin, to disturb my train of thought? I sit in meetings and all I can think about is you. I see you in the NICU and I can't help but wonder what it would be like to kiss you again. You're turning my thoughts from my work and driving me insane.' He gave her a little shake, exasperation flooding through him.

'I know we've both been doing our best to avoid each other but it's clear that there's something wrong. You were sick. I could hear you courtesy of the thin walls and terrible plumbing pipes.' His hands had gentled now and she could feel the exasperation change to the strong awareness that seemed to exist permanently between them. 'What happened? Is there something wrong in the NICU? What is it, Janessa? Are the girls OK?'

'They're fine. Better than fine. So gorgeous and strong and healthy and…alive.' On the last word, all the strength seemed to leave her and she sagged against Miles. 'They're so alive, Miles. So alive. Not like my little boy at all. He died.'

The tears slid down her cheeks and Miles immediately gathered her to him, shifting them around so that he could sit up against the headboard of the bed and hold Janessa close.

'My Connor,' she said between hiccups. 'I couldn't face holding him. The staff were wonderful, caring and doing all they could for us. They tried to encourage me to hold him, to say goodbye, to achieve closure, but right then and there I…I couldn't. I felt so weak, so useless, so scared.'

'Oh, Nessa,' he whispered, feeling her pain.

'Then, later on, I couldn't sleep. The nurse on the ward

was wonderful and when she asked me if I wanted to try and say goodbye to Connor, I agreed. She arranged everything, she was amazing. I was escorted down to the mortuary, to the small viewing room, and…I saw him. I held him. My baby. So still. So cold.' Janessa sniffed. 'So…lifeless.' She shook her head, her words barely audible. 'I was too young. My life with Bradley was over. We just couldn't get past the loss of our baby. And then…my mum died. My beautiful, sweet, loving mum. I lost so much.'

Miles listened to her talk, stroking her hair, hearing her heartbreak in every word she spoke. It was obvious she hadn't dealt with the pain of her past…but, then, until he'd met her, neither had he. He'd just forged ahead, putting his past away. He knew how she felt but at least, being there for her, holding her, helping her…hopefully she'd be able to move forward, just as she'd helped him to start letting go of his own past.

'After I buried Connor, the doctor said it wasn't wise to try for another pregnancy too soon. Bradley and I…we were both so young and in pain. We took it out on each other, blamed each other, but in the end we knew we would never be able to go back to the young carefree teenagers we'd been before Connor was born. I felt as though my life was over. That there was nothing more for me, no happily-ever-after.'

Miles shook his head. 'But you were strong. Perhaps stronger than you realised because look at what you've managed to accomplish. You went to medical school, worked hard, trained hard, no doubt determined to specialise in neonatology, to help other confused and hurting mothers. The people who have been through the same or similar experiences are the ones who can offer the most hope, the most compassion and the most understanding to those who follow. Your experiences have made you a better doctor, Nessa, even if you don't see it that way. You are a strong and incredibly intelligent woman. You're amazing.'

Janessa allowed his sweet yet strong and powerful words to wash over her, dissolving more of the protective walls she'd built around herself. Was that how he saw her? As a strong woman? Filled with compassion? Why was it that she couldn't see herself that way?

'You also looked after your father when he was ill. Sheena told me how you were his sole carer until his death.'

'And I grumbled about it at times,' she added. 'It isn't easy to look after a parent, especially when you can see their health failing right before your eyes.'

'It's not meant to be easy. The hard times only make us stronger. Easy to say, difficult to work through but still so very true.'

Janessa knew he was right and the fact that he'd been through his own heart-wrenching experiences made her listen to his words. 'So is that how you view your own negative experiences, Miles? How can you turn what happened to you into a positive?' She asked the question quietly, hiccupping a little now that her tears had stopped.

Miles rested his head against the wall and slowly exhaled. 'I don't know, Nessa, but for a while there I had to force myself to get out of bed, to remember to breathe in and out every day, to push through the pain of my loss and try to find some sort of silver lining. My wife and son died and there was nothing I could do.'

'You were unconscious. You were hurt as well,' she pointed out, remembering what he'd told her.

'I woke up to…nothing.' He tightened his hold on her, loving the feel of her in his arms, the support and comfort she was allowing him to take from her. 'It's a day that's forever burned into my brain. The happiness of being on the train, of being with my family, of looking out the window at the incredible view, and then…nothingness.'

Janessa looked up at him, his square jaw clenched with stubbornness, his eyes staring off into the distance. 'The pain and heartbreak at being left so alone isn't a nice feeling, especially when your family was ripped from you so suddenly, but yet you went on. That takes strength.'

Miles looked down into her beautiful brown eyes, slightly red-rimmed from crying, but even so she looked gorgeous. 'What else is there to do?'

'Give up? Walk away from medicine? Change jobs? Lock yourself away? But you didn't do any of that.'

'Neither did you,' he felt compelled to point out.

Janessa gave him a crooked smile. 'A real mutual admiration society, aren't we?'

'We've got to stick together in this world.' He nodded, but his gaze dipped down to her lips.

'Yes.'

Miles swallowed and brought his free hand up to caress her cheek. 'You are so lovely, Janessa.'

She gasped at his words, her heart starting to pound wildly in her chest. She wanted him. She wanted him so badly she felt as though she was going to burst with desire. How could he elicit such emotions from her so effortlessly? Her breathing started to increase and she licked her lips as his gaze caressed her.

'I am so sorry for the pain you've been through, for what you've lost, but right now all I can think about is kissing you.'

'Oh.' The small word came out on a hiccupping breath and she found that she couldn't stop from staring into his come-hither blue eyes.

'Ever since the day the girls were born—which seems like half a lifetime ago, rather than just a few weeks—I haven't been able to stop thinking about how perfect your mouth felt against mine. About how perfectly you fit into my arms. About how perfect we are together.'

She wanted it, too. Wanted nothing more than to follow through on her heart's desire but she paused, just for a second. 'But we can't. We work together. We have—'

Miles shook his head and placed a finger across her lips, stopping her words. 'Shh. I don't want to rationalise this, Janessa. I've spent too much time trying to figure things out, trying to deny the way being near you makes me feel, but the truth of the matter is that you make me feel alive again.

'For the past seven years since Wendy's death, I've been existing, going from one job to the next, in order to help out where I could but also to close myself off from the world. It's easy to move through the world, to appear fine and healthy when you know how. You smile, you nod, you provide your expertise. You receive thanks, you shake hands, you go on your way, heading off to the next place where you do it all again. No one gets close enough to touch the real you, deep down inside. Everyone is kept at arm's length. Everything is under control. Or at least that's how my life was…until I met you.' His finger outlined her trembling lips and Janessa's eyelids fluttered closed as she accepted the caress.

'Miles.' His name was a breathless whisper. 'I want this, too, but—'

'You don't want to get hurt when I leave,' he finished for her, shifting slightly to bring her a little closer to him.

'Yes.' She opened her eyes and looked directly into his.

'I can't promise anything, Janessa, only that I want to spend more time with you, to hold you close, to kiss you. I never thought I would *ever* become interested in a woman again and the fact that I have, the fact that I want you, that I can't stop thinking about you, that I want to kiss you every time I see you, is a miracle within itself. I didn't think I had the capacity to care for anyone as deeply as I do for you.'

'So…what are you saying? That you'll stay? That you'll remain in Adelaide once the girls have been separated? That you want to keep seeing me? Spending time with me?'

Miles looked down at her mouth, tempted to lie, to promise her whatever she wanted, just so he could kiss those perfect lips of hers…but he knew he couldn't. She'd been hurt so long ago and the fact that she was still so incredibly cautious only showed him just how deep that hurt had gone. It also showed him that he owed her one thing right now, and that was the complete truth.

'It's tempting, Nessa. So very tempting, and that in itself is something new. I've always been in control, had things mapped out, known exactly what's happening next, but not now.' He spoke so clearly, so articulately, and it was just another facet to him that she was coming to love.

Love?

Janessa ignored the thought, focusing on the here and now because on a romantic level the 'here and now' always ended with a generous serving of pain and sadness later on. Why was it that he had to go? Why did he have to leave? To move? Wasn't it worthwhile, staying here? Seeing whether these wonderful sensations that had existed between them since they'd first met meant anything?

'Janessa?' Miles saw confusion, anxiousness and longing cross her face, and he knew she was just as confused as he was. 'You once asked me if there was any hope for a "happily ever after" for control freaks such as us.'

'Mm-hm?'

'I think there might be.'

'Really?' She edged closer, hope filling her heart as she leaned up towards his mouth, wanting more than the touch of his fingers on her neck, her cheeks, her lips.

'Yes.' The word was a whisper of promise. What was coursing between them, filling the room with energy and repressed tension, was too strong for either of them to cope with right now. 'I want you, Janessa. Don't ever think that I don't.'

'Show me, Miles.'

'Oh, honey, I want to.' He closed his eyes as though in pain. 'Believe me, I want to.' He brushed his thumb over her lips once more before gently easing himself away. Where he found the strength, he had no idea but now, when she'd been upset, when she was tired, when both of them had no real answers to their present dilemma, he also knew he couldn't take advantage of her. She was too special, too precious. She wasn't just *some woman*. She was an *important* woman in his life. That was the realisation he'd reached tonight and as such she deserved far more than he could presently give.

'But we both need to get some sleep.' He stood with his back to her as he collected himself, slowly exhaling before walking around the bed. 'Rest.' He reached out and brushed some hair from her forehead. 'More meetings in the morning.'

'Yes.' Janessa captured his hand in hers and sat up, kissing his knuckles. 'Thank you, Miles.'

'For?'

'For being a gentleman. For listening. For comforting.'

Miles's heart was throbbing in his chest and he clenched his jaw for another long moment, wanting her so badly but knowing it wasn't right…not yet. He gave her a crooked smile and pushed his free hand through his hair. 'Glad I could help.' He stood there for a moment, just looking at her, feeling his superhuman strength start to drain. 'Good heavens, you're beautiful,' he ground out, and then, before he succumbed, he let go of her hand and headed towards the front door.

'Miles?' Janessa was on her feet and heading after him as quickly as she could. He stopped by her open front door and spun around eagerly to face her. 'What does this mean? About us? *Is* there an us?'

He could hear, could see all her vulnerabilities. She was being open with him, allowing him to see the real Janessa, and she couldn't have given him a stronger reason to give her the answer she deserved. 'Yes. Yes, honey. Whether we like it or not, there is an *us*.' He wasn't sure how she'd take that news. They'd both verbalised their feelings, their uncertainty, their hesitation in moving forward.

Janessa nodded slowly, then took him completely by surprise when she stepped forward and wrapped her arms about him. Her body, soft and glorious against his own. 'If there really is an "us", then there's also a "we", and I think *we* should at least kiss goodnight,' she murmured, and when his arms slid eagerly around her waist, she brought his head down so their lips could meet, both of them giving in to the powerful sensations that zinged between them.

She was perfect. So sweet, so supple, so sensual. She was sugar and spice and all things nice, and yet he wasn't sure whether standing here, holding her, kissing her was the right thing to do when his need for her continued to increase.

Groaning with regret, Miles eased back after a few minutes and set her at arm's length—her inside her door, he in the corridor outside.

'Now. Get some sleep. We'll...talk more later on today.'

Janessa sighed and smiled at him, her eyelids half-closed with relaxed sensuality. 'OK.' Still, she didn't move. She just stood leaning against the wall, looking at him with a little half-smile on her lips. It was very disconcerting and extremely distracting, especially when he was trying to do the right thing.

'Uh…how about we have breakfast together?'

She nodded. 'Sounds great.'

'I have fresh fruit and bagels.'

Her smile increased. 'I'll make fresh coffee. Your place or mine?' She giggled a little and it was all Miles could do not to gather her up and close her door with him firmly on the other side of it with her. He shoved his hands into his pockets and balled them into fists.

'Yours.'

'Set your alarm clock for the usual time. I've been relying on it to wake me up for the past few weeks. Tomorrow morning shouldn't be any different.' Her smile was now wide, sleepy and inviting. He clenched his jaw so tight, his head began to ache.

'Until then.' And before he could be affected by her any more, he reached forward and pulled her door closed, effectively shutting her in and himself out. Quickly, he opened his own door and went into his apartment, being mindful to be as quiet as possible as he walked straight to the bedroom and fell onto the bed, burying his face in the pillows.

Janessa was incredible, gorgeous and driving him to distraction. The last time he'd felt this way about a woman, the last time he'd allowed a woman to get this deep beneath his carefully groomed exterior, he'd married her. He and Wendy had enjoyed a few wonderful years together but then she'd been taken from him, leaving him all alone.

Now, out of the blue, he'd found Janessa. Funny, clever, evocative Janessa, and he knew he was in real danger of losing his heart.

CHAPTER TWELVE

THEY met for breakfast the next morning, enjoying coffee, bagels and fruit whilst deciding to spend as much time together as their schedules would allow.

Ever since the safe delivery of Ellie and Sarah into the world, the planning for their first operation of inserting the tissue expanders had accelerated. The different specialists Miles had requested to assist him with the surgery would be arriving in the next few weeks. However, the major surgical procedure, the actual separation, wouldn't take place until Miles deemed the girls healthy enough to endure an intense anaesthetic.

Until then, there were still several planning sessions and extra scans to be completed. The planning for a surgical procedure for separating conjoined twins was extensive. Of course, this extra workload also meant that any free time Janessa and Miles might previously have enjoyed was sucked away by meetings and paperwork.

They also had to juggle the press, to ensure that no one from the media could sneak into the NICU to take photographs of the twins. Charisma, the hospital CEO, was controlling this as best she could, but it meant that Sheena and the girls were often hidden away in a corner of the NICU where even the other young mothers weren't able to pry.

Official photographs had been taken of mother and daughters and Sheena had given a few interviews earlier on, and once that was out of the way they were able to focus completely on maintaining the health of the twins.

Throughout it all, Janessa and Miles tried to eat at least one meal together every day, and as they didn't keep conventional hours, sometimes they found themselves sitting in the hospital cafeteria at three o'clock in the morning, quite content to talk and share with each other.

The fact that Miles knew of her past, knew of her heartbreak and the inner turmoil she'd experienced only made it easier for her to talk to him. He understood. He'd been in a similar position and by the same token she found herself wanting to know about his life, wanting to know where he went to medical school, how often he saw his parents and siblings.

Sometimes he looked as though he was about to clam up, to not give a straight answer to what she wanted to know, but every time he would take a breath and talk. He was so generous and it also showed Janessa that he really was invested in the 'us' that existed between them.

Still, they continued to take things one step at a time. They enjoyed spending time with each other and they enjoyed working together. The more they talked, the more they understood that this attraction, which seemed to have existed between them almost from the instant they'd met, was only intensifying with each passing moment.

Still, she knew their time together was limited. Miles was a man of great skill and importance in the world of conjoined twins. His expertise would always be in demand and she had no idea where or how she would fit into any plans he might make. It was the only thing that worried her but she tried her best not to show it, putting on a brave face, being happy whenever they were together yet always waiting for that axe to fall.

'This is my favourite and worst part of the day,' Miles said one evening as he stood at Janessa's apartment door, drawing her into his arms.

'Well, that's not at all ambiguous,' she drawled.

'It's my favourite because I get to kiss you, but the worst because we must part.'

'You're so poetic,' she remarked as she brushed her fingers lovingly through his hair, pulling out a piece of confetti. 'Can you believe the girls are already one month old?'

'The time does seem to be flying by at the rate of knots.'

'It was so sweet of you to organise that little party for Sheena in my office.'

'Sweet?' He quirked an eyebrow at the adjective.

'Thoughtful?'

He raised the other brow.

'Masterful?' she tried, but only caused his expression to turn more quizzical. 'Stroke of genius?'

'Ah, that's better. Genius. I like the sound of that one.'

Janessa laughed, unable to believe she could be this happy as he brought her closer and captured her lips with his. She gasped a little, just as she did every time when that first electrifying contact was made. Then she would sigh and lean into him, loving the slow and perfect movement of his mouth on hers.

Miles listened to her, supported her, argued with her—when it was warranted—and held her so securely in his arms whenever he said goodnight. They were a couple and they didn't hide it. Everyone knew, and was very pleased, about this latest development between the two neonatologists.

'It's about time,' Sheena had said, happy for both her friends. 'I could tell the instant I saw the two of you together that you were meant for each other.' She'd clapped her hands. 'So? What happens next? Will you be staying in Adelaide, Miles?'

'Um…' Miles had looked at Janessa, at the woman who had the ability to fill him with the strongest sense of belonging. 'Charisma has approached me about extending my contract here at Adelaide Mercy.'

'Wow.' Sheena had been surprised. 'Charisma will no doubt do everything she can to secure your services.'

Miles had smiled and it had been then Janessa had noted that the smile hadn't reached his eyes. Was he possibly considering staying here at Adelaide Mercy? To be with her? She couldn't help but think that he'd miss the travel, miss the excitement of helping other sets of conjoined twins. He had so much expertise and knowledge it almost seemed a waste of talent to hold him to just one place.

Even now, as he held her in his arms, as he kissed her so completely, so passionately, she couldn't help but wonder if he would stay because it was what he wanted to do, or if he was considering staying because this was where she was?

'Well, my genius,' she murmured as she closed her eyes and rested her head on his chest, not bothering to hide the fact that his kisses had made her breathless. 'I was looking in my diary and noticed that on Friday afternoon both of us have a block of two whole hours where there are no meetings, no scans, no ward rounds, no anything.'

Miles frowned but there was a twinkle in his eyes as he eased her back a little to look into her glorious face. 'Really? Can that be possible? You don't actually mean we might have some…leisure time?'

Janessa laughed. 'It does look that way.'

'Hmm.' He smiled. 'What did you have in mind and does it involve your car?'

'Well, well, well. A genius and a mind-reader.'

'Airfield?'

'Airfield,' she agreed. 'You can drive the car and I'll fly the plane.'

'Sounds like a plan.'

'A plan for five days in advance.' Janessa grimaced. 'Here's hoping that nothing—'

Miles pressed a kiss to her lips, effectively cutting off her words. 'Don't even say it. Let's just hold on to the dream of Friday.' He kissed her again, then put her from him. 'Sleep sweet, my Nessa.'

'See you in the morning,' she replied as she reluctantly eased from his arms. Leaning against the door after she'd closed it, she hugged her arms close, feeling bereft of his touch. She loved him so much and she wondered if she had the strength to give him up.

A fax had been sent through to the NICU for Dr Trevellion and it had arrived on her desk along with all the other faxes for the NICU. The letter had been from a hospital in the UK, requesting his valued expertise with the case of another set of conjoined twins that were due to be born around Christmas.

When she'd read the letter—purely by accident at first— her throat had gone dry and her stomach had churned, making her feel instantly ill at the thought of Miles leaving. He hadn't said a word to her about the offer and she wondered whether he was going to accept.

How could he not? He was a man with such an incredible skill and thanks to him and a team of highly skilled professionals, he was able to provide a healthy and separate existence for babies who were born conjoined. How could she possibly ask him to stay? To turn down the job in order to be with her?

How was she going to face not seeing him? Not holding

him? Not being with him? Not kissing him? He was her joy, her elation, her happiness. It had taken her so long to find him and now...now that she had...she was supposed to let him go? It wasn't fair!

Hearing him shuffling around next door, she put her hand up to the wall, knowing she would do her best to be happy, to enjoy the time they had left together. She desperately wanted—no, *needed*—to be close to him. Her Miles. Her life. Her love.

Miles pressed his hand to the wall, desperately wanting to be with Janessa. So many times during the past few weeks he'd wanted to pick up a sledgehammer and smash a hole in the wall that separated them. He wanted to be with Janessa, not just for now but for ever.

The knowledge had stunned him and it was then he'd finally admitted that his feelings for Janessa were those of love. He loved her. He'd fallen in love again and that in itself was a miracle. For far too many years his life had been lonely and empty and he'd worked hard to fill it and be satisfied within his professional life at least. Everyone in the neonate world knew of Miles Trevellion but Janessa was the only one who *knew* him.

The discussions they'd had, not only about the twins but about the advances in medical technology, the memories they'd shared of their past, of their babies whose lives had been cut so short and the painful hurt that had followed, bonded them closer. He recalled the quiet, reflective moments when they'd been flying in her Tiger Moth, looking at the calm scenery below, relaxing in each other's company.

All of these moments, such as holding her close, offering comfort when they'd been unable to save little Philip or after their first meal together when she'd turned her head and his lips had been pressed to hers in a glorious tantalising accident…they were all perfect and wonderful and he wanted so desperately to stay, to be with Janessa, to make more memories, to move forward with his life rather than going around in circles.

Earlier that day, he'd received a phone call from the hospital in the UK, the same hospital that had faxed over an invitation for him to lead a team of neonatologists in separating the next case of conjoined twins, which had only just been diagnosed. The hospital director had been insistent for Miles to accept as soon as possible. The sooner planning could start, the better—but for the first time in seven years he'd hesitated, and he'd hesitated because of Janessa.

For the first time he had been unsure of what to do, of what was best—not for his patients—but for *him*. Spending time with Janessa, holding her, being with her, kissing her… If he left, if he accepted the job offer, he wouldn't be able to do any of those things.

She'd once asked him what he was running away from, why he travelled so much. At the time he'd been unwilling to give her an in-depth answer but now that he'd had some time to really think about it, he realised he hadn't been running away from anything but rather running towards her. He hadn't known it at the time, of course. Travelling and being busy had most certainly helped his mental thought processes to deal with the loss of his wife and child, but after seven years he was ready to start living again and he wanted to do that living with Janessa.

On Friday, Janessa tiptoed her way gingerly through the morning, almost waiting for something to go wrong, for the block of time she and Miles had set aside to be eaten up with something else—but it wasn't.

'Go and enjoy,' Sheena said as she finished expressing some breast milk. Both of the girls were starting to put on weight and soon the first of their many surgeries would begin. 'We're all doing just fine here. It's time you and Miles spent some time away from the hospital.'

'Yes.' Janessa frowned.

'Something wrong?' Sheena asked as she buttoned up her shirt.

'Nothing. Everything.'

'Oh. Is that all? Come on. This is me, Nessa. Don't you think that I can't see straight through you?'

'I love him, Sheenie.' The words came out on a sigh, a sad sigh, filled with resignation.

'You don't sound too happy about it.'

'We can never be together.' She spoke as though there was no hope for tomorrow. To even contemplate a life without Miles made her heart constrict with pain, it made her stomach twist into knots and it made her want to sit all day and do nothing. Without Miles, she felt her life would lose all meaning.

'What?' Sheena sat up straight and glared at her friend. 'Why ever not?'

'He's been offered another job.'

'Great. He's a man of talent and skill. It's not an uncommon occurrence. What's the problem?'

'What's the problem?' Janessa sprang to her feet, needing to pace, but there was no room—the small NICU cubicle had no room. 'The problem is that I want him to stay here in Adelaide, with *me*. I can't let him do that.'

'Why not?'

'Because there are other little babies out there who need his expertise. He's so brilliant and incredible at what he does that I can't let him stop doing it just because I want him to be with me. That's a little selfish, don't you think?'

'So…go with him.'

Janessa paused. 'What?'

'Go with him.'

'But…uh…what about you? The girls? My friends? My job? My house has almost finished being built. What about that?'

'Oh, nonsense. All of that is irrelevant. Now that you've met Miles and fallen in love with him, *he* should be your first priority. Not me.'

'But, Sheena, I promised I would always be here to help you.'

'And you will. It doesn't mean that you can't do something else for a while. Why not go with Miles? Help out as part of his team of experts. You're more than qualified and now, because of Ellie and Sarah, you'll have had experience in this elite field.' Sheena laughed. 'Nessa, the girls are going to be spending the rest of this year, at least, in this hospital. They're going to be well cared for and we both know I'll be fine. First I was their incubator. Now I'm their snack machine.' Sheena rolled her eyes and laughed at herself before standing and crossing to Janessa's side.

'If you love Miles—*really* love him, Ness—then you do what you need to do to be happy. Don't you go thinking about me or the girls or the hospital or your house. None of us are going anywhere and we'll always be here for you, just as we know you'll always be there for us.'

Janessa listened to what her friend was saying and sighed. 'OK. Let's say, for a start that Miles does want me to go with him to the UK, to be a part of his team. What happens when *that* case is finished and he gets offered *another* case? You forget. I've been following this man's career for years. I've read the articles he writes for the leading neonate journals, I know he likes to move around. It's who he is. It's what he does.'

'It's what he *did*.' Sheena's smile broadened. 'I've seen the way you look at him and I've seen the way he looks at you, and I have to say that both of my friends have been bitten by the same bug. The love bug.' She wiggled her fingers at Janessa as she said the words but Janessa just couldn't smile at the action, her insides churning with confusion and indecision. Sheena instantly sobered and gave her friend a hug.

'This isn't a bad thing, Ness. It's a good thing. You've fallen in love. For real this time. You're not an impulsive teenager any more. This is real and good and right and everything else that's wonderful.'

Janessa stood there and processed Sheena's words, realising that true happiness might well be within her grasp. That if what Sheena said was true, if Miles cared for her as much as she cared for him, there might be the slightest hope that they could work things out.

'I have to go find him.'

'Atta-girl,' Sheena said with a wide grin on her face. She watched her friend blow a kiss to the sleeping twins and race out of the NICU.

Janessa had arranged to meet Miles at her car, and after quickly changing she headed to the old shed behind the residential wing. He'd already opened the double doors in order to drive the car out and for a moment she couldn't see him.

She paused, her gaze searching frantically for him. Was he here? He had to be here. They were supposed to meet here. And then she caught sight of him, bent down low next to the car, rag in hand, giving the paintwork a polish. Her heart turned over with love for him.

She stood there, watching the way his muscles flexed beneath his shirt, the way his legs were powerful and strong, the way he cared for her car in exactly the same way as her father had. He was a kind, caring and considerate man and she was instantly struck with overwhelming regret that her father had never been able to meet this most extraordinary man.

'Hey,' he said when he looked up and saw her. 'Just giving her the once-over. Almost ready to go.' When Janessa didn't move, Miles stopped what he was doing and tossed the rag back onto the work bench. 'Is everything all right? The twins? Sheena?'

'They're fine. Everything's fine. We're good to go. But… do you mind if we take a slight detour first? It's not far. About two blocks from here.'

'OK. Sure.' He opened the passenger door for her, pressing a quick kiss to her lips before hurrying around to slide behind the wheel. They both put on their seat belts and Miles turned the key in the ignition, the engine purring instantly to life. 'Oh, yeah. This car is the best.'

Janessa just smiled as she gave him directions. Soon they pulled up outside a house that was almost finished being built. There were a few workmen around, banging and hammering, but apart from the unfinished landscaping, the house looked almost complete. They climbed from the car and then leaned against it.

'This is my house,' she said to Miles. 'My new house,' she clarified. 'The other one burnt down.'

He nodded. 'I remember Sheena saying something about that on the day we met.'

Janessa sighed, allowing him to pull her into his arms, snuggling in as close as possible. 'It seems so long ago. That first day.'

'A lot has happened,' he agreed, thinking of the way he loved her so completely.

'Yes.' They stood there for a few minutes, just watching, both of them lost in their thoughts. Finally, it was Miles who broke the silence.

'Is this where you think we should live?'

'Well…' She looked up at him and eased away. 'Yes and no.'

'Great. Not ambiguous at all.' He took her hands in his and studied her closely. She linked her fingers with his and squeezed their hands, wanting to bind them together for ever.

'Miles…these past few weeks that we've been together have been the happiest of my life for many, *many* years. Even before that, from the moment you walked into my NICU, being bossy and demanding and jet-lagged…telling me I looked too young to run a NICU—'

'Young and beautiful and way too tempting for a man who was completely exhausted,' he interjected.

'Well, yes.' She smiled at his words, feeling her cheeks get a little hot. He chuckled at her embarrassment and brushed a kiss across her lips. 'Miles, what I'm trying to say, very badly, is that…' She paused and took a deep breath. 'I don't think you should stay.'

'What? At the residential wing any more? Do you think we should move in here, to the house?'

'No. That's not what I meant.' She took another deep breath. 'What I mean is…I know about the job,' she confessed. 'The fax you received was mixed up with my faxes, and I'm afraid I was halfway through reading it before I realised it wasn't for me. I'm sorry. I should have said something earlier.'

'The job in the UK?'

'Yes.'

'I wasn't going to mention it.'

'Why not?'

'Because I'm not going.'

'But you *have* to. Those babies *need* you.'

'You want me to go? To leave Adelaide?' He swallowed over the sudden dryness in his throat. Didn't she want him? He was positive that she loved him, even though she hadn't said the words…yet. Was that why she'd brought him to her house? To show him that she would be fine, living here, without him?

'Miles, you are so incredibly talented and there are babies in the world who need you.'

'More than you?' The words were asked quietly, softly but earnestly.

Janessa slowly shook her head, her eyes intent. 'No, but I can't be selfish. I can't keep you all for myself. It's your own fault for being so terrific.'

'I see.' He thought for a moment. 'So you're saying I should take the job in the UK? That I should go and help those little babies?'

'Yes.'

'Because you can't be selfish?'

'No.'

'Because you love me?'

'Yes.' She gasped, only realising belatedly what she'd said. She met his gaze and found his eyes twinkling with delight.

'Well…if that's the case, then I'll definitely have to accept that job and I'll also let the hospital know that I'll be bringing you along with me.'

'Really? You want me to go with you?'

He stared at her, an incredulous look on his face. 'Why would you think I'd go *anywhere* without you?' he asked, and it was only then that she heard the tenderness in his tone. 'I need you, Janessa.'

'What?'

'I need you,' he repeated, and tugged her back into his arms. 'It doesn't matter whether I'm working at Adelaide Mercy or in the UK or in Timbuktu! If I'm with you, I'll be happy. I had planned to talk to you about all of this at the airfield. I even thought of having someone sky-write a note asking you to marry me. But when I called Myrna and enquired about sky-writing, she said you were the pilot who usually did that.'

'Ma-ma-marry?' Janessa was stuck on the one word.

'Janessa, honey. I love you.' His words were plain, simple, straightforward. Good, old-fashioned honesty. That was what she was getting, and a slow smile crept onto her lips.

'You love me?'

'Are you going to keep asking questions or are you going to answer some?'

'Uh…sorry.' She gave her head a little shake, needing to clear it in order to take in everything he was saying. Miles loved her! He wanted to marry her! 'Of course I'll answer questions. What questions would you like me to answer?'

'Do you really love me?'

'Oh, Miles. Yes. Yes, I do. I have for quite some time now, although I couldn't admit it to myself. I was too scared to say anything in case you didn't feel the sa—'

Miles silenced her the best, most enjoyable way he knew how. Janessa instantly gave herself up to his kisses, leaning into him and wrapping her arms tightly about him. 'Nessa,' he groaned when they finally broke apart. 'You will marry me, won't you?'

'Yes. How could you doubt that?'

He kissed her again and once more received no complaints. 'And you will come to the UK with me?'

'I'd follow you to the ends of the earth. I don't mind if we travel because home is where the heart is…and my heart belongs to you.' She kissed him.

'And I don't mind,' he said, 'if we stay put for a while. It's been a very long time since I've put down roots and, thanks to you, I'm ready to start again.' He indicated the house in front of them. 'A new home for a new beginning.'

'Yes. Although I don't think Charisma will be too happy at the cha—'

Miles kissed her, cutting her words off once more.

'Are you just trying to cut me off so you can—?'

Another kiss.

'Miles!'

Another kiss before he laughed. 'I'll take any excuse I can to kiss my fiancée,' he remarked.

'Fiancée?' Janessa blinked slowly at the realisation.

'You *did* just agree to marry me, didn't you?'

'Yes. Yes, I did.'

'Excellent news.' He paused. 'You do realise I'm not just asking you to join me overseas because I love you.'

She raised her eyebrows. 'There are more reasons?'

'Yes. You're a highly skilled neonatologist and I'd be insane to pass up this opportunity to ask you to join the team. I know,' he continued quickly, 'that it will mean applying for leave from Adelaide Mercy and leaving the family you've gathered around you, but we'll return. We'll be back. After we've finished in the UK, we can return to Adelaide.'

'What if another case of conjoined twins comes up? Miles, I don't want to hold you back. You're incredible with the way you work, the way you care, your expertise.'

'We can assess things on a case by case basis together…
at least until we're ready to have children of our own.' The
words were said quietly…more quietly than anything else
he'd said.

'You want children?'

'Don't you?'

'Yes. Yes, I do. I want to have children with you, Miles.'
Her tone was quiet but he could hear the veiled fear behind
her words.

'We'll make sure everything goes smoothly. We have the
best resources, the best teams right here at Adelaide Mercy,'
he encouraged. 'The point is that whatever we face, we'll
face it together.'

She nodded in agreement, feeling his strength and cer-
tainty flow through her. No longer would they be alone.
Together they would make a new family, a second chance
at love and life. With Miles by her side, Janessa knew there
wasn't anything she couldn't face, and she smiled up at the
man of her dreams—her fiancé.

'Together,' she agreed, and knew that all her dreams
really would come true.

* * * * *

SPECIAL CARE
BABY MIRACLE

BY
LUCY CLARK

MILLS
BOON

First published in Great Britain 2011
by Mills & Boon, an imprint of Harlequin (UK) Limited,
Eton House, 18-24 Paradise Road, Richmond, Surrey TW9 1SR

© Anne and Peter Clark 2011

ISBN: 978 0 263 88601 6

Harlequin (UK) policy is to use papers that are natural, renewable and recyclable products and made from wood grown in sustainable forests. The logging and manufacturing process conform to the legal environmental regulations of the country of origin.

Printed and bound in Spain
by Blackprint CPI, Barcelona

Will turned to face her. 'You won't be alone, Sheena.'

It wasn't until he urged her closer that she realised she'd spoken her concern out loud. Will leaned towards her, capturing her lips with his. Sheena's eyelids fluttered closed as she sighed into the kiss, drawing hope and strength and a yearning desire to always have this man in her life, to have him beside her, as the father of her children as they lived together for the rest of their lives. Was it possible to believe in such a fairytale? Throughout her entire life she'd wanted the fairytale, the happily-ever-after ending.

Now here she was, outside the home of Will's parents, with Will close to her, kissing her, making her feel cherished, wanted, needed, loved. She kissed him back with all the love in her heart, wanting him to know that she'd never stopped loving him, that hurting him all those years had been the worst moment in her life and that she really wanted nothing else than for the two of them to make a 'proper' family with her girls. It was the fairytale...but she knew of old that fairytales never came true.

Lucy Clark is actually a husband-and-wife writing team. They enjoy taking holidays with their children, during which they discuss and develop new ideas for their books using the fantastic Australian scenery. They use their daily walks to talk over characterisation and fine details of the wonderful stories they produce, and are avid movie buffs. They live on the edge of a popular wine district in South Australia with their two children, and enjoy spending family time together at weekends.

Recent titles by the same author:

DOCTOR DIAMOND IN THE ROUGH
THE DOCTOR'S SOCIETY SWEETHEART
THE DOCTOR'S DOUBLE TROUBLE

For Sheena and Will—never 'dare' a writer!
You two are awesome.
Pr 23:4–5

CHAPTER ONE

THE string quartet began to play and Sheena finished fussing with her friend Janessa's bridal veil. Sheena, Kaycee and Janessa were all in a small side room next to a large aeroplane hangar.

'Only *you* would get married in an aeroplane hangar.' Kaycee, one of the nurses Sheena and Janessa had worked with for years, couldn't help but smile.

Sheena laughed, knowing it wasn't the first time Janessa had heard such a comment.

'Well…I *am* a pilot as well as a doctor. Besides, this airfield was part of my childhood. My dad loved to fly and my mum loved to watch him. Now that they're both gone, I guess I feel closest to my parents when I'm here,' Janessa replied with a nostalgic sigh.

'There.' Sheena stepped back and surveyed her closest friend. The two women were as close as sisters and today she was so proud of Janessa. 'You look radiant.' Sheena so desperately wanted everything to go perfectly. Happiness had been a long time coming for Nessa, but since she'd met Miles Trevellion just over three months ago her life had changed for the better.

Sheena tried not to sigh at the romance that had blossomed between her two friends, wishing it was her instead.

She'd given up her one chance at *true* love ten years ago and it was a mistake she'd have to live with for the rest of her life.

'Thanks for everything,' Janessa said, her words filled with meaning. 'You're the best sister a girl ever had.'

Sheena felt tears start to well in her eyes and quickly blinked them away. 'I'd do anything for you,' she replied, hugging Janessa carefully, emotion rising within her.

'All right, you two,' Kaycee said. 'No tears or we'll be another fifteen minutes fixing our make-up and I doubt Miles will be able to contain his impatience.'

'True. True,' Sheena remarked as Kaycee handed her a bouquet of white roses. The two bridesmaids wore long, ruby-red dresses with sexy slits up the sides. Janessa accepted her bridal bouquet of ruby-red roses and held them in front of her with slightly trembling hands.

'Stunning.' Sheena nodded in approval before the photographer came in to take one last photograph of the three women together.

'Time to head down the aisle,' Kaycee said, and, squaring her shoulders, walked out of the little room, leaving Janessa and Sheena together for a brief moment, the music from the quartet surrounding them.

'I'm so happy for you, Nessa. Really. No one deserves this more than you.'

Janessa blew Sheena a kiss.

'Ready?' Sheena stepped out the door, ensuring the train of Janessa's dress didn't get tangled. They walked on the red carpet laid out in the hangar, which had been decorated with a mixture of roses and wild flowers. Garlands hung around the hangar and also on Janessa's beloved Tiger Moth biplane, which was just outside the door.

Everyone stood as Kaycee started to walk down the aisle, between the rows of chairs which had been set out for the guests. Sheena smiled once more at her friend then turned to look towards the groom standing at the other end of the aisle.

Miles was waiting impatiently for his bride. Beside Miles stood his father, acting as best man as Miles's first choice for best man—Will Beckman—was still in America and had been unable to make it back for the wedding.

Sheena was relieved at that. She and Will had history and a shared romantic past that hadn't ended happily. Sheena turned back and gave Janessa one more smile before holding her bouquet in front of her, shoulders back, head held high. Time to walk slowly but surely down the aisle. She lifted her foot, took one step, glanced up to where Miles was waiting… and faltered.

Will!

He was standing there. Between Miles and his father. Will was here. *Will was here!*

She blinked her eyes once…twice…as though trying to clear her vision, trying to tell herself that she'd imagined him standing there, looking so devastatingly handsome in a tuxedo, a red boutonniere pinned to his lapel, his hair slightly ruffled by the cool July breeze outside.

She blinked again. It was definitely him. Will was now standing beside Miles, the two men sharing a quick but firm handshake and pat on the back. He'd made it just in time for his best friend's wedding.

Sheena's mouth went instantly dry, her heart starting to pound wildly in her chest, the noise thrumming through her body, almost deafening her. She gripped her bouquet tighter, channelling all the panic and fear, which seemed to have hit her like a tidal wave, into the stems of the flowers.

How could he be here? Miles had told her only yesterday that Will was unable to make the wedding because he'd been delayed by a sick patient. Until then, Sheena had been psyching herself up to see Will again. She'd gone over polite little sentences in her head in order to make small talk with him. She'd pondered whether he'd changed much during the past decade. She'd stressed over his reception of her—would it be friendly or antagonistic? She'd lost sleep over the prospect of seeing him again so when Miles had told her Will wouldn't be able to make it, she had been intensely relieved.

And now he was here! He'd made it. She had no idea how or why but... She blinked again, clearing her vision, registering the scene before her. Nervous anxiety exploded within every cell of her body, her stomach flipping and turning. She gripped the flowers even tighter, trying in vain to steel herself. She would have to speak to him now, smile politely, be cool and calm, yet she felt anything but. It was necessary to have contact with him, given that he was the best man and she was the maid of honour, but for all the different scenarios she'd worked through in her mind, she now found she couldn't remember a thing.

Will was here. At the end of the aisle. Standing next to Miles, his tuxedo making him appear crisp, debonair and excessively sexy. Her heart skipped a beat and she tried not to remember what it had been like to kiss him.

Will was in the same room as her—breathing the same air—for the first time in ten years. It couldn't be...but it was. He had come and now *she* had to face him.

Sheena swallowed convulsively, her gaze trained solely on the man who had once meant the world to her. Will Beckman. They'd been so in love...and then it had ended. *She* had ended it and Will had hated her for it.

'Sheena?' Janessa's concerned tone from behind snapped Sheena back to the present. 'Something wrong?'

Sheena turned and looked at Janessa. 'Will is *here*.'

'Oh, great.' Janessa beamed. 'He made it. Miles will be

so happy. Go. Go, Sheenie. That's your cue.' Janessa urged her friend forward and there was nothing else for Sheena to do except to turn, paste on a smile and walk down the aisle.

Because of the shock she'd just received, it was a wonder she could actually remember how to walk, let alone do it in time to the music. Will was here. The thought played over and over in her mind, as though stuck, and each step she took brought her closer towards him.

The aisle seemed to stretch on for ever and if she'd had half the chance, she would have turned tail and bolted as far away as possible... but she could never do that to Janessa. Sheena kept her eyes trained straight ahead, smile fixed firmly in place, one slow step at a time.

All too soon, she was standing opposite him, everyone turning to see the bride walk down the aisle—Sheena and Will on opposite sides of the makeshift altar. She knew she should be watching Janessa but she couldn't resist a quick glance his way...and was startled to find him looking at *her*.

Quickly averting her gaze, her heart started pounding even faster against her ribs and she glued her eyes to her friend, unable to believe he'd caught her sneaking a glance at him. She had no idea how her legs were still holding her up as her entire body was shaking with adrenaline at being so close to him. Good heavens, he was handsome but, then, he always had been. So handsome. So tall. So...Will.

Her breathing had now almost reached the point of hyperventilation. She parted her lips to allow the pent-up air to escape, wondering what sort of reception she would receive from him. She wouldn't blame him at all if he didn't speak a word to her but she hoped, more for Miles's and Janessa's sakes, that that wasn't the case.

Janessa finished her walk down the aisle and Sheena accepted the bridal bouquet, glad to have something to do. She watched as her two friends held hands—eager to be married, love, honour and devotion shining clearly from their faces.

Throughout the nuptials, Sheena risked quite a number of glances at Will, her mind still processing the fact that he was standing not six feet away from her. Was he still angry about the way things had ended between them? Had he managed to forgive her sometime during the past decade? Had he moved on with his life? Found someone to spend his time with? She quickly checked his hands but found them ringless. Still, that didn't mean he wasn't attached. It didn't matter to her whether or not he had someone—all she'd ever wanted for Will was his happiness.

'I now pronounce you husband and wife,' the minister announced, and Sheena jolted her thoughts back to the present, unable to believe the ceremony was done and dusted. Had she been in la-la land the whole time? 'You may now kiss your bride.'

Miles leaned forward and lifted the veil from Janessa's face before sliding his arms around his new wife's waist and drawing their bodies into close contact. Sheena couldn't help but smile at his antics, knowing Miles was determined to kiss his new wife thoroughly.

She was incredibly happy for both her friends and, with a bright smile still on her lips, she glanced over at Will, astonished to find him once more looking back at her. Sheena's heart skipped a beat and she couldn't help but gasp, her eyes widening in surprise. She knew she should probably look away, pay attention to her friends, but she couldn't. She was like a deer caught in the headlights, his blue eyes as rich and deep and compelling as they'd always been.

His gaze flicked from her eyes down to her lips before quickly scanning her body in a visual caress that filled her with heat and flooded her body with a longing she'd long since forgotten. Did he still like what he saw? She hoped she looked good, especially considering that three months ago she'd given birth to twin girls…and not just *any* twins but conjoined twins. Her figure, she knew, was more curvy than it had been ten years ago. Did he still find her attractive? And why did it matter so much to her?

Janessa once more brought Sheena's thoughts back to the present as she reached around for her bouquet. Sheena snapped her eyes away from the alluring Will Beckman and realised that she'd missed the inaugural kiss and that everyone in the hangar was now clapping and cheering the newlyweds.

The bride and groom started back down the aisle, stopping to receive warm wishes from their friends and family. Sheena stepped forward, as did Will. He was the best man. She was the maid of honour. Kaycee, the other bridesmaid, would be partnered by Miles's father, who was the other groomsman. Sheena took another step closer to Will and breathed in a strong, calming breath…or at least that was what she'd planned to do. Instead, she breathed in the earthy, fresh scent she'd always equated with him and tried not to sigh with longing.

With another step he stood beside her, crooking his elbow in her direction, ready to escort her down the aisle behind the happy couple.

'Hello, Dr Woodcombe.' His tone was brisk, crisp and efficient, as though he were simply saying good morning to a member of staff at a ward round. Sheena slipped her hand around his elbow, heat suffusing through her at the touch. She tried not to be concerned with his impersonal greeting. They had been a couple a long time ago but surely the fact that they *had* been together afforded her something more than a perfunctory greeting. She licked her dry lips, belatedly remembering she was wearing far more make-up than she was used to and it wouldn't do to have all her lipstick disappear before they started posing for photographs.

'Hello, Will.' She tried to ensure her own voice was without emotion. She tried to clear her throat but there was nothing there for her to clear. She continued to keep her pasted smile in place as guests snapped pictures of the wedding party. 'I see you managed to make it in time. Well done.'

He glanced briefly down at her as they took another few steps and stopped as both Janessa and Miles paused to hug and greet more well-wishers. 'No doubt you probably wished I hadn't made it at all.'

She was stunned that his comment was so spot on. 'What makes you say that?'

'I saw the look of shock on your face before you started to walk down the aisle.'

She closed her eyes for a brief moment. Oh. Had he? How embarrassing…how telling. His comment made her feel naked, stripped bare as though after all these years he was still able to see right through her, that he still had some sort of power over her. She hated feeling so exposed. 'Miles wanted you here. That's all that matters.'

They took another step forward, another camera flash lighting the air around them, both of them smiling politely.

'I understand congratulations are in order,' he said after a moment, his words clipped.

'For?'

'Did you not give birth to two little girls?'

'Oh. Yes.' At the mention of her daughters, Sheena's smile became natural, her eyes sparkling with happiness, yet at the same time she felt highly self-conscious discussing her daughters with Will. The main reason she'd turned down his proposal all those years ago had been because she'd been unable to have children, and now she had *two*.

'I'm sorry, Sheena,' her specialist had said when she'd been about eighteen years old. 'The chances of you ever having children are extremely slim. Your endometriosis is too severe.'

When Will had repeatedly talked of his plans for a large family and how much having children meant to him, she'd known she would never end up spending her life with him, even though back then she'd loved him dearly.

Now, though, she had Ellie and Sarah. Her babies, her girls, and they were her two incredible miracles she'd been assured by the finest specialists would never happen.

'How are they coping?' he continued when she didn't elaborate. 'Of course I've received status updates from Miles but it would be good to have the mother's opinion of the situation, especially as she's a trained paediatrician.'

'As a paediatrician, I have to say they're doing incredibly well. As a mother…' She paused for a moment and smiled. 'I have to say that they are the most beautiful, wonderful little girls on the face of this earth.'

Will clenched his jaw at her words, annoyed with himself for being affected by the sweet smile on her face. She hadn't changed much in the ten years since they'd parted. Her hair was shorter and she looked tired around the eyes, even beneath the make-up.

Sheena. A mother. The woman who had told him she couldn't marry him because she could never give him children. Well, she'd been able to give some other man children so perhaps there had been other reasons why she hadn't wanted to be with him but hadn't been courageous or honest enough to admit them. Never again would he allow himself to succumb to her. Once bitten, twice shy and all that. She'd had her chance and she'd rejected him. He'd moved on and he congratulated himself for being professional and polite towards Sheena.

They took another step down the aisle and stopped as more people greeted the bride and groom in front of them.

'Hang on, what did you think I was congratulating you for?' he asked a moment later.

'Uh…nothing.' She shook her head.

'You may as well tell me everything because we're going to be stuck halfway down this aisle for another few minutes. Besides, if you've achieved more milestones in your life, how am I to congratulate you if I don't know about them?' Although his words seemed polite, she could hear slight curiosity in his tone. Was he as curious about her as she was about him?

'It's no big deal.' She shrugged a shoulder. 'It's just I signed my divorce papers last week.' She went to take another step forward but found that Will had stopped. She looked up at him.

'You're not married?' There was a hint of incredulity in his tone.

'That's generally what the word *divorced* means, Will,' she countered.

'And you thought I was offering congratulations on that?'

'You did mention that Miles had been giving you updates.'

'On the *girls*, not your private life.'

Sheena shrugged, knowing that even if Miles had let something slip about Sheena's present life, it would never have been done with malicious intent. Janessa and Miles both wanted Sheena to be happy with someone new, but she was the mother of twins and her girls had to be her main focus from now on. The chances of she and Will reuniting as a couple wasn't on the cards either. A decade was a long time and both of them had clearly changed.

'In a way, my divorce is sort of worth celebrating.'

'How so?'

'I'm ending a part of my life which, ever since I was told I was pregnant, has given me nothing but grief. Now, at least, I can focus solely on the girls.' There was complete commitment and determination in her tone. 'I'm going to be the best mother I can possibly be.'

'You always were full of determination.' Will glanced down at her and she was surprised to see a small half-smile teasing his mouth. 'Some might say stubborn—'

'Hey!' she interrupted, but found her own lips twitching into a smile.

'But we'll stick with determined for now.'

'Thank you.' Sheena was secretly pleased that after a few minutes in each other's company, Will had felt comfortable enough to tease her a little. Was it possible they could form a relationship that was more than just professional? A loose friendship perhaps?

Even when they'd been dating, they'd always been good friends and right now, given that she wasn't looking for any sort of permanent relationship with any man, she needed as many friends as she could get.

Of course, there was no doubting Will's appeal. The man was still the most handsome man she'd ever seen and with the way she was still tingling with excitement at being so close to him, it was clear he still maintained that unassuming sensuality she'd first been attracted to all those years ago.

They managed to take another few steps down the aisle, drawing closer to the end. The heat from his body, the scent of whatever aftershave he was wearing, so earthy, so spicy, settled around her, enticing her to remember just how close they'd been in the past. Soon she would be able to let go of Will's arm and at least put a bit of breathing room between them before they had to pose for more photographs. When they finally reached the end of the aisle, Sheena quickly slipped her hand from his arm.

'Excuse me. I'll be right back,' she murmured, before slipping away from where the photographer and everyone else was busy snapping photographs of the bride and groom. She knew as maid of honour she should be there, that she should stay by Janessa's side, helping her with whatever she needed, but…well, Janessa had Miles now and Sheena needed some air.

Heading around the outside of the hangar, the heels of her shoes sinking into the grass, she walked to the small bathroom and ran her hands beneath the cool water for a moment. She wanted to splash water onto her face, to shock her thoughts back to reality, but she couldn't even do that because of the make-up she was wearing.

High heels, dresses, make-up, fancy hairstyles—they just weren't her, and right at that moment, even though she loved Janessa and Miles very dearly, all she wanted was to be back at the hospital with her little girls. Kissing them, talking to them, feeding them, loving them. She closed her eyes, missing them so badly it was starting to hurt.

Seeing Will again had rocked her neat and ordered little world from its axis. Her comfortable life had been turned upside down and inside out at the first sight of him.

The fact that he still looked incredible didn't help at all. Where she'd thought she'd be able to put what had happened between them into the past, to look forward to her new life with her girls—even though she knew the next nine months weren't going to be an easy road—her anxieties had hit the roof the instant she'd seen him standing at the other end of that aisle next to Miles.

Will Beckman. She closed her eyes, remembering how incredible it had felt being held by him, being close to him, laughing with him, kissing him. She sighed, breathing out her memories with soft longing. However, that was all in the past.

'Sheena?' Kaycee called. 'Are you in there, honey?' A second later, Kaycee walked into the small room. 'Oh, there you are. The photographer needs us.'

Sheena turned, putting on a smile for her friend, knowing she would not let Janessa down even though she felt like hiding in the bathroom for the rest of the day. 'Ready when you are.'

They headed back out to where Janessa and Miles were posing against *Ruby*, Janessa's beloved biplane that her father had lovingly restored and named after her mother.

'They look so happy,' she murmured.

'Yes. They do,' a deep voice replied from just behind her, and she turned, a little startled as she'd been expecting Kaycee to answer. 'Are you all right, Sheena?'

'I'm fine.' She swallowed over the obvious lie. Being near Will, standing close to him, talking to him, made her feel anything but fine. He was the reason she was in a dither but there was no way she was going to confess that to him.

Kaycee headed off to find Miles's father so that the entire bridal party could be reassembled for more photographs. Will leaned in closer, his breath fanning Sheena's neck as he spoke. 'Liar,' he whispered softly, before easing away.

'What do you know about it?' she asked as they both headed over to where Miles was helping Janessa up onto the wing of the plane, ensuring her wedding dress and veil didn't tear. The heels of Sheena's shoes once more sank into the grass as she walked and she realised she must look highly undignified…but at the moment she really didn't care.

Will stopped walking and looked at her. 'I know you, Sheena. I know you better than I know myself sometimes and I know when you're lying.'

She scoffed at that but knew he spoke the truth. He *did* know her, just as she knew him equally well. 'Fine. Then I'm not all right. OK?'

'Because of me?'

'Yes, because of you. I…hadn't expected to see you today. Janessa said last night that you weren't able to make it.'

'I was only able to make it because the patient I've been caring for stabilised early this morning, giving me a short window in which to fly from Melbourne to Adelaide and attend the ceremony. At this stage I'm not quite sure how long I'll be staying as we're due to be flying back to the States later this evening.'

'Transferring a patient from Melbourne to Philadelphia?' When Miles had told her Will wouldn't be able to make it because he was transferring a patient, Sheena had assumed Will was still in the States, not already here in Australia.

'Yes. Two-year-old boy with early signs of rheumatoid arthritis. Some vascular colleagues have developed a new way of assisting young children with this disease and have asked me to consult in an orthopaedic capacity, hence why I've flown to Australia to escort the patient and his family to the States.'

'That sounds like incredible research, Will.' She could talk about medicine with him, especially as it meant the conversation wasn't focused on her. 'You were always so good with sick children. You have a knack of making them feel relaxed and cared for.'

Will paused for a moment then cleared his throat. 'Thank

you, Sheena.' Her words had surprised him. He'd been prepared to see Sheena again, prepared to keep his distance,
to treat her merely as the mother of the conjoined twins he
would one day help separate. What he hadn't banked on were
the effects of her smiles and sincere words. He'd also expected her to be married and the news that she was recently
divorced had thrown him. He shook his head. It didn't matter
if she was single, it didn't matter if she looked as incredible
now as she had ten years ago. She was still the woman who
had turned down his marriage proposal and then years later
married another man and had had children—children she'd
told him she would *never* be able to conceive.

'You're a brilliant doctor, Will, and I know your work can
be rather intense,' Sheena continued. 'Being an orthopaedic
paediatrician who specialises primarily in neonatology car-
ries with it a heavy workload. Miles has often talked of the
work you've done together and now other specialities are
appreciating your gift.' She looked up at him. 'Does the work
you do make you happy?'

He frowned at the question, finding it a little odd. 'Of
course it does. I wouldn't do it if it didn't challenge me or
make me happy.'

'Good.' She nodded. 'I'd hate you to be hiding yourself
away in your work.'

'What's that supposed to mean? That because you turned
my marriage proposal down a decade ago, I'd be so lost without you I would throw myself into my work and forget about
living?'

Mortification crossed Sheena's face. 'No. I merely meant
that as a vibrant, handsome man it would be a great shame if
you focused solely on work.' He continued to glare at her and
she started to feel a little uncomfortable. 'Despite what you

might think, Will, I've only ever wanted you to be happy, to be able to fulfil your dreams.'

He caught a glimpse of Kaycee, the other bridesmaid, heading in their direction, with Miles's father in tow.

Will eased a little closer to Sheena, his voice low, his eyes sharp and piercing. Sheena tried not to gasp at the darkness around him. 'Are you saying that you turned my proposal down because you didn't want to destroy my dreams?'

She'd never seen him look like that before—ever. This was a new expression, a different side to Will, and in that one moment she realised that perhaps she didn't know him as well as she'd previously thought.

'Yes.' The word was barely a whisper and she tried to step back, to put a bit of distance between them, but the heels of her shoes had sunk into the grass.

'And what about the other man you married?' Will continued. 'Did you care about his dreams?'

Sheena winced a little at Will's words. Did he think her devoid of all emotion? Pain pierced her heart to think he thought ill of her. 'Of course I did.' She frowned as she answered, conscious of keeping her voice down so they didn't disturb Janessa and Miles. She was aware that at any moment they'd be called on to stand side by side and smile brightly for the camera but first there was something she needed to say.

'You know nothing about my life, Will. A lot can happen to a person in ten years and that's exactly what has happened to me—a lot. My relationship with Jonas is none of your business, just as your own relationships over the past decade have nothing to do with me. We were a couple. We broke up. We moved on.'

'Agreed, but—' he leaned even closer, his blue eyes flashing with dangerous excitement '—aren't you the least bit curious?' His gaze dipped to encompass her parted lips, unable to believe the way he'd felt watching her eyes light up with emotion. He'd always been attracted to her, even more so when she'd been angry. He breathed in, tantalised by the strawberry scent he'd always equated with her. He looked at her eyes again, admiring the way they'd widened in surprise at his nearness.

It was clear he could still affect her and he tried not to preen a little at that realisation. 'Curious about me?' His tone was deep, rich, sensual, yet with a hint of menace, drawing her in, hypnotising her. 'I'm definitely curious about you. I want to know what you've been doing. Why you finally married and had children, especially when you told me you couldn't.'

Her gaze was fixed on his mouth, her heart pounding as she watched his lips form the words. 'I find myself wanting answers to the questions that have been buried in the back of my mind for so very long…and given I'll soon be in Australia, caring for your daughters, seeing you every day, I intend to get them.'

CHAPTER TWO

SHEENA paced back and forth in front of the crib that held her two very special little girls. Her agitation level was high, her anxiety was through the roof, and for some reason she seemed unable to stop wringing her hands.

Ellie and Sarah, her two beautiful babies, were sleeping peacefully in their specially designed crib, the girls conjoined at the hip. Sarah had her thumb in her mouth and Ellie sucked on a pacifier. They may be conjoined but the six-month-old twins most certainly had their different personalities. Sarah, so gung-ho, letting everyone know she was around, whilst Ellie was placid and patient.

The pacing, however, didn't cease. Back and forth Sheena went. Wringing her hands, heart pounding wildly. The girls had been moved one month ago from the neonate intensive care unit to a private room in the paediatric wing. They were still garnering a lot of media attention, especially with the date of their impending separation drawing closer every day.

'You can do this. You can do this,' Sheena said over and over, wiping her hands down her pale pink skirt. She fidgeted with her cream-coloured shirt and checked her short black hair in the mirror, her blue eyes wide with fear. Anyone watching her might think she was nervous and apprehensive because in a few days' time her daughters would be undergoing one of the biggest and intricate surgical procedures of the medical profession…but that wasn't the case.

'You can do this. You can do this,' she repeated, giving her hands a shake before starting to wring them once more.

Her girls had already had several smaller operations to insert tissue expanders, helping them to grow extra skin so that when the separation was complete, there would be skin to cover the open wounds around their hips. They'd also had many anaesthetics, especially when having CT scans. This was so the neonate team could quite clearly see what veins and arteries the two girls shared. As a paediatrician herself, Sheena was well aware of all the negatives and positives surrounding these procedures and whilst she'd been anxious and concerned for her girls each and every time they were wheeled away, it was nothing compared to the complete and encompassing agitation she was feeling now and it was all because of Will.

Seeing him at the wedding had been nerve-racking enough, without him saying that he was curious about her. When he'd leaned forward, looked at her so intently with those big blue eyes of his and a look that could still weaken her knees, she'd known she was in trouble. She knew she'd hurt Will all those years ago when she'd rejected his proposal, but she'd had to. Loving him the way she had, she'd chosen to make the sacrifice of breaking it off while there had still been a chance for both of them to find some sort of happiness with someone else.

He had desperately wanted children. She hadn't been able to give them to him. In her mind, it had been as clear as that. She'd rather he hated her for rejecting his proposal, for breaking their relationship, than agreeing to marry him and then having him reject her when he discovered he could never have that family he'd always dreamed about.

Hearing him say he was curious about her, about the decisions she'd made in her life since they'd parted, had caused a mass of tingles to wash over her in anxious anticipation. He'd been so close, his breath fanning her cheek, his lips moving almost in slow motion as his rich, earthy scent, tinged with hypnotic spices, had wound its way around her, causing her to almost hyperventilate.

A second later, Kaycee had marshalled them all into position for the next group photograph, Sheena powerfully aware of every slight move Will had made. When the photographer had asked Will to place his hand around Sheena's waist, her body had become a riot of suppressed excitement at being so close to Will once again. His hand hadn't been shy or tentative but instead he'd drawn her close, as though it had been the most natural thing in the world. As they'd smiled for the camera, she'd felt the heat radiating out from his body, felt his veiled determination in the quest he'd just started and could feel the high level of awareness they'd both felt at being so close to one another again.

When they'd shifted positions, this time standing behind the bride and groom, almost facing each other, her hand on Will's shoulder, his hand resting in the small of her back, Sheena had found it not only mentally distracting to be so close to him but increasingly difficult to keep her smile in place as Will had been moving his thumb in slow, small circles, driving her to distraction.

'Stop,' she whispered between her polite smiles.

'Why? I know you like it.'

'Will!'

'I can't help it if I have intimate knowledge about you, Sheena.'

'So you're going to deliberately use it against me? To drive me wild with annoyance?' The photograph was taken and they were told they could move. Will, however, held her for a second longer.

'No. To drive you wild with *longing*.' His deep, dark voice had washed over her and even when he'd released her from his hold, she wasn't able to move for a whole thirty seconds. His eyes told her he was determined to follow through on his quest to extract from her the answers he required.

Then, before she'd had a chance to suss him out further, before she'd been able to get a firm hold on exactly what he wanted to know, Will was forced to leave the wedding before the reception even started because his patient in Melbourne required his immediate attention.

Sheena had been left with a sense of impending doom hanging over her head for the past three months. Every now and then she would wake from her sleep, gasping with that wild longing he'd promised her she'd feel. How was it that after so many years he still had the ability to affect her?

'Breathe. Breathe,' she whispered again, trying to listen to that small, still voice in her mind that was desperate to calm her down.

'Hey, Sheenie.'

Sheena jumped and whirled round, her eyes becoming even wider as someone entered the room. A split second later she relaxed and breathed a sigh of relief as Janessa walked towards her.

'Oh, Nessa. You scared me.' She pressed her hands to her chest.

Janessa hugged her friend, the two women as close as sisters. 'What's wrong? Is it the girls?' Janessa immediately looked across at the twins, lying in their specially designed crib. As one of the neonatologists assigned to the twins, Janessa was completely in love with both her goddaughters, and was providing the best care possible for them.

Janessa's husband, Miles Trevellion, was the neonate surgeon in charge of the entire team of specialists responsible for the upcoming separation of the twins. During the past six months, Miles and Janessa had been Sheena's stabilising support but now Sheena wasn't at all sure they'd be able to do anything about the impending doom that awaited her.

'The girls are fine. Perfect. Beautiful. Fine.'

Janessa looked closely at Sheena. 'You're pacing. You're wringing your hands. You're…highly agitated.' She continued to watch her friend, thinking quickly. 'In fact…I haven't seen you this agitated since my wedding.'

Sheena stopped pacing and flung her arms out wide. 'There's only one man in the world who can bring me to this level of agitation!'

'Will.' Janessa nodded. 'Do you know, when you spotted him at the other end of the aisle, I had the briefest thought that you might turn tail and run.' She smiled warmly at her friend, her words carrying no malice.

Sheena laughed without humour, the sound holding a tinge of repressed hysteria. 'I was highly tempted but I wasn't going to ruin your big day.'

'And I thank you for that. What I don't quite understand—' Janessa sat down in one of the comfortable chairs '—is that you've known for months that Will would be treating the girls. Besides, you both seemed OK at the wedding.'

'That's only because neither of us wanted to make a big fuss on your special day but now he's not here for a few hours, he's not here to pose and smile for the camera. He's here for at least the next two months and I'll no doubt be seeing him almost every single day of those two months.'

'Are you worried that the old spark might rekindle?' Janessa waggled her eyebrows up and down for emphasis.

Sheena closed her eyes, not ready to admit that the 'old spark', as Janessa termed it, had been reignited at the wedding…or at least something had been awakened. Seeing that determined look in Will's eyes had made him seem ruthless, dangerous, tempting…and that had excited her.

She sighed with confusion and looked at her friend, starting to pace again. 'I don't know,' she told Janessa. 'I'm the type of person who likes to understand her parameters so I can work within them. I've had to make some very difficult decisions throughout my life, I've had to endure a lot of unfun things, but the whole time I at least knew where I'd come from and where I was going.' She shook her head. 'That doesn't happen with Will. He twists me up inside and turns my otherwise intelligent mind to mush with just one of his gorgeous, deep, smouldering looks.' Sheena stopped pacing, her hands now clutched against her chest.

'Wow. This guy really does wind you up, doesn't he?' Janessa stated rhetorically.

'Arrgh. What am I supposed to do?' Sheena covered her face with her hands then indicated the door. 'He's coming here *today*, Nessa. He'll be here soon. Will! Will is coming here. To see me and the g—' She stopped talking, suddenly finding it difficult to breathe as the impact of her situation seemed to hit with full force. She felt hot and cold and fanned her face with her hands as she tried to calm her breathing. She didn't resist when Janessa forced her to sit.

'You've gone as white as a ghost. I had no idea that Will sent you into such a tizz. Quick, put your head between your knees before you faint.' Janessa urged Sheena's head down. 'Now stay there while I go and get a paper bag.'

Sheena closed her eyes, doing as she was told. Why was it that the mere thought of seeing Will again could affect her in this manner? Was it because he was determined to find answers? Would she be able to give him answers that would satisfy him? They'd met in England while both working on their registrar rotations. They'd become friends then started to date. They'd become serious, more deeply involved than Sheena had thought possible.

Then her rotation had come to an end and the week before she'd been due to return to Australia Will had proposed. Seeing the devastation on his face, the shock, the disbelief when she'd told him she could never have children, that it was a medical impossibility, had broken her heart but confirmed the truth of why she'd needed to turn him down. There was no way she could give him the happiness he deserved. Sheena had finished the last week of her rotation, avoiding Will wherever possible, and had then returned to Australia, to her life without him.

Now Will was one of the world's leading orthopaedic paediatric specialists for conjoined twins. He was coming here to care for the daughters she'd been told she would never have.

Her *miracle* babies.

The door to the room opened. 'Quick. Give me that bag,' Sheena urged, and, with head still down between her knees, she held out her hand.

'Hello, Sheena.' The deep, rich, unforgettable tones of William Beckman filled the room and Sheena froze for a second before dropping her arm, lifting her head and standing up. The sudden action, especially as she'd had her head down, made her feel dizzy and she stumbled.

'Whoa. Easy.' He was by her side in a flash, his firm, muscled arms slipping about her waist as he drew her close, steadying her against him. 'No need to get up on my account.' The vibrations from his voice rumbled through her as she placed a hand weakly against his chest, memories of the last time he'd held her like this, been this close to her, within kissing distance, flooding through her mind as she slowly raised her gaze to mesh with his.

Blue eyes met blue eyes and she sighed, transported back

to the day they'd spent together at Brighton. Two Aussies, out to find a bit of sun during a typical English summer. Having a few days off from the hospital, they'd headed off to Brighton, standing on the pebbly beach, their arms about each other as they'd watched the sun disappear and the stars start to twinkle above them.

They'd both been so happy.

Sheena sighed, allowing herself this one brief moment of reflection, her gaze still locked with his. How was it possible that after all this time she was still so affected by his nearness? As she continued to stare into his eyes, she saw that hint of darkness, that strong, powerful difference she'd witnessed at the wedding. He quirked an eyebrow at her.

'Feeling better?' The words were rich and deep and resonated throughout her entire body.

Sheena stared at his lips, hoping her mind was capable of understanding what he'd just said. It was clear that she was uncomfortable but with the way he'd just caught her sitting, it brought instantly to mind the very first time they'd met. Sheena had been lying on the floor, trying to get a tiny toy car out from beneath a heavy cupboard in the paediatric playroom. She'd located the toy car, stood and then thrust the car high into the air in triumph.

The children around her had clapped, impressed with her rescue skills, and it hadn't been until one of the children had pointed out that another doctor had entered the playroom that Sheena had even known he'd been there all along, watching her every move—*and* she'd been wearing a skirt. After they'd been dating a while, he'd confessed to her that it had been the sexiest toy rescue he'd ever witnessed.

She'd handed the car back to the child, all the time staring at Will in a way that had made him incredibly aware of the instant tension buzzing between them. When he'd held out his hand to introduce himself, she'd stood there for several seconds before shaking it.

'Sheena?' he prompted, trying not to breathe in her sweet, strawberry scent.

'Uh… Um…' As though only just realising she was still in his arms, she instantly shifted, moving away, putting some distance between them. 'Yeah… I'm… I'm fine. Thanks.' She waved her hands in the air, as though she was trying to make the past minute or two disappear. 'And you? How are you since I saw you last?' Her gaze flicked over him in a quick but thorough appraisal and she swallowed, unable to believe he looked better than he had at the wedding.

'Fine.'

Had his lips just twitched when he'd said that? She thought she'd detected a slight twitch. Was he amused by her silly antics? With the fact that she'd been head down, tail up when he'd first walked into the room, before becoming dizzy?

She watched as he put his hands into his pockets and with that one move it was as though he'd switched on his professional persona. *Dr* Will Beckman was now in the room. 'I trust the past three months have been good for you and your girls?'

'Yes. Yes, they have.' She nodded for extra emphasis, a little intrigued with his politeness and the way he seemed intent on keeping his distance. From the way he'd left things at the wedding, saying he was curious about her, she'd half expected him to waltz in here and pin her with twenty questions. 'They've both responded well to the surgeries.'

'I'm pleased to hear that.'

'Oh, by the way, how's your patient with rheumatoid arthritis? The one you flew to Australia to collect back in July?'

Both of Will's eyebrows rose in surprise, revealing a

glimpse of the Will she'd known in the past. It was sort of strange to be around him, familiar with his facial expressions and mannerisms and yet not really knowing the man he'd become during the past decade. She was seeing two sides to him and realised the brisk, direct man, the one who seemed to harness a hint of darkness about him, the one who'd both startled and excited her at the wedding, was the one she knew she needed to be wary of.

'Doing well. Thankfully he responded extremely well to the new treatment and was able to return to Australia about a fortnight ago.' He nodded, pleased with the satisfactory outcome of that situation.

'That's wonderful news. I've often thought about you… er…about you and him and his…you know…his case and the research and treatment and…everything. I'm glad it all worked out.'

Will gave her a curious look. 'I'm astonished that with everything you've had going on with your girls you would have even given him another thought. Then again, you always were a considerate doctor, especially when children were involved.' His words were spoken softly, tenderly and then, almost as though he'd caught himself praising her, he quickly straightened his shoulders and clenched his jaw, his expression changing from one of open appreciation to an unreadable mask. He crossed his arms over his chest and inclined his head towards the crib.

'Aren't you going to introduce me to your daughters?' His tone was professional once again.

'Oh. Right. Of course. How silly of me.' Sheena shook her head as she walked over to the crib where the girls lay, unable to believe she'd momentarily forgotten they were even in the room. Ellie was lying there, eyes open, content simply to look around the room. Sarah, thankfully, was sleeping. 'Hello, baby,' Sheena crooned as she stroked Ellie's cheek.

Ellie's little eyelids fluttered closed for a moment before she looked at her mother. 'I didn't know you were awake.' Sheena leaned over and brushed a soft kiss over Ellie's forehead.

'Ellie, this is Will. Will, this is Ellie. Sarah, the rowdy one of the two, is thankfully sleeping.'

'Rowdy, eh?' There was a slight thickness to his tone as he watched her with the babies. She looked so right, so complete standing there, touching their soft skin, kissing them.

'They may be conjoined but they have very different personalities. It's as though they really are two halves of the same whole.'

He nodded, desperate not to be affected with the way she looked near the babies. So calm and happy and...right. He clenched his jaw, hardening his heart against the sight before him. He'd come here to treat the girls, to be a part of the team that would separate them and give them the best chance at living normal, healthy lives. Nothing more. The fact that he wanted answers from Sheena was a bonus and perhaps once she provided him with the truth about why she'd rejected his proposal ten years ago, he'd finally achieve closure on that chapter in his life. He was certain that she'd lied to him, that she'd used the possibility of infertility as an excuse. The evidence of that lie was before him right now. Two babies— *Sheena's* babies.

He nodded. 'That's the way it is with the majority of conjoined twins. One rowdy, one quiet. It's also the way it is with twins in general, especially identical ones.'

'Miles says the same thing.'

'I guess, as we've both been working in the field of separating conjoined twins for quite some time now, that we share similar views and opinions on the subject.'

'You're the experts. All I know is that Sarah is the one who screams the loudest, who eats the most and who demands all the attention. Ellie, however, doesn't seem to be at all jealous of her sister's vivacity. Ellie's very quiet, very content. Some days I worry about her more.' There was a wistfulness to Sheena's tone and she brushed another kiss across Ellie's forehead. 'My quiet achiever. See how, even though she's awake, she doesn't move or wriggle or make too much noise?'

Will nodded. 'She doesn't want to wake Sarah. She's smart. Sarah may have the sass but Ellie definitely knows what's what.'

Sheena laughed. 'I guess you're right. I've never thought of it that way.'

And he'd never thought he'd hear that sweet, relaxed laugh of hers ever again. When she'd left England to return to Australia at the end of her rotation, his world had been devastated. Since then, he'd only been back in to Australia for brief visits to see his parents and siblings, and each time he'd made sure there had been no way he would ever run into Sheena—the woman who had broken his heart into tiny pieces. This time, though, there had been no avoiding the issue. First they'd been thrown together at Miles and Janessa's wedding and now they'd be seeing each other almost daily because of her daughters.

Now here he stood, back in Australia, back with Sheena, looking down at *her* children in the crib. The little girls were gorgeous and definitely had their mother's colouring in their bright blue eyes and dark hair. So incredibly beautiful.

He'd always wanted a big family. Little girls and little boys, and he'd wanted them with Sheena. The perfect family. Having been raised in a large, loving home himself, he'd carried this ideal picture with him, only to find that life never turned out the way you planned.

'How is it that you can know so much about the girls when you've only just walked into the room?' Sheena glanced up at him, amazed at his skill. 'You were always so good at diagnosing patients, having a bond with them after only a few minutes in their presence. I always envied you that ability.'

When he looked at her, he was astonished to find her blue eyes filled with wonderment and appreciation. He swallowed over the sudden dryness in his throat. Flashes of the times they'd spent together, the way they'd laughed, the way they'd shared intimate moments, the way she'd broken his heart… The images flicked through his mind, one after the other, before he closed the mental door in his mind and hardened his heart.

'I've been working with conjoined twins for quite some time now, Sheena. Recognising their individuality is one of the first aspects of effective care and one that most professionals in this field acquire quite quickly.'

Sheena placed one last kiss on Ellie's forehead before straightening. She hadn't missed the way his blue eyes had turned from calm and collected to dark and stormy. She knew him so well that at times it was easy for her to read his expressions. It shouldn't be that way. Not after all these years.

The fact that their paths had crossed again, under the most far-fetched circumstances, meant nothing. The twins were all that mattered and as she stroked her fingertips lightly down Ellie's cheek, causing the moppet to close her eyes and relax, Sheena knew she had to find a way to put aside her past relationship with Will and focus on what needed to be done. Ellie and Sarah were the two people in the world who mattered most to her and she couldn't let them down by becoming a basket case of repressed memories simply because Will was here.

She cleared her throat, still stroking Ellie as her baby fell asleep. 'Have you had much of a chance to look at scans or operation reports? The tissue expanders have worked wonderfully, although the skin took a little longer to stretch than Miles originally thought.'

'Miles has kept me apprised on both of the girls since before they were born.'

'Oh?' She looked at him then, quite surprised. 'I had no idea he'd been in such close contact with you for so long.'

'I was finishing up on another case in Philadelphia. Twin boys who were joined at the spine.'

'Good heavens.' Sheena placed a possessive hand on Ellie's little stomach while the little girl slept alongside her sister. 'Are they all right?'

'Both boys are doing very well. They were almost eight months old when we separated them but now they're fourteen months and both starting to walk around.'

'Wow. That's amazing. Did Miles work with you on that case?'

'Yes. We've worked together many times during the past decade. In fact, it was through working with Miles that I initially entered the field of conjoined twins.' Will paused and frowned for a moment. 'It gave me something new and challenging to focus on.'

Sheena turned away from the crib and took a step towards him. Will immediately drew himself to his full height, his backbone ramrod straight, his defences in place. Although the action may have been involuntary, it told her a lot. This was the man who had been very important to her all those years ago, the one man in the world who had really understood her, and while they gazed at each other now, she realised that while there still might be an underlying level of attraction simmering beneath the surface, they needed to rise above it, to move past it and to get on with the job at hand.

'Will, I can't thank you enough for coming, for accepting the job as orthopaedic surgeon to my girls. It means the world to me to know they'll be in such safe hands.'

'They need my expertise. I'm honoured to provide it. It's as cut and dried as that.' His words were clipped and he clenched his jaw. Sheena knew of old that that meant he was either highly uncomfortable, embarrassed or trying to hold on to his temper. In this instance, she wondered whether it wasn't all three.

'I also don't want...' She stopped and laced her fingers together, desperate to keep her composure. 'I mean...I would be horrified to think that you might think that...' She stopped again, biting her lip.

She was nervous and unsure. Will could tell quite clearly from the way she was trying not to wring her hands or bite her lip. It annoyed him that after all this time apart, after everything he'd been through in the past decade, he could still read this woman like a book. It was as though everything about Sheena was burned into his memory and would remain with him for ever.

'We have a past,' he jumped in, saving her the trouble of expressing what he could see clearly written all over her face. His words were spoken in a clipped and firm tone that indicated he'd made a decision and was following through with it. 'We were together—so we know each other well. Things didn't work out. We moved on.' He smoothed a hand down his silk tie before shoving both hands into the pockets of his trousers. 'Now, purely for professional reasons, our paths are once more crossing. We're both very different people now.'

'You're right.' She nodded. 'I mean, you have a life I know nothing about and I have...well, I have the girls to think about.'

'What about your ex-husband? Doesn't he figure in the life of your daughters? Despite what may or may not have happened within your marriage, I had at least expected to see him here, helping you.'

'Er…no.'

Will shook his head as though disagreeing with her. 'The parents' marital problems don't figure at all in the equation of the actual separation of conjoined twins. It's the babies that matter most.'

'I couldn't agree more.'

'So where is he?' He was still frowning, as though not really wanting to talk about this but still wanting to get things completely straight.

'He's gone. Out of my life. Wants nothing to do with the girls.'

Will's expression eased to one of professional concern. 'You're all alone? A single parent?'

'I am.' Her voice wavered as she said the words and there was deep sadness in her eyes. Was it regret for her defunct marriage? All Will knew was that when she stood there, looking up at him, her blue eyes wide and sad with the corner of her lower lip caught between her teeth, he had to remain strong.

Years ago, he'd loved this woman completely. She'd been vitally important to his life but that time was long past. He wasn't responsible for protecting her any more. Neither was he responsible for her happiness. He couldn't allow himself to become ensnared by her again.

Balling his hands into fists in order to stop himself from going to her, Will breathed deeply before nodding once and turning on his heel. He was only here for the babies, not their mother. Yet, as he walked out of the room, he was positive he could feel her watching his every move.

CHAPTER THREE

THAT evening, after Sheena had fed and changed the girls, tucking them in so they were ready for their evening sleep, she said goodnight to the night sister and made her way from the ward to the hospital's residential wing.

It was close to midnight, the hospital corridors all but deserted, and she looked forward to getting to her small apartment. She knew she could get a good five to six hours' sleep before the girls woke, ready for their breakfast. They were both so lovely, so special and so perfect. Other people might look at the girls and see twins who were joined at the hip but when she looked at them, she saw only Ellie and Sarah, two different little girls, and she loved them completely.

What she longed for most at the moment was to be able to hold them and cuddle them without needing help to get them in and out of the crib. As it was, with the tissue expanders still in, it only made holding them even more difficult, but there was no way she was giving up her cuddles, even if it probably drove the staff around the twist because she needed help each time. Tomorrow the tissue expanders would come out and then early on Monday morning the surgery to separate them, which Miles estimated would take a good twenty hours—maybe more—would begin.

Her girls. Her babies. They'd lived in the hospital all their

lives and so knew nothing different, but she did. She was
their mother and she was determined to provide for them
both, to give them the best chance at life. Still, Miles had already discussed the pros and cons of the impending surgery
with her. They all knew the risks, but to leave the twins as
conjoined would cause them not only psychological complications but health complications as well. They all knew that
separating the girls was the right course of action to take but
still…she was their mother and if anything should happen to
either one of them…

Sheena stopped walking, trembling with sudden fear, the
burning need to just hold her babies one by one overwhelming her. Tears threatened and she closed them, instantly
trying to regain a hold over her emotions, calming her mind
down, at least until she managed to get back to the privacy
of her room. Leaning a hand against the wall, she swallowed
over the lump in her throat.

'Sheena?'

She whirled round at the sound of her name, startled at
being discovered and very surprised to find Will standing in
the corridor not far from her. Sheena quickly straightened,
dropping her hand and sniffing, pulling herself together.

'Will. Is there something I can help you with? You look
lost.'

'I am. I was looking for the cafeteria.'

She nodded. 'You've come down one extra floor. The
cafeteria is directly above us.' She impatiently blinked the
impending tears away, unable to believe that Will, of all
people, had caught her at a weak moment. 'There won't be
any food on offer, just coffee.'

He nodded but didn't move. He should just turn, walk to
the stairwell and leave her alone. He should keep his distance but it was clear she was upset. He'd never been able

to resist Sheena when she'd been sad. The need to cheer her up, to support her, was powerful and one he couldn't ignore. Whatever had happened between them in the past could be put aside, at least for a short while.

'Are there any restaurants open outside the hospital? Preferably close? Food would be appreciated. My stomach kept growling all through that last meeting.' He gave her a sheepish smile and Sheena wished he hadn't. He was far too adorable, far too irresistible when he looked at her like that.

'Wow, that meeting ran very late.'

'You're telling me,' he scoffed. 'Restaurants? Any thoughts?'

Glad of the distraction, she mentally went through the restaurants close by. 'Um…there are a few places still open at this time of night. Two Italian restaurants and also a vegetarian café. Ah, but I've just remembered that you're not a big vegetarian fan, so I guess it'll be Italian for you.'

'Well, if you've remembered that I don't like vegetarian food, you'll also remember that I don't like to eat alone. Come on. Let's go.' He started walking towards the door at the end of the corridor, closing the distance between them. 'Are the Italian places within walking distance or do we need to take a taxi?'

Her eyes widened at his words. 'Wait. I can't go with you. I'm going to bed.'

Will stopped beside her and looked down into her up-turned face. 'I'm willing to bet you haven't had a proper meal for at least three to four days. Am I right?'

'Yes.'

'It's settled, then.' He smiled and her heart almost skipped a beat. Good heavens, he was even more handsome than he'd been a decade ago. Her heart started pounding a little faster, the earthy, fresh scent she'd always equated with Will teasing her senses once more.

'But, Will...'

He rolled his eyes and shook his head, somewhat bemused. 'It's just dinner, Sheena. Not a lifelong contract, and the longer you argue with me, the later you'll get to sleep, and if I know you, which I do, you'll be back on the ward bright and early to accompany the girls to Theatre.'

Sheena bristled a little at his words, annoyed that he'd made valid points. It *wasn't* a lifelong contract. It *was* just dinner and she *was* hungry. 'Of course I'll be on the ward. They *are* my girls. It's my responsibility to care for them.'

'And it's my present responsibility to eat. Let's go, Woodcombe.' He placed his hand beneath her elbow and urged her towards the door.

Sheena pulled her arm free of his grasp, heat burning through her at where he'd touched her. 'I'm coming. No need to manhandle me, Beckman.'

'I'm hungry. Let's hustle.'

'You always were bad-tempered when you needed food.' They walked outside into the cool October air and Sheena now wished she'd brought her cardigan instead of leaving it in the girls' room. Then again, she hadn't expected to be leaving the hospital to have dinner with Will Beckman.

They walked through the hospital grounds, the silence around them starting to grow tense and a little uncomfortable. In order to help her flustered nerves, which he'd had the audacity to ruffle, Sheena found herself pointing out different buildings as they walked along. It was strange to be making small talk with Will but, then, in many respects, he *was* a stranger.

'That's the pathology building and down that way is the medical school. That large building is the administration building and this,' she said as they walked past a small brick chapel, 'is where I like to come and just think, to just ponder, to just stop.'

Will looked at the little chapel with its white-painted door, brown bricks and the little steeple on top. 'A place of solitude.'

Sheena shrugged. 'We all need one.'

As soon as they reached the roadside, where the taxi rank was situated, Will walked to the first taxi and held the door open for Sheena.

'Where ya headed?' the driver asked them as Sheena sat in the back, trying to keep her distance from Will.

'Giuseppe's, please,' she told him, and a moment later they were driving through the streets of Adelaide at midnight.

'Wow. Everything looks just as I remembered. The country town trying to be a big city.' He smiled as he said the words.

Sheena frowned. 'Don't some of your family live here? I can't remember.'

'My parents and one sister. She's married with children and lives just around the corner from my parents.'

'I'll bet your parents are glad to have you home for a while.'

He nodded. 'They are.'

Sheena sighed, her tone wistful. 'I always envied your family. Whenever you spoke about them, it always sounded so…wonderful. Lots of siblings, lots of mischief.' She nodded to herself. 'That's what I want for my girls…well, the mischief part at any rate.'

She looked down at her hands, surprised to find they were shaking. 'Right now, though, I just want them to be healthy.' She swallowed over the lump in her throat.

'The projected outcomes for the surgery are good, Sheena.' Will placed a hand over hers, needing to offer her hope.

'I know.' She forced a smile. 'It's never easy for a mother when her child is sick or needs surgery. Over the years, I've watched the parents of my little patients as their child was wheeled away to surgery and the devastation and fear and pain and anguish reflected in their eyes is now permanently lodged in my throat.'

'We have a great team together and Miles knows what he's doing.'

Sheena quickly shook her head. 'I'm not concerned about the team. I know everyone will do everything they can for my girls. I'm confident with that. What I'm not confident about are these maternal emotions. I never thought I'd have them and now that I do, they're…intense.'

'In a way, I envy you.' Will's words were soft and he dropped his hand from her shoulder. 'You're a parent. You have children. That's special.'

Sheena looked at him. 'It is special.' Her words were a whisper then she cleared her throat, asking the question that had been burning through her since the wedding. 'You've never met…anyone else? I'm not trying to pry, Will,' she rushed on hurriedly.

'Sure you are,' he countered, thoughts of Beatrice coming to his mind. He and Beatrice were well and truly over, had been for the past two years, but he had to admit he would feel strange telling Sheena about his aborted engagement. 'But why shouldn't you? Why shouldn't I? I've already told you I'm curious about you and I'm determined to get answers.'

'You deserve them.' She nodded. 'We can clear the air tonight. Start afresh tomorrow.'

'Just like that?' He was a little surprised at her words. 'One hundred per cent honesty?'

'Yes.'

The taxi slowed before he could say anything more and soon they were climbing out and paying the driver. Neither of them spoke as they were welcomed by one of the waiters and led to a table. Sheena waved to the few other patrons in the restaurant, all of whom worked at Adelaide Mercy.

'How are the girls tonight?' one woman asked. Sheena recognised her as one of the dieticians and smiled politely.

'Growing more and more every day.'

'Good to hear.'

'You're well known,' Will said, after she'd been asked a few more questions. He held out her chair for her and waited until she was seated before sitting down opposite her.

'I'm the mother of Adelaide's conjoined twins, a minor celebrity.' She spoke with forced joviality, then sighed and shrugged. 'I've become used to it, especially at work.'

'The press don't bother you?'

'Charisma, Adelaide Mercy's CEO, and the rest of the PR department take care of those things. Apart from when the girls were born, I haven't really been hounded. The PR department discuss the information with me and give their recommendations, such as which journalists to speak to and who to stay clear of, but other than that things haven't been too bad. My main focus is to look after the girls.'

'That's good to hear. Many parents of conjoined children are often hounded by the media for photographs and update reports. You do know that things will heat up again with the impending separation surgery?'

Sheena nodded and sipped at the glass of water the waiter had just poured for her, declining the offer of wine as she was still expressing milk for the twins. 'Miles took me through the drill.'

'Good.' Will opened the menu and after a moment of perusing it gave his order to the waiter, as did Sheena, and once he'd left them alone, Sheena put both hands on the table and leaned forward a little, not wanting her voice to travel to the other patrons.

'Shall we begin?' It all seemed so strange, so civilised but Sheena rationalised this was probably better than ranting and raving and getting way too emotional. Calm and controlled. Open and honest. It seemed the best way to proceed.

'Now?'

'Why not? You go first. Ask away.'

Will nodded then jumped right in. 'When you rejected my proposal, were you telling the truth about not being able to have children?'

Sheena tried not to wince at his accusatory tone and tried not to take it to heart. Will had obviously thought about this as his question had rolled immediately off his tongue with no hesitation whatsoever. She'd agreed to provide him with answers and she was going to follow through. If there was any hope that she and Will could find some common ground, that they could put the past behind them and hopefully become friends, it would be good not only for them but for the girls as well. She would do *anything* for her girls and if it meant being uncomfortable whilst sorting things out, then it would all be worth it.

She swallowed and nodded. 'Yes. I had bad endometriosis. The chances of me conceiving were, I was told, impossible.'

'And yet you have twins.'

'And yet I have twins,' she agreed, that same secret smile touching her lips. 'Miracle twins.' She breathed the two words as though they were her heart and soul. Will found that puzzling yet interesting.

'So if you knew you couldn't have children, why did you marry?'

Her expression changed, a small frown furrowing her brow. 'Jonas didn't want children. He was a plastic surgeon I met at a paediatric conference on facial reconstruction. We hit it off, started dating and I was determined not to make the same mistakes I'd made with you. So I told him upfront that I was unable to have children and he was happy about it. He'd said he was focused on his career, that he had expensive tastes and that children didn't fit into his life at all. We were…compatible, and so when he proposed I accepted.' She looked down at her hands, clasped together in front of her, trying not to feel highly self-conscious at discussing her marriage with Will.

'When my gynaecological surgeon contacted me about a new surgical technique of removing the endometrial cysts from my ovaries, I was interested. He said it would alleviate a lot of my pain.'

Will was surprised to hear her speak of pain. 'Were you always in pain? I don't remember you ever complaining of abdominal pain.'

Sheena laughed without humour. 'When you've had the pain for most of your life, you learn to deal with it. Anyway, the surgery worked. The pain was dramatically reduced and then two months after the surgery, when I returned for an ultrasound, it was discovered I was pregnant. Naturally I was over the moon and I thought Jonas would be, too.'

'He really didn't want the children?'

She shook her head. 'He really didn't. He said I'd lied to him, telling him I could never have children and then conceiving only twelve months after we were married. He said

I'd violated our prenuptial agreement and that it was grounds for divorce. Within the week he'd contacted his solicitor, packed up my belongings and made me leave the house.'

'He kicked you out!' Will couldn't help but see red at some other man treating any woman in such a fashion, let alone Sheena. 'That's disgusting.'

Sheena shrugged and sighed. 'He was well within his legal rights. Besides, at least he was honest. At least he didn't pretend he was happy when he wasn't, unlike my parents.'

'*Your* parents?'

'My parents are very wealthy, very prominent solicitors in Sydney.'

'They're alive? I'd always thought they'd passed away as you never spoke of them.' He shook his head. Why didn't he know all of this? The two of them had been so close, or so he'd thought.

'We don't talk. We haven't spoken in…' She paused for a moment as she tried to calculate. 'Well over two decades— ever since my fourteenth birthday. I was at boarding school and had been told by my teacher that my parents were sup- posed to pick me up and take me out for the day. They never showed. I called the house, worried that they might have had an accident, that something bad might have happened, but I was told by Harrington, our butler, that my parents had flown overseas that morning on urgent business and wouldn't be back for six months.'

She looked down at her hands and gave a small shrug. 'They'd forgotten me—again. I didn't hear from them during the rest of my time at boarding school. Then, as soon as I turned eighteen, their contract—as they called it—with me expired and I was told by one of their solicitor colleagues hired to handle my "case" that I was on my own.'

'Oh, Sheena.' Will felt her pain and wanted to be there for

her, to touch her, to let her know how disturbed he was to learn of her past. He wasn't entirely sure what sort of reaction from him was appropriate when rehashing the past with an old girlfriend…so he sat and waited for her to continue.

'Apparently, when my mother discovered she was pregnant with me, she said she felt as though her world had come to an end. My father wasn't interested in her any more because she was large and fat—her words, not mine.'

Sheena shook her head, trying not to feel hurt and betrayed, but she couldn't help it. After all these years, the cold, impersonal way in which she'd been raised still had the ability to hurt her. It also made her determined *never* to do that to *her* girls. 'She even once told me that if the doctor who had first confirmed her pregnancy hadn't been part of their social set, she would have had an abortion. However, she couldn't deal with the possibility of being ostracised by her friends, most of whom had the odd child or two, so she decided to continue with the pregnancy.'

'What? How old were you when she told you that?'

'Seven. I remember asking her why she never came to see me at boarding school, why she never attended the school concerts I took part in, why I was driven to and from school by a chauffeur rather than my father. Of course, I had no idea what the word *abortion* meant so I asked my teachers.'

'I had no idea.' He shook his head. 'Why didn't you tell me any of this before? How come I don't know this about you?' It also made him wonder whether he'd been so wrapped up in creating his own perfect family picture that he hadn't bothered to dig a little deeper where Sheena was concerned.

She shrugged. 'I didn't talk about it at all. Period. My parents didn't share a caring bone in their bodies—except perhaps for each other, and even then I'm not so sure. My mother demanded a C-section delivery, simply because she refused to give birth naturally, and then when she'd regained her pre-pregnancy figure my father started paying her attention again. I was only endured because to do otherwise would have brought ridicule from their elitist friends. To them, having "offspring" was considered acceptable, even though they didn't raise me.'

Will thought for a moment, recalling some of the conversations they'd had or, more correctly, the times he'd talked about his family, not realising that Sheena had *never* talked of hers. 'And then there was me. Always going on about my parents and my siblings and my nieces and nephews.'

'You didn't go on.' She smiled. 'I loved hearing your stories. I loved them so much and I could tell that family was so very important to you. You *needed* children, Will, so you *needed* a wife who could give you that.' She shook her head sadly. 'That wasn't me.'

'So you turned me down. Instead of talking to me, instead of sharing with me, instead of trusting me, you simply decided to run away?'

'Hey, I didn't run away. It was extremely difficult for me to do what needed to be done. I was raised in a non-communicative household and then a boarding school so I've never been any good at talking about my feelings, but I didn't run away from you.' She tried not to raise her voice, to keep her tone on that calm, even footing she wanted, but it was difficult when he was accusing her.

Will shook his head. 'No. Not buying it. Those may have been the reasons you *told* yourself you couldn't accept me but deep down inside you were scared. I can see that now. You were scared of opening up, of getting close to someone. You probably thought that one day I would slap you down the way everyone else around you had done, and so you rejected me before I could reject you. A pre-emptive strike.'

Sheena knew his words were close to the truth. She *had* been scared, scared that he would one day come to really hate her...and she hadn't been able to live with even the thought of that. 'Or that if I'd said yes, if I'd accepted your proposal and we'd got married, you would have eventually come to hate me for not being able to give you the one thing you've always wanted—a great big happy family.

'And if you *had* married me, those gorgeous girls wouldn't just be yours, they'd be ours. *Our* miracle. Instead, they belong to another man...another man who doesn't even want them.' The last words were said with utter disgust.

'Which is why I intend to give them all the love I have and more. Those girls are my life and I will do anything and everything to ensure their health and happiness. Even when I had a lot of bleeding early on in the pregnancy and even when I had to stay bedridden, feeling as though I had no other purpose in life than to be a human incubator, nothing else mattered other than giving my babies everything I had to give. From the instant I was told about them, I've loved them with every fibre of my being. And I shall continue to be there for them, to provide them with a happy home for the rest of my life.' Vehemence laced her tone, pride stiffened her backbone and determination was written all over her face.

When the waiter arrived with their food, his presence almost startled her and she realised she'd become too intensely focused on herself and Will. The rest of the restaurant came back into focus—the sights, the smells, the surroundings. The waiter smiled politely, wished them a brief *'Buon appetito'* then left them alone once more.

Will quietly picked up his fork and twirled it into his pasta before lifting it to his lips. 'Mmm,' he said a moment later. 'Delicious. Good choice of restaurant, Sheena.'

That was it? Wasn't he going to ask any more questions or had he discovered all the answers he needed? Confusion swam through her and as she started to calm down, she realised the waiter had unfurled her napkin and placed it in her lap. An uncomfortable silence started to settle over them and Sheena wasn't sure what to say to alleviate it.

'Why don't the girls have your husband's surname?' Will asked after a few minutes, his words so abrupt that Sheena almost dropped her fork to her plate. 'I've noticed on their charts that they're both listed as Woodcombe.'

Sheena shrugged. 'As Jonas wasn't interested in the girls and as I hadn't changed my name when we married, it seemed ridiculous for us to have different surnames.'

'You didn't change your name.' He pondered the words, intrigued that she'd chosen to remain a Woodcombe given that she had no ties to her family heritage. Had that been because the process was too time consuming, or because deep down inside she'd known her marriage to Jonas would never last?

'My medical degree is in the name of Sheena Woodcombe. Whether or not I'd changed it, I'd still have to practice as Dr Woodcombe. It just seemed simpler to leave things as they were.'

'It didn't bother your ex-husband?'

'No. Why? Would it bother you?'

Will pondered her words for a moment then leaned forward a little. 'Not that it has anything to do with our present situation, but if we'd been married, would you have changed your name?'

Sheena nodded, her decision almost instant, as though at some point she'd given it some thought. 'More than likely. Besides, when we were together I was still a registrar and didn't have my paediatric consultant qualifications.'

'So it's all logistics to you?'

'I've had to be logical. It was the only defence I had against the way I was raised. Closing myself off, being logical about all things was the only way I could cope. Janessa was the first person ever to break through my barriers… and…' She took a calming breath, reminding herself that she was being completely honest with him tonight. 'And you were second.'

'And what about Jonas? Was he the third?'

'No. Jonas never broke through my barriers. I loved him but it was more companionship. A marriage I could be in so that I had someone to share things with, to discuss my day with. Marriage is all about someone else being a witness to your life and at that time I was very lonely. I had Janessa and I had my work and that was it.' She shook her head. 'I don't expect you to understand as you have a plethora of siblings and loving, caring parents who are actually interested in your life, who *want* to talk to you, who *want* to spend time with you.'

'I do understand, Sheena.' He nodded slowly. 'I've been living overseas for well over a decade now and although I am in contact with my parents, they don't know much about my life. About the way I'm always working to stave off loneliness.'

'You've been lonely?' Sheena's heart started to ache for him, to ache for this man who had meant so much to her.

'Don't sound so surprised, Sheena. Loneliness can happen to people even if they have a big family around them. Being an only child to indifferent parents doesn't give you a monopoly on the emotion.'

'Uh…' She shook her head. 'No. I never meant to imply that it did.' She bit her lip and asked again the question she'd asked during the taxi ride to the restaurant. 'Didn't you…?

I mean…I thought you would have met someone else. I thought by now that you would be married with that large family you always wanted.'

Will looked down at his food and placed his fork on the side of his plate, lifting his gaze to give Sheena his full attention. He'd asked about her and she'd replied. It was only fair that he do the same.

'I did meet someone else. Beatrice. We met through work. She was a lawyer advising on a medico-legal case I was involved with. We dated, became engaged and then…' He stopped and shook his head. 'I broke it off. We were heading off to the printer to do a final check on the invitations as they were due to be sent out the following day and I…' He stopped again and ran a hand over his face as though he couldn't believe what had transpired.

'It *felt* wrong. I can't explain it any other way. Everything about the wedding, about spending the rest of my life with Beatrice, just felt…wrong.' He could still hear Beatrice telling him that he spent more time at work than with her. That work was his first priority whereas *she* should have been. He had known that that would never change.

He was dedicated to his job and, as he'd told Sheena at the wedding, it made him happy. He'd buried himself in work when Sheena had left and it had taken quite a few years for him to start dating again. Finally, though, he'd been able to move on and when he'd met Beatrice, he'd thought he'd once more found happiness.

He'd been wrong…again.

Will cleared his throat. 'I knew I couldn't enter into a marriage with doubts and I realised that Beatrice deserved better than me. She deserved someone who would worship the ground she walked on, who would be there for her at the end of a hard day's work, someone who could spend their weekends with her.'

He picked up his wineglass and twirled the liquid, looking into it but not seeing it at all. Sheena watched him closely. He was miles away. She could see the pain in his eyes and in his furrowed brow as he recalled his past.

'I was always being called away to an emergency or would be stuck late in Theatre or would be in meetings or on call over the weekend. I was often either interstate or overseas consulting on different cases, especially with conjoined twins. It completely frustrated her. I guess in the end it all took its toll because I could see Beatrice was coming to resent my job, even though she admired my dedication.' He put the glass down without taking a sip. 'That was when I came to the conclusion that she deserved better.'

'It's difficult doing the right thing—especially when it tears you up inside.' Sheena spoke softly, remembering the way she'd felt when she'd turned down Will's proposal, knowing that he deserved better. Even now, sitting across the table from him all these years later, she still felt the pain of that day. 'I'm sorry it didn't work out for you, Will. Truly I am.' There was deep sincerity in her tone.

Before he could reply, a man approached their table.

'I heard you were in my restaurant and I had to come and say hello to the beautiful mother. It is good to see you in here and not be sending you takeaway.' The elderly Italian, suave and debonair, pulled Sheena to her feet and kissed both of her cheeks soundly.

'It's good to be here, Giuseppe.' Sheena smiled at the man, genuinely pleased to see him.

'And the babies? They are fine? Growing big? I am sorry that I have not been in to see them more. Business has been busy.'

'Don't you worry about it. The girls are both growing big but visitors will be restricted for the next month or so.' She glanced at Will, then back to the proprietor. 'Their surgery will start soon.' There was a hint of anxiety in her tone. Will was sure Giuseppe hadn't picked up on it, but he could tell. It appeared that talking about the major surgical operation caused Sheena quite a bit of distress—and rightly so. The lives of her baby girls would be in jeopardy. While the assembled teams responsible for the surgery were all experts and were all doing every test possible to avoid complications, sometimes unforeseen problems arose.

'In fact,' she continued, 'please allow me to introduce you to the leading orthopaedic surgeon on the case, Will Beckman.'

Will stood and held out his hand to the restaurateur.

'Ah. Dr Will. I have heard Miles talk of you.' Giuseppe disregarded Will's proffered hand and instead grabbed him by the shoulders, leaning up to kiss him on both cheeks. 'You are most welcome to my humble restaurant and, please, you must accept that you are my guests this late evening.'

When both of them started to protest, he held up his hands. 'I insist. I will leave you now. You no doubt have much to discuss, but remember—when you are at that hospital and you are hungry, you call Giuseppe and I will prepare you fresh food and send it straight away.'

'Thank you.' Sheena leaned over and kissed his cheek. 'You're a good man.'

'And we will have Ellie's and Sarah's first birthday party here,' he declared. 'It will be bigger and better than Miles's and Janessa's wedding reception.' He placed a hand to the side of his mouth and said in a stage whisper, 'But we won't tell Miles and Janessa that.' Letting out a large belly laugh, Giuseppe headed back towards the kitchen.

'He's jovial, isn't he?' Will stated rhetorically as they sat back down.

'He is.'

'So this is where Miles and Janessa had their reception. I was sorry I had to leave early.'

'Everyone understood, Will. You had a sick patient to care for. Miles was thrilled you'd made it to the ceremony, so was Janessa, but this place looked like something out of a romantic fairy-tale. Giuseppe and his staff had hung twinkle lights around the room with big bouquets of flowers on each table. Crisp white tablecloths, white covers with big red bows on the chairs…' She trailed off and slowly shook her head. 'He really outdid himself.' Sheena sighed, wistful and relaxed, even if it was for just a moment.

Will couldn't help but watch her. Outwardly she'd changed but only slightly. Her hair was much shorter now than when they'd been together and where he'd loved her long hair, he couldn't get over how perfect the short cut, as her hair bounced and curled slightly around her face, suited her. Dark hair, pale skin, blue eyes, pink lips. That was Sheena.

'Giuseppe's a good man,' she continued as she took a sip of her water. 'Genuine, too.'

'That's an odd comment to make.'

'Not really. The hospital has been contacted by so many different firms. People who sell baby clothes, baby furniture, baby toys, all wanting me to use their products with the twins so they can give a "used by Adelaide's own conjoined twins Ellie and Sarah Woodcombe" endorsement. It's quite ridiculous.'

'But I'll bet you've stood your ground and didn't endorse a single product, right?'

'Right.'

'And yet you're more than happy for Giuseppe to organise, six months in advance, the girls' first birthday party?'

'If he wants to. As I've said, he's genuine. He cares about what happens to my girls, and to me. It's nice. He's not in it for the publicity.'

Will finished his last mouthful and dabbed at his mouth with a napkin. 'Are you sure?'

'Definitely. I have to believe I'm still a good judge of character.'

Was she talking about him? Did she not trust her judgement where he was concerned? 'You've had reason to question it?'

Sheena shrugged carelessly and pushed her plate away, her food only half-eaten. 'My divorce was finalised three months ago, Will, so, yes, you could say that I've had reason to question it.'

'Fair enough.' The wistfulness had disappeared from her eyes and he could tell she was getting more and more tired with each passing moment. He wanted to see happiness light her features again, to listen to her talk with optimism and spirit. He offered her dessert or a coffee but she turned both down and suggested they call it a night.

They said goodbye to Giuseppe and thanked him for their meals, taking another ten minutes just to get out of the restaurant, but when they were in the taxi, heading back to the hospital, Sheena leaned her head back against the seat, her eyes closed.

'Tell me more about Miles's and Janessa's reception,' Will said softly.

'Why?'

He shrugged. 'I wasn't there. You were.'

'They have the whole thing on DVD.'

Will exhaled with resignation. 'You know I hate sitting down and watching those things.'

She opened her eyes, giving him a small smile. 'I remember.'

'I'd much rather hear about it from you.'

'OK, but you still might not be able to get out of sitting down and watching the whole two-hour DVD—with running commentary from both Miles and Janessa.' She chuckled and when they arrived back at the hospital allowed him to hold the door for her. She was tired, and as they walked along she tripped, her feet tired and clumsy, but Will was there to steady her, leaving one arm about her waist afterwards.

She talked softly, telling him about the reception and how Miles hadn't been able to keep his eyes or his hands off his bride. 'I've never seen Janessa or Miles so happy, and even now, three months on, they're both still ecstatic.'

'Yes. It is nice.'

The entire time she talked and the entire time he listened, she was acutely aware of the way his arm hovered lightly at her waist, supporting her in her exhausted state in case she stumbled again. When she shivered due to the very early morning breeze, he quickly slipped off his suit jacket and placed it around her shoulders. She wished he hadn't because then his scent only encompassed her even more.

She wasn't even quite sure what she was saying any more, her mind sluggishly trying to recall events that had happened at her best friend's wedding. All she was aware of was his nearness, his arm at her waist, his jacket around her shoulders. His scent, his touch, his heat. It flowed through her, bringing dormant parts of her that she'd buried way down deep pulsating back to life.

As they entered the residential wing, Sheena stopped

walking and Will dropped his arm as she turned to face him. 'Anyway, this is where I'm staying. It's lodgers only past this point, I'm afraid. If you came in, you'd need to sign the register and give proof of identification, and it's all too much rigmarole for this time of night.'

'Early morning,' he corrected, as she slid his suit jacket from her shoulders and handed it back with thanks.

She shrugged and crossed her arms over her chest, both as a means of guarding herself from him but also to help her keep warm after the loss of his jacket. 'I guess I'll see you in the morning.'

'I guess you will.'

She paused. 'Thanks again for dinner…and the chat. I hope I've been able to put your mind at rest, to give you the answers you were looking for.'

'In a way, yes. I think I've realised tonight that ten years ago I didn't know you as well as I thought I did. Perhaps, when you turned me down, you did do the right thing after all.'

'Oh.' Why was it that his words pierced her heart and made her feel bereft? Standing here, looking at him, and now being the mother of two gorgeous girls, she wished on all the wishes in the world that she could go back in time and *accept* his proposal. They would have been married, she would have had the surgery and she would have conceived *his* children, and they all would have lived happily ever after.

But that wasn't the way things had turned out. To all intents and purposes they were strangers…strangers who shared a past.

CHAPTER FOUR

ON FRIDAY, the tissue expanders were removed, Miles and Janessa more than happy with the way the girls were handling the preparation for their up-and-coming long surgical procedure. Today was Sunday and the girls had just returned from the radiology department, where they'd undergone yet another scan. Their surgery was scheduled for the following morning and tensions were high.

Sheena knew it was all necessary and that the more information the surgeons had before the big day the better, but each time the girls needed scans they had to be anaesthetised and Sarah always woke up grouchy.

Sarah shifted in the crib, accidentally kicking Ellie, and by the time the porters had wheeled the crib back onto the paediatric ward, both girls were crying.

'Oh, I know. I know,' she crooned to both of them, quickly settling the crib and touching both of their cheeks. She pressed kisses to Ellie's forehead and then to Sarah's, but both girls cried on, part sleepy, part annoyed and part hungry.

'It's all right. Mummy's here. I'll get your bottles.' She pressed the buzzer on the wall, indicating she needed some help from one of the staff. The girls couldn't be left alone while she went off to get bottles of her expressed milk, which were stored in a fridge in the staffroom, especially as they were still coming around from an anaesthetic.

Raquel-Maria stuck her head around the door. 'Bottles?'

'Yes, please.' When she'd left, Sheena pressed a hand to her breasts, feeling the let-down pain of milk release, which often happened around the girls' feed time. It would mean that she would soon need to express some more milk, and while she knew it was the best thing for her babies, to be drinking her milk complete with antibodies, she had to admit she often felt like a cow at milking time.

'But you're worth it,' she crooned to the two of them, still kissing them and whispering to them in a quiet and controlled voice.

'I hear it's feeding time,' a deep voice said from the doorway, and when Sheena looked up, she saw Will standing there, holding two ready-to-drink bottles of expressed milk.

'Yes. What are you doing here?'

'Checking on my patients. Raquel-Maria told me to bring these to you so I guess I'm also helping with the feeding.'

Sarah started to cry even harder and it didn't matter whether Sheena liked having Will in the room to help out or not, the girls needed feeding.

'Help me raise the crib so it's at an angle—they feed better that way.'

Will nodded, put both bottles down on the table and helped Sheena to turn the handles located on either side of the crib, which then angled the entire mattress, making it easier to feed the girls.

Sheena had only seen him sporadically since their impromptu dinner the other night. She knew the theatre team, which included Will, had been meeting for hours on end to go over every aspect of the surgery. He'd been around several times to assess the girls but at no point had he referred to their conversation at dinner. She hoped that meant he'd received the answers he'd been looking for and that they could keep their relationship professional and focused on the girls. Sheena needed all her mental strength to cope with what was happening tomorrow.

'You take Ellie. I'll do Sarah. She's already starting to work herself up and if she doesn't feed properly, she'll be sick.'

Will agreed and quickly tested both bottles by shaking a few drops from each onto his wrist, ensuring the milk was the correct temperature before handing one bottle to Sheena. She went round to the right side of the crib, bending over Sarah a bit more. 'Shh, darling. Mummy's here. Mummy's here. It's OK. Everything's OK,' she crooned softly, and ever so slightly Sarah's cries started to subside.

Sheena bent her finger and put her knuckle near Sarah's mouth to initiate the sucking reflex and the baby quietened a bit more. With a lightning-quick move, she swapped her knuckle for the teat of the bottle before Sarah could protest and, with Ellie already drinking the bottle Will was holding, the room was soon plunged into a welcome silence.

'That's better,' she said with a sigh, trying her best to stop Sarah from guzzling the milk.

'She certainly has a good set of lungs on her,' Will murmured, a half-smile on his lips.

'That's for certain.' They both fell silent, listening to the girls drinking from their bottles with little murmuring noises of satisfaction.

'Are you looking forward to them starting solids?'

'Most definitely, they're growing so rapidly. While they were quite small when they were born, they weren't as small as Janessa first feared, and both of them have fantastic appetites. A nice five and a half pounds for Sarah and five pounds for Ellie.'

'That *is* quite good for twins. You said you were bedridden for the last few months of your pregnancy.'

'It was safer for the girls. There was no way I was going to miscarry, and with being in hospital…well, I didn't have anywhere to live anyway so it was best for all.'

'Do you have somewhere to live now?'

'Not anywhere outside the hospital. It seemed pointless to be paying rent or a mortgage when I'm spending all my time here. There are nights when I sleep in this room and other nights when I sleep in the residential wing. I've recently gone back to consulting a few half-days per week in the clinic and, quite frankly, finding somewhere to live isn't a high priority at the moment.' She stroked Sarah's cheek, maternal love in her voice as she spoke. 'The girls need me here.'

Will agreed with her sentiments but it seemed odd to him that she had no place she could call home. She was a strong woman. He'd always known that about her, but to see her like this, alone in the world, a single mother without the support of her parents, about to face an emotionally taxing forty-eight hours with her daughters' impending surgery, only highlighted just how strong she was.

'Everyone needs roots, Sheena.'

'And that's what I'm doing for my girls. They're going to be in hospital for at least the next three months and then I'll buy a house, put down roots and start my own happy home. I want to have that perfect, fairy-tale family life you often talked about. I want the laughter and silly little squabbles and the making up and the sorting out. I want Sarah and Ellie to have the type of home life I always dreamed of but never had.'

Will pondered her words for a moment, reflecting on the

squabbles he'd had with his brothers and sisters—the loud family dinners, the strict rules and regulations his parents had enforced, all designed to love and protect their brood. It was what he'd wanted, that idyllic picture of family, and Sheena intended to paint her own version…without a father for her girls.

He knew she could do it. He knew she would struggle and be severely challenged along the way and the briefest part of him wanted to be around to help and to advise and be challenged alongside her…but he knew that was impossible.

While Ellie and Sarah were indeed gorgeous girls, they weren't his. He hadn't come to Australia to play father figure to another man's children. He'd come as a surgeon, one responsible for leading the team of highly skilled orthopods in the separation procedure of the twins. He looked down at Ellie, who had almost finished her bottle, her face relaxed in contented pleasure, her stomach full, completely unaware of what awaited her.

The next day might well be the biggest day of her young life but she didn't know it. She was small and helpless and trusting. What if, when she grew up, she trusted the wrong person? What if someone teased her or bullied her at school? What if she fell in love with a boy who didn't love her back?

Will swallowed over the instant need to protect her—not only Ellie but Sarah as well. These girls had no father figure in their life, not even a grandfather who could step in and provide guidance.

But these weren't his children. He had to keep reminding himself of that.

Will removed the bottle when Ellie finished feeding, looking over at Sarah who had also finished. She lay there, wriggling her feet and hands a little, her big blue eyes wide open, eyes that were exactly the same shade as her mother's.

He couldn't believe how much the girls looked like Sheena. Even though they were only six months old, they were both incredibly beautiful—as was their mother.

Sheena looked at him and held his gaze, neither of them speaking but both saying a lot with their eyes. Will could see a mixture of confusion and despair behind her brave front. When she bit her lip, he knew she was nervous and worried about something. Well, of course she would be. The next forty-eight hours were going to be some of the most intensely emotional hours she had faced. He wanted to go to her, to hold her, to reassure her, to tell her that everything would be all right, that he and the team of doctors had successfully separated other sets of conjoined twins who had been even more intricately connected than Ellie and Sarah, but he didn't.

Sheena looked away, moving to stand in front of the girls, rubbing and gently patting their chests. Ellie stayed asleep and Sarah started to relax even more, her eyelids starting to flutter closed, getting heavier by the moment.

Sheena started to hum a soft lullaby, the sweet melody filling the small private room. Sarah instantly responded to the sound and soon the twins had successfully slipped back into slumber.

Will allowed her song to wind its way around him. She had such a beautiful voice and the words of love contained in the lyrics were sung with such heartfelt intensity. He could recall his own mother singing to him as a child, the sounds strong and reassuring, and he'd been able to close his eyes and fall asleep secure in the knowledge that with his family around him he would always be safe.

Her voice broke as she finished the song, emotion rising to the fore. The room was plunged into silence as she pulled a blanket over the girls and tucked them in. Then she stepped back, shoved her hands into the pockets of her denim skirt and looked at Will.

'Thanks for your help.' Her tone was thick, and Will could see her anxiety and concern for her girls was increasing.

'You're welcome.' He shoved his hands deep into his pockets, too. They both stood there, looking at each other, remembering what had attracted them to each other in the first place all those years ago as well as fighting the present attraction, which seemed to weigh heavily about them. 'I'd forgotten just how lovely your voice was.'

Sheena smiled but it didn't reach her eyes. Her lower lip began to wobble. 'It's nice of you to say so.' She clenched her jaw and blinked a few times, trying to hold on to her emotions. Why wasn't he leaving? Why was he just standing there? She was almost at breaking point and a few of the looks he'd given her already had let her know that he had no intention of picking up where they'd left off.

Her breathing rate started to increase and the tears came into her eyes, refusing to be blinked away. 'I don't want to hold you up. You probably have a lot of things to do and organise.' She wiped a hand impatiently across her eyes, sniffing and swallowing over the large lump in her throat. Her chin wobbled again.

'Sheena—' he began, clearly seeing her distress.

'Just…go. Please?'

'You're worried about the girls. That much is evident.' He felt so helpless, standing there with his hands in his pockets. What he wanted desperately was to go to her, to put his arms around her, to comfort her, to help her, as he had so often in the past.

'Of course I'm worried about them. I know you say that everything is going to be all right but—' She broke off, the tears and emotions overcoming her. 'They're my babies.

Mine.' She looked at him then, tears streaming down her cheeks, lips pursed together between the gasps of air she was dragging into her lungs. 'I never thought I'd ever have children and now that I do, I want to protect them and keep them safe and do everything I can for them and give them the chance of a normal life and...' She let the sentence drift off, hiccuping a little. 'I love them so much, Will,' she said through her tears, 'and if they...if something goes—' She broke off, shaking her head, then whispered between her sobs, 'I'm terrified.'

'Oh, Sheenie,' he ground out, and within the next instant he'd covered the distance that separated them and hauled her into his protective arms.

How on earth was he supposed to resist this woman when she needed him most? He stood firm and held her in his arms, bringing her as close to his body as he dared. Memories flooded through his mind as he breathed in her scents, allowing the essence of Sheena to wash over him. Will closed his eyes, resting his chin lightly on her head as she buried her face into his shirt and continued to cry.

It would be far too easy to slip back into old habits, of thinking about her in a romantic light. That wasn't why he was here and he had to find the strength to at least keep himself one step removed from her...but it was extremely difficult when she was this upset. He tightened his hold on her.

As her sobs began to subside, her breathing became deeper and she settled against his chest, her hands tucked beneath her chin. She wasn't exactly sure how long they stood there but even as the hiccuping became less, Will made no move to pull away. Sheena kept her eyes closed, breathing in the fresh earthy scent that always drove her to distraction.

Feeling his arms about her, being so close to his firm,

muscled body, listening to his heart beat beneath his chest… these were the little things in life she'd thought she'd never get the chance to experience again. When she'd rejected his proposal, it had broken her heart. The look of surprise, of disbelief, of complete anguish that had been present in his features, his blue eyes changing from sincere to stormy, had been a sight burned into her memory.

Never again had she thought she'd be enfolded in his arms, drawing comfort from him, but here she was, feeling safe and secure and protected. Her breathing was almost back to normal now and still he made no move to pull away.

Was it the past that was making him stay where he was? Or was it possible that Will had really forgiven her for refusing his proposal and was ready to move on with their friendship? The fact that the underlying attraction between them had never died was clearly evident but she had no idea what it might mean.

She could feel a sneeze starting to build and sniffed, trying to make it go away, twitching her nose to try and get rid of it. She wanted to stay here in Will's arms and not worry about anything else. She pursed her lips, trying to hold back the building sneeze, but knew it wasn't doing any good. A shudder began to ripple through her body and if she didn't pull away from him now and quickly get a tissue… well, it wasn't going to be pretty.

Jerking back, forcing his arms to suddenly let her go, Sheena spun around and all but lunged for the tissue box. She wrenched out a tissue just in time, sneezed and then blew her nose. She tried to blow quietly so as not to wake the girls, and when she was finished she picked up the tissues and turned to put them in the bin—only to find the room empty.

Will had gone…again.

* * *

Will continued to scrub his hands, his mind focused on what lay ahead. Doing his best for his patients was what he'd always done, but this time it was different. This time it was personal and he knew he wasn't the only one in the operating suite who felt the same way. Both Miles and Janessa were here, along with a lot of the other Adelaide Mercy theatre staff.

Of course, there were also staff who had only arrived the day before, such as Marta von Hugen, a colleague from Philadelphia, with whom both he and Miles had worked with on several occasions. Marta would be in charge of the second team of specialists as surgery of this magnitude meant that staff worked on a rotating basis. Ensuring the health and alertness of all involved with such extensive surgery was of paramount importance.

Will looked at the scans that were up on the viewing box in the theatre room. He'd studied them so completely that he felt he knew every inch of them. As far as the operation went, he'd been faced with far more complicated surgery and had been successful with all of them.

'It looks good,' Miles said, coming to stand beside him at the scrub sink.

'Clean,' Will agreed. 'Parapagus twins are the most straightforward when it comes to separation.'

'Should only take somewhere between fifteen to seventeen hours.'

Will nodded, both of them knowing that they'd been in surgery far longer with other conjoined twins over the years. With Ellie and Sarah being conjoined in the lower body, side to side, and given that they didn't share any major veins or arteries, the surgery should indeed be straightforward.

Still, that didn't stop Will from being concerned about Sheena.

'You're frowning,' Miles pointed out. 'What's wrong? Have you found something the rest of us have missed?'

'Do you know what Sheena's planning to do all day while we're in surgery?' He looked back down at his hands, using the special nailbrush to ensure all dirt was definitely gone.

'As far as I know, she's going to fill in at the paediatric clinic and then work on the ward.'

'She's going to work?' Will was instantly concerned.

'She's a fully qualified—and might I add completely brilliant—paediatrician, and as quite a few of her colleagues are here working with us, offering to hold the fort is her way of helping and keeping her mind busy so she doesn't dwell on the girls.'

Will pondered that for a moment then nodded. 'I guess I'd want to keep busy if it were my daughters undergoing extensive surgery.' He elbowed off the taps and turned with his hands held upwards to receive a sterile towel from one of the nurses. He didn't want to be thinking about Sheena at this time, or her well-being, or how she was coping, or anything else for that matter. Of course he was concerned about her, just as he would be about any other parents of conjoined twins, but right now he needed to keep his head in the game. 'Time to be completely focused,' he murmured.

Miles nodded. 'It's never easy operating on someone you know and love. Those little girls are my goddaughters and I love them very much.'

'There is something special about them,' Will agreed, a small smile tugging at his lips. It had only been a matter of days since he'd met Ellie and Sarah but he knew that both girls had already infiltrated his heart. He'd tried telling himself that they were just another set of conjoined twins, that they were the same as all the other twins he'd operated on over the years, but he knew he was lying to himself.

As he continued to gown and glove, the theatre nurse tying his mask in place, Will looked to where the six-month-old twins had been anaesthetised and were waiting for their surgeons to start this operation.

Soon he stood beside Miles, the two men so in tune with each other that they were able to communicate with simple glances and looks. Right now, both of them seemed to be wearing the same expression, that of complete focus on what was about to happen.

'It's just the same as any other operation,' Will remarked, and Miles nodded.

'Switch off the personal, switch on the professional,' Miles agreed.

They stood there silent for the next minute, waiting for the go-ahead from the anaesthetist. The little girls looked so tiny with tubes and leads coming from them, their radiographs up on the view boxes around the room. On either side of the central theatre were two smaller theatres, which would be used once the girls had been separated.

Paul, the anaesthetist, looked at them and nodded, indicating he was ready. Will looked to Miles. 'For Sheena,' he said softly, and Miles gave an imperceptible nod of agreement.

After addressing the theatre staff, Miles began the slow and careful process of making the first incision. This operation was not about speed, it wasn't about a quick fix. It required a methodical and painstakingly perfect process. No mistakes. Will stood back and watched as his friend and the rest of the team set to work.

When it was time for him to step forward, he looked again at his friend and could see that Miles was smiling beneath his theatre mask.

'All yours,' Miles remarked, his voice upbeat.

'Thanks. Good to hear that tone in your voice, mate.' The

staff shifted around, the orthopaedic theatre nurses coming forward while the others took a much-needed break.

'Let's just say there haven't been any unwanted surprises.'

'That's the type of news I like to hear.' Will checked with the anaesthetist. 'Status?'

The anaesthetist rattled off his statistics before smiling brightly at Will. 'Both Ellie and Sarah are doing remarkably well,' came the jovial reply.

'Excellent.' Will straightened his spine as he looked down at the draped little bodies in front of him, the large conjoined pelvic bone neatly exposed. Separating the girls meant that they would be able to lead normal, healthy, happy lives. Two little dark-haired girls and their dark-haired mother. Three beautiful ladies…all on their own.

Will felt a surge of protectiveness pierce his heart at this thought but quickly dismissed it. He wasn't a part of Sheena's life any more and yet he'd already come to care deeply for her little girls. He wanted the best for Sarah and Ellie; he wanted to make sure they had every advantage growing up; he wanted them to know how precious they were.

Although he and Miles had told themselves that this surgery was just like any other, that there was nothing different about these babies as opposed to the others they'd operated on, they'd also known that they'd been lying to themselves.

Will paused as he looked down at the girls, a brief moment of panic and fear gripping him. What if something went wrong? What if a problem arose that they'd been unable to anticipate? Would Sheena ever be able to forgive him? The last thing he wanted to do was to cause her pain. After talking with her the other night, he'd come to realise that he was as much at fault for their break-up as Sheena. If only he'd asked her more questions, taken a real interest in *her* rather than simply assuming her life had run a similar course to his own. He'd been blinded by love, blinded by the fact that he'd found his happily-ever-after and had assumed that, because Sheena had admitted her love for him, they would be together for ever.

He'd bought the engagement ring, barely able to contain his excitement at the promise of a rosy future with the woman of his dreams. Then, when she'd turned him down, he'd plummeted, stunned and shocked when she'd confessed she couldn't have children.

For the first time in his life the perfect fairy-tale family picture he'd always had firmly in his mind had started to shake, the foundation of imagination and anticipation nowhere near as solid as he'd thought.

Now, as he was about to perform this intricate surgery on Sheena's beautiful girls, he couldn't help but ponder that if things had gone differently between Sheena and himself, if he'd been less pushy and she'd been more open, these little darlings might have been *his* daughters.

Having always longed to be a father and with those dreams having been cut off with Sheena's rejection, his hopes and dreams had been pushed aside while he'd focused on his career, knowing that medicine was absolute and something he could control. Until he'd met Beatrice, he hadn't realised how much he'd locked his heart away, but being back near Sheena made him realise that what he'd felt for Beatrice paled into insignificance when he was around the mother of these gorgeous twins. She'd allowed him to spend quality time with Sarah and Ellie, and seeing the way they were coming to recognise him when he walked into the room, loving the way they would smile and gurgle and make cute little noises, had unlocked those dreams of parenthood from his heart.

Two little girls—without a father.

Was it possible that if he returned to Australia, if he came home to Adelaide, if he and Sheena could find a basis for a solid friendship, he might be able to fill that void? Surrogate father? It wasn't picture perfect, it wasn't what he'd always dreamed of, but for some reason these two angels had well and truly captured his heart. Even in the short amount of time he'd spent with them during the past few days, watching the way they interacted with Sheena, smiling at the way Sarah always seemed to be the one causing a ruckus while Ellie preferred to keep things calm, Will had been captivated by these twins.

They were different from his other patients because he cared about their mother. That made all the difference in the world. These girls needed him. Sheena needed someone to lean on, someone who knew her well, and with determination coursing through him he decided that he wanted to be that person. First of all, he needed to do what he'd come here to do and focus on this surgery. He'd mentally walked through the operation so many times that it only took a moment to get his thoughts neatly ordered once more.

He raised his gaze to look at the highly skilled staff ready to work with him.

'Let's begin.'

CHAPTER FIVE

WILL was exhausted but elated, and as he stripped off his theatre garb excitement started to grow as he thought about the look on Sheena's face when she saw him heading towards her. She would be tense, nervous, worried. He would smile and she would instantly know that every thing was all right. That her girls were fine.

As he exited Theatres, all ready to give her the good news, he was astounded to discover she wasn't there. He knew she'd planned to work in the paediatric clinic but clinics would be well and truly finished by now. Perhaps she was on the ward. He headed to Paediatrics, still elated at what he and the team of specialists had achieved.

There was always relief when everything had gone according to plan and there was always a strong sense of satisfaction when both babies were doing well after such intense surgery, but this time, with Ellie and Sarah, the two little girls who had completely captured his heart, he felt as though he'd just been handed the moon. Now he could offer that moon to Sheena.

He couldn't hide the smile on his face as he entered the paediatric ward, his gaze eagerly scanning for Sheena. Raquel-Maria and Clementine, at the nurses' station, saw him coming and immediately returned his smile.

'You're out! By the look on your face, it's all good news,' Raquel-Maria commented.

'Yes. Where's Sheena?'

Raquel-Maria shook her head. 'She's not here. She was about an hour ago, but then she left. We thought she'd gone to Theatres to wait.'

Will continued to scan the ward, just in case the women were wrong. 'Try paging her. Calling her. Anything!' Even as he said the words, he was racking his brain to try and figure out where she might have gone. Where would Sheena go? To be alone? To think? To wait?

'She's not answering her phone,' Raquel-Maria said, concern in her tone. 'I wonder where she might be?'

The chapel. The words popped into his head and he remembered the other night, as they'd been walking to catch the taxi to Giuseppe's, she'd mentioned she liked going to the little chapel to think and relax and become one with her thoughts.

'Never mind, Raquel-Maria.' Will headed for the ward door. 'I know where she might be.' He walked briskly along the long corridors, barely able to contain the urge to run through the hospital, desperate to find her, desperate to give her the good news.

Her girls were fine.

He stepped out into the cool October night air and walked across the courtyard to the small brown-brick chapel. She needed to know. Her girls were safe. She needed to know because already half the hospital had received the news and he didn't want the mother to be the last to know.

He pushed open the door with an eagerness that surprised him. He needed to see her, to deliver the news that would bring a smile to her face. He wanted to see that smile, so bright, so wide, causing her eyes to sparkle with happiness.

There were several wooden pews on either side of the aisle, the chapel lit with the glow of large candles, the scent of fresh spring flowers filling the air. There was only one person in the chapel, kneeling down, hands resting on the back of the pew in front, head bowed.

Sheena.

Will rushed down, not caring that he was interrupting her thoughts. 'Sheena!' He didn't speak loudly but it was loud enough for her name to echo softly around the walls. She immediately looked up, seeing him coming towards her, entering the row she was in. She rose to her feet, her face filled with anxiety and pain, her heart pounding with ferocity against her ribs such as she'd never felt before.

Will was here. He must have news about her girls.

'They're fine. They're good. They're better than good.' The words tumbled from his lips, desperate to give her relief from the torment he could see on her face.

'Oh. Oh!' She covered her mouth with one hand as her eyes filled with tears. 'My girls?'

'They're perfect. They handled the surgery with ease. They're strong, those two. Real fighters.' There was great pride in his voice as he spoke. 'There were no complications. Everything went according to plan. Miles and Janessa are monitoring the girls closely in Recovery and everything is perfect. They're *perfect*,' he repeated, his tone conveying his elation.

'Oh, Will. Thank you.' She sniffed and threw her arms about his neck, hugging him close. It was the most natural thing to do, to hold him close as she allowed the emotions of relief and happiness to wash over her. 'Thank you. Thank you. It seems such an insignificant thing to say when I feel so much more, but I can't thank you enough.'

Will's arms automatically slid around her waist, keeping

her near. She felt good in his arms. Right. As though she belonged there. As though she'd *always* belonged there. Will pushed the realisation away, knowing he would ponder it in more depth much later. Now that the initial surgery was complete, he might be able to give more thinking time to figuring out what might happen next.

'It's been my pleasure,' he murmured near her ear, content to breathe her in. 'Those girls are fighters. Strong. Independent. Determined. Like their mother.'

'Oh, Will.' Sheena pulled back to look at him. 'That's so…' She swallowed, only realising then just how incredibly close she was to his mouth. His glorious, masterful mouth. Her gaze dipped from his eyes to look at his lips before she met his eyes again. 'Sweet,' she finished on a whisper, and swallowed, the tension and awareness increasing between them until it was so nearly palpable there was nothing left to do but acknowledge it in the only way they knew how.

They stood there, staring at each other for one more second, and Sheena could take it no longer. With her heart filled with thanks, with elation, with hope, she reached up a little higher and urged his head to dip a little lower, causing their mouths to meet.

She thrilled at the instant touch, the light, feathery sensation as though they were both testing the reaction, both wanting this to happen but also very unsure. There were a lot of what-if's surrounding them and as she stood there, her arms around his neck, her lips brushing once more across his, her breath mingling with his, Sheena shoved all her reservations, all logical thought completely out the door.

This was Will, the man who had not only been instrumental in assuring her girls were safe and healthy but the man who had the ability to set her heart on fire. She wanted this and she could feel it in the way he held her, the way he brushed his mouth over hers, that he wanted it too. Both seemed intrigued to discover whether their experiences over the past ten years had changed anything. The world had always rocked off its axis when they'd been together and with the way he was making her feel now, it appeared that was still the case.

'Sheena,' he murmured against her mouth, kissing her again, unable to believe how incredible this felt.

'Shh,' she whispered. 'It feels so good. Just kiss me, Will.'

He did as she'd bidden, not about to let her down. There had always been a frighteningly natural chemistry existing between them and it was clearly still there, even after a decade of separation. Slowly he allowed his mouth to re-acquaint itself with hers, knowing what she liked and what would bring her the most joy.

Holding her close, her body pressed against his, her mouth tilted upwards for his pleasure, he continued to bring them both to the heights, not rushing but giving them both exquisite torture. 'You taste the same. Like always. Sunshine and strawberries.' His tone was thick, husky and filled with desire.

With her breathing erratic from his masterful kisses, Sheena sighed and relaxed against him, the emotions of the past few days starting to subside. 'It was always like this. As though fireworks exploded inside me.' As she rested her head against his chest, her arms slack around his neck, she listened to the thumping of his heart beating beneath his chest. So strong. So vibrant. As it had always been.

'Do you remember our very first kiss?' Will asked a moment later, and Sheena couldn't help but smile.

'I was just thinking about that myself. We'd just finished a gruelling thirty-six-hour shift with that nasty motor vehicle accident.'

'We'd been spending quite a bit of time together.'

'Two Aussies working in London,' she finished. 'I was tired and on my way back to my accommodation and you insisted on walking with me.'

'It was three o'clock in the morning, Sheena,' he protested. 'I wanted to make sure you were safe.'

'You walked me to my door at the old nurses' home and we stood on the step, in the cold, staring at each other.'

Will eased back and looked down at her. 'You looked so tired and exhausted but I could tell you were excited, I could see it in your eyes.'

Sheena smiled up at him, her arms still about his neck as they both took a trip down memory lane. 'You shuffled your feet, you put your hands into your pockets and you tried not to stare at my lips.'

'You had the most gorgeous mouth…you still do.'

Sheena felt a thrill of delight buzz through her at his words, amazed that after so long apart the deep-seated need for him was still very much alive.

'I wasn't sure whether you'd let me kiss you or deck me one.'

'I was hoping you'd give in to the thing that was between us—it was so electric, wasn't it?'

'You hesitated with your key. You didn't put it straight into the lock and go inside. You stopped and looked at me and you didn't seem to want to head in.'

'I didn't. I wanted you to kiss me.'

'And I did.'

Sheena sighed. 'And it was the most perfect kiss I've ever experienced.'

'Really?' Will smiled, trying not to preen like a peacock at this news.

'Yes…although this kiss wasn't so bad either.'

'Wasn't so bad?' He smiled down at her and her heart melted. 'I think I'm going to ignore that but only because we need to go and see your girls.'

Sheena breathed in deeply and slowly eased out of his arms. 'Yes. My babies.' She nodded, although Will could sense a hint of hesitancy in her words.

'Is something wrong?'

'What?' She looked at him in the dim light of the church. 'No. Nothing's wrong.' She smiled and nodded. 'Let's go and see them.'

'Right.' He stepped back so they could exit from the seats and as they walked down the aisle of the small, quiet chapel, he could sense the excited anticipation radiating from her. She'd been through so much, especially today, and finally she had the opportunity to go and see her daughters after their life-changing surgery.

As they walked through the hospital, it was apparent that the good news had travelled fast and everyone they met seemed to beam brightly with happiness at the news that the girls were doing well.

'Fantastic news, Sheena,' one nurse said as they passed in the corridor.

'So happy for the babies,' a cleaner said as they rounded a corner.

Will was happy to share in Sheena's elation as she received comments from her co-workers but what surprised him was the level of elation coursing through him. It was odd simply because he'd performed far more difficult separation surgery, which had dragged on for far longer than today's operation, and still hadn't felt this level of happiness. Why was he so happy? So upbeat?

He glanced at the woman walking beside him, the woman who was smiling so brightly he knew her cheek muscles must be hurting. She looked so incredibly beautiful with her eyes sparkling and her cheeks all rosy. He swallowed and licked his lips, surprised to find the taste of Sheena still lingering there.

It was then he realised it wasn't just the successful operation that had him so happy but the fact that he'd kissed Sheena. It was something he'd promised himself he wouldn't do, but how was he to know that the attraction he'd felt for this woman had only been lying dormant, waiting to be reawakened with her sweet laugh, her sunny smiles and her alluring scent?

'There you are,' the theatre sister remarked as they headed into the theatre block. 'Janessa and Miles have been expecting you.'

'Sorry.' Sheena clasped her hands together as she walked along the corridors and more people offered their happy thoughts at the joyous outcome for the girls. All of it—the sights, the sounds, the smells—became muted. All she could hear as she advanced towards the theatres where the girls were being monitored was the sound of her pounding heart.

Her girls, her beautiful babies, had been separated. They were both alive and progressing well. It was the news she'd only prayed she'd hear, but now that the moment of actually seeing them was upon her, she was gripped with fear. Not fear for her girls but rather fear for the enormous task ahead of her.

Was she up to the task of being both mother and father to her twins? Up until now she hadn't been able to focus on anything else except the surgery. Now that it was over, she felt as though she had the weight of the world on her shoulders. Her feet started to drag and she licked her suddenly dry lips, her eyes wide with concern.

'Sheena?' Will stopped and waited for her when he realised she'd slowed down. 'What's wrong?' he asked, the smile sliding from his face as he watched her closely.

She stopped, swallowed and tried again, feeling silly for voicing her fears out loud. 'I'm…I'm scared, Will.'

'Scared? What about? The girls are strong, they're fighters and they're fine. They're both healthy. Of course, they'll each require further surgery but that's all minor and quite a few weeks away. For now, though, everything is looking better than expected, better than the surgical teams could have hoped.'

'I know. I know, and I appreciate everyone's efforts, their skills, their support, their caring, but…now it's all up to me.'

Panic was beginning to rise in her voice and anxiety was written all over her face. 'In six months,' she said, 'Miles and Janessa will head off overseas, doing their own thing, helping others, and that's good. I'm really happy for them. Everyone else here at the hospital has their own lives despite how much they care for my girls. I'll leave the hospital and I'll be all alone. I have nowhere to take my girls when we leave here and wherever we end up, I'll be raising them on my own and what if—?'

Will leaned forward and placed a finger across her lips to stop her talking. He *had* thought of kissing her to shut her up. It was what he would have done in years gone by and although they'd just shared a few kisses, he had no idea what any of it meant. Had she simply been grateful for what he'd done for her girls? Had she been overcome with relief? Had she used her situation as an excuse to be close to him and, if so, why? What did she want from him? Right now, though, he could see she was confused and anxious about her girls, about her life, her future. Calming her down was the first step to figuring out what was really going on.

'What if you're fine? You, the girls—all fine. This is the

next stage, Sheena. The next chapter.' His tone was calm but firm and he held her gaze, watching as her panic slowly subsided as his words wound themselves around her. 'You've been in survival mode since the girls were born, probably even before that with your husband leaving you in the lurch.' The protective urge he felt towards Sheena came to the fore again and he had to quickly hold it at bay.

'Everything over the past six months has been building towards this day, this hour, this second. That's quite intense. All of your energies have been focused on coping with feeding, bathing, changing and sleeping. They're your girls, Sheena. The babies you thought you'd never have, and for the first time in their lives your girls are currently in separate cribs. *Separate!* That's huge.' He placed his hands on her shoulders and looked down into her eyes, intent on helping her through this.

'It's only natural to have questions, to be worried and concerned, but you can't let that scare you. You're stronger than that. Let's go and see them. Soon you'll be able to hold them. You'll be able to smother them with kisses, to bath them, to dress them in clothes that don't need to be specially made. You've given them the chance to lead normal, healthy lives and that's the one thing every mother wants for her children. You'll be able to cuddle them, one at a time. Or you could have Ellie in one arm and Sarah in the other. And if that gets too much or your arms get too sore, call me. I'm eager to have a cuddle with each of those gorgeous girls. You hold one. I'll hold the other.'

Sheena couldn't help but smile at his words. She sighed, feeling calmer, more in control, better able to cope, and it was all thanks to Will. Not only had he assisted with the intense surgical procedure which had separated her girls, he'd put her mind to rest against the fear and trepidation that had been slowly building throughout the past six months and had only just hit her—square in the face—throughout this day.

'It's just like you to know exactly what to say to make me feel better. Thank you, Will.' His words had given her courage and hope. 'I know it's not going to be easy. I know I'm going to need support and help, and as I'm not very good at asking for either, I guess I'll have to learn.'

Will agreed and dropped his hands back to his sides, pleased he'd been able to help out. He'd also been serious when he'd suggested she call him if she needed help. 'Just take things one step at a time. For now you're surrounded by people who care for you, Sheena. Once you leave the hospital, don't forget there are a lot of community support services as well. You won't be on your own.'

Excitement started to replace fear and she couldn't contain it as her eyes flashed with delight. 'I *do* want to see them.' Love filled her heart. 'I'm *desperate* to see them, and you're so right, Will. This is the next chapter of my life. It's not going to be an easy road but I'll do it. I have to face my fears sometime, right?'

'That's the Sheena I know.' He winked at her as she once more started to walk, eager now to see her daughters. She was facing her fears with her head held high and he was incredibly proud of her for that...which only made her even more difficult to resist.

When he ushered her into Recovery she stood there, looking at her daughters, who were, for the very first time, sleeping in separate cribs. Janessa and Miles, along with several other specialists, were attending the babies, but when Sheena entered the room they stepped back, smiles on their tired faces as she walked slowly towards her girls.

'Thank you,' she murmured to the room in general, the

words heartfelt and filled with sincerity, but her gaze was solely trained on her babies. She shook her head as though she couldn't quite believe it. 'They're separated.' The words were whispered, catching against the emotion choking her throat, but in the quiet of the room, everyone heard.

She reached out to Ellie, tenderly brushing her fingers across the baby's face before leaning down and kissing her daughter. Then she turned and walked over to where the other crib was situated and did the same thing to Sarah, a gentle caress and then the kiss of a mother who loved her babies very much.

From his vantage point in the doorway, Will watched the entire scene and when he felt his own throat start to thicken, he looked around the room, watching as other people followed Sheena's actions, all of them almost as happy as the mother herself that everything had gone according to plan, with no surprises during the surgery and no complications thus far.

Sheena reluctantly tore her gaze away from her beloved babies to look at everyone in the room—the nurses, the doctors, the surgeons, some, like Janessa, who were lifelong friends, and others, like Marta, who she'd only met the day before.

'Thank you. Thank you all so much.' She clutched her hands to her chest, her words sincere.

Then she looked over at Will and while the look of appreciation and thanks was still definitely in her eyes, they seemed to soften as they rested on him. 'I still can't believe this has really happened.' She swallowed, her tongue flicking out to wet her dry lips, and Will felt a tightening in his gut. Her lips. Her gorgeous, succulent, perfectly plump lips. Lips that not ten minutes ago had been pressed to his.

'It's good to see,' Miles remarked, coming to stand beside

Will as Sheena fussed over her two girls. 'A mother who is so in love with her daughters.'

'It's very good.' Will continued to watch Sheena's every move, as though unable to look away from the mesmerising sight. She was so at home with her girls and even though she'd confessed her doubts, he knew they were all for naught. Anyone seeing her with Sarah and Ellie would think the same.

'It's not going to be easy—the road ahead. She's going to need a lot of help,' Miles remarked.

'Agreed, but she's a natural mother with a healthy dose of common sense. She'll be terrific,' Will added.

'Especially if she has help. From people she trusts. People she's known for a long time,' Miles said. 'People like Janessa and myself…and you.'

'What are you trying to imply, Miles?' Will asked, tearing his gaze away from Sheena to look at his friend with a hint of impatience.

'You're someone she trusts, Will.'

'And?'

'And you're due to return to Philly in about five weeks' time.'

'Yeah. So?'

'So…what happens after that? What do you really have waiting for you back in the States? Beatrice didn't exactly take your broken engagement quietly and as she's now a permanent hospital lawyer, it can't make life all that enjoyable for you.'

'What are you getting at, Miles?'

'Why don't you return to South Australia? Your parents are here. Some of your siblings are here.' He paused and said more quietly, 'The people you really care about are all here.

So what's keeping you in the States? Think about it.' Miles slapped his friend on the back before returning to his duties.

Will pondered his friend's words. He couldn't deny he'd given some thought to how his life might change if he moved back to Australia permanently. Sorting out his past with Sheena had helped free up a lot of mind space. It had also made him realise why things had felt wrong with Beatrice. He knew he could have cut back his hours at the hospital when Beatrice had asked him to, if he'd really wanted to, but he could now admit that that hadn't been what he'd wanted.

If he came back to Australia he would definitely cut back on the hours he worked, especially if it meant he could spend more time with Sheena and the twins. It was no secret that those little girls had stolen his heart and he knew he'd do anything for them.

He'd been planning a life with Beatrice and he knew that had they had children, he would have been a hands-on father. Still, he wouldn't have made the work sacrifice *just* for Beatrice. He thought about Sheena, about if they were together and if *she* had been the one to ask him to cut back his hours. Would he have done it?

He frowned a little as he realised the answer. It was yes.

CHAPTER SIX

TWENTY-FOUR hours later, Will went to see how Sheena and the girls were coping. The twins had been in induced comas in order to help them heal and recover. He knew the head anaesthetist, Paul, had been around to review them, and from what Will had just read in Ellie's chart, it looked as though she was doing a little better than Sarah.

He'd only left the hospital once, to return to his parents' house where he was staying, for a quick shower and change of clothes, before coming back to monitor his small patients. He knew he should try to get more sleep but the simple fact of the matter was that he was worried about not only Ellie and Sarah but Sheena as well.

She was sitting in a comfortable chair opposite where her daughters slept, their individual cribs pushed as close as possible. Will stood there, watching her sleep, unable to believe how peaceful she looked. She deserved some peace, some support, some help. He knew she was overwhelmed by the huge job before her but he knew of old that she had so much inner strength she'd do fine…but she'd still be alone.

'Hey,' Miles said softly behind him, and Will turned, unaware his friend had even come into the room. 'How are the girls?'

'Vitals are all good. Sarah's running a bit of a temperature, but it's being closely monitored.' Will angled his head towards the door and both men exited, eager to allow Sheena to sleep for as long as possible. 'Sheena's exhausted,' Will told his friend as they headed towards Miles's small office situated off to the side of the paediatric ward.

'How do you think she's really doing?' Miles asked as the two men sat down.

Will thought carefully before answering. 'She's had a lot to cope with but I think sleeping will help her the most at the moment, allow her body and mind to relax.'

'And how are *you* doing?'

'Me?' Will gave his friend a quizzical glance. 'I'm fine. The operation was a complete success so it looks as though those two little girls can live out very normal, very healthy lives with their mother.'

'I was referring to you seeing Sheena again. It appears you've both managed to work through whatever happened all those years ago.'

'Yes.' Will stood and shoved his hands into his trouser pockets. 'It's all behind us.'

'And you don't think there's any way the two of you can… reconcile?'

'Trying to play matchmaker, Miles?'

'You and Sheena were good together all those years ago. I remember. Now when I see you two together again it just seems…oh, I don't know…right somehow. Janessa and I think the four of you would make a great family.'

'No.' Will immediately shook his head. 'While there might still be some remnant of attraction between Sheena and myself, it doesn't mean there's a future as a family.'

'But you want a family. You've always wanted a family.'

'But this family doesn't belong to me. Those girls—'

'Have no father.'

'That doesn't mean it's up to me to fill the position.' Will paced angrily around Miles's office, back and forth in the small space. 'I've always wanted *my* family. To father my own children. I don't even know if Sheena can *have* more children.'

'There's a slim chance she can,' Miles informed him. 'Her gynaecologist is waiting until she's finished breastfeeding the girls before he makes any decisions, but as far as I've been told, her endometriosis is still bad. It's not as bad as it used to be but as far as I know, she may need to have further surgery, possibly an oophorectomy.'

Will was stunned. 'Why didn't anyone tell me? Why didn't Sheena tell me?'

Miles shrugged. 'She's a strong woman, Will. She's been used to coping with big decisions on her own for quite some time now and she'll keep on coping. Unless she has someone she can lean on…now and then.'

Will frowned, pondering his friend's words. If Sheena needed another operation, if she had an oophorectomy, then she would never be able to have any more children. Ellie and Sarah would be all she'd have and it made those little girls even more precious.

'When did everything become so difficult?' he remarked, shoving his fingers through his hair. 'Ever since I was little, I just wanted to grow up, become a doctor, meet a nice woman, get married, have children and live happily ever after.'

'I know what you mean. That's how I always thought my life would pan out and I thought it had, before my first wife died.' Miles nodded solemnly. 'It's not about where we think we'll end up but how we get there. Janessa's shown me that. She's lost so much in her life and yet those losses have only made her stronger. Sheena's the same. Nessa says that's why the two of them are such close friends, because they've both been to that dark place where they have to endure a lot in order to fight their way out.'

Miles met Will's gaze fair and square. 'You deserve happiness, Will. So does Sheena. She's a woman of substance and she'll deal with whatever comes her way and she'll do it on her own if she has to and I have no doubt that she'll do a bang-up job, but wouldn't it be great if she didn't have to? Wouldn't it be great if she had someone who loved those little girls as much as she did to help her raise them?'

'The twins have a father. He should be here, raising them, supporting Sheena.'

'But he isn't. He's a self-centred, egotistical pig who kicked his pregnant wife out of her home and then divorced her for breach of contract.' Miles gritted his teeth. 'Life isn't fair and Sheena knows that.'

'She really is going to keep soldiering on, isn't she?' Will stated rhetorically. 'Whether I'm in her life or not, she'll move forward, she'll raise those girls on her own, even though she's incredibly scared.'

Realising that Sheena would do what needed to be done, would continue, without any support if necessary, to raise her girls, had helped to dispel the picture of the perfect fairytale family he'd always carried within his heart.

Life wasn't fair. Things hadn't worked out between Sheena and himself all those years ago. Was it possible that he really was being given a second chance? Ellie and Sarah weren't biologically his daughters but they still needed a father.

Will spun on his heel and headed out of Miles's office, back towards the girls' private room. He stopped outside the door and looked in through the small window at Sheena. Although there were blinds on the window, he could see between the slats. She still sat in the chair, laptop on her knee as she stared at something on the screen. Shifting slightly, Will could see she was studying the various radiographs of her daughters as though she still couldn't believe they were now separated.

He could tell, just by looking at the slight slump of her shoulders and the way her head seemed too heavy to hold upright, that she was exhausted but he also knew her stubbornness of old. She wouldn't sleep, at least not properly, until she was certain that both her girls were out of danger. Being a trained paediatrician, she knew that the first twenty-four hours were critical and that monitoring the babies was of utmost importance.

Walking quietly into the room, he glanced at Sheena and saw that although the laptop was on her lap, her eyes were closed. He headed over to the cribs and smiled down at Ellie, sleeping all on her own, with no Sarah to accidentally kick her awake. He was pleased Sheena had insisted the cribs be pushed as close together as possible as research had shown that once conjoined twins were separated, they could often suffer feelings of abandonment. After all, for their entire existence they'd always had someone else right there beside them. He brushed his finger across Ellie's cheek and smiled. She was gorgeous, adorable and so like her mother.

He looked at the machines that were giving readouts of oxygen saturations, EEG and fluid intake and output. He unhooked his stethoscope and placed it over Ellie's chest, listening to her heart rate, confirming it against the EEG. Pleased with her progress, he shuffled around to check on Sarah, frowning a little at the differing readouts. The fluid intake and output wasn't as steady as Ellie's and Sarah's heart was beating at a slightly higher rate. He checked it with his stethoscope, confirming the readings from the machine, and ensured the oxygen non-rebreather mask, which was over her mouth and nose, was securely in place.

'How's she doing?'

Will quickly turned to look at Sheena, sitting in the chair, unsure, in the dim light, whether her eyes were open or closed.

'She's stabilising so that's good.'

'I didn't hear you come in.'

A small smile tugged at his lips. 'Good, because I was trying not to wake you. Have you managed to get much sleep?'

'No, but, then, I'm used to it,' she said on a sigh. Shifting slowly, as though her muscles were a little stiff, she placed the laptop on the table beside her and stood. She wiggled her shoulders and turned her head from side to side before putting her arms up above her head and stretching. 'I was just thinking earlier that I should set up the small camp bed and lie down properly, rather than dozing on and off in the chair.' She smothered a yawn. 'I think the dozing makes me more tired.'

'I think the lack of sleep and high stress levels are what's causing your exhaustion,' he returned, but Sheena could hear the caring note in his words. Will still cared for her and where she'd initially thought it was only because she was the mother of his patients, after the kiss they'd shared in the small chapel, she was desperate to believe it was due to their shared past.

'You have a point. What about you? Have you managed some sleep? That was one gruelling operation you all performed yesterday.'

'I've grabbed a few hours here and there. During the surgery we were working in teams with planned breaks so none of us became exhausted.'

'And I appreciate that. Honestly, Will, saying just a simple "Thank you" to everyone feels so…inadequate.' She walked over to Ellie's crib and looked down at her little girl. 'My babies are no longer conjoined and while I understand the medical side of the surgery and appreciate everyone's skill, the fact of the matter is that my daughters are now able to grow up and lead a more normal life. That's huge.'

Will hooked his stethoscope back around his neck and shifted to stand at the base of both cribs. 'It's what every mother wants for their children. A normal, happy life.'

'Yes.' She rested a hand on Ellie's head, her thumb moving back and forth, caressing her child, who was sleeping peacefully. 'I know there are still long days ahead, especially with Sarah.' She swallowed painfully. 'You know, I never thought I'd be one of those mothers who panicked and fretted over their children. I'm a trained paediatrician. I've seen so many different things happen to children and I have the knowledge and medical expertise to be able to help others. Now, though, I look at these two and realise that I could hold every medical degree in the world and still not have a clue what to do if both of them are screaming and crying at the same time.' She forced a laugh but he could hear fear and uncertainty in her words.

'You're borrowing trouble, Sheena. It's probably one of your biggest weaknesses. You over-think and then you panic and, while you're internally strong and can accomplish anything you put your mind to, you have to let go of all the questions that surround your future. Believe me when I say that you're going to be fine.'

'Do you really think so?'

Will crossed to her side and looked down into her face. 'I know so, Sheena. You're…amazing!'

Sheena's heart started to beat wildly against her chest at his words. 'Really?'

'I would never lie to you.'

Sheena wasn't sure what to think, what to say. He was standing close, so close she could breathe him in, the kisses they'd shared in the chapel coming instantly to mind. Her gaze momentarily dipped to his lips and she was about to ask him about the kisses they'd shared when a small cry, more like a hiccup, came from Ellie. Sheena immediately returned her attention to her daughter. And there in her crib, amongst all the tubes and monitoring paraphernalia, Ellie opened her eyes for the first time since surgery, and looked at her mother.

'Oh. Oh, Will. Look. She's awake!'

Will looked down at beautiful little Ellie, and the baby gave them a sleepy smile.

Love, pure and simple, flowed through Sheena as she bent and kissed her daughter. 'Oh, it's so magnificent, so perfect. Oh, Ellie, honey. Mummy was so worried about you.'

'Yes,' Will agreed, unable, in his elation at seeing Ellie awake, to resist dropping his arm around Sheena's shoulders. 'I think you're going to do much better than *fine*.'

'I need to hold her, Will. I need to hold her.'

'Let's make that happen,' he said, and together they wheeled all the machines that were attached to Ellie over towards the comfortable chair and within a few minutes Will had lifted Ellie from the crib and placed her, for the first time, in her mother's arms.

'Oh, my sweet Ellie. My gorgeous girl.' Sheena held her close and Will couldn't help but kneel down beside the chair, slipping his arm back around Sheena's shoulders, elated when she leaned over and put her head on his shoulder, the two of them staring down at the still sleepy baby.

'This is one of the most precious moments of my life,' Sheena whispered. She lifted her head and turned to look at Will. 'I'm so happy you were here to share it with me.'

Will nodded. 'I'm honoured.' And it was the most natural thing in the world to lean closer and press a kiss to her lips.

It was another twenty-four hours before Sarah decided to settle down, to stop scaring her mother by indulging in high temperatures, and opened her eyes.

Sheena's heart instantly lifted when she saw her daughter's wide blue eyes looking up at her from the crib. 'You're all right. My beautiful Sarah.' Sheena kissed her daughter who, now that she was awake, was already making herself known.

'She's going to give you lots of grey hairs when she's older,' Janessa remarked. Her friend was seated in the comfortable chair, giving Ellie a bottle.

'With the way she peaked a high temperature, I'd say she's already started,' Sheena countered, desperate to pick Sarah up but knowing it was difficult with the tubes and drains still attached to the baby. She pressed the buzzer, letting the staff at the nurses' desk know she needed some help, but as Sarah was starting to work herself up into a real frenzy, Sheena bent over the crib and brushed kisses onto Sarah's cheek. The baby girl tried to hold out her arms to her mother but couldn't because of the drips, which only caused her crying volume to increase.

'Shh. Shh. Mummy's here. Mummy's here,' Sheena crooned. 'It's all right. I'm here.' Thankfully, Sarah started to respond to her mother's voice and when Raquel-Maria came in, Sheena smiled. 'Sorry to disturb you from your duties,' she said to the nurse.

'Sarah's woken up?' Raquel-Maria's smile was wide and

filled with delight. 'Well, of course I can *hear* that she's awake. Oh, how wonderful. That's just wonderful. I take it you want to feed her? Right, then. Let's get you settled.'

A few minutes later Sheena was seated in another comfortable chair, silence filling the air as Sarah greedily suckled at her breast. It was incredible to be able to hold her children one at a time and to feed them, rather than having to constantly express milk. 'Oh, baby. Slow down,' she crooned, settling Sarah a bit better. 'The last thing you need right now is a tummyache.'

'Too true,' Janessa remarked. 'Look, Sheenie. Ellie's fallen back to sleep with just the last bit of her bottle left, but when I try to take it from her mouth, she starts madly sucking again.'

'I know. She often does that. It's so cute.' Sheena sighed and looked across at her other daughter. 'They're both going to be fine. Sarah's awake now and they're both going to be fine.' There was determination in Sheena's tone, mixed with a healthy dose of relief.

'Yes, they are,' Janessa agreed. 'Both Miles and Will are extremely happy with their progress and no doubt Raquel-Maria is off phoning them to let them both know that Sarah's awake.' Janessa looked at the clock on the wall. 'I give Will…under ten minutes before he gets here.'

'He won't just drop everything and race here.'

'Why not? Technically, the girls are his only patients, although now that the major surgery is over, I have to tell you that Charisma is looking to headhunt Will for the hospital.'

'Really?' Sheena looked away, focusing her attention back on Sarah as she tried to process this news. If Will stayed, that would mean he would be here in Adelaide longer than his currently scheduled two months. Could it be possible that they could be granted more time together to figure out what on earth was happening between them? Was the attraction they still felt only residual? Would it stand the test of time? Would she be able to open up to him completely, tell him her deepest, innermost thoughts and secrets? She didn't know but having more time definitely increased the odds.

'H-how long do you think Charisma wants him to work here?' She tried to make her words sound as though she were asking the question about any other member of staff, as though Will working here at Adelaide Mercy was really nothing special.

'Stop trying to be so casual about it.' Janessa saw through her bluff neatly. 'I know you far too well. Of course you want Will to stay.'

'What makes you say that?'

'I've seen the way the two of you look at each other.'

Surprised that they'd been so closely observed, Sheena raised her eyebrows. 'What way?'

Janessa smiled. 'The way Miles and I look at each other.'

Sheena shook her head. 'No. Will does not look at me the way Miles looks at you. Miles worships the ground you walk on. He would get you the moon if you asked him to.' She shook her head again. 'Will doesn't look at me like that.'

'Oh, no? Then why was it that I almost walked in on the two of you kissing yesterday?'

'What?' Sheena's throat went instantly dry and her cheeks tinged with pink as heat washed over her. 'You...'

'I came to check on the girls and opened the door—saw you sitting in this chair, holding Ellie, Will kneeling beside you, locking his lips to yours.' Janessa's smile was very bright. 'So?' Excitement filled her friend's voice.

'So?' Sheena replied.

'So...what does it mean?' Janessa blurted. 'Are the two of you back together? The old feelings have come to the surface once again and if Will stays here in Adelaide, you'll be able to—'

'Whoa! Whoa, there.' Sheena held up her free hand. 'For a start, Will and I are not back together. He kissed me quickly on my lips because we were caught up in the moment. That's all. Nothing romantic about it. Ellie had just woken up and it was…' She shrugged as she searched for the right words to describe how she'd felt. 'I don't know…it was…it just felt right. Like a celebratory kiss.' There was no way she was telling Janessa about the kisses she and Will had shared in the chapel.

'Are you trying to tell me that you're not well on your way to falling in love with Will all over again?'

Sheena swallowed. 'No. I'm not saying that at all. I'm saying that I'm confused and emotional and…I rejected him, Janessa.' She shook her head as though that one strike against her could never be fully removed. 'I refused his marriage proposal. It doesn't matter whether we've cleared the air or not, no man is going to come back for more when he's already been rejected.'

'But Will is no ordinary man, Sheena. From what I've seen, he's not the sort of man to let a past mistake stand in the way of true happiness.'

Sheena absorbed Janessa's words, hope starting to rise. 'Do you really think so?'

'I do. Now, tell me straight. Do you still have feelings for him?' Janessa persisted.

Sheena looked away, then back to her sister, knowing she couldn't lie. 'Yes. Of course. We had a past. I keep remembering the good times we shared and all the things we wanted to do. We were happy. I want that happiness again.'

'Good. Admitting it is the first step. Uh…' Janessa

thought of another question. 'Do you want these feelings to continue to grow?'

'Yes, but—'

'Ah. No buts. Do you want Will to reciprocate these feelings?'

'Well, of course I do but I hurt him—'

'Shh.' Janessa cut her off. 'Let it go. Let the past and the hurt and the rejection and everything that went along with it…go. That's the first step in gluing this relationship back together.'

'Nessa, it's not that simple. I have the girls to think about now. I can't put my needs and desires before theirs. They need me and I need them. I don't have time for any sort of romance. I'm a mother first and foremost and unlike my own mother, who didn't give me the time of day, I intend to be there for Ellie and Sarah, to let them know without a doubt that they are truly loved. There's simply no time now for romance.'

As she finished talking, Will walked into the room and Sheena's heart instantly jumped with delight. Her mouth lifted in a smile and her eyes sparkled with happiness.

'Right,' Janessa said softly, not believing her friend for a moment. She glanced pointedly at the clock. 'Eight and a half minutes. Not bad.'

'Quiet,' Sheena said, but turned and smiled at Will. 'Hi.' She couldn't help the way her heart thrummed with delight the instant he appeared, the way her breath caught in her throat at the sight of him and the way she could feel a blush suffuse her cheeks at being noticed by him. Thank goodness she was already sitting down because with the demanding and protective way he'd entered her room, like a knight coming to rescue his princess, Sheena knew her knees wouldn't have been able to support her. Was Janessa right? Was Will still interested in her? Sheena could only hope. The fact that he had indeed come to the room less than ten minutes after Raquel-Maria had left to notify him surely meant something? Right?

Of course, given that he was such a brilliant doctor, he would be concerned about his patients, but Sheena wanted to believe it was more than that. After the moments they'd shared yesterday when Ellie had initially woken up after the long, life-changing surgery, Will had been so pleased that he'd been there to witness it. He'd been as excited as Sheena that Ellie was doing so well. Was he like this with all his patients and their parents, or was it just her? Was she special to him?

Twice Will had kissed her. Twice she had responded. Were they really moving towards some sort of reconciliation and they hadn't even realised? Was he able to forgive her for turning him down all those years ago? It seemed so and if things did progress, if they *were* able to rekindle their relationship, would he be able to accept Ellie and Sarah as his own? Sheena watched him as he immediately came to her side and knelt down beside the chair, hope filling her heart.

'I was told Sarah had woken up. That's excellent news. I only wish I'd been here for it, as I was with Ellie.'

'I'll bet,' Janessa murmured beneath her breath, a secret smile on her lips.

Sheena ignored Janessa and looked from Sarah, who was sleeping contentedly in her arms, to Will…his face so close to hers. 'Yes. My darling Sarah opened her eyes, dragged in a deep breath and screamed until she was fed.' Sheena told him.

Will's deep, rich chuckle was her answer. 'I can well believe it.' Tenderly he stroked the baby's head. 'Hello, Sarah,' he whispered. 'Good to have you back with us.' Sheena watched Will closely, a lump in her throat at the way he seemed to adore her girls. Their heads were almost touching as he bent and placed a kiss on Sarah forehead. 'So small. So precious. So special.'

'Yes.'

When he looked at her, the rest of the world seemed to melt away and all that was left was the two of them and the girls. The possibility of a family. Her heart was linked with his, pounding in unison to the same rhythm.

With the increase in her breathing rate due to his nearness, due to the way his gaze seemed to bore into hers with repressed need and desire, Sheena parted her lips to allow the pent-up air to escape. Her tongue slipped out to wet her dry lips and she swallowed, wondering if she was imagining the way Will's mouth seemed to be drawing closer to her own.

Was he going to kiss her again? Was it that he was happy that Sarah was awake or was it something else? Was this really happening? Confusion continued to war with barely veiled passion that seemed to burn through her whenever he was this close.

'Sheenie,' he whispered, his breath fanning out to warm her, to caress her, to lure her closer.

Almost…almost…

Beep, beep, beep.

'Blast!' Janessa murmured, digging in her pocket to switch off her pager at the same time that Will instantly straightened, putting distance between himself and Sheena. The outside world returned with a bang. Will stood and straightened his tie before shoving his hands into his pockets.

'Sorry. Don't mind me,' Janessa said.

Sheena could quite clearly see the look on her friend's

face, the one where she was trying not to grin too widely at the 'almost kiss' she'd witnessed.

'It's the unit,' Janessa remarked after looking at her pager. 'Sorry, but I need to go. Will, can you help me put Ellie back into her crib, please? Then I'll leave you to help Sheena.'

'Of course.' Will carefully worked with Janessa to wheel the machines connected to Ellie back towards the crib, and after Janessa laid the baby on the soft mattress he quickly checked Ellie's vitals, ensuring the machines were working correctly.

'Now that Sarah's awake,' Janessa continued, brushing her finger over Ellie's cheek, 'Charisma will no doubt schedule the press conference for first thing in the morning. You can give your prepared statement, have your photograph taken with the girls and then hopefully the media will leave you in peace.'

Sheena groaned. 'The press conference. I'd forgotten about that.'

'Well, I'm needed in the NICU, so I'll leave the two of you to discuss the ins and outs of PR…and anything else that might come to mind.' Janessa winked at them before heading to the door. Soon Sheena and her girls were alone with Will once more.

'Do I really have to do the silly photo shoot?'

Will nodded. 'PR helps with the hospital budget,' he pointed out, but jerked his thumb towards the door. 'What's with Janessa? She was acting a little strange, don't you think?'

'Janessa saw you kiss me yesterday.' As well as witnessing the 'almost kiss' they'd just shared, she wanted to add, but as Will hadn't actually kissed her, she didn't want him to think she was jumping to conclusions.

'Ah.' Dawning realisation crossed his face and he shoved

his hands into his trouser pockets again. 'That would explain it.' He paused as though completely uncertain what to say next. He looked at her, she looked at him and the rest of the world seemed to disappear. It was how it had always been when they were alone together. Sheena could sense the tension increasing between them and when Will held her gaze for a moment, the increase in her breathing rate was automatic.

'We were good together,' he murmured, still standing beside Ellie's crib as though he needed to keep some distance between them.

Sheena nodded. 'Always. We were friends first, though.'

'We were,' he agreed.

'Do you think…?' She paused and swallowed. 'I mean, is it possible for us to become close friends again?'

Will shook his head and closed his eyes for a moment before meeting her gaze once more. 'I want to be friends, Sheena. I've really missed just being with you, talking to you. We share the same sense of humour, the same outlook on things. I think, after you left, that's what really hit me the most. That my friend was gone…gone from my life.'

'I'm here now,' she offered quietly. 'Perhaps reconnecting through the girls is our second chance to rekindle our friendship.'

He nodded. 'Perhaps it is.' Friendship was a good place to start but he had to confess that sharing in her quiet moments with Ellie and Sarah, feeling the joy and elation pass through her as she held her girls, made him want more than just friendship. Deep down inside, he admitted he wanted to be a part of her life. He wanted to help her make decisions, to spend more time with the girls, not only in a medical capacity but as an important person in their lives.

Sarah shifted a little in Sheena's arms and Will smiled.

'Is Sarah getting too heavy?'

'I think it's time to put her back in her crib.' Sheena looked down at her baby and smiled. 'It's so wonderful to be able to hold both of them individually. So...' She searched for the right word.

'Heart-warming?' Will suggested.

'Exactly. See? We're still very much in tune with each other. Friendship is a good place to start.'

Will came over and together they settled the still sleeping baby into her crib and again Will checked the machines to ensure they were working correctly and performed Sarah's observations, pleased with the outcome.

'She's definitely over that fever,' he said, bending down to kiss Sarah's head. 'Clever girl.' He turned and looked at Sheena, who was trying to smother a yawn.

'Let's get this small camp bed set up for you so you can get some proper rest, rather than just napping in the chair.'

Sheena nodded, talking as they set up the bed. 'Now that Sarah's woken up from the induced coma and they've both been fed and changed, exhaustion seems to be swamping me at every turn.'

Will smiled. 'It's to be expected. You've been through so much, Sheenie.' He turned down the covers for her and waited while she slipped off her shoes and lay down, her hand covering her mouth as she yawned yet again.

'Your girls are fine,' he murmured as he knelt beside her and pulled the covers up, gently tucking her in.

Sheena yawned, wanting to talk to him some more, wanting to thank him for everything he'd done, but her eyes refused to stay open one second more.

Her breathing instantly settled and he knew she was asleep. Tenderly, his fingers swept her hair back from her forehead and his gut tightened as he looked down at this sleeping beauty. Bending down, he brushed a kiss across her lips. 'Sleep sweet, Sheena,' he murmured, before walking to the chair and sitting down. He intended to stay here, to monitor the babies and give Sheena the opportunity to have a proper sleep. As the three of them slept soundly, Will nodded. Relaxing back into the chair, he felt a sense of contentment he hadn't felt in well over a decade. It felt right to be here. With Sheena. With the twins. It felt right to be watching over them.

'Three beautiful girls,' he whispered into the quiet room, then smiled.

CHAPTER SEVEN

FOR the next few days Will spent quite a bit of time with Sheena and the twins, pleased that Sheena was allowing him the opportunity to really get to know her daughters. Now that both Sarah and Ellie were awake it wasn't long before they were both off the monitoring equipment and going from strength to strength.

'Is it Ellie's turn for a bottle or is she due for me to feed her?' Sheena asked him over Sarah's cries, as she finished changing Ellie's nappy. Will was about to put Sarah into the bath and was ensuring that the clear protective, waterproof bandage was secure over the wound site. Sarah, however, wasn't enjoying being stripped naked and was quite vocal about it.

'Sarah's due for the bottle after her bath. You feed Ellie while I wrangle this minx into the bath.' As he spoke, he bent down and blew a raspberry on Sarah's tummy, surprising the little one so much she was actually quiet for a split second before resuming her cries. He chuckled, the warm sound washing over Sheena with delight as she settled in the chair with Ellie. Unbuttoning her top, she settled the baby to her breast, then looked over to where Will was carefully lifting Sarah into the bath, the baby splashing a bit to begin with before settling down to the soothing warmth of the water.

'Phew!' Will looked down at the little girl. 'You certainly have a good set of lungs, sweet Sarah,' he told her, and was rewarded with a smile. He looked over to where Sheena was feeding Ellie, surprised to find her watching him. Sheena smiled.

'Peace and quiet…if only for a moment. Ah, Sarah, I envy you. What I wouldn't give for a relaxing bath.' Sheena closed her eyes and leaned her head back against the chair. 'Even for ten minutes, just to soak and unwind and have no demands on my time.' She opened her eyes and smiled at Will. 'I guess being a single mother to two little munchkins, my bath dreams are over. At least for the next five years until they start school.' She chuckled to herself.

Will nodded, listening to her words and mesmerised by the sight of her sitting there, babe in arms, looking so incredibly beautiful and serene. It was clear that she loved her daughters very much and there was no hint of the fears she'd confessed to him almost a week ago outside the operating theatre. He knew they were still there, simmering beneath the surface, but he also knew that she was internally strong enough to cope with whatever life threw at her.

Sarah splashed, demanding his attention once more, and he gave it, murmuring sweet words to her. Both girls had come along in leaps and bounds since the surgery almost a week ago and he couldn't have been happier with their progress.

Ellie was starting to close her eyes, her little world peaceful and content. Sheena was starting to feel the same. Ever since the surgery she'd felt as though she could now start to move forward with her life. It wouldn't be too much longer until the girls would be allowed to go home…but first she had to find a home for them to go to.

'We'll get there, won't we, my beautiful Eleanor?' she murmured, stroking her baby's head.

'I've never heard you call her Eleanor before,' Will remarked, glancing over. 'How did you choose their names? Any particular reason?'

Sheena nodded, sadness creeping into her eyes. 'Ellie and Sarah were the names of my imaginary sisters when I was growing up.'

'Imaginary?' There was no censure in Will's tone, only intrigue.

'When I was at boarding school, especially during the holidays when all the other girls went home to their families and I was left to rattle around the property all on my own, I used to imagine I had two older sisters who would be there, too. The three of us would go off into the woods around the boarding house and we'd explore together and have wonderful adventures.' Sheena smiled at the memory of her schoolgirl dreams. 'Then at night I'd imagine that they'd push their beds next to mine, one on either side to protect me, so I wasn't all alone in the large empty dormitory.'

'How old were you?'

'About six or seven.'

Will's heart constricted at her words, feeling empathy for little Sheena and anger at her parents for leaving her all alone.

'As I grew older, I would still imagine quiet yet determined Ellie and loud, protective Sarah by my side, always in the back of my mind for whenever I needed them most. I have no idea where I initially pulled the names from but when I knew I was having twin girls, those were the two names that seemed to fit perfectly. My girls—only this time, it would be me who would always protect them.'

Will looked away from her, swallowing the lump that had

lodged in his throat. He glanced down at Sarah, still happily splashing away, and discovered his vision was a little blurry. 'Why did you never tell me any of this? About your childhood?' he asked.

Sheena shrugged. 'I guess for so long I didn't want to remember. It was a time in my life I tried hard to forget. Besides, you used to tell me the most wonderful stories about your family, about your siblings and the mischief you used to get up to, and it was all so alive and colourful and real. It helped push the bleakness of my own childhood further into the back of my mind and it's only been recently, since I've had the girls, that I find I can think back to that time without being swamped with feelings of complete desolation and rejection. That time is gone. I can't get it back. I have to look forward. I have a future with my girls and I want it to be bright and alive and colourful. Filled with love and laughter.'

Will nodded in approval. 'That's the way to do it. Move forward.'

There was a strength to his words that made Sheena wonder whether he'd been referring to something other than her childhood memories. She watched as he took Sarah from the bath and wrapped the little girl carefully in the towel, picking her up to cuddle her dry. He was so good with both the girls and it was clear as Sarah snuggled into him that they were both becoming attached to him.

Was that a good thing? She knew Will was only supposed to be working at Adelaide Mercy for another month before he was scheduled to return to Philadelphia. Would he return? Would he stay here and accept the job Charisma had offered him?

On the day after Sarah had woken up, the CEO had headed up the press conference, with the media being allowed to photograph both girls, lying in their separate cribs, and the hospital staff who had been responsible for the life-changing surgery. When Charisma had been giving her report, she'd mentioned to the press that she was hopeful of securing the services of Dr William Beckman for the next two years but they had yet to work out the details of the contract.

Since then Will hadn't mentioned it to Sheena and she hadn't wanted to ask or pry. The friendship they were both working hard to maintain was still so new and she didn't want to pressure him one way or the other. Whatever he decided, whether to stay or go, had to be his own decision and she would respect whatever he chose. Would he con- sider staying in Adelaide as moving forward with his life? She hoped so because having him around, talking to him, sharing these special moments with her girls, was something she'd come to quickly treasure.

'Speaking of moving forward...' he remarked, clearing his throat, and Sheena could sense uncertainty in him. It was in the way he straightened his shoulders, pushing them back and raising his chin slightly, that helped her to recognise the feeling. His firm arms still securely held a squirming Sarah but even though her daughter wriggled, there was no danger of Will dropping her.

'How would you feel about taking the girls out of the hospital tomorrow?' He turned back to the change bench and laid Sarah down, quickly fixing a disposable nappy into place, ensuring the bandaged area was thoroughly dry.

'Out?' Sheena was surprised by this suggestion. 'Oh... um...I hadn't even thought about that.'

'You've been cooped up in this room for well over a week.'

Sheena carefully switched Ellie to the other breast and when her daughter was once again settled, she glanced up at Will. 'Do you think it's all right to take them out? Where

would we go? What would we do? How would we get there?
I don't have a car.'

'Whoa, there.' Will chuckled as he finished dressing
Sarah, who was once again squirming and registering her
displeasure at being dressed. 'Don't go stressing about this,
Sheena. For a start, I think the girls are both perfectly well
enough to head outside. Tomorrow is supposed to be a nice
day, not too hot, not too cold, and I thought perhaps we could
start with the park. A walk. In the sunshine. A bit of fresh air
and Vitamin D.'

'But I don't have a pram.'

'The hospital has one. Even a twin pram so the girls can
be propped up and take a look at what's going on around
them.'

Sheena's mind was working overtime, puzzling its way
through scenarios.

'If you think it's too soon—' he began, but Sheena held
up a hand to stop his words.

'I'm just trying to work things through. I'd need to pack
a bag for each of them. Change of clothes, extra nappies, express some milk. It'll be a lot of work. A lot of preparation.'

'True.' He lifted a bathed and dressed Sarah into his arms
and came to sit in the chair next to her. 'Twins are a lot of
work and require a lot of preparation. Going out, for even
an hour, means you pack the same amount of clothes and
paraphernalia as you would if you were going out for the
day.'

'How do you know so much about what to pack and how
to change nappies and bath squirming little girls?'

'I used to help my mother with my younger siblings. I
think I first changed my brother's nappy when I was about
six or seven. It was disgusting but that's the way things

went in a large family. The older ones helped to care for the younger ones.'

'Sounds great.' Sheena smiled at him, watching as he held Sarah in his arms, the little mischief-maker blowing raspberries and waving her arms about with joy. Ellie could hear her sister and started to wriggle, trying to see what was going on. Sheena eventually gave up and laid Ellie over her knee in order to expel any wind.

Sarah leaned towards her sister, arms held out towards her, as Ellie reached for her twin. Will quickly laid Sarah on his knee so both girls were lying on their stomachs, holding hands across the small gap between the two chairs.

'They love each other,' Sheena remarked. 'No matter what else happens in their lives, they'll always have each other, and that makes me very happy.' She exhaled slowly, then looked at Will. 'OK. Let's take them out tomorrow.'

'I can see you're concerned and I know it's a big step for you,' Will soothed. 'But the girls are healthy enough for this next adventure.'

'So long as we don't get hounded by any press and we can just enjoy ourselves, I think you're right that it's time for an adventure of a different kind. One that doesn't involve a trip to either the operating room or Radiology.'

'Agreed, and they'll be safe in the care of their loving orthopaedic surgeon and their paediatric mother. No dramas.'

'Promise?' Sheena reached out her free hand to him and he instantly took it, squeezing it with reassurance.

He nodded with determination. 'Promise.'

Later that evening, as Sheena sat in the chair, Sarah feeding in her arms, she thought about Will. He'd been so close, so attentive, so wonderful to her and the girls these past few days. Although she'd had many other friends stopping by to help out, Will's presence had made a difference *to her*.

She knew he was their surgeon, that he was obliged to visit them, to make sure their wounds were healing nicely, but after the kisses they'd shared, Sheena had started to open up to the old feelings she'd tried to hide from. Will had been a major part of her life and for so long she'd tried to repress the way he'd made her feel, but now…was it right to want him back in her life? Would she get hurt again? Would the girls? It was clear they loved him, especially Sarah, who always seemed to calm more quickly whenever she was in Will's arms.

'You've got good taste,' Sheena whispered to her daughter as the baby finished her evening meal. Ellie was still sleeping but would no doubt wake for her feed the instant Sarah was finished. She knew she'd never be bored, raising twins on her own. There would be always something that needed to be done.

She closed her eyes as she thought about Will's idea of taking the girls to the park the next day, feelings of panic racing through her. She knew she'd become institutionalised, having been confined to the walls of the hospital grounds for such a long time, and that even heading to the park for a few hours would do her and the girls the world of good, but she couldn't help the feeling of apprehension that had ripped through her when Will had first suggested it.

'They'll be safe…' She could hear his voice so clearly in her mind, picture his face before her, breathe in his scent all around her. Sheena sniffed again, then frowned as she realised she really *could* detect his earthy scent. Opening her eyes, a smile came instantly to her lips as she saw him standing there…with one hand behind his back.

'Hi. I didn't hear you come in.'

'I wasn't sure whether you were asleep or not. Sarah is.' Will looked down at the baby sleeping contentedly in her mother's arms without a care in the world.

'I was just thinking,' she murmured, and stood, carrying Sarah back to her crib. 'How about you? How has the rest of your day been? Still writing up my girls' operation for a journal article?'

'The article is coming along nicely.' He waited, trying not to be impatient to give her the surprise he'd spent the better part of the last two hours organising. He was starting to feel like a kid at Christmas!

She tucked the blankets around the sleeping babe, being careful of the bandaging before turning to face him. 'I'm excited and nervous about tomorr—' She stopped. 'Will? Why are you holding a loofah behind your back?'

'Darn. You saw it.' He held out the loofah, which was on the end of a smooth wooden stick. 'It's for you.'

'Uh…thanks…' Sheena accepted the gift, not at all sure what was going on. 'I'm a little confused. Are you saying that I smell?' She sniffed her clothes. 'You're probably right. With stuff coming out both ends of the girls, it's no wonder I stink.'

'Stuff? Is that the technical term the paediatric association is using nowadays?'

Sheena laughed. 'Yes, as a matter of fact it is, and you were supposed to say, "You don't stink, Sheena." But instead you nitpick my vocabulary, which I might add may not be all that coherent at this time of night.'

'Will you be quiet? I'm trying to give you a present here and you're rambling on.'

'The loofah is my present?' She looked at the item in her hands and gave it the consideration Will obviously thought it deserved. 'Then again, I thank you and promise to use it for my lightning-quick shower tomorrow morning. Honestly, since the girls were born I've learned the true meaning of "quick" showers. Usually, they're both nice and calm until I'm standing naked in the bathroom about to turn on the water and then you can bet they *both* wake up and start crying. It's a conspiracy.' She shook the loofah at him.

'You really are nervous about tomorrow, aren't you?' Will stated, humour laced with impatience in his tone. 'You're babbling faster than a brook. Now, if you'll just listen, I'll explain about the significance of the loofah.'

'Oh. The loofah has significance?'

'It does.'

There was a brief knock at the door and a moment later Raquel-Maria came in. 'You wanted to see me, Will?' she asked.

'Yes. Would you mind keeping an eye on the girls for about three minutes, please?' With that, he took Sheena's free hand in his and gently pulled her from the room. 'Bring the loofah,' he instructed.

'How did Raquel-Maria know to come in then?' Sheena asked as she glanced at her babies before allowing Will to tow her from the room.

'I asked her to give me five minutes just before I came in.'

'Will? Where are we going?' Sheena asked as she walked along beside him, loofah still in her free hand. 'And why did I need to bring the loofah?' They walked down a long corridor towards the maternity ward.

'Because I've organised a surprise for you,' he said as they walked into Maternity. They received some odd looks from people, some smiling, some intrigued, some just con-fused…much like her. 'The maternity ward is the only place where there are baths,' he said as he held open a door that led to one of the private bathrooms.

Sheena went through and then stopped, her eyes wide with complete surprise. In the room was a decent-size tub filled with sweet-scented bubbles. There were no lights on in the room because it had been lit with about a hundred—or so it seemed—little tea-candles. A nice new fluffy towel hung over the rail and next to it was a large fluffy robe and fluffy slippers. The lights from the candles seemed to twinkle brightly, making the room cosy and relaxed.

'For you,' he murmured. 'You mentioned earlier today that you probably wouldn't be able to enjoy a bath for at least the next five years. I decided that was too long for you to wait. You've been under enormous stress lately and now that both girls are well on the road to recovery, I think you're overdue for some "Sheena" time.'

'But…' Sheena was gobsmacked. She looked from the bath to the glowing candles back to Will. 'I…have to feed Ellie.'

'I've checked the fridge and there's more than enough milk there for Ellie, which means you can definitely spend some time soaking in the tub and letting all your stress and cares go.'

'You're going to…look after my girls?' Sheena was still trying to come to terms with what he'd arranged.

'If you're OK with that, yes. I love spending time with your girls, Sheena. Please let me do this for you.'

Sheena looked at the glorious bubble bath again, almost itching to slip into the soothing water and let all her stresses go. 'I can't believe you've done this for me.' She held up the loofah. 'An incredible bubble bath complete with my own personal loofah.' She giggled, still somewhat surprised at this unexpected turn of events.

'You deserve it, Mother of Adelaide's previously con-joined twins.' Will raised her hand to his lips and pressed a slow, soft kiss to her skin. 'Take all the time you need but, above all, relax.'

He released her hand and stepped from the room, leaving her in peace. Sheena stood there for a moment, breathing in the glorious sweet scents surrounding her and noticing some other little treats Will had prepared in the room. Off to the side of the bath was a small table with a plastic champagne flute and a bottle of non-alcoholic wine. Sheena poured herself a glass and took a soothing sip before stripping off and sliding into the water.

As the bubbles and water surrounded her body, she closed her eyes and sighed, unable to recall a time when she'd been afforded such a luxury as a soak in a tub. The stresses of the past few months started to slip away, her thoughts relaxing along with her body.

Will couldn't have given her a more gracious and precious gift other than some time to herself. He was quite a man and her feelings towards him were intensifying with each passing moment.

Will was standing by the cribs, watching the girls as they slept, when Sheena walked back into the room almost twenty minutes later. She was dressed in the fluffy robe and slippers, the towel and her clothes folded neatly in her arms.

'Wow.' She stopped just inside the door, gasping at the sight before her. Just as he'd done with the bathroom, Will had placed small tea-light candles around the room. There weren't nearly as many here but it still managed to create a romantic, relaxed atmosphere and Sheena couldn't believe how excited that made her feel. 'It looks…incredible in here, too.'

'I'm glad you like it,' Will murmured, pleased with her

response to his idea. He picked up a tea light in his hand and a moment later the light went off.

'How did you do that?'

'They're battery operated. There was no way I was going to risk real candles in here, not with the girls so close.' He switched the candle back on and placed it on the shelf. 'I saw that same thought flick across your face just now, concerned the candles were too close to the girls.' He took a few slow steps forward, coming to stand in front of her before he leaned in to whisper something near her ear. 'I know your expressions all too well, Dr Woodcombe.' It had been a mistake to lean in close. He'd known it would be because the glorious scent from her bath hung all around her, but he hadn't been able to resist. He eased back, putting a bit more distance between them, and she came further into the room, placing her things on a nearby table before going to check on her girls.

'Both sleeping soundly. Sarah hasn't woken. Ellie finished her bottle about ten minutes ago and she's been changed and settled, as you can see.'

Sheena bent and kissed both her daughters then tucked the fluffy robe closer around her body, conscious not only of the fact that she was naked beneath but also that Will would know that as well.

'Now, why don't you go and get changed while I set up the next part of the surprise?'

'There's more?' Sheena's eyebrows rose in disbelief. 'Will, you don't have to do this. The bath, the candles, the—'

He stepped forward and pressed his finger to her lips. 'Stop trying to control everything. Just for the next hour, while the girls continue to sleep, let yourself continue to relax.'

Sheena edged back a fraction, her lips suffusing with heat

where his finger had touched her, and the sensation started to spread throughout the rest of her body. Perhaps Will was right. Perhaps putting on some clothes was the best way for her to feel a little less self-conscious, but she also needed a few moments away from him to pull herself together.

'OK. Good idea.' She quickly crossed to the dresser by Sarah's crib and extracted some clean clothes from her pile. 'Won't be a moment,' she said, heading into the small bathroom attached to the girls' room. It only housed a shower, toilet and handbasin. No big, glorious bath. Once she had changed, still deciding to wear the cute fluffy slippers, she stepped back into the room—and stopped.

Not only were the tea-light candles twinkling their lights around the room but Will had pushed the chairs to the side, and spread a red-and-black checked picnic rug over the hard floor. A few cushions were scattered around the edge of the rug and in the middle was a cheese and fruit platter, a plate of mini-muffins and some biscuits. Will stood at the door to the room, accepting a tray with a pot of tea and two bone china cups from Raquel-Maria.

He turned and saw her standing there, surveying his handiwork. 'Oh. You're out faster than I'd anticipated. Never mind. Sit down. Make yourself comfortable.' He carried over the tea-tray and knelt down on the rug.

'How…did you do all this? The food? The cushions?' Sheena shook her head in bemusement as she sat down on a cushion and snagged a grape from the platter.

Will smiled but slowly shook his head. 'I'm a man of mystery and never divulge my secrets.'

Sheena laughed and settled more comfortably on the cushions. 'It's been…amazing, Will. The loofah, the bath, some time away from the girls, and now *this*.' She waved a hand at the late-night supper spread before them and sighed.

'Thank you.' Her tone was filled with sincerity. 'For…everything.'

Will heard the honesty in her words as well as the appreciation. 'It was most definitely my pleasure, Sheena Andromeda.'

She giggled at the name. 'I can't believe you remember *that*.'

He seemed surprised. 'The day that you decided to choose your own middle name because you weren't given one? Yes, my dear Dr Woodcombe, I do,' he remarked as he handed her a plate. As she put some food onto it, he spoke quietly.

'We'd just finished a gruelling shift—me in Theatres, you with an epidemic in the children's ward. We sat outside the front of the hospital, looking up at the stars, talking softly about our night. You told me that one child you'd been caring for had three middle names and that you had none.'

Sheena's smile was bright. 'And you told me to choose one. "Choose a name, Sheena. Anything you like and tonight I will christen you with your new name". That's what you said.'

Will lay down on his side, propping himself up on his elbow as they revisited the past. 'You laughed, pointed up at the sky and said, "I choose Andromeda".'

'And you immediately christened me Sheena Andromeda Woodcombe.' Shyly she looked down at the food on her plate before meeting his gaze. 'That's one of my favourite memories. When things in my life aren't going the way I'd planned, that's one of the memories I take out, dust off and think about.'

'It's one of my favourite memories, too,' he confessed. They both fell silent, the years they'd been apart disappearing as their familiarity and the sense of ease in each other's company washed over them.

'Life seemed so simple back then.' She sighed, and hugged one of the cushions to her chest, needing some contact, needing to feel close to him but knowing she couldn't possibly ask him to hold her. That would be far too dangerous.

'We were young.'

She nodded. 'Yet we felt so old. We thought we knew everything.'

'But it turns out not nearly as much as we should have.'

'I'm so glad we've been able to start afresh,' Sheena remarked, her gaze flicking between his eyes and his lips. Did the man have any idea just how irresistible she found him?

'So am I,' he murmured, unable to help but notice the way she was looking at him. Now that they'd sorted through a lot of their past, he was well aware of the mounting tension coursing between them. He'd kissed her twice—almost three times—and having that small sweet taste of Sheena had only unlocked the cravings he'd kept hidden away for far too long.

'Don't look at me like that, Sheena,' he whispered quietly into the sudden stillness of the room, the only sound that of two little girls breathing deeply as they slept.

'Then you shouldn't have given me such a wondrous evening, Will. No one has ever done something so unselfish for me. Usually, whenever I get a treat, there are strings attached.' She frowned for a second and looked at him with concern in her eyes. 'There aren't any strings attached, are there?'

He thought about her parents, about the boarding school, about her ex-husband, and how it honestly did seem as though Sheena had lived her life always waiting for the axe to fall. Well, not with him. 'Only that I like seeing you smiling, seeing you relaxed and being able to unwind after everything you've been through.'

'And that's it?'

'That's it.' He sat up and faced her, knowing it was best to ease the tension surrounding them. 'Now, before the girls start to wake up, can I interest you in some cheese? Or perhaps milady would like some more grapes. A mini-muffin, perhaps?'

'You've organised way too much food,' she said with a laugh, pleased he'd managed to break the intense atmosphere. She wanted him. There were no two ways about it but she also knew it was completely the wrong time of her life to be worrying about romance. Friendship—now, that was something she could handle, and for the next fifteen minutes they sipped tea and nibbled at the food until Sarah woke up, demanding their attention.

All in all, though, when Will finally took his leave after helping her to pack away the rug and set up her camp bed for the night, Sheena couldn't resist standing on tiptoe and kissing his cheek.

'You're a *good* man, Will Beckman, with an equally *good* heart. That's a rare quality nowadays. Thank you again for my wonderful and relaxing evening.'

Will shoved his hands into his pockets to stop himself from hauling her close but smiled and nodded. 'You're more than welcome. Now, get some sleep because tomorrow is another big day, both for you and the girls.'

'And I'm so happy that you'll be there to share it with us.'

'There you are.' Miles walked over to where Will was sitting in the hospital cafeteria, the smells of bacon, eggs, sausages and grilled tomatoes filling the air. Miles pulled out a chair and sat down next to his friend, giving him closer scrutiny. Unshaven, crumpled shirt, no tie. 'I've been looking for you. Aren't you supposed to be taking Sheena and the girls out for a few hours?'

Will frowned and glanced at his watch. 'I'm not due to meet her for another hour.' He looked more closely at his watch and then checked one of the clocks on the wall in the cafeteria. 'What? My watch battery must have died.' He quickly finished his half-drunk coffee and rose to his feet. 'Did she ask you to come and find me? Is everything all right? Are the girls fine? I checked on them just after two o'clock this morning and they both seemed fine.'

Miles raised an eyebrow, taking in his friend's attire. 'Interesting look you have there. Is it the new dishevelled surgeon look you were after? Because I think you've achieved it.'

'I couldn't sleep. Too much on my mind.'

'You've been out walking, haven't you?' Miles asked rhetorically, knowing his friend of old. The two men headed out of the cafeteria, talking as they walked. 'Your all-night walking and thinking escapades usually only happen when you can't figure things out. Now, I know the twins are fine because I've already been around to see them, so that can only mean it's their mother who's been keeping you awake. She's clearly messing with your mind.'

'How do you even know what's in my mind?' Will spluttered, and became even more annoyed when Miles had the audacity to chuckle.

'Because I've been in your position, mate. If it's love that's bothering you, don't even try to work it out.' They rounded the corner into a longer corridor and continued their way to the paediatric unit. 'I tried to fight love and look…' He held up his left hand, where a gold wedding band gleamed. He laughed again. 'I've never been more happy in my life. Janessa is…everything I've ever wanted in a woman and, where for years I thought I'd never find happiness again, it jumped up and slapped me right between the eyes the instant I saw her.'

'You think I've fallen in love with Sheena?'

Miles snorted. 'I don't think you ever *stopped* loving her. She may have broken your heart ten years ago but back then she thought she was doing the right thing, but right or wrong and no matter what you may have been able to trick yourself into believing, it's as plain as the nose on your face that you still love that woman…and her adorable girls.'

'Who *doesn't* love those girls?' Will tried to smooth his crumpled shirt. He'd meant to head back to his parents' house and change his clothes before taking Sheena and the girls out but now he'd run out of time.

'True, but not the way you do. I've seen you with them and both Ellie and Sarah have you wrapped firmly around their tiny fingers. As for their mother—well, whenever you two are in the same room the tension buzzing between you is almost enough to power the entire hospital.'

Will frowned in puzzlement. 'It can't be that obvious.'

'It is to me but, then, I've known both of you for quite some time. I remember what the two of you were like the last time you were together and I can see the same things happening. Those long looks, those meaningful touches, those secret smiles.' Miles over-dramatised his words with wide hand gestures. Will felt a smile start to tug at his lips. 'Add to all of that the fact that I'm a man wildly in love with his wife,' Miles continued, 'and I want every other man to be as happy and as fortunate as I am.'

'And you think I'd be happy with Sheena?'

'I think the only time you've ever truly been happy was when you were with Sheena. Which brings me to my next question.'

Will stopped and faced his friend. 'Don't ask it. I've been

asking myself all night long how I really feel about her and I still haven't come up with any answers, only more questions.' The main question was whether he'd be content not to have any natural children of his own. He loved both Sarah and Ellie as though they were his own. With the amount of time he'd spent with them, it was now second nature for him to change them or give them a bottle or simply cuddle them.

Sheena hadn't restricted him in any way, accepting his help and advice, but he could still see concern in her eyes. She wasn't sure whether he was going to stay in Australia or whether he was going to go back to the States. He hadn't been able to talk to her about it because he wasn't sure himself...yet.

'All right, then,' Miles continued. 'Let me ask you this question. How do you feel when you think of her spending her life with someone else?' Miles received an immediate growl as his answer.

'I can't even go there,' Will confessed, his jaw clenched, his fists tight, his heart instantly in pain.

'Interesting.' They started walking again, drawing closer to the paediatric unit. 'You and Sheena are good together, Will, but communication wasn't your strong suit ten years ago—on both sides. Don't let it hold you back this time.'

'I don't intend to. I want to be part of their lives,' Will said as they stopped just outside the door to the paediatric unit.

'But?' Miles prompted.

'What if Sheena can't have any more children? What if Ellie and Sarah are it?'

Miles nodded. 'And there goes your big family picture.'

'I know it might sound pathetic but I always pictured myself surrounded by a lot of children.'

'What about adoption? If Sheena can't have any more

children, how about considering it? There are many children out there just waiting to be loved.'

Will nodded but didn't make any remark. Instead, he opened the door to the unit and instantly heard a baby crying.

'That's Sarah,' he said, quickening his pace.

'How can you tell? Just from a cry?' Miles was totally amazed.

'Sarah's cry is deeper than Ellie's and a heck of a lot louder, too.' Will entered the room and found Sheena trying to quickly finish dressing Ellie, calling to Sarah in a soothing tone.

'I'm coming, Sarah,' she said. 'Mummy's almost finished. Shh, darling.'

'Hey. Sorry I'm late.' Will headed to Sarah's crib, his heart turning over when she instantly held out her arms to him, wanting him to pick her up. No sooner was she in his arms than her cries subsided and she snuggled into him. Will closed his eyes and hugged the little girl tight. She was *his* Sarah, just as Ellie was *his* Ellie.

And Sheena? Was she *his* Sheena? Was he fortunate enough to still have her love him? He hoped so.

CHAPTER EIGHT

As THEY headed out into the sunshine, Will pushing the pram with ease, Sheena slipped her sunglasses on and made sure the little sunhats were shielding the girls' eyes properly. Will slipped the hood of the pram into place and breathed in the fresh air.

'They're both blinking rapidly,' Sheena said with a smile on her face. 'They're not used to being in direct sunlight.'

'All that's going to change. Now that the main surgery is over, they're both going to start moving more and crawling, and before you know it they'll be running around creating more mischief than you can imagine.'

'Oh, help. Don't say that.' Sheena laughed. 'I feel so silly for being nervous about bringing them outside.'

'You're nervous?' he asked as they headed towards the botanical gardens situated near the hospital.

'I know. I guess it's because all they've known of life are the four walls of the hospital.'

'They've never been outside before?'

Sheena shook her head. 'Although they were healthy before the surgery, the risk of being outside, of catching a cold or getting sick in some way, was just too great. Miles and Janessa were in complete agreement and none of us wanted to make any mistakes in case it delayed the surgery.

Besides, when they were conjoined, they were such a media novelty that even when *I* went out of the hospital grounds I was often photographed and asked questions.'

'So this is their very first time?' He nodded, feeling proud that he was here for such a momentous occasion.

'Yes.'

'Then you have every right to be silly or nervous or what-ever other maternal emotions you feel.' He winked at her as he pushed the pram along and Sheena felt sparkly inside from his attention. It had always been that way with Will. He just needed to look at her, smile at her and her body came alive with tingles.

She quickly looked away and focused on the girls, making sure they were comfortable. Due to the bandages, the girls were unable to sit up properly but they'd angled both babies so that they could see quite clearly the world around them.

Sheena held open the gate to the gardens as Will pushed the pram through and as they walked around she couldn't help but feel as though a huge weight had been lifted from her shoulders.

'I've been so scared,' she confessed to Will as they found a nice place to spread a rug and sit down, the girls content to remain in the pram. They faced the pram towards them and as Sheena talked, Will pulled faces at the girls, making them giggle. 'Trying to imagine my life outside the hospital gave me nightmares.'

'That's understandable.'

'It is?'

'Of course.' Will handed the girls a soft toy each and turned to face Sheena. 'Your life has been in a state of flux for the past year. Now that the girls have come through the surgery, your life with them can begin. Coming out today was the first step towards looking to the future, and you've accomplished it with ease.' He leaned over and took her hand in his, raising it to his lips. 'You're a strong, incredible woman, Sheena Woodcombe, and you'll be able to handle anything life throws at you.'

Sheena nodded, tingling from his touch, loving the attention but well aware that in the way he spoke he wasn't including himself in any scenario. Did that mean he wasn't going to stay in Australia? Was he going to return to the States but didn't know how to break it to her? They'd agreed to be friends and even though there was a high level of tension buzzing between them whenever they were in the same room, both had been conscious of not following through on it. Re-establishing their friendship had been the most important thing but Sheena had been well aware that with every moment she'd spent with him, whether it was bathing and changing or feeding the girls, she was coming to rely on him more and more. So much so that when he left, when he exited her life, she'd be left with a gaping hole of sheer emptiness that she doubted she'd ever be able to fill.

Even thinking about it now made a lump form in her throat and she looked away from him, over into the trees around them. She sat up straighter, her attention captured by a person hiding behind one of the trees. Her eyes widened when she realised he had a camera and that a large telephoto lens was pointed in their direction.

'The media.'

'What about them?' Will asked, noting the change in her demeanour.

'They're over there.' Sheena shook her head, annoyed that the very first time she'd brought the girls out of the hospital, they'd been followed. Her first instinct was to pack everything up and return to the sanctuary of the hospital as fast as possible but she'd learned through her PR briefings that it was better to face the music and give the photojournalists the scoop they were after.

'Relax,' Will said softly. 'We'll invite him over. He can take his pictures and then we'll be left alone.'

Sheena nodded. 'Agreed, but I don't like it. My daughters aren't a sideshow.'

'No. They're two little girls who have captured the hearts of many,' Will said. 'Including me.' He pulled Sheena to her feet and embraced her in a protective hug, not caring who saw them. 'I'll be right by your side,' he reassured her. 'No one's going to hurt my girls.'

Within another minute Sheena found herself standing behind the pram with Will by her side as they smiled for the camera, the photojournalist as pleased as punch to be allowed to take his photographs. The whole time she smiled, Will's last words were running around in her head. *'No one's going to hurt my girls.'* Did that mean that he'd accepted them? That he wanted them? All three of them? Hope began to increase deep within her.

'Make sure you send us a copy,' Will said as he started to wheel the pram back towards the hospital. By the time they arrived back in the paediatric unit, Sheena was mentally exhausted and so were the girls. With Will's help, she settled them in their cribs, singing a lullaby to help them drift off to sleep.

'I think that's enough excitement for one day,' she murmured, delighted when Will brought her a soothing cup of herbal tea. 'You remembered.'

'Of course I remembered. Whenever we were working nights, you used to complain that you never got to have your soothing cup of herbal tea.'

'I never complained,' she said, going to the window to

look out at the sunny afternoon. Will came to stand beside her, sipping his own cup of tea.

'I beg to differ.' He chuckled, the warm sound washing over her. She turned slightly, putting her cup on the thick window ledge between the vases of flowers still blooming brightly.

'Will?'

'Yes?'

'What's happening between us?'

He smiled at her words. 'We're being friends.'

'I know, and I like it very much, but…' She didn't have to say another word as he put his cup down and pulled her into his arms. Closing her eyes, she rested her head against his chest, listening to the steady beat of his heart.

'We're at a crossroads, Sheena.' She felt him shake his head. 'Not just as a possible couple but as singles as well. I have big decisions to make. You have big decisions to make, and in some ways, until those decisions are made, we won't know how to move forward.'

Sheena opened her eyes and looked up at him. 'How about you make my decisions and I'll make yours? That way, the pressure can be off,' she suggested with a crazy smile.

He looked at her and returned her smile. 'If only it was that simple.'

'Seriously, though, is there anything I can help with? Any questions you want answered? We weren't too good at communicating properly all those years ago, so let's make sure we don't take that road again.'

Will thought about things for a while before nodding. 'OK. Well, I do have a few questions. The first one being about your endometriosis. Are you in any pain? Will you need further surgery?'

Sheena eased out of his arms and saw the concern on his

face. 'The pain isn't too bad, nowhere near as bad as it used to be, and, yes, there's a high probability that I'll require an oophorectomy, possibly a bilateral one, which will mean definitely no more children for little ol' me.'

'Oh, Sheenie.' There was anguish in his eyes. 'How do you put up with it? Always to be in pain and knowing that with surgical intervention the pain can be removed? You're so brave, so strong.' And he wanted to hold her for ever and take away all her pain. He wanted to protect her and her girls for the rest of his life.

'I put up with it because now that I've had the girls, I'm incredibly hopeful. I want more children, Will. I feel incredibly greedy saying that, especially as I've already been blessed with two gorgeous girls, but…' She trailed off. She wanted more children, almost desperately so, and she wanted them to be Will's. Hers and his. Just as she'd dreamed about all those years ago. 'The doctors were wrong about me before and perhaps…just perhaps they're still wrong when they say there's an incredibly small chance of me conceiving again. So I put up with the pain and I'll continue to do so if it means that there's a tiny chance.'

'So long as your health isn't at risk.' They both knew the risks. 'The chance of conceiving is irrelevant if it means you become sick.' He shook his head. 'The thought of you—' He broke off, unable to say the words out loud. Instead, he put his hands on her shoulders and looked deeply into her eyes. 'You're too important, Sheena. To your girls, to Janessa and Miles…and to me.' He swallowed the lump in his throat. 'Promise me you'll look after yourself.'

Sheena met his gaze, unable to believe the intenseness of his blue eyes. 'I promise.'

'Good.' He breathed out in relief before crushing her to

him. 'You are so special to me, Sheena. So incredibly special.'

'As a friend?' she asked, and he eased her back to look down into her upturned face.

'Not *just* as a friend, and I think we both know that.' A small smile tugged at his mouth. 'I've found it difficult to keep my hands off you ever since I returned to Australia, but I knew I had to.'

'We needed to talk.'

'And we did. I want us to stay on the same page, Sheena, to be constantly communicating with each other.'

'I want that, too, Will. I'm still so sorry for what happened all those years ago and for the way I handled things, but—'

Will didn't want to hear her apologies so silenced her the best way he knew how and covered her mouth with his own. Sheena gasped in surprise then leaned into him, relaxing against his body, winding her arms about his neck. Closing her eyes, she knew this was the place she'd longed to be for such an incredibly long time. In Will's arms once more. Being kissed with more than a brief brush of his lips against hers. This was real. *This* was what she'd dreamed about.

Her mouth was smooth and warm and, oh, so ready for him. It was as though her lips had been made specifically for *him* to kiss, and he was relishing every second. Their scents mingled together as he slowly slid his hands up her back, drawing her as close as he possibly could. When she groaned, he took that as an invitation to increase the intensity of the kiss.

Her mouth opened beneath his and they went on a mutual journey of becoming reacquainted. It was exciting, enthralling and exhilarating, and she couldn't get enough. Never before had his kisses made her feel like this, and she realised that there was definitely something different. Was it maturity? They'd both been through a lot in the past ten years and that had to change a person. He felt so familiar and yet so different, and it was that difference that made her eager to explore, to know more of this new Will who had once again captured her heart.

His kisses continued to turn her entire body to mush and she leaned closer into him, not only wanting his firm body pressed against her own but to find more stability to keep her from sliding to the floor in a boneless mess.

It was Will's turn to groan as he continued to hold her close, still giving and receiving in equal portions, feeding his need. She was everything he remembered and more, and finally, when he thought his lungs would burst if he didn't drag oxygen into them, he reluctantly lifted his head from hers but didn't relinquish his hold on her delectable body.

With their breathing slowly returning to normal, Sheena looked up at him. 'Wow!'

'Yeah. Wow. I mean, it was always good between us but that was…'

'Different.'

'But good different,' he confirmed, and she nodded in agreement.

'Wh-what are we supposed to do now? Where does that incredibly sexy, incredibly passionate kiss leave us?'

'Shaken,' he replied with a laugh, but let her go to pace the room, pleased the girls were still sleeping soundly. 'I have to decide whether to accept Charisma's job offer or to continue with my work and research in the States. You have to decide where you want to live, where you want to put down roots with your girls. We need to decide whether to pursue this undeniable attraction or to pull back and just remain friends.'

Sheena covered her face with her hands. 'Why can't anything in my life be simple?' she asked rhetorically, before lowering her hands and stepping forward into his pacing path.

'What do you think about…dating?'

'Dating?'

'Sure. For the rest of the time you're here in Australia, we still work on our friendship but we date as well. There's no point in denying the attraction between us any more, Will, and it might possibly lead to more confusion, which is the last thing we both want.'

'So we date.' He nodded as though the idea had merit. Where the girls were concerned, they both knew they worked well together, but if they had plans to solidify their relationship, to lead towards marriage, they needed to make sure they were definitely on the same page.

Was it possible he would be able to have the fairy-tale family after all? Himself, Sheena and the girls? Could they make this work? It wasn't the fairy-tale family he'd envisaged all those years ago but did it really matter? Dating might help them both to be sure. He'd rushed into things ten years ago and it had ended in disaster. He wasn't going to be that foolish this time around.

'You're a good catch, Will Beckman.'

He smiled at her words, almost relieved to hear her say them. 'Is that so?'

'Yeah.' She returned his smile, her earlier annoyance and frustration with the media being replaced by a calm, serene sigh that only Will's relaxing presence could evoke. He reached out and cupped her cheek with his hand, his thumb tenderly caressing her soft skin. She leaned into his touch and relaxed.

'So…if we're serious about this dating thing, how do you feel about meeting my family?'

At his words, Sheena jerked her head upright and stared at him.

'Uh…that's a little…uh…quick, isn't it?'

'Sheena?' He spread his arms wide. 'I have to return to the States before Christmas. That's not that far away.'

'True. True.' She took a few calming breaths, then nodded. 'I guess it's only fair that I meet your family. Especially as you've already met mine. The girls, Janessa and Miles,' she said by way of explanation.

'I guess I have.' He reached for her again, taking her hands in his. 'It'll be fine. My parents will adore you.'

'Are you sure?' Now that he'd suggested the meeting, she couldn't help the nervous butterflies that were zinging around her stomach. 'I've never met anyone's parents before. Jonas's had both died and I hardly knew mine. What am I supposed to do?'

Will smiled at her, surprised at her nervousness yet unable to believe how adorable she looked. 'You be yourself.'

'Do I need to get them a gift? Isn't it customary to bring a gift when you meet parents for the first time?'

Will shrugged. 'Bring the girls. My parents love children and will definitely consider spending some time with Adelaide's star twins a very special gift.'

Sheena nodded and tried once more to calm her breathing. 'Are you sure about this?'

'Positive. If we want to move forward, Sheena, we need to do this.' He leaned forward and brushed one of those rich and tantalising kisses over her mouth. 'Trust me.'

She breathed out slowly, her entire body trembling as she nodded. 'OK.'

CHAPTER NINE

'I'M TERRIFIED!'

Sheena paced around the girls' room before stopping to check that the baby bag was packed with everything she might need. She'd expressed milk, and the bottles were stored in the special milk compartment. There were enough nappies for her to stay away for a week—at least, that was what Janessa had said.

'Relax. You'll be fine,' Janessa soothed.

'I don't know how to meet parents, Ness. I've never met anyone's parents before…well, except for your dad.'

'You know Miles's parents. You met them at the wedding.'

'That's hardly the same. I wasn't in love with their son.'

'I should hope not,' Janessa retorted, then stopped. 'Wait a second. You said…'

'I know what I said and I can't dwell on it right now. Weren't you nervous when you met Miles's parents? What did you do? What did you say? Maybe I can learn something to say.'

Janessa waved her friend's words away. 'You're taking the babies, Sheena. No offence, honey, but no one's going to be interested in you. Babies have that effect on people, especially your two little darlings.'

'Will's hiring a car and the hospital is providing child car seats. This is the first time the girls have travelled in a car. What if we have an accident?'

Janessa walked to her friend and put her hands on her shoulders. 'Will you calm down? Will's parents don't live too far away. It's about a ten-minute drive from the hospital. Everything is going to be fine.'

'Is she still in a flap?' Will asked as he walked into the room.

'Yes. Come and silence her in a way only you know how. I'll take the baby bag down to the car. You two can bring the girls.' Janessa turned and left them alone, Ellie and Sarah were all dressed up in a pair of matching floral dresses, their dark hair tied up with red bows in little fountains on top of their heads. They looked adorable, as did their mother, apart from the flap she was in.

'I have something for you,' Will said, and it was only then Sheena realised he had one hand behind his back.

'Another loofah? This is hardly the time for a bath.'

He laughed. 'That stopped you from stressing for a moment. Here.' He shifted and pulled, from behind his back, a beautiful bouquet of brightly coloured flowers.

'Freesias.' Sheena gasped. 'The biggest bunch I've ever seen. Oh, Will.' She accepted the flowers and bent her head to sniff them appreciatively. 'They're gorgeous. Thank you. Thank you so much.'

Will beamed. 'I know you already have a room full of flowers but these aren't for the girls—these are for you.'

'And I love freesias. They're my favourite.'

'I remember.'

They stood there. Oblivious to anything or anyone else. Absorbed in each other for what felt like minutes but in reality was only a few seconds. His intense blue gaze was like a visual caress as he took in her comfortable shoes, three-quarter-length designer jeans and a blue shirt that clung to her feminine curves. She looked incredible, her short dark hair framing her face, her blue eyes, her pink cheeks, her plump, kissable lips.

Will swallowed. 'You look stunning, Sheenie.'

She put the flowers down for a moment and then looked at her clothes. 'Are you sure? Because I can go and change if you don't think this is appro—'

Will stepped forward and kissed her. 'I *do* like this method of relaxing you,' he murmured after a moment. 'Let me put these flowers into some water for you and then we'll take the girls down to the car,' he said, reluctantly releasing her from his arms.

A minute later, he walked over to the cribs, where the girls were wide awake.

'Hello, sweet Sarah,' he crooned, and was instantly rewarded with the biggest grin Sheena had ever seen her daughter give anyone. Her daughter had good taste. Sarah waved her arms at Will, desperate to be picked up, and he didn't disappoint her, scooping her up and pressing kisses to her cheeks.

Ellie started to grizzle, which she only did when she thought she was being left out. Sheena instantly collected her daughter and took her over to Will so he could say hello to her. Ellie rewarded him with big smiles and leaned forward, her arms outstretched. Will shifted Sarah over and accepted Ellie as Sheena handed her over.

'They both adore you,' she murmured with a smile.

'The feeling's mutual. Right, time to go.' Will looked at her. 'Ready?'

'As I'll ever be.' She spread her arms wide and let them fall back down to her sides in a gesture of surrender.

'Excellent. Then let us away!'

Janessa was at the car, waiting for them at the front of the hospital. Sheena and Will clipped the girls into their car seats before heading off, waving goodbye to Janessa as Will drove them from the hospital. He reached over and took her hand in his.

'Still OK?'

'Yes. It felt strange the other day when you took us to the gardens but this is…well, this is really giving the girls a taste of normal life.'

Will nodded. 'It happens often to people who have prolonged stays in hospital.' They continued to chat as he drove carefully towards his parents' home. He turned off the main road, heading into an older suburb, the trees high, the gardens lush and green from the recent rain. They passed a little creek with a small play park next to it. Will pointed to it.

'Before they made that area into a park, it was sort of like a mini-quarry and my brothers and I would spend a lot of time playing there, creating imaginary games of intergalactic war, often refusing to allow our sisters into the game at all. Then the girls would run and tell Mum or Dad and we'd be instructed, in the most direct way possible, to allow them to play, and of course the girls used to really mess the game up. Where we boys were content to roll around in the dirt and hide behind the rocks and shrubs for protection against the high-powered laser blasters contained in our index fingers as we tried to save the omniverse from imploding, my sisters wanted to tidy the place up and make delicious mud pies.' He grinned widely. 'It was all very stereotypical.'

Sheena laughed. 'It sounds like…fun.'

'It must have been so difficult for you, growing up alone.' He rubbed his thumb over the back of her hand. The love and trust that ran between himself, his parents and his siblings was incredibly strong and while, over the years, he might not have been able to see them as much as he would have liked, the bond was still there and as strong as ever. He knew his mother would instantly warm to Sheena but would Sheena allow herself to accept such open love? From the little she'd told him about her parents and the lack of affection they'd shown their only daughter, he hoped she really was able to leave it behind her and move forward.

'I can't imagine what it must have been like for you but of one thing I am absolutely sure, and that's that your daughters will have a fantastic time growing up with you as their mother. They'll laugh and argue and learn how to deal with the world, and you'll be able to enjoy it all with them.'

Sheena felt a tightening in her chest at his words. 'I hope so. It's what I've always wanted from the moment I first discovered I was pregnant.'

'My mother always said that being a parent gives you the chance to enjoy a second childhood,' Will continued, 'and you get to do it with all the knowledge of an adult so you don't make silly mistakes like thinking you can ride your bike off a ramp constructed with some bricks and a plank of wood, and do a loop in the air and land perfectly on two wheels.'

Sheena pushed aside her internal panic and smiled at him. 'You didn't?'

'Oh, I did, and had a cast on my arm for eight weeks to prove it.'

'I'm starting to be thankful I had girls, not boys.'

'Oh, don't let gender fool you. Sarah has enough fight in her to give you a run for your money and Ellie...' He glanced at the girls, who he could see in the rear-view mirror. 'Well, the quiet ones are usually the most stubborn.'

She nodded in agreement. 'You know them so well, Will. I have no idea how I'm going to cope with one girl who's stubborn and one who's a fighter.' He brought the car to a halt outside a charming yet nostalgic brick-veneer home as Sheena once more battled her own insecurities. It didn't appear that she would be able to suppress them, especially when today she would be surrounded by all the reminders of everything she'd missed growing up—a loving family. What Will had said was true. She *did* have the opportunity to have a second childhood, to leave her own upbringing behind and start afresh. Still doubt niggled. 'How am I ever going to cope alone?'

Will switched off the engine and turned to face her. 'You won't be alone, Sheenie.'

It wasn't until he urged her closer that she realised she'd spoken her concern out loud. Will leaned towards her, capturing her lips with his. Sheena's eyelids fluttered closed as she sighed into the kiss, drawing hope and strength and a yearning desire to always have this man in her life, to have him beside her as the father of her children as they lived together for the rest of their lives. Was it possible to believe in such a fairy-tale? Throughout her entire life she'd wanted the fairy-tale, the happily-ever-after ending.

Now here she was, outside the home of Will's parents, with Will close to her, kissing her, making her feel cherished, wanted, needed, loved. She kissed him back with all the love in her heart, wanting him to know that she'd never stopped loving him, that hurting him all those years ago had been the worst moment in her life and that she really wanted nothing else than for the two of them to make a 'proper' family with her girls. It was the fairy-tale…but she knew of old that fairy-tales never came true.

'Sheena,' he whispered against her mouth, their breathing slightly erratic. 'I can't stop thinking about you, wanting you, needing you and—'

'There you two are.' The joyful female tones cut through the air and Will broke off from what he'd been saying and slowly pulled back, obviously not caring whether his mother had seen them kissing or not. He let go of her hand before climbing quickly from the car to come around to her side and open the door for her.

As Sheena stepped out, his mother came to their side and openly embraced her son. Will hugged his mother back, not at all embarrassed by the display of emotion. Sheena felt a lump rise in her throat at the sight. Will was a grown man but the love and respect he had for his mother was clearly evident. She opened the back door, only to discover that both the girls had enjoyed their first car ride so much that they'd drifted off to sleep.

'They're asleep,' she announced with a hint of incredulity in her tone. 'I mean, I'd heard of parents driving their children around in the car in order to get them to go to sleep but I didn't think that it actually *worked*.'

Will's mother chuckled and stepped forward, peering around Sheena to see into the back seat of the car. 'It's very true, my dear. I remember driving around these very streets with a car full of children, desperate for them to go to sleep so I could at least have some peace and quiet, especially if Stephen was working late. Oh, aren't they adorable? So precious,' she remarked of the twins before turning to face Sheena. She opened her arms wide and wrapped them around Sheena in much the same way that she'd hugged her son. 'And I'm very happy to meet you, too, Sheena.'

In the next instant Sheena found herself enveloped in the warmest, sweetest maternal hug she'd ever experienced. She closed her eyes, wanting to savour every second, the fairy-tale dreams she'd had back in school coming back to life in that one moment. This woman didn't know her at all, yet Sheena felt complete acceptance. Was this how her baby girls felt when she cuddled them? All warm and secure and loved? How wonderful!

'I'm Mary,' Will's mother said as she released Sheena. 'And you are very, very welcome. Now, let me help you get these adorable creatures out so you can come inside. I've already put the kettle on.'

Unsure whether the girls would wake up or stay asleep but knowing she couldn't leave them in the car, Sheena and Will unpacked the pram from the back of the car and then carefully transferred the girls from the car seats to the pram. Thankfully, Sarah stayed asleep but the instant they moved her, Ellie woke up, smiling brightly up at Will.

'Oh, look at the gorgeous smiles on this one,' Mary cooed, and was more than happy to carry the baby bag into the house while Will and Sheena manoeuvred the pram through the door.

'Are you all right?' Will whispered near Sheena's ear once they were inside.

'I'm fine. Why?'

He smiled down into her face. 'You looked a little dazed when my mother hugged you. I probably should have warned you that she's a very demonstrative person.'

Sheena quickly shook her head. 'Oh, I'm not worried about that. I think it's marvellous.' With happiness sparkling in her eyes, she shrugged one shoulder, feeling a little self-conscious. 'It's just that…well…I've never been hugged by anyone's mother before. Not even my own. It was amazing.'

Will stared at her as he comprehended her words. 'You really have no concept of what a family is like, do you?'

'I used to watch Janessa and her father interact, amazed at the way they talked so openly and freely with each other. She took his death pretty hard but with her help I've learned that pulling a family together from people around you can also give you what you need, even if the people aren't blood relatives.'

'And that's your grounding in family life?' He wasn't being critical, he was simply astounded.

'I guess so.'

'Then allow me to show you a different sort of family life. The sort of family life you deserve to have with your girls.'

As they stepped into the front entryway of the house, a loud squeal came from the hallway. A second later a toddler ran past them, quickly followed by a boy of about three. A woman laughed somewhere in the house and a deep masculine voice asked when it was going to be time for a coffee break. Sarah slept on while Ellie looked eagerly around at this new scenery.

The walls of the house were decorated with many different photographs, some in black and white, some in colour and all of them framed with mix-and-match frames. There were vases of flowers on most of the tables and an upright piano in the corner. There were paintings, knick-knacks and lace doilies around the place. So incredibly different from the spacious, impersonal mansion where her parents lived. There had been no personal photographs on the walls there, only expensive artwork. Her mother had only worn the latest in couture whilst Mary wore a comfortable cotton dress with little rosebuds all over it, which definitely matched her sunny disposition.

Will wheeled the pram through to the kitchen, which Sheena soon discovered was the main hub of the house as it contained an enormous wooden family table and ten chairs. A woman was sitting on a stool at the kitchen bench; Mary was calling to her husband, who was busy hammering in the backyard, and children were running everywhere. The smell of a freshly brewed pot of coffee filled the air, along with chocolate-chip cookies, which were cooling on a rack.

As Will rushed forward to greet the woman who she quickly realised was not only one of his sisters but also six months pregnant, Sheena clutched her hands to her chest and nodded. This was right. This was what it should be like. All noise and laughter and smiles and talking, everyone mingling with each other but still somehow understanding what was going on. This was family…a *real* family.

Ellie wriggled, eager to be free from the pram, and Sheena instantly unclipped her from the safety harness. Mary was the first to hold out her hands, eager for a cuddle with the baby. Will instructed his mother on the best way to hold her and how to be careful of the bandaging that was still in place beneath Ellie's pretty cotton dress.

Ten minutes later Sarah awoke on her usual default setting of crying loudly for attention. Thankfully for her, she had plenty of people there just waiting to give it. Stephen begged for a cuddle and, just as she did with Will, Sarah settled almost instantly.

'She likes the men,' Sheena whispered to Will, then frowned humorously. 'That might be a worry one day.'

He chuckled and slipped his arm about her shoulders. 'We'll cope.'

We'll cope? She tried to remain cool, calm and collected at his words, aware that he might not have even realised he'd said 'we'. However, it did make her wonder that even if Will was really serious about their burgeoning relationship, was *she* really ready to move forward?

She wanted Will in her life, almost to the point of desperation, but was she really any good for him? She'd loved him so much all those years ago that she'd had to let him go. She'd known he'd wanted a family and that she hadn't been able to give it to him.

Well, now she *could* give him a family but what if he wanted more children? His sister was pregnant with her fourth child and from the photographs around the house it was clear that his other siblings also had gone forth and multiplied.

There was absolutely no guarantee that she'd ever be able to conceive again. Her doctors had told her that her pregnancy with Ellie and Sarah had been a miracle. Even *they* weren't quite sure how it had happened. It gave her hope. Hope that one day she'd be able to have Will's baby.

Will deserved to have a whole gaggle of children. He deserved to live in a house like this, one filled with photographs and toys and miscellaneous paraphernalia. He deserved this life…and she simply didn't know if she was capable of giving it to him.

CHAPTER TEN

LUNCH with his parents and his sister Anna was such a laid-back, relaxed affair that instead of feeling highly self-conscious, Sheena found herself laughing along with the others. Compared to the stiff dinner parties she'd occasionally been allowed to attend with her parents, the Beckman clan carried on as though they were from another planet. Or perhaps it was *her* upbringing that had been out of this world? What she was experiencing with them was normal and it was the type of upbringing she was determined to give her girls.

Throughout the morning she'd talked with Will's sister, asking about Jesse, who was running about the place, and little Lester, who had only been walking for the past three months. She'd watched Mary give Ellie a bottle and had been astounded when Stephen had offered to change Sarah's nappy.

'Along with Mary, I've raised five of my own and I wasn't one of those old-fashioned fathers who stepped back and let the wife do everything. No, siree. I was in there, changing nappies, bathing babies, cleaning up messes and fixing toys.'

'A hands-on dad,' Sheena had said with a laugh as she'd accepted Sarah so she could feed her. Ellie had been almost done with the bottle and Mary had cradled her carefully, humming a sweet song. Ellie's eyes had closed, content that everything was perfectly fine in her little world.

'Have you had enough milk for both of them?' Anna asked now as she collected Lester and held him on her side, careful to avoid her baby bump.

'I have. I've been very fortunate in that area.'

'That's good. With this one…' she inclined her head towards Lester '…my milk dried up within a month. Then again, he was a whopping ten pounds, seven ounces when he was born *and* he was a week early!'

'A healthy baby indeed,' Sheena remarked as Anna yawned.

'I think I'll go have a lie-down and get the boys to have a rest. If I'm not up when you leave, may I just say that it was lovely meeting you and your girls, Sheena.'

'Thanks. It was wonderful to meet you, too,' she said, smiling brightly.

'Would you mind if we popped into the hospital to visit? I'd love you to meet my husband and my eldest boy. He'll be sorry he missed meeting you all.'

'Of course. I'd be delighted.'

Anna nodded and headed off just as Will brought Sheena a cup of tea. He set it down on the table before sitting next to her, putting his arm about her shoulders as she continued to feed Sarah.

'Ellie's sound asleep,' he said, glancing over to where his mother was reclined in her chair, Ellie asleep with her head on Mary's shoulder. 'And Dad's eager to have another hold of Sarah once you've finished feeding her.'

Stephen had gone off to help Anna settle her two boys but had already promised to return for another cuddle with Sarah. 'They really love children, don't they?' she said.

'Absolutely. They're very involved with their grandchildren and helping out my siblings whenever they need them.'

Sheena turned to look at him. 'They're amazing people, Will. You're so blessed to have them.'

'*We* could be blessed together, Sheena. The four of us. You, me, Ellie and Sarah.'

Sheena swallowed over the lump in her throat. 'A family?'

'Yes.'

'But, Will… what if I can't have any more children? You deserve to have more, to be a hands-on dad just like your own father and be involved in your children's lives. I can't give you that prom—'

Will leaned over and kissed her mouth. 'You taste so sweet, so perfect,' he murmured against her mouth, breaking away for a second so both of them could drag in a breath.

'It's always like this when I'm with you. So powerful. So perfect,' she added, her words breathless as she leaned towards him, eager to have his mouth on hers once more. He didn't disappoint her but he did manage to slow it down a little, to ease the frenzy of the kisses both of them seemed to need so desperately.

She was close. His mouth was on hers, his tongue tracing the edge of her lips, tasting her, tantalising her to distraction. She moaned a little sigh against him and sank deeper into his arms. He held her close, thrilled at the way she was responding to him, elated that he could still affect her in such a way and delighted that he'd been handed a second chance to do so.

'You can't always kiss me into submission every time I'm saying something you don't agree with,' she murmured, trying not to disturb Sarah, who was almost asleep as she finished feeding.

'Why not? Don't you enjoy it?' He waggled his eyebrows

up and down suggestively, and she smiled at him and shook her head.

'Put your arrogance away and be serious. What if I—?'

A loud, ear-splitting scream filled the air, piercing their quiet solitude, cutting off what Sheena had been about to say. After the scream came an almighty crash, as though a car had just driven through the front of the house.

Will sprang to his feet, heading in the direction of the noise. Sarah jumped, then pulled away, spluttering and crying at being disturbed. Sheena quickly buttoned her top and by the time she'd shifted Sarah to her shoulder and then stood, Mary was by her side, arms opened wide to receive the babe.

'Ellie's still asleep. I've put her in the pram,' the experienced grandmother said.

'Jesse? Jesse?' They could hear Anna calling throughout the house and a moment later Lester's cries filled the air as the baby woke from his sleep because of the commotion.

'Give me Sarah and go and see if Will needs help. Stephen will look after Lester.'

Sheena nodded and handed her grizzling daughter to Mary. Will was moving through the four-bedroomed house like lightning, opening and closing doors to check that everything was all right...until he came to Stephen's study.

'The door's jammed shut,' he said when he saw Sheena in the hallway.

'Jesse?' Anna came into the hallway from one of the rooms where she'd put Lester down for a nap. 'Where's Jesse?' She was as white as a sheet. 'He fell asleep with me on the bed but he's not there. Will?' Anna was starting to panic as Will and Sheena tried to push open the door to Stephen's study.

'It's jammed,' Will said. 'Something is blocking the way.'

'We'll have to get in through the window,' Sheena said. She could hear Sarah still crying in the front room and Mary singing to her. Lester was crying in one of the nearby bedrooms and Stephen was attempting to calm his grandson down. Anna looked so pale that Will quickly helped her to sit on the floor.

'We'll find him. We'll sort everything out,' he reassured his little sister, before heading outside to get a ladder. Sheena stood in the hallway, and the noise surrounding her started subsiding. She heard a small whimper coming from Stephen's study.

'Jesse?' she called with calm authority. 'Jesse? Can you hear me?'

Another whimper was her only reply but it was proof that he was in there and as they were unable to open the door, it was logical to surmise that something had fallen down, pinning Jesse and blocking the doorway.

'Jesse, I want you to stay very still. OK? Just like a statue. Uncle Will and I are coming to get you.'

'Jesse? Jesse?' Anna was panicking and there was the hint of mild hysteria in her tone. Sheena instantly turned to face the young mother.

'Anna.' She placed her hands reassuringly on Anna's shoulders, trying to calm her down. If Jesse heard the panic in his mother's voice, it might make him more upset and he could do things that could cause him further damage, especially if he was pinned under something heavy. 'He's in there. I can hear him. My guess is that he's trapped beneath whatever is blocking the door but it's of the utmost importance that we keep him calm and still until Will can get to him. You can speak to him but you *must* remain calm and controlled.'

'Yes. Yes.' Anna tried to breathe in and out more slowly.

Stephen appeared in the hallway a moment later, a pink-cheeked, wet-eyed Lester in his arms.

'Sheena!' Will called from the front of the house. 'Sheena, I need you out here.'

'Coming,' she called, then turned to look from Stephen to Anna. 'Jesse needs to stay calm and still. Just talk to him, let him hear your voices. Reassure him.'

'Right you are, Sheena,' Stephen replied, nodding wisely. Sheena quickly headed out the front door, where she found Will positioning a small stepladder near the partially open front window, which was situated a metre and a half from the ground.

'I can't get it open too far due to the locks on the window but it should be wide enough for you to squeeze through,' Will said.

'OK.' She instantly climbed the ladder, glad she'd decided to wear trousers instead of a skirt, and shifted sideways, putting her foot up on the window ledge. Pushing aside the curtains, she shimmied and squeezed her way through the small gap, almost getting stuck a few times and knocking over something that had been positioned near the window, but within a few minutes she was through.

'The bookshelf has come down,' she called as she turned and unlocked the window from the inside so that Will could push it open the rest of the way and climb through to help her. 'Jesse? It's Sheena. Uncle Will's friend. Just stay still, sweetheart,' she called calmly, still unsure exactly where the little boy was.

'Good heavens!' Will said as he climbed through the window, almost tripping over a mountain of books on the floor. 'Dad. I'm going to need your help in lifting this bookshelf.' Will spoke in a tone that was calm and controlled yet the hint of urgency was evident in what needed to be done.

'Right you are, son,' came Stephen's calm voice.

'What's happening?' Anna said from the other side of the door. 'Is he all right? Jesse?'

At the sound of his mother's voice, another whimper sounded from beneath the pile of rubble and Sheena quickly scrambled in that direction. Within several seconds Stephen was through the window and into the room, both he and Will shifting around to position themselves on either side of the large wooden bookcase.

'Can you see him?' Will asked, almost ready to lift.

'I think I can see his foot. See? Just there.' She pointed to an area in the middle of the room where she'd managed to shift a few of the books out of the way but couldn't do any more until the bookcase had been lifted away.

'Yes. Good. It's all right, Anna. We'll have him out in a jiffy,' Will called reassuringly to his sister. Sheena could hear the love and reassurance in his tone and her heart swelled with pride for this man. He was so good, so caring, so loving to those around him. He was *her* Will. She didn't want to let him go, not ever, but…could they work things out? Would he be happy with only Ellie and Sarah? Two girls who weren't biologically his children?

Will looked over at his father and nodded once, the two men not needing any other words to communicate what had to happen next. Together they hefted the large bookcase out of the way and instantly Sheena scrambled to where Jesse lay buried beneath the books and papers that had been in the bookcase, pushing them out of the way in order to get to the little boy.

'There you are. Keep still. You're all right,' she murmured, desperate to reassure the little boy as her hands felt over his limbs, checking his body. Once the bookcase was upright and out of the way, Stephen opened the door to let

Anna in while Will came and knelt down on the other side of his nephew.

'How is he?'

'Check his right leg for me,' she instructed as she pressed her fingers to Jesse's carotid pulse. 'Hey, there, Jesse. Can you hear me?'

Her answer was a whimper but the little boy didn't open his eyes. 'Pulse is strong. Breathing is good. Bit of a lump on his head where it connected with the shelf.' She lifted his eyelids to check his pupils and he whimpered and turned his head away, moaning, more in annoyance than in pain. 'Ahh…we have cognitive function.'

'Oh, Jesse. Jesse. You scared Mummy,' Anna said as she rushed into the room, almost tripping over the paraphernalia that was littered about the place, but Stephen was by her side, steadying his pregnant daughter. Mary stood in the doorway with a quiet Sarah securely in her arms, Lester clinging to her leg.

'Don't touch him just yet,' Will said when it appeared Anna was ready to scoop her boy up into her arms. 'Just let Sheena and I make sure he's OK. Almost done.'

'I'm so glad the two of you were here,' Mary murmured. 'See, Anna? No one better than two trained doctors and one of them your big brother to help out and take care of Jesse. It'll all be fine.'

'Although it does appear he may have broken his leg,' Will told his sister. 'I'll need to see an X-ray to confirm it but—'

'What? An X-ray? Is it that bad? Will he need to go to hospital?' Anna started to breathe more heavily and Sheena instantly looked at the expectant mother, concern for Anna's blood pressure now starting to worry her. 'I need to call Jeff. He needs to know what's happened. Oh, my poor Jesse. A broken leg. X-rays. Hospitals.'

'He's fine, Anna. Fine. Just a broken leg and as I'm an orthopaedic paediatrician, I'm the perfect person to look after him. He'll be just fine,' Will reiterated. 'Mum, do you have any children's paracetamol? Or ibuprofen?'

'Can you give ibuprofen to a child his age?' Anna asked.

'You can if you're an orthopaedic paediatrician and know the correct dosage,' he returned, and winked at his sister. 'I'm here, Anna-banana.' At the use of the childhood nickname, his sister gave him a watery smile. It was the most perfect thing he could have done. 'I'm not going to let anything happen to my precious nephew.'

'Come on, love,' Stephen said, helping his daughter to her feet. 'Let's give Will and Sheena some room. Come and sit down and put your feet up. We don't want your blood pressure rising too far.' Stephen looked at his son before he left, mouthed the word 'Ambulance' and received a nod from Will.

A moment later Mary returned, minus Sarah and Lester, who were apparently now with Stephen, bringing not only medication but some bandages as well. Jesse had opened his eyes but was more than content to lie still and have everyone make a fuss of him. Sheena took the bandages and searched around for something stable to act as a splint.

'What were you doing in Grandpa's study?' Mary asked him softly as she bent over him and kissed his cheeks. Will administered the medicine, knowing it wouldn't take too long to take effect.

'I wanted da big book. Da one with all the pictures of the horsies.' Jesse told his grandma. 'It was berry high up and I climbed and I climbed and then it was stuck.'

'You should have come and asked a grown-up to get it for you,' Mary scolded lightly, and Jesse's eyes began to tear up.

'I sorry, Grandma,' he said, and within a moment was

crying, although Sheena had the feeling it was more because he was upset at having disappointed his grandmother than because of any pain. Carefully, Sheena and Will applied the splint and bandage to Jesse's right leg.

'How are you feeling now, little man?' Will asked his nephew.

'Am I still in trouble?' he asked softly, reaching for Sheena's hand and holding it tight. She smiled at his words as Will lovingly shook his head.

'No, matey. You're not.'

'Then I feel better,' he confessed, and Sheena couldn't help but laugh, the action helping to release her concern. It also made her wonder what the rest of her life was going to be like, being a mother to two small girls.

'One day Ellie and Sarah are going to be three years old, just like Jesse,' Sheena mused out loud, shaking her head as though she couldn't quite believe that day would come. 'How am I ever going to cope?'

Mary chuckled. 'You'll do fine. You simply take each day at a time and deal with whatever life throws at you. Never borrow trouble.'

Will was pleased with his mother's sensible advice but he could hear the depth of Sheena's words. 'You do realise that where Jesse is one little boy trying to get a book down from a bookshelf, you'll have two little monkeys getting into mischief. Double the trouble.'

'And from what I've seen, Sarah will be the one to lead the charge,' Mary added as she headed out of the room to check on everyone else.

Sheena shook her head in bemusement. 'It's so hard to imagine. Both of them running around, doing their own thing.'

'Living their lives like normal little girls.' Will smiled

and reached over, taking her free hand in his and giving it a squeeze.

'Normal and filled with mischief.' Uncertainty gripped Sheena's heart and she bit her lip, unsure what her future held. 'What have I got myself into?'

Will chuckled before brushing a kiss to her lips. 'A whole world of love and laughter.' Which he was determined to share with her.

They stayed beside Jesse, making sure he didn't move until the ambulance arrived.

'Hey, Sheena. Hey, Will,' Dieter, one of the paramedics from Adelaide Mercy, greeted them. 'What are you two doing here?'

'This is my nephew,' Will explained, and as he and Sheena went to stand to give the paramedics some room, Sheena found her hand gripped firmly by Jesse.

'Stay,' he whimpered, and she could hear the panic behind his words.

'Of course I'll stay with you, sweetie,' she reassured him, and helped the paramedics transfer Jesse to the stretcher. Even when he was secure in the ambulance, Jesse still refused to let go of her hand and Sheena knew she'd have to stay with him. Her mind raced ahead, thinking of Sarah and Ellie.

'You'll need to go in the ambulance if he's not going to let go of your hand,' Will pointed out as he came and sat beside her in the rear of the vehicle.

'I realise that because it's important to keep Jesse as calm as possible. Would you mind taking care of the girls? Driving them back to the hospital? I can meet you there.'

Will tried not to let his jaw drop at her words. 'You...trust me that much? You'll entrust your girls to my care?'

Sheena leaned over and kissed him. 'Of course I trust you.

You *love* my girls. That much is quite clear to anyone who watches the three of you together. You honestly love them, Will, with all your heart, and I know you'll always protect them and keep them safe.'

He swallowed once, twice before answering. 'I will.' His tone was husky but it was also laced with determination. 'Right, then. I guess I'll see you back at the hospital.' He kissed her once more before saying goodbye to his nephew and climbed from the ambulance so that Dieter could shut the rear doors.

As Will watched the ambulance depart, he couldn't believe the gift Sheena had just given him. Complete and utter trust for her daughters. Sheena could see how much he loved Ellie and Sarah. She could see that he wanted to protect those little girls for ever and she was willing to let him do it. She was willing to let him into her life and that was the biggest gift of all.

He'd let her down in the past. He realised that now. He hadn't spent the time to really get to know her, to understand the upbringing she'd endured, how sad and lonely she'd been. He'd been so wrapped up in finding the woman he wanted to spend the rest of his life with, so happy that he'd get to have his picture-perfect fairy-tale life that he hadn't *seen* Sheena for who she was deep down inside.

Since he'd returned to Australia and spent more time with Sheena, and her girls, he'd come to discover how sad and lonely she'd been all her life. He understood now why she'd never talked about her past or her endometriosis, but back then he'd only considered his own happiness and had blamed her when she'd turned his proposal down.

He'd let her down in the past but as he headed into the house to care for her beautiful daughters, he vowed that he wouldn't let her down again.

CHAPTER ELEVEN

WHEN they arrived back at Adelaide Mercy, Sheena handled Jesse's care, requesting X-rays to see if the little boy had sustained a greenstick fracture. Anna arrived just as Jesse was being wheeled to Radiology and finally the little boy was more than eager to let go of Sheena's hand when he had his mother right beside him.

'Hi, Sheena,' the triage sister said with surprise as she walked into the nurses' station where Sheena was writing up Jesse's notes. 'I didn't know you were scheduled for a stint in A and E today.'

'I'm not.' Sheena smiled and quickly explained about Will's nephew Jesse.

'So…where are the girls?' Sister was clearly puzzled.

'Will's bringing them back to the hospital.' Sheena looked at the clock on the wall. 'In fact, they should be back by now. Perhaps he's getting them settled in their room. It's been a big day. Do you mind if I use the phone to ring the ward and check?'

'Go ahead,' Sister remarked, a secret smile touching her lips. 'You and Will seem to be very close. At least, that's the impression we all have from the photo in today's paper.'

'Paper?' Sheena turned with the receiver to her ear and accepted the cut-out picture Sister offered. It was one of the photographs from the other day in the park when the photo-journalist had caught them out, although it wasn't one of the ones they'd posed for. Instead, the paper had decided to go with the photograph of the babies in the pram, Sheena and Will sitting on the blanket, Will raising her hand to his lips. She read the caption below.

Sheena Woodcombe, mother of Adelaide's newly separated conjoined twins Ellie and Sarah, finds a quiet moment for romance with lead orthopaedic surgeon Will Beckman in the botanical gardens.

Sheena stared at it, stunned that she seemed to be some sort of celebrity and that people were interested in her love life.

'So I guess this means there *is* something going on between you and Will?' Sister fished. 'Is it serious?'

'As a heart attack,' Will remarked as he walked towards them. Sister quickly cleared her throat and returned to her duties as Will stared at the piece of paper Sheena held in her hands. She turned to face him and replaced the phone receiver in its cradle.

'You're here. Where are the girls?'

'All tucked up in their beds. Aunty Nessa is more than content to stand there and watch them sleep.'

Sheena sighed and smiled up at him. 'Good. Thanks for taking care of them.'

'No problem. Where's Jesse?' he asked as he took the picture from her fingers.

'Radiology.'

'You look great in this picture. It's definitely not my best side, though.'

Sheena chuckled. 'You're so vain.'

Will put his head on the side and looked at her. 'You don't mind about this?'

Sheena slowly shook her head. 'Not really. Perhaps before today I would have had a bit of a rant and rave about the media but...I don't know, today has changed things. Brought perspective.'

'Really? In what way?'

'In the way that a little boy climbing on a bookcase and hurting himself could have been a lot worse. In the way that families care and interact and show love for each other. In the way that even though I feel I'm floundering in a sea of parental confusion, everything will turn out right in the end. The media can take photographs and print what they like. They don't know the *real* story behind that moment. They don't know *me* and they probably never will. My girls are no longer conjoined and therefore no longer high-profile news. They're going to be able to grow up and enjoy normal lives. The past belongs in the past.'

She smiled and sighed as she said the words. 'And it feels great to say all of that out loud.'

Will nodded and reached for her hand. 'Come with me.'

'But I'm waiting for Jesse to return from Radiology,' she said as Will led her from the nurses' station.

'Call Dr Woodcombe in Paediatrics when Jesse returns, please,' he instructed the triage sister as they walked past. He was quiet as they took the stairs up to Paediatrics, walking along the busy corridors until they were back in Ellie's and Sarah's room.

'Janessa, would you mind waiting outside for a moment? I just need to propose to Sheena,' Will remarked, his words and tone direct.

'Uh? What? Uh...sure. Whatever you say,' Janessa said, as Will's words penetrated the haze around their friend.

Janessa headed out of the room and closed the door behind her.

'You're proposing?' Sheena asked as both of them peered into the cribs, smiling at the two little girls, who were sleeping soundly.

'I thought I'd give you a heads-up this time so I didn't take you completely by surprise.'

'Very considerate of you.' She couldn't help the wide beaming smile on her face. He was going to propose? Really? Her heart rate picked up as her mind processed the information but she forced herself not to jump ahead with a million and one questions, but instead to relax and focus on the moment.

He crossed to the vase that held the freesias he'd brought her that morning and plucked one out before turning to face her. He twirled the bloom in his fingers.

'I hope this goes better than last time,' he murmured with a slight frown.

'It will,' she replied encouragingly.

'Oh. Good. That certainly gives me a confidence boost.' He cleared his throat and took one small step towards her. 'I love you.'

'Strong beginning,' she whispered, her heart leaping with joy at hearing those words from his lips.

'Shh.'

'Yes. Of course. Sorry.' She nodded once. 'Please. Continue.'

Will laughed then took another step towards her. 'I have always loved you, Sheena, and I am so grateful that you've been able to have children and that those children were conjoined and that I was asked to come and look after them. The past belongs in the past. Hearing you say those words made me realise that you were right.

'It's the future we should be concerned about. The girls' future—*our* future—and I want that future to start right now. I love your girls, Sheena. I love them with every beat of my heart and I will continue to love them for the rest of my life. And, yes, before you ask, I would love to have more children but not at the expense of your health.

'*You* are far more important to me than the possibility of having more children. We have two beautiful girls and they'll fill our life with so much sunshine we'll need to wear dark glasses.'

Sheena chuckled and then gasped as he took one last step towards her and slid his arm about her waist, drawing her close to him. As he pressed her body against his, she sighed with delight, her gaze taking in his gorgeous mouth for a moment before she looked deeply into his mesmerising blue eyes.

'Sheena.' Her name was a caress on his lips. 'Will you do me the honour of becoming my wife?' He handed her the single freesia as he spoke the words and she accepted it with a nervous smile.

Sheena swallowed and licked her suddenly dry lips. She was about to give her answer when Sarah started to fuss.

'And could you be quick with the answer because I think *our* daughter is about to wake up?'

Sheena's smile was as bright as the love in her heart. 'I can't believe this is actually happening. That I'm so fortunate to have you back in my life, to be able to contemplate a future with you. I love you, Will. So very much. And I'm the luckiest woman in the world to be able to have a strong, protective man like you to call my husband. I want to build a life with you and the girls. The four of us together as a family, and if any other children come along—the more the merrier. Thank you for loving my babies and wanting them to be your own. I'm honoured.'

Will's smile was dazzling as he lowered his head, claiming her lips in a kiss that held all the promise of a wonderful future together. In the background, they both heard Sarah's fussing turn to grizzles and in another moment those grizzles would turn into her cries for attention, and when those cries came, they would need to part to go and attend to her before she woke Ellie…but until then Will was more than content to kiss his new fiancée, their hearts forever joined with the purest love.

EPILOGUE

'QUIET. Quiet, please!' Giuseppe demanded as he walked through his restaurant, which was closed for a private function—the function being the first birthday celebration of Adelaide's first previously conjoined twins, Ellie and Sarah Beckman.

The restaurant had been decorated in blue, which was Sarah's favourite colour, and yellow, which Ellie had declared she loved. Frills and flowers and lace and soft toys in the chosen colour theme were placed around the room, making it feel more like a toy factory than a restaurant.

'Quiet. Quiet, please!' Giuseppe called again. 'The mother and the father want to propose the toast.'

The family and friends gathered to celebrate Ellie and Sarah's first birthday all shifted back to their seats. While the girls were too young to ever remember this day, Will had arranged for his father to film the proceedings. 'That way we can embarrass them on their twenty-first birthdays by replaying it,' he'd lovingly suggested to his wife.

Will stood, scooping Sarah into his arms, shifting her around so he could put his other arm around Sheena's shoulders. 'Thank you, Giuseppe,' he called as the noise died down. Sheena bent to pick up Ellie, the little girl resting her head on her mother's shoulder as she looked out at the crowd before them.

Miles and Janessa were standing not too far away, almost ready to leave for their next adventure—in the UK, looking after the next set of conjoined twins. They'd delayed their departure specifically to be here today. 'There's no way I'm missing my nieces' first birthday,' Janessa had declared, and Miles had readily agreed with her.

Anna, Jeff and the rest of their brood, along with a brand-new granddaughter for Mary and Stephen, sat not too far away. Kaycee, Raquel-Maria, Clementine, Charisma and many of their other friends from the hospital were there as well, all smiling and beaming brightly at the two gorgeous little girls who had brought such happiness into their lives.

Two months ago Will had surprised Sheena with a glorious pre-wedding gift of a five-bedroom home with a large backyard only fifteen minutes from Adelaide Mercy. Both Will and Sheena had decreased their hours at the hospital in order to spend as much time with their girls as they could, the four of them bonding together in perfect harmony.

Will had applied to officially adopt the girls but in his heart they already were and always would be *his* sweet Sarah and *his* elegant Ellie. He cleared his throat and looked around the room at everyone who had come to celebrate with them, then his gaze settled on his wife.

His wife. *His* Sheena. He loved her more today than he had for the past ten years and he knew she felt the same way. They talked daily, about deep and meaningful things, about plans they had for their future.

She looked up at him and smiled brightly. 'I love you,' she said softly, before he bent and brushed a kiss across her lips.

'Love you right back,' he murmured. Their wedding two

months ago had been a quiet affair held in the backyard of their new home. Intimate and relaxed, just the way they'd both wanted it, and two weeks ago, when the girls had finally been released from the hospital, their lives had begun in earnest.

'Friends,' Will began, feeling Sarah already impatient to be down and crawling around the floor, getting her pretty blue dress all dirty. He smiled. That was his girl. No doubt she'd have Ellie into all sorts of mischief before the evening was over and he looked forward to discovering what they would do next.

'Thank you all for coming to help us celebrate the first birthday of these two very special girls. Sheena and I had many things to say, many people to thank, but Sarah's eager to be down and enjoying herself once again so in order to acknowledge her impatience—no doubt for the incredible cake Giuseppe has created—please, all raise your glasses of milk as we toast Sarah and Ellie.'

'To Sarah and Ellie,' everyone toasted, clinking their glasses of milk and laughing.

Sarah squirmed once more in her father's arms and Ellie snuggled into her mother but as soon as Will put Sarah down, Ellie immediately erupted with energy and was eager to be off after her sister.

Will drew his wife close and pressed another kiss to her lips. 'We're going to have our hands full,' he said.

'Even fuller than we ever expected,' she murmured, her words punctuated with deep meaning. She eased back to look directly into his eyes. Just after their wedding, Sheena had needed to have two cysts removed from her ovaries, as well as be treated for her increasing endometriosis. Both she and Will had been told that if they wanted to try for more children, there was an extremely small window of opportunity, and until today, when Sheena had returned to see her surgeon for a review, she hadn't dared to hope for such incredible news.

Sheena smiled up at him, her heart bursting with love as she nodded, tears beginning to glisten in her eyes.

'What?' Will was stunned.

'I'm pregnant. I only found out an hour ago, and you were finishing up in surgery and then with coming here and… We're going to have a baby. The ultrasound is booked for tomorrow and I'll need to take things even easier and—'

Will pressed his mouth to hers in complete happiness. 'We're going to have another baby! I can't believe that we've been so blessed already with the girls and now we're—'

Sheena employed his tactic and kissed him quiet, knowing he wouldn't mind.

'We already have the fairy-tale family,' she murmured against his mouth. 'But this new baby will be the crowning glory.'

'And he will be loved and cared for as much as his big sisters,' Will announced with joy.

'He? Who said anything about it being a boy?'

Will winked at his wife. 'Trust me!'

* * * * *

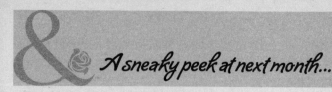

A sneaky peek at next month...

CAPTIVATING MEDICAL DRAMA—WITH HEART

My wish list for next month's titles...

In stores from 2nd September 2011:

❏ Cort Mason – Dr Delectable — Carol Marinelli

& Survival Guide to Dating Your Boss — Fiona McArthur

❏ Return of the Maverick — Sue MacKay

& It Started with a Pregnancy — Scarlet Wilson

❏ Italian Doctor, No Strings Attached — Kate Hardy

❏ Miracle Times Two — Josie Metcalfe

Available at WHSmith, Tesco, Asda, Eason, Amazon and Apple

Just can't wait?

Visit us Online

You can buy our books online a month before they hit the shops! **www.millsandboon.co.uk**

0811/03